CRITICS AND READERS PRAISE

INSIDIOUS

"Coulter keeps the two plotlines equally engaging—and the reader guessing—all the way to the satisfying resolution of each."

—*Publishers Weekly*

"Two very intriguing mysteries . . . you can't go wrong with a Coulter book, as she has proven time after time."

—*RT Book Reviews*

"Both story lines are exciting and gripping. . . . This is another winner by the *New York Times* bestselling author. Readers should be prepared to laugh and to care about these characters, as they try to solve the two mysteries."

—*Working Mother*

"Catherine Coulter knows how to weave and web incredibly heinous crimes that make you think and shudder."

—*Mrs. Leif's Two Fangs About It*

"[*Insidious* is] a fast-paced, quick read. . . . The intriguing story lines hold your interest as they shift back and forth between the two cases and hurtle you toward an exciting ending to find out whodunit in both cases. Definitely a page turner."

—*The Poisoned Martini*

"You outdid yourself on this one. The best one yet. I had a very hard time putting it down. I had to take my wife to the doctor today and while I was waiting, I was getting almost to the end of the book. I was so engrossed in the story that I did not realize my wife was leaving."

—Tom Muller

THE FBI THRILLERS

Insidious (2016)

Nemesis (2015)

Second Shot (2014): Eleventh Hour *and* Blindside

Power Play (2014)

Bombshell (2013)

Backfire (2012)

Split Second (2011)

Twice Dead (2011): Riptide *and* Hemlock Bay

Whiplash (2010)

KnockOut (2009)

TailSpin (2008)

Double Jeopardy (2008): The Target *and* The Edge

Double Take (2007)

The Beginning (2005): The Cove *and* The Maze

Point Blank (2005)

Blowout (2005)

Blindside (2003)

Eleventh Hour (2002)

Hemlock Bay (2001)

Riptide (2000)

The Edge (1999)

The Target (1998)

The Maze (1997)

The Cove (1996)

A BRIT IN THE FBI THRILLERS (WITH J. T. ELLISON)

The End Game (2015)

The Lost Key (2014)

The Final Cut (2013)

CATHERINE COULTER

INSIDIOUS

POCKET BOOKS

New York   London   Toronto   Sydney   New Delhi

Pocket Books
An Imprint of Simon & Schuster, Inc.
1230 Avenue of the Americas
New York, NY 10020

This book is a work of fiction. Any references to historical events, real people, or real places are used fictitiously. Other names, characters, places, and events are products of the author's imagination, and any resemblance to actual events or places or persons, living or dead, is entirely coincidental.

First Pocket Books paperback edition March 2017

POCKET BOOKS and colophon are registered trademarks of Simon & Schuster, Inc.

For information about special discounts for bulk purchases, please contact Simon & Schuster Special Sales at 1-866-506-1949 or business@simonandschuster.com.

The Simon & Schuster Speakers Bureau can bring authors to your live event. For more information or to book an event, contact the Simon & Schuster Speakers Bureau at 1-866-248-3049 or visit our website at www.simonspeakers.com.

Manufactured in the United States of America

10 9 8 7 6 5 4 3 2 1

ISBN 978-1-5011-5029-6
ISBN 978-1-5011-5030-2 (pbk)
ISBN 978-1-5011-5031-9 (ebook)

ACKNOWLEDGMENTS

Fred (Ski) Ludwikowski—thank you for recommending Sherlock's birthday present from Savich, a new ankle piece, the 9mm Glock 43. She is really enjoying it, practices fast-drawing between floors on the elevator.

Angela Bell, FBI, Office of Public Affairs—even though I didn't bombard you with questions and situations with this book, knowing I could have is gold. Having you there with every answer merits an eternal thank-you.

The town of Malibu—thanks to all the inhabitants I spoke with, both inside and outside the Colony. You guys are the angels atop the LaLa Land Christmas trees.

Karen Evans—as always, the light in my window, the premium in my tank, the apples in my pie. You are a princess.

1

Missy Devereaux, whose real name was Mary Ann Duff, fluffed her hair as she pretended to look in the store window, scanning behind her, wondering if he'd followed her to Las Vegas. And then she saw him, across the street, ducking behind an old gray Volvo in the thick Las Vegas Strip traffic. He looked thin in his baggy jeans and his loose-hanging dark blue shirt. She couldn't see his face—he wore dark sunglasses and a Giants baseball cap.

It wasn't fair. She'd just landed a six-month stint here at the Mandalay in a Beatles musical retrospective, hoping for half a year of peace and calm without a stalker to tie her stomach in knots, but here he was, after only four days. She'd been so careful when the taxi picked her up at her cottage in Malibu nearly a week before—had the driver drop her off at LAX, a terminal away from the airline she'd booked—but still he was here, watching her, following her. All she'd wanted was her life to return to normal. She'd done everything she could. She'd gone to the cops to see if they could stop him. Movie star stalkers were old hat to the Calabasas Sheriff's Department, responsible for handling all the criminal problems in Malibu. They had a protocol in place, a pleasant older cop had told her four months before, they would talk to him if she would point him out. What, she'd asked, would her stalker do when he got tired of following her around? Attack her? The friendly older cop only shook his head, avoided answering that question. That same day, Missy bought a Becker Ka-Bar knife, a fixed blade three and a quarter inches long, with a three-inch handle. It was made of Cro-Van steel, the salesman had told her, and was favored by sailors going back nearly to the ark. She liked the sound of that, carrying something badass enough for the marines. She liked the feel of the Ka-Bar, too, solid, and ready to go in its sheath hooked onto her waistband.

The cops hadn't caught the stalker, even following their protocol.

She kept fluffing, touched on some lip gloss, and continued to stare into the window. She didn't see him now, but she knew he was there, watching. She was so used to feeling acid burning her gut, so used to the overwhelming urge to run as fast as she could, that she didn't at first recognize the bolt of rage that splashed through her. She felt her adrenaline spike, felt her blood pumping hard and fast, the mad mix making her shake. For the first time she let the heat of anger wash over her, and she saw clearly who and what he was—nothing. She wasn't going to let him destroy her life. Not anymore. She turned on her heel and worked her way through the gridlock traffic on the Strip, not even aware of the horns honking, the tourists jostling her or the wolf whistles. All her focus was on that miserable little man who probably spent his nights licking her publicity photos.

She saw him straighten, stare at her, then draw back when she started running toward him, not away, her Ka-Bar in her hand.

She heard growling, realized it was from her, and yelled, "You miserable little worm! I'm going to carve out your tonsils!" He sprinted away, Missy after him, running fast and strong. She'd been a blimp in high school, but all that had changed when she'd turned twenty. Six years later, she was in top-flight shape, ran three miles every single day, worked out at Sam's Muscle Bar, in L.A. Catch him? Not a problem. He wove through crowds of tourists on the sidewalk, knocking some out of his way, going around others, and Missy followed in his wake, closing in on him. He ran past the Venetian hotel with its Grand Canal and gondolas floating past, knocking two people aside, leaving them cursing after him. When the crush of tourists became too thick, she ran in the street, close to the sidewalk, and gained on him more. When he turned right, toward the Wynn hotel and looked back over his shoulder, she saw it clear as day—fear. *He's afraid of me!* It was heady to see that look after so many months of aggravation and, yes, fear. Now it was his turn. She felt fierce, unstoppable. She amped up her speed.

He was tiring fast as he ran into the huge hotel garage, nearly empty this time of day, Missy on his heels. She lost him for a moment in the shadows, then spotted him running across to the far side of the garage that opened onto the gardens of the Wynn. She was nearly on him now. Without hesitating, Missy took a flying leap and landed on his back, wrapping her arms around his neck. He fell forward under her weight, half on the grass, half on the concrete garage floor.

"You move, and I'll slice off your ear!" She pricked his neck with her Ka-Bar, enough to draw a drop of blood, to show him she was serious. He became still as a stone. So he wasn't a complete moron. She jerked off his ball cap, grabbed a tangle of brown hair, and pulled his head back. She elbowed off his sunglasses and looked down into a thin, good-looking face, marred by some acne scars on his forehead, and pale brown eyes filled with fear. Of her. Of her Ka-Bar digging into his neck. He didn't outweigh her by more than twenty pounds. She felt triumphant; she'd brought him down, and not a cop in sight. Missy leaned close, thought about biting him but didn't. She whispered in his ear, "You're the one who's scared now, aren't you, you creep? Who are you? Why have you been stalking me?"

"I don't know what you're talking about. I never saw you before in my life. You started ch-chasing me and

I-I saw the knife. I ran." His voice was high, twitchy, with a bit of a stutter that pleased her immensely.

"You puking little liar!" She jerked up his head by the hair, dug the knife a bit deeper. He groaned, music to her ears.

A man's deep voice from just above her said quietly, easily, "Please don't carve him up here, ma'am. Mr. Wynn wouldn't be pleased. I'm Del Conroy, head of security."

Missy stilled, craned her neck to look up into a hard face, at odds with that smooth cowboy voice. He was older, with iron-gray hair cut short, a white shirt and slacks. "Please don't stop me, Mr. Conroy. I'm Missy. Missy Devereaux. I want to carve him up, but I won't if he tells me why he's been stalking me."

"A stalker? And you brought him down. Well done." He squatted down beside her. "Nice to meet you, Missy. And what's your name, sir?"

"I didn't do anything. She attacked me!"

Conroy studied the young man's face, spotted the midwestern accent, stood. "Up you go, Missy, I've got this now, if you don't mind." And he scooped her up beneath her armpits and set her on her feet. Both of them stared down at the man, who was rubbing his neck. Missy saw the smear of blood from her Ka-Bar and smiled.

Conroy said in the same calm, soothing voice, "I suggest you don't move or I'll let her cut your ears off." He turned back to Missy, who was still breathing fast and hard, not from all the running, but from the adrenaline rush. "Talk to me."

Missy's foot was raised to slam down on his back if he moved. The urge to kick him was nearly overpowering.

"Talk to me," Conroy said again.

"Phew, well, okay. Like I said, this out-of-shape worm is a stalker, been lurking around corners for months, even followed me here from L.A." And Missy couldn't stop herself, she kicked him, not very hard at all, really, since she wasn't in her boots, only sneakers.

He lurched to the side, hugging himself, and yelled, "You saw what she did. I'm going to have her arrested; I'm going to press charges. I didn't do anything. I was walking down the Strip, minding my own, and she starts screaming at me and waving that knife! I want you to call the police."

Del Conroy, a retired cop himself and head of security at the Wynn for three years now, knew that very probably nothing was going to happen to this guy, and hated it. He said politely, "Sir, again, what is your name?"

"Blinker—well, that's my nickname—I'm John Bayley. I have a good job. I'm a fine citizen."

"Why does anyone call you Blinker?"

"I'm a bond trader. I'm fast, I can make a trade in the blink of an eye."

A bond trader who was a stalker? That was a new

one, even to Conroy. He said, "Please give me your wallet, Mr. Bayley."

The man pulled out a butt-flat alligator wallet, good quality, Conroy saw, and handed it to him. A California driver's license, three credit cards, an AAA card, a gym membership for Fit Bods in Santa Monica, a couple of hundred-dollar bills. "You want to tell me what you're doing here in Las Vegas, Mr. Bayley?"

"Just like the other hundred thousand mutts wandering the streets out there, I'm here to unwind from the high-stress job I've got—see shows, play some machines—until this crazy girl came after me with a knife."

"You're thirty-two."

"Yeah. Let me up."

Conroy memorized the address in Santa Monica and gave Mr. Bayley back his wallet. "Get up, Mr. Bayley. We'll go back to my office and call the police." Del Conroy prayed the guy had prior charges, or he'd get off without a doubt.

Missy became vaguely aware of people's hushed voices and looked up to see a good dozen bystanders watching the little drama. She slipped the knife back into her pocket, tossed her head until her beautiful hair swirled and danced, and gave them a huge wave. "Come see me sing at the Mandalay tonight! I'm in *The Beatles Retrospective*." She turned, shook Del Conroy's hand. "Thank you for keeping me from sticking my knife in this pervert's neck. But I wanted to, I really did."

"I know, but you didn't. You did good."

"I didn't do anything! It's you who's going to jail!"

"Be quiet, Mr. Bayley," Del Conroy said. He turned to Missy. "Keep that Ka-Bar in its sheath, Ms. Devereaux. You don't want the cops to see it. How'd you get it through airport security?"

"I bought it here, at Larry's Pawn Shop. Why would the cops care? I was defending myself."

"Better to play it smart. With Mr. Bayley ranting how you sliced him up, they'll probably take it anyway."

Well, that didn't sound right. Missy eyed her stalker. "It's over now, anyway, you pervert. I know who you are and I'll soon be free of you. You're going to leave me alone or you'll be going to jail for a good long time. And me? I'll be normal again." She felt so very fine she started to sing her favorite song, "Twist and Shout."

2

Marty Sallas moved quiet as a thief, which he was, to one of the side windows of the small pastel-blue house, his glass cutter in his hand. It was a good fifteen minutes from the Strip, in a quiet middling residential neighborhood. Perfect, really, for what he had planned. He'd kept his eyes on his princess—called Legs by everyone in the cast of *The Beatles Retrospective*—for the past two days, ever since he'd noticed a rich guy coming on to her. Last night he'd seen the dude give her an expensive emerald-and-diamond bracelet from Laszlo's, a not-so-subtle inducement to hit the sheets. Tonight the rich guy wasn't with her, he was playing high-stakes poker again at the Mandalay, where he'd seen her singing and dancing in her show. Molly Harbinger was her name, but to Marty, she was his princess who would give him her crowned jewels. He looked at his watch, lit a cigarette. Of course he'd stick the butt in his pocket. Soon now, Molly should fall into bed, exhausted after her three-hour workout in the show.

Marty used the time to think about how he'd spend the money he'd get from this job. He was considering the San Juan Islands off the coast of Seattle, perfect weather this time of year, not like this hellhole, and who cared there'd be no hot girls hanging out drinking beers? He'd buy himself a wet suit and swim in Puget Sound. He had to pay off Alf, a security guard at Laszlo's, who'd texted him the particulars about the bracelet. The rich dude had shelled out fifteen big ones. So one thousand to Alf. It always paid to keep his boys happy.

Marty froze when the kitchen light came on at the rear of the house. He moved around so he could see into the kitchen. Why wasn't she in bed, getting her beauty sleep? He'd seen her caress the rich guy's hand just that afternoon, over two glasses of chardonnay, the bracelet sparkling in the dim bar light, and heard her thank him again, tell him she had two shows tomorrow, and she needed to get to bed early, but—lovely pause—she was off Monday. The guy had bowed out gracefully, no doubt he'd wet-dream his night away. Marty hoped he would win big at poker and give her more bling. The princess deserved that.

It was after midnight and there she stood, wearing pink pajama boxers and a tank top, drinking water over the kitchen sink. *Back to bed, princess, back to bed, time's a-wastin'. Come on, honey, it don't pay to hang around in one place too long.*

He heard a man's wheedling voice but couldn't make out the words, then the princess yelled, "I told you to get out of here, Tommy! What you did this time tears it. You gambled away all the money I've saved. Get out now, you loser, I don't want to see your stupid face again."

Marty had thought she'd already drop-kicked Tommy, a car salesman she'd been seeing over on Marian Avenue. No loss, the jerk. The fact is, he'd believed she was alone. Where was Tommy's car? Marty didn't like this, didn't like it at all. He had to be more careful.

Whatever, boot the jerk out, princess. Get your beautiful self back into bed and into dreamland, and I'll give you something to guarantee a good night's sleep.

Marty eased back toward the front of the house and hid himself in a mess of red bougainvillea. He was waiting patiently for Tommy to come trooping out the front door, when he heard a motorcycle coming down the quiet street. It was moving slow, as if the driver was looking for an address. At this hour? What was wrong with people? Even in Las Vegas regular people slept at night. It was only delusional brainless yahoos flying in here from who-knew-where who stayed up all night.

The motorcycle stopped in front of the house, idled. What was this crap? Had Tommy called a friend to pick him up? Or was it someone else sniffing on Marty's turf? Nah, another thief wouldn't be cruising around on a loud-ass motorcycle. He'd be hiding, like Marty, biding his time. Marty cursed low. All he wanted was to get in, lay a chloroform mask over his princess's nose, watch her snap awake, then breathe in and pass out, three seconds, tops. He'd find that bracelet and get out with no one the wiser, but no, he couldn't catch a break. First a boyfriend and now this motorcycle, and who was this guy? He heard the front door slam. So Tommy had called a buddy to come get him. Everything was all right. Tommy climbed aboard and the motorcycle revved and rocketed down the street. No more drama. Neither idiot was wearing a helmet.

Marty would give her another twenty minutes at least. If she was mad at the boyfriend, it'd take her longer to calm herself and float off to dreamland. He waited, listening, and now there was only the sounds of crickets, a coyote in the distance, but nothing else except a light desert breeze.

Finally Marty pulled the glass cutter out of his pocket and walked quietly toward the second-bedroom window.

Then he heard something, like a door opening real quiet, like someone sneaking around who didn't want to be heard. No, impossible, it couldn't have come from the princess's house. She was alone. But his heart still pounded. Maybe he was getting too old for the business. He waited, the glass cutter poised in his hand.

Marty pressed the button on the side of his watch, lit up the face. Nine minutes after one o'clock now. He hadn't survived this long by being stupid. He waited another five minutes. Nothing, no light, no sound. Everything was as it should be. The neighbors were all tucked in, pets snoozing, Tommy and his motorcycle buddy watching a late movie, guzzling beer.

Marty carefully carved a small circle in the glass, gently lifted it out with tape, and stuck his hand through the opening to unlock the window. He hoisted himself up and carefully eased inside the second bedroom, more an office, he thought, seeing the small desk, the laptop, a chair. He quietly closed the window, no sense taking a chance that a sudden noise outside would awaken her. He stood a moment in the darkness, listening, then pulled out the cloth wrapped around a small bottle of chloroform from his jacket pocket, and soaked it good. He walked silently to the door, opened it, looked out into the darkened hallway. There wasn't a sound, not even an air conditioner, and that was good, it meant the princess was fast asleep. Would she have the bracelet on the nightstand next to her? That would make things easy. In his line of work, though, Marty had learned early on that something that easy happened maybe once in a decade.

He crept toward her bedroom, at the end of the hall, his sneakers soundless against the wood floor. The bedroom door was open. He slowly looked around the edge of the door.

And nearly fainted. He managed to keep his shriek in his throat, but the figure bending over his princess sensed his presence, turned, and Marty saw his face in the shaft of moonlight coming in through the bedroom window. He was wearing goggles smeared with blood and had a bloody knife in his hand. As the man jerked away from the bed, Marty saw his princess covered with blood, saw her head bent at an impossible angle, saw blood still oozing from her neck, all in a millisecond. And he could smell the blood, thick and hot and coppery. Marty ran back down the hall, threw a bookshelf down behind him. He heard the killer's shoes hitting the wood floor in the hall behind him as he ran back into the small office. Marty dove out the closed window headfirst, cutting his hand on his way through, but he didn't slow. He rolled to his feet, clutched his hand to his chest, and ran to where his car was parked three streets away. Only when he was driving away did he look back. He didn't see anyone. Had the man seen his face? Would he be able to find him?

Marty's heart pounded and he was still panting from his run and from stark terror. He'd never been so afraid in his life. He felt the pain in his cut hand only then, smelled his own blood, only not nearly as thick and fetid as the smell in the princess's bedroom.

It wasn't until later, after his hand had been

stitched in the ER across town, and he was cruising on morphine, did he feel rage at what the monster had done. He'd stuck that knife into the princess—his princess—he'd slit her throat. And then he'd come after Marty.

3

FBI Special Agent Dillon Savich looked up at the light tap on his open door to see Special Agent Cam Wittier looking ready to jump out of her skin. What had her boss, Criminal Division Unit Chief Trey Morgan, told her? Savich waved her in. Before he tapped the key that darkened MAX's computer screen, he knew she'd seen the grisly murder scene photo. He said matter-of-factly, "That's one of the crime scenes from a particularly nasty set of tourist murders in Bar Harbor, Maine. People expect to enjoy themselves there, not get knifed to death in their motel rooms.

"Five dead as of yesterday. The police chief called me early this morning, asking for help. But enough of that. Come on in, Agent Wittier. Sit down."

Cam settled herself, crossed her legs, and smiled at the man she'd always thought was as sexy as a Wild West sheriff at high noon. She'd pictured how he'd look moseying around in a long yellow duster and a pair of black boots with spurs, of course, when she'd first met him at a computer-coding class he'd given at Quantico. It was a bummer he was married to Sherlock, a good friend and kickboxing partner, and had to stay a fantasy, a no-go forever. Life, Cam sometimes thought, looking at Dillon Savich, was out of sync for her.

Savich said, "Trey told me about those crooks in suits in Philadelphia—two bankers and three of their lawyers, was it?—you took down for fraud and embezzlement. And recovered twenty million dollars they'd stashed offshore. Congratulations. He told me he did a punk-rock duet with you as your reward."

"Thank you, sir. It was a lovely reward, since Trey likes to dance when he celebrates. The only problem is he had no idea how to dance to punk rock, but that small detail didn't slow him down. Quite a sight.

"He told me I was to be on special assignment with you, sir. But he didn't tell me what it was about."

"Call me Savich or Dillon."

She tried it out. "Dillon. Please call me Cam, not Camilla, as in Prince Charles's longtime love. My dad named me after her, said she had more guts than the queen." She shut up, seeing his smile was distracted. It was understandable. Here she was being a motor-mouth, since she was still flying high over bagging those overdressed scum in her fraud case. After seeing the huge smile on the federal prosecutor's face, she knew she had an "in," that her chief might give her another plum assignment. Who knew Dillon Savich would request her?

"Cam, I asked for you because you're a good boots-on-the-ground investigator. Your boss tells me you can see connections others don't, and you're a pretty good interviewer, gifted at getting people to trust you. Let me add that Sherlock recommended you. She was very impressed when you tied her legs around her neck at the gym. To be honest, though, the biggest plus you have for this assignment are your L.A. connections. Even Mr. Maitland believes you'll be a perfect fit for this particular case. Let me add you're a lifesaver, since the unit is swamped."

She basked in his words. "Sir— Dillon, what would you like me to do for you?"

"We have a Serial out of Los Angeles who broke pattern and jumped state lines. He killed an actress in Las Vegas Saturday night, and that makes the whole business federal. We'd like you to go to L.A. and coordinate with all the various sheriff's departments and the LAPD and catch this guy."

She held back from jumping out of her chair and pumping her fist, but her eyes were shining. "My mom's been keeping me up to date on those murders. She called me when the murder in Las Vegas hit the news yesterday, said she'd worked with that young woman who was killed, Molly Harbinger, last year. Mom thought she was talented, could really sing and dance, and she was still wide-eyed and sweet, not to mention gorgeous. Same M.O., killed in her own bed like the other four? About midnight?"

He nodded.

"Mom's neighbors are really on edge since the third

serial murder. It was in the Colony, you know, in Malibu, and a lot of people knew the murdered girl, Constance Morrissey. She was always nice, Mom said, probably sleeping with Theodore Markham, the influential producer who was renting her his house, not that anyone cared. My parents had never met the other murdered actresses."

Savich nodded. "We don't have much of anything on the four murders in L.A., but in Las Vegas—I think we've caught ourselves a break. I spoke to Police Chief Moody, who knew all about the Serial and was happy to hand it off to the FBI. There are anomalies in the murder Saturday night."

She was sitting so far forward in her chair, Savich was afraid she might tip over onto his desk.

"The Serial's M.O. is cutting the alarm wires, then coming in through the back door. But in this case, in addition to the back door being broken open, a glass cutter was used to cut a circle out of a window in the second bedroom to open the lock. Chief Moody tells me he's convinced there was a burglar in the victim's house that night as well as the Serial. The burglar saw the Serial or the murder scene and ran for his life. He threw himself back through the window to escape, left big jagged shards of glass outside and he cut himself. Forensics found blood drops leading away from the house. The shape of the blood splatter showed the wounded man was moving fast, probably running all out.

"Believe it or not, the same man ended up in the Valley ER early Sunday morning to get his hand stitched. He used a phony name and address, paid cash. We have him on video at the hospital. He was wearing a hoodie, so the cameras didn't get enough of his face to identify, but the blood means DNA for us. If he's in CODIS, we'll have a name right away. The chief put a rush on it."

"Going to a local ER wasn't especially bright," Cam said. "If he'd been thinking straight, he'd have wrapped it up and driven a hundred miles to another town."

"Agreed. A sketch artist is working with the doctor who stitched him up. We should be hearing soon from Agent Poker in Las Vegas."

Her eyes lit up. "His name is Agent Poker? Is that a joke?"

Savich grinned. "Special Agent Aaron Poker requested Las Vegas, said he knew he'd fit right in, and evidently he does. I'm thinking it's his own little joke. He's been there four years now, and has a good close record. I spoke to Aaron this morning, and needless to say, he's pumped, and all over this."

Cam said, "So another criminal—a burglar—might identify the Serial. Now there's irony for you."

"If he pans out, and talks, I'll personally offer to clean his slate, buy him a beer and a pizza.

"You'll have a lot of politics to untangle in L.A." Savich looked at MAX's screen. "The first murder was February 26th, a twenty-four-year-old actress, Davina Morgan, from Lubbock, Texas. That was in Van Nuys, LAPD jurisdiction. The second was April 2nd, in San

Dimas, which is a sheriff's jurisdiction. Her name was Melodie Anders, twenty-six, from San Diego. Constance Morrissey, your parents' neighbor, was murdered May 3rd in Malibu, again a local sheriff's jurisdiction. The fourth victim was Heather Burnside, twenty-eight, from Atlanta, Georgia. She was killed in North Hollywood, LAPD, June 2nd. For whatever reason, the Serial then traveled from there to Las Vegas in order to murder Molly Harbinger this past Saturday.

"Cam, I told you one of the reasons we selected you is because of your L.A. connections. You were born and grew up in Malibu, and as you know, Connie Morrissey's murder happened in the Colony, not far from your parents' house. Your folks are actors. They're still active, aren't they?"

"Oh yes. I guess you could say acting is their life. They play stock characters now, mostly. Movies, TV, anything they can get. They enjoy working as much as Michael Caine, Dad told me, only for a lot less money." She gave him a fat smile, showing nice white teeth and a dimple in her left cheek. "I do know the alligators in this particular swamp and they're a special breed. Their brains, well, they don't work quite like ours do."

"You mean normal, like cops?"

She laughed. "My folks think an alien deposited me in the hospital nursery, since I've never had any interest in the business. Thank you for asking for me, Agent Savich— Dillon."

He smiled at her. "Try to remember that only bad guys call me Agent Savich."

"When you have them in a half nelson, right?"

"Sometimes. With the murder in Las Vegas, we have five dead movie stars, all young women, in four different jurisdictions. The Serial's M.O. is always the same. He cuts the alarm wires, comes in through the back door, cuts their throats during the night when they're in bed, asleep. There's never been any signs of a struggle. Then he's gone. Clean, fast, silent. Now, something that's been kept out of the news: he takes their tablets or laptops and their cell phones."

Cam sat forward. "Any idea why? You think he's afraid there's something to connect them to him?"

"We don't know yet, but we know they're important to him. This past Saturday night in Las Vegas, not even the burglar surprising the Serial was enough to rattle him. Even when he couldn't catch the burglar, he didn't panic. He went back and took the victim's Toshiba and her cell phone that she'd left charging on her night table. Very cool, very together.

"Molly Harbinger had a boyfriend, name's Tommy Krug, a car salesman. Agent Poker said the guy wouldn't stop crying, admitted he was there until sometime after midnight. A buddy picked him up on a motorcycle. The buddy is a blackjack dealer at the Mirage casino, verifies Tommy's alibi. The two of them went to Tommy's place and played cards."

Savich gave her Agent Poker's email and cell phone. "If you have questions, or as Aaron gets more information, he'll call you or you'll call him.

"But you're not going to Las Vegas, Cam, you're

going to the Lost Hills Sheriff's Station in Calabasas, to work with a Detective Daniel Montoya. He's the lead on Connie Morrissey's murder. He was also the first to realize we had a Serial. He's been working the case, and he'll be the one to brief you."

"Why won't I be working with the LAPD? The last murder was in North Hollywood and they have more resources. Why a sheriff's detective?"

"First let me tell you about Montoya. He's thirty-one years old, a year out of Army Intelligence, and fairly new to the job. He was bright enough and experienced enough to get promoted into a newly retired detective's slot. He's got the background for it.

"As I told you, he was the first to figure out we were dealing with a Serial and alerted all the law enforcement agencies in the L.A. area. It took Montoya and three murders to get that far, even though the first two victims were both young actresses who had their throats slashed and their computers and cell phones taken. And why is that? I wonder." He arched an eyebrow at her.

Hallelujah, Cam knew something about that. "So many young people in L.A. are would-be actresses. On the Hollywood food chain, the victims were still guppies. They were all hoping to luck into that one glowing role that would put them on the red carpet, but hardly any of them ever walk it. My parents told me these women were a very long way from being household names. So, to the detectives, at the beginning at least, they'd simply be individual cases."

Score one for Wittier. "So that's one question you've answered. Another you'll have to address is how and why the Serial picked them.

"We don't want you staying at your parents' house while you're on the job, it could get complicated. You'll be staying at the Pinkerton Inn in Malibu. As you know, the Calabasas sheriff's station handles Malibu. The sheriff—"

"—Dreyfus Murray. I know him, Dillon. My mom dated him before she met my dad. Way back in the day."

And with those few words, she knew she'd proved her value to him. Of course, she would bet her next paycheck he already knew all about Dreyfus Murray.

"That should assure your cooperation with that office, unless your mother broke his heart and he hasn't gotten over it."

"Nah, he's been married twenty years. Mom said they're good friends, wife, too."

"Mr. Maitland spoke to the LAPD chief of police Martin Crowder. They've known each other a very long time, he told me, and he could speak frankly." He paused, raised a brow.

"I'm sorry, I don't know him."

"That's okay. Chief Crowder is a bit peeved that his people won't be running the case, but he's resigned to it. He informed Mr. Maitland that the LAPD would have tagged the Serial by now if two of the murders hadn't happened in outlying sheriffs' districts. David Elman, head of their Homicide Special Section, had already spoken to the sheriffs' people. Mr. Maitland asked him to arrange a meeting at LAPD headquarters tomorrow with all the sheriffs' detectives and LAPD detectives who've been working the case, get everyone together, face-to-face, with Montoya. Make it perfectly clear you're in charge, Cam, that it's you who will decide what directions to take them.

"I'll download all the separate murder books to your iPad so you can review them on your flight to L.A. this afternoon—autopsy reports, crime scene reports, bios of all the detectives working the cases.

"You'll have to start by not shooting any of them at the meeting tomorrow. I doubt the sheriff's department detectives will give you any trouble, but you never know. Sherlock told me you deal well with male egos at the gym."

An eyebrow went up. "Me? I marvel at her skill at that, Dillon. There's never any bloodshed."

Since he marveled as well, he couldn't disagree.

4

Savich watched Cam Wittier stroll through his unit, taking her time because there were eight agents to touch base with, and, of course, there was Shirley the unit secretary. Cam had her smiling and talking—about her health, her family's health, about all her pets' health. That was smart. Any agent with a brain knew the unit secretaries ran the FBI universe. Shirley was grinning from ear to ear when she handed Cam her airline tickets and itinerary.

He'd picked the right agent to work with the local cops in L.A. It wouldn't be easy with all those territorial egos vibrating when a *federale* walked through the door. There was something about Special Agent Cam Wittier, something shining and vital. Energy seemed to pulse in the air around her. She could draw people in like a magnet, maybe even some of those suspicious L.A. cops who would think she was there to bigfoot them. Yes, he'd picked right. If an outsider had a chance of navigating the alligator-infested waters of L.A. without undue carnage, it was Wittier.

Sherlock appeared in his doorway. "She'll knock 'em dead, Dillon. The way she reads people, not to mention that brain of hers—it's all good. I've come to haul you off to lunch. I'm thinking maybe some Chinese—"

His cell belted out Jessie J's *Bang Bang*.

He answered and heard a whispery voice, thin as old parchment. "Dillon?"

"Venus? Is that you? What's wrong?"

"Yes, Dillon, it's Venus. I daren't speak louder. Someone might hear me, the wrong someone."

"Venus, I can hear you fine. What's going on? What's wrong?"

"Dillon, someone's trying to kill me." Dillon stared at his cell. Kill Venus Rasmussen? Was she losing it? No, not Venus. At eighty-six she still had her shark brain, still ran Rasmussen Industries with an iron fist. He'd spoken to her a couple of weeks before, and she'd been fine.

"Talk to me, Venus."

Her voice sounded a bit stronger now, but still muffled. Was she hiding in a closet, a handkerchief over the phone, so no one would hear her? "Last night we were celebrating Alexander's acquisition of some quite-valuable Japanese watercolors from the Fukami collection for the Smithsonian. Well, of course I did some groundwork for him, helped him convince Mrs. Fukami to donate the watercolors, but he pulled it all together, well, mostly. We had champagne after dinner and I only drank enough for two toasts. An hour later, after I was in bed, I began shaking, my stomach cramping, and I threw up. Veronica—you know Veronica, my companion—she called my doctor and he was there in fifteen minutes. He said it was an old lady's stomach, sensitive to food I'm not used to. That's what he said the first time, too." She snorted. "Dillon, the thing is, the first time wasn't bad, but then it happened a second time, and then a third time. And I keep getting 'old lady's stomach' tripe from him. Dillon, I know it wasn't because I'm a sensitive old lady. This time it was really bad, much worse than before. I felt ill for three hours. I told Dr. Filbert I wasn't allergic to anything—he already knows that, of course—that it had to be something else. I reminded him I'm eighty-six years old and after all these years I know my body. This wasn't old lady's stomach; this is something else entirely. I told him I believed I was being poisoned. He didn't laugh, smart man, even said I could go to the hospital and be tested, but I wasn't about to do that. You know what the media would do if they got hold of a tidbit like that."

He heard her draw in a deep breath. "I looked up some poisons on the Internet by myself. Dillon, I think it may be arsenic. And whoever is feeding it to me came close to killing me this time."

He couldn't get his brain around what he was hearing. He knew Venus wasn't an alarmist. She was solid as a rock, and sharper than his dad's hunting knife. "Have you told anyone in the household of your suspicions?"

"Of course not. I'm old, but I'm not a moron."

Good, that was the Venus he knew, tough and no-nonsense.

"Dillon, I'll admit it, I'm frightened, but more than that, I'm angry. Someone close to me, someone in my household, is trying to kill me. I mean, it's not like I'm tight-fisted with Guthrie or Alexander. For goodness' sake, Alexander is my heir apparent. He will eventually run Rasmussen Industries after I step down. Or I'm dead. As you know, both Alexander and his father live with me, so neither of them have any big expenses to deal with. They both have all the money they need. And Hildi, I'd bet my last dime she's happy, painting to her heart's content. Years ago I settled a lot of money on her, hired a manager to see to both her and little Glynis. Well Glynis isn't so little now, is she?"

"We'll talk about all that when we get there. Twenty minutes, Venus."

"Thank you. I'll tell Veronica and Isabel that you're coming for lunch. I don't want anyone to know why you're really here." She paused, then she spoke through her pain, loud and clear, "I can't bear it, Dillon. What if it's one of my family? Could any of them hate me so much they want me dead?"

After he punched off, Savich told a puzzled Sherlock exactly what was going on as they walked to the garage. Neither of them wanted to accept it. If it was true, if Venus was being poisoned, it was a betrayal they couldn't imagine.

Sherlock said as she fastened her seat belt, "Your plate's full, Dillon, but there's no way you can say no to your grandmother's best friend. Do you remember that article about her in the *Washington Post* a couple of months back? They called her a local treasure."

"That fits her well," Savich said as he pulled the Porsche out into traffic. "Can you imagine how she feels thinking one of her own family wants to murder her? I know Guthrie and Alexander are both, well, not exactly selfless, loving human beings, and I know there's resentment there on Alexander's part. I'm afraid what this would do to her if it turns out to be poison and one of the family is responsible."

"Venus is tough, one of the toughest people I've ever met. Whatever happens, she'll deal with it, she always does. Don't worry, Dillon. We'll help her figure this out. We won't let anything happen to Venus."

5

The Porsche was impatient to move out on such a bright warm day in June, but Savich couldn't let his baby roar, not in the city. When he turned onto 19th Street NW, Sherlock said, "Venus may be wrong, Dillon, about the arsenic. Her symptoms weren't very specific, and you know how easy it is to get misled about medical problems on the Internet."

"You're right, for most people. But remember I told you Venus regularly beats my mom at Scrabble? And Mom's a whiz. I have to doubt Venus would ever be misled. We'll have Dr. Amick in the forensics lab test her for all the toxins and poisons he might think could have been used." And Savich made the call, got the ball rolling.

Five minutes later, he pulled the Porsche to the curb in front of what Realtors everywhere called the Grand Chateau, Venus Rasmussen's home for more than fifty years, the A-list Washington property.

Sherlock always loved visiting this house. Venus had

told her a famous architect, Andre Pellier, had built the three-story pale yellow brick French chateau in 1911. He'd been lavish with terra-cotta and limestone floors, a sweeping staircase, a mansard roof, and tall dormer windows. Full-grown oak trees were thick around the house, their leaves shading all but the double front doors. Several embassies had asked to purchase the house over the years, but it was always a nonstarter.

Venus had remodeled the mansion in grand style in 2006, and now she shared it with her eldest son, Guthrie, and his son Alexander, as well as her longtime companion, Veronica Lake. Together they occupied only four of the eight large bedroom suites.

"I wonder exactly how large this place is, Dillon."

"Around fourteen thousand square feet, if I remember correctly." He came around and opened her door, as was his habit.

Sherlock said, "I hope Alexander isn't here. He'd blow his stack if he believed we suspected him."

"We won't have to deal with Alexander today. Venus only wanted the three of us. Also, neither Alexander nor Guthrie know about this yet."

She sighed. "To want to kill your own grandmother? I don't see even Alexander doing that. Still, if it is arsenic, and it is one of the family, my money's on him. But it would break Venus's heart if it were any of them for that matter. I sure hope she's mistaken about the arsenic."

"If she's not, it could be someone outside the family, who, for whatever reason, wants her dead."

Isabel Grant, Venus's housekeeper since Moses, Isabel would say and laugh, opened the door, welcomed them in. Isabel was tall and thin, her salt-and-pepper hair worn in a severe chignon, showing very pretty ears with diamond studs. She was dressed as she usually was in a plain dark dress and sensible shoes. Sherlock remembered Isabel had once told her the original thirteen fireplaces still worked, but now they were seldom used, what with central heating installed in the sixties.

Isabel shoved her glasses back. "Agent Savich. Agent Sherlock. I'm so glad you could come so quickly. Ms. Venus is very upset, why, she won't tell me. I do know she was ill last night. If you're here, it's something bad, isn't it? No, no, I can tell it's not for my ears yet." She eyed both of them. "You two look very professional and very dangerous."

Sherlock blinked and patted her arm. "That's good to hear, Isabel. How are your daughter and the twins?"

Isabel smiled so widely they saw her gold molar, so pleased she was to be a grandmother. "Yvette called me last night, said she was so tired, she'd fall asleep in the babies' bathtub if she'd fit. But she's happy as can be. Follow me. Ms. Venus is in the living room waiting for you. Whatever is wrong, I know you will fix it."

They followed her through the large terra-cotta foyer and turned right into the grand living room. Venus was alone, holding what looked to be a glass of iced tea in her hand. Where was her companion, Veronica? Venus didn't rise. It looked to Savich as if she'd been crying. That shook him. He'd seen her cry only two times—at his grandmother's funeral, and when he'd been a small boy, at the funeral for her husband, Everett Rasmussen.

Savich had known her all his life for the simple reason that Venus and Savich's grandmother Sarah Elliott had been girlhood friends. He remembered Venus breaking down at his grandmother's grave site, and he'd held her, swallowing his own tears.

Savich and Sherlock each leaned down and hugged her. Sherlock looked closely into her eyes for signs of lingering discomfort. Thankfully, she didn't see any. Sherlock sat beside her, Savich on the chair facing them.

"It's nice to have you both together with me again, under your grandmother's painting, Dillon. I wish the circumstances were different."

He looked up at the large painting by his very famous grandmother that hung over the fireplace. "I remember as a boy looking up at that windswept coastline of Brittany, wondering what it would be like to be right there, the seawater cold and wet against my legs, the wind tearing at my shirt, and bowing the trees—" He broke off the familiar poignant memories.

"Half a dozen museums have come around to woo me, buy me outrageous gifts, to get me to bequeath that painting to them. But no, Sarah's painting will remain in the family. She gave it to me after Everett died, to help me feel again 'the boundless energy of life,' as she put it." It was Venus's turn to fall silent, and then she said, "I miss her, Dillon, every day when I look at that painting, I think of her and her immense talent, and everything we shared throughout the years—the laughter, triumphs, the tragedies. I suppose she told you stories of our time in Paris back in the bad old days?"

"Yes, she did, but I always thought she edited out the good parts."

Her sharp green eyes turned bright. "I certainly hope so. I've always believed that's why we're all young once, to do stupid, wicked things that will amuse us until we die."

After Venus's husband had died in an industrial accident in one of his steel plants in Pittsburgh, she had overcome the shock and grief and filled the breach and taken over his kingdom. She'd earned the title of Queen Rasmussen, and soon no one doubted she was in charge. She made all her business decisions without sentiment. One made enemies wielding that much power. For decades she was an undisputed mover and shaker in Washington. Now, at eighty-six, she was an icon.

Savich said, "Venus, our forensics lab is sending over a tech within the hour to take a sample of your blood and hair. Dr. Amick requested a urine sample as well. We'll know very soon if indeed someone is trying to poison you. But I want to proceed on the assumption that you're right. So tell Sherlock and me about the first time you got ill. Where you were and who you were with, and when."

Venus opened up a small black notebook, thumbed

to the first page. "Guthrie, Alexander, and I were at the Ambassador Club on K Street three weeks ago, Wednesday. No celebration, only a simple dinner out. I ordered the lobster chasseé, a specialty of the chef there who invented it. I do remember it was a bit too spicy for my taste, but their champagne cocktails were divine. I drank two, but spread out over two hours, then I had a cup of decaf coffee."

Savich leaned toward her. "At the club, did anyone come by, stay any length of time to visit?"

"When I'm out in public there are always people who want to schmooze. Check to see if I'm senile yet, I suspect."

Savich laughed. "Not much chance of that. Did any of them get near your food?"

"Frank Zapp—you know him, Dillon, he's been one of my accountants for a dozen years or so—he stopped by, and I asked him to have a seat. He had a cocktail with us. I asked after his wife, and he told me she was leaving him. Not much to say to that except to commiserate, and he soon left. I believe two others came by—a city councilman I met at the mayor's office and a member of the board of regents at the Smithsonian whom I've worked with, but the visits were short, too short for any of them to slip poison into my lobster."

Sherlock said, "When did you get ill, Venus? What were your symptoms?"

"We got home about ten o'clock. Veronica helped me to bed, but I had a lot on my mind. There's a merger we're working on with a family-owned company outside Boston. They're not happy, but they need our money desperately and they're having trouble accepting the consequences. I got a sudden terrible headache that made my head spin, an upset stomach with cramping pain. And I felt nauseated. The worst of it lasted about thirty minutes. I didn't even buzz Veronica, simply took some antacid and some Tylenol. Then everything was fine again. I called my personal physician, Dr. Filbert, in the morning, and he told me it was probably from the lobster chasseé, too much for my eighty-six-year-old stomach. It made sense. I hated it, but I accepted it."

"Did you tell anyone you were ill?"

"Certainly. I mentioned it to Guthrie and Alexander. I was concerned they'd gotten ill as well, but they hadn't. Veronica agreed with the doctor. I believe she phoned the chef at the Ambassador's Club, asked if the lobster had made anyone else ill. But no one else had called."

"Tell us about the second time."

"That was last Friday evening. I was with Guthrie and Alexander again. Hildi and Glynis should have been there, but Glynis wasn't feeling well and her mother stayed with her. We had dinner at the Wallingford Bistro over in Foggy Bottom. I had some consommé and a house salad, basically a Cobb with some roasted pine nuts artfully scattered on top. Nothing at all iffy, not after my experience with the lobster.

"I started feeling nauseated and shaky when we arrived home. I had some terrible abdominal pains and an upset stomach. The room was spinning. This time, Veronica wanted to call an ambulance to go to the emergency room. I called Dr. Filbert instead, and he thought it was my old lady's stomach again—but to cover himself, he wanted to order a hundred tests, all of them unpleasant and undignified. I told him I'd think about it, see if the symptoms passed. Guthrie and Alexander were at home with me. Like Veronica, both of them wanted to call an ambulance, but I was feeling better by then. They both seemed satisfied with what Dr. Filbert said."

"My daughter, Hildi, called the next day when she found out, but she wasn't too worried, said I was an iron horse. As for Glynis, her headache was gone and she was out shopping."

Savich knew Venus's granddaughter, Glynis, was the jet-setter in the family. She never seemed to be happy, no direction in her life, always racing to fill her time with buying designer clothes and globe-trotting to the latest "in" spots. She'd been divorced twice, had no children. Had she really been ill? Who knew.

And Hildi, her mother. Savich remembered his grandmother grinning and shaking her head over Hildi. "Venus never imagined birthing a hippie artist, yet she did, all the way down to her tie-dye and Birkenstocks." He also remembered his grandmother telling him that Venus had paid off a man she called a "creep," who'd married Hildi for her money after getting her pregnant with Glynis, to disappear from the Rasmussens' lives without so much as a by-your-leave. How had Hildi felt about that?

Venus paused a moment. "Do you know, Dillon, Hildi turned fifty last month? Can you imagine? My own child turning fifty! Of course, Guthrie's fifty-eight, but people of my generation never really think of men as getting old—they simply fall over of a heart attack at some point." She fell silent, looking down at the rich nap of the Persian rug beneath her feet.

She looked up finally. "A lot of politicos have dinner at the Wallingford, so we spent most of our time meeting and greeting, which is why I rarely go out to a restaurant anymore. It's exhausting, but Guthrie urged me to go, said he really liked the chef's way with artichoke risotto. No, none of our visitors from the first time at the Ambassador Club were there, as I recall." She raised eyes drawn with strain to Savich's face. "And then this last time. Last night. It was horrible, much worse. I was here, at home, with Guthrie and Alexander. Hildi and Glynis dropped by. Mr. Paul served us coffee and apple pie. It happened fast—after ten minutes, I could hardly stand, the room was spinning so. And I noticed my urine was dark, almost black. And that's when I researched poisons on the Internet and found my symptoms perfectly fit arsenic poisoning. Then I knew someone, maybe someone in my family, someone of my blood who lives with me, and claims to love me, is trying to kill me."

6

Sherlock said, "Venus, let's take one step at a time."

Isabel appeared in the doorway. "Agent Savich, there's a Bill Carlson from the FBI here."

"Good. He's arrived earlier than I thought. He'll draw your blood, Venus, take a couple of strands of your hair and the urine sample Dr. Amick from our forensics lab requested. We may know in a couple of hours what we're dealing with."

"I do hate needles," Venus said. "Always have. Still, it's better than an ambulance ride."

"That's the truth," Savich said, and patted her hand. As he spoke, he studied her elegant face, saw she was in control again. She was looking back at him, her eyes sharp, determined and intelligent. He knew she had to be focusing on her son and grandson, Guthrie and Alexander, as the ones trying to murder her, impossible for her not to since they'd been there with her on all three occasions. However horrible such a betrayal might be for her, he saw she would pull through this. She would go on.

Savich rose. "Come on in, Bill. We're ready here."

The blood draw was quickly over. Bill was good with a needle and stuck her vein on the first try with hardly an intake of breath from Venus. "Beautiful veins you have, ma'am," Bill Carlson said as he patted down a cotton ball over the puncture site and pressed on it. "Now, a couple strands of your hair. You press on the cotton pad and it'll be over in a flash." And it was. "Now we need a urine sample." He handed her a small plastic container, her name written on it in Magic Marker.

Venus took the container, nodded to Savich and Sherlock, and left the living room. She returned a few minutes later with a small paper bag, handed it to Bill Carlson.

"Thank you, ma'am. Agent Savich, I'll put a rush on this and call you as soon as I know."

They heard Isabel speaking to him in the entrance hall, heard the front door open and close.

Sherlock said, "With your permission, Venus, another team will arrive later to pick up the ingredients from your dinner last night and to go through the kitchen and pantry. If there's anything questionable there, they'll find it."

Venus laughed. "I can only imagine the look on Mr. Paul's face."

Savich pictured Mr. Paul's aesthete's face, his mouth

pinched, and a manic gleam in his black eyes. "It can't be helped. From now on I'd like all your meals to be prepared outside the house and delivered here until we get a better handle on this. Isabel can do the ordering. Don't eat anything except what's delivered, all right? That also includes from Veronica. She's not here because you haven't spoken to her about this, correct?"

Venus looked both miserable and angry. "No, I've only spoken to you. I sent her out to run some errands for me."

Savich said matter-of-factly, "I think we should call Isabel in now, only Isabel, no one else. I'm sure you realize, Venus, if Sherlock and I are going to be of help to you and keep you safe, we can't keep what we're doing a secret from your family. If the tests show any kind of poison, we'll need to have you examined to make sure you're all right, and then we'll need to talk to your family, all of them."

"I'm sure my family will want to help, at least that is my profound wish."

Venus called in Isabel and recounted the story she'd told Savich and Sherlock. Isabel was speechless at first, then furious that such a thing might be possible in the Rasmussen household. "Isabel, we're not even certain yet of any of this, you understand," Venus said. "And please keep this discreetly held."

Isabel nodded, her eyes brimming with tears.

"It will be all right," Venus said, and hugged her

close. "You and I have dealt with many things in our years together, we'll manage this as well. Don't worry."

Isabel pulled back to look at Venus. "Of course I'll worry! What's happening, it's not right. It's evil. But it can't be one of the family, oh no."

Savich said, "Yes, it is evil, Isabel. We're here to find out if it's true and then we will all take care of it. Now that you know, order in Venus's meals. And let's begin with lunch."

Venus patted Isabel's shoulder. "I'm in the mood for some nice chicken consommé, crème brûlée, and a Caesar salad from *L'Etoile*. Dillon and Sherlock, will you please stay for lunch?"

"Thank you," Sherlock said. "It will give us more time to talk while we wait for your lunch to arrive."

"Isabel, if you would make the order, then tell Mr. Paul we have two guests for lunch, one of them a vegetarian. Please have Mr. Paul place anything left from our dinner last evening in cartons, to be tested."

Isabel nodded and said to Savich and Sherlock, "Mr. Minendo at *L'Etoile* is very fond of Ms. Rasmussen. I will call him right now with her lunch order. He will oversee the preparation himself." She looked from Venus back to them. "No one will touch her food." Then she left the living room.

Savich said, "Venus, you were telling me about the third time, last night, that you were ill, but you didn't give me details. Let's go over that now."

She shook her head. "I didn't call for help. I waited it out, then decided it was time to help myself. I looked up symptoms of poisoning on the Internet. It was easy enough to find. Arsenic can cause every one of my symptoms." She paused a moment, looked at them. "Dillon, Sherlock, let me say how grateful I am that you believed me without hesitation. I appreciate that."

Savich said simply, "You are the most down-to-earth person I know, Venus, not to mention the smartest. Now, this third time, the symptoms were really bad."

"Yes, but I gritted my teeth and endured. Maybe I should have gone to the ER, but I decided if the media got hold of that, it wouldn't be good for the company, or my family."

Sherlock said, "Venus, you're very powerful, you've influenced many lives over the years. I'd say it's impossible for you not to have made some enemies. Does anyone stick out in your mind, anyone who has personal reasons, or who might profit a great deal from your death?"

Venus smoothed her pale veined hands over her black silk trousers, ran her tongue over her lips. "As for personal reasons, I certainly hope not. As for financial gain, I could prepare a list. In business one tries to become a resource and a partner, more valuable alive than dead. Ah, there is Ellis Vaughn, a senior accountant I had to fire three months ago. My COO showed me proof he was embezzling from us. I let him go rather than call in the police, mostly because I knew his wife and three kids, and I liked them. But there are always people like that in one's life. His trying to get revenge doesn't make sense to me. And how would an accountant have gotten to my food, anyway?" She swallowed, looked away. "I've told you, only Guthrie and Alexander were with me each time."

They saw tears swimming in her eyes. "It's a horrible thing to imagine, Dillon. One of my own flesh and blood. I don't want to believe it, even now, even with last night being so bad."

"Make the list, Venus. We'll go over it later. Let's talk about Alexander. Have you noticed anything unusual in his life lately? Some change in his mood? Anything at all?"

"I'm sure you know Alexander can be a prick—don't look shocked, you two. Even old ladies know how to lay something obvious out in modern language. He's embarrassed me more than once with his sense of entitlement, acting like some kind of crown prince. I recall he was rude to you the last time we met at the art museum benefit. Implied it was somehow low class of you to spend your life dealing with criminals. Of course, he'd never say anything outright against you to my face, but I apologize for that. He's my grandson, but—"

Sherlock leaned forward and laid her hand over Venus's arm. "With Alexander, there's always a but. Has anything changed in your relationship with him, Venus?"

Venus smiled at Sherlock. "I knew Dillon had hit the jackpot the very first time I met you. No, Alexander is still very much himself. I'd hoped all the hurly-burly competition of working in a top law firm would teach him to think a little less highly of himself. He's always been sharp as a tack, but he's still got a lot to learn about leadership, about how to deal with people if you want them to work hard for you. I'm finding teaching him that slow going." She shrugged. "Anyway, though I've never told him outright, I assume he knows I have picked him to take over for me when I retire or pass on to the hereafter. Not either of my children—not Guthrie or Hildi. Hildi, because life is all about her painting. I had hopes for Guthrie, but after his wife died he lost interest in everything, including his life. Although Glynis is bright, she has no interest, no ambition. I pray that will change. I think her free-spirited mother, Hildi, gave her too little structure when she was growing up. And of course she grew up without a father.

"So my successor is Alexander. Last year I arranged a position for him as a consulting lawyer for the Smithsonian—they were pleased enough that a Rasmussen family member would be associated with them in a role like that. They provided a small office for him in the tower. He's concerned with the provenance of their newly acquired collections, rather than simply focusing on making money, as he did with that law firm in New York. Of course, he doesn't appreciate my pressing him into that position, but I felt it was important for him to be involved in bettering the community, in giving back. Our family has never failed to do that. I'd hoped he'd settle in after a time, but I'm afraid he's not very happy there."

Savich imagined that all Alexander—never Alex— wanted was to leave Washington in his rearview to run Rasmussen Industries from a newly relocated headquarters, most likely New York. He never seemed much interested in giving back. He recalled that Alexander had been eased out of the prestigious law firm in New York—Rathstone, Grace, and Ward—in his second year. Why? Was he not up to it? Or was it malfeasance? "Venus, why was Alexander let go from Rathstone, Grace, and Ward?"

She seamed her mouth. So there was something there, something Venus didn't like to talk about. Savich let it go. He'd ask Alexander in interview. "What about his personal life? Is he seeing anyone?"

"After he and Belinda divorced three years ago, he did go through a rough patch. I know he's escorted high-powered women to various functions from time to time, but as to anyone special, he hasn't said anything to me nor would I expect him to. He's very private."

Savich said, "All right. Let's talk about Guthrie."

"I dearly love my son. I can't imagine he would be responsible for this. If such a thing did ever come to his mind, it would fall right back out. His life is easy and comfortable, predictable, and he dearly likes that. He's always been rather indolent, in fact, and utterly indifferent to woes not his own, which is a pity because he has a very good brain. I think my husband

and I spoiled him rotten, not intending to, of course, but it was the early years of the Vietnam War and so many young men were dying and we loved our son, wanted the best for him.

"Like Isabel, I agree this is evil. Guthrie isn't evil." She shook her head, looked at them straight on. "The only worthwhile thing Guthrie ever managed to accomplish was to marry the woman who gave birth to his second son, Rob—so bright, so eager to eat life right up."

Savich cocked his head, surprised to hear Rob's name. Robert Rasmussen was the black sheep of the family, wild to a fault as a teenager, arrested for joyriding, marijuana, and a couple of bar fights. He'd escaped prison only because Venus had pulled strings. "Rob? You've heard from him?"

Venus was silent.

Savich said, "It's been what, Venus, ten years?"

"That's neither here nor there," Venus said. "He has nothing to do with this." She rose slowly, not waiting for Savich to help her. They heard Isabel coming.

"Mr. Paul is setting out Dillon and Sherlock's lunches, Ms. Venus, and *L'Etoile* just delivered yours. All of you are free to come to the dining room whenever you wish."

"A moment," Savich said, and took himself off to the modern kitchen, the size of two New York apartments, to speak to Mr. Paul personally. He was greeted by the smell of Spanish risotto and several classic Gallic shrugs from Mr. Paul, who accepted his apologies with raised brows and rolling eyes. His opinion was that some malcontent in the steel business, possibly a German, had crept into the kitchen and done this foul deed. He turned up his nose when the lovely lunch from *L'Etoile* arrived. The chef there, he believed, was a commoner with no imagination.

He served Savich and Sherlock his Spanish risotto, freshly baked rolls to die for, and a salad of poached pears. As Savich took a bite of the risotto, better than his own, he had to admit, he thought again of Rob. Venus had seemed to mention him by accident. Why? Was he back? Had he contacted her, asking her for money? Was Venus still protecting him? Was Rob Rasmussen a seasoned criminal now, maybe the one responsible for this? The more Savich thought about it the more he was convinced Venus was right. It was poison.

Sherlock bit into a roll, closed her eyes at the taste. Then it was back to business. It was like she was reading his mind when she said, "Dillon once told me Rob was more than a bit wild, but he always liked him. He said Rob was a straightforward guy who never made excuses. Dillon and Rob had a fight once, you know. Dillon couldn't remember what it was about. Since he was four years older than Rob and trained, he put him on the ground in no time, held him down. What was it he said to you, Dillon?"

"I remember he was gushing blood from his nose. When I pulled him to his feet, he tore off a sleeve and pressed it hard against his face. Then he started laughing and said no matter I'd bloodied his nose I was still a wuss and he guessed he owed me a beer."

Venus smiled but didn't say anything. What was happening? He'd hoped that story would open a spigot, but it hadn't.

Savich went with his instincts. "Venus, you know I always liked Rob, but I couldn't ever figure out how to help him, how to make him see that occasionally doing something other than shooting himself in the foot could be a smarter choice. Then he was simply gone, into the army. Ten years I haven't heard his name spoken. Until today. You sounded pleased when you mentioned him. Have you seen him?"

"I'd rather not talk about him now, Dillon. I'd like to keep Rob out of this—this mess. I didn't mean for his name to slip out. I'm old, it happens."

As they were preparing to leave a half hour later, after a dessert of orange sorbet, Savich pulled Venus gently against him. "I know you're sure it's poison. I know you're scared and you're angry and you feel betrayed. But we don't know about any of it yet. Don't jump ahead and make yourself crazy. We'll be speaking with our forensics lab this afternoon, and I'll call you. Do think about that list, Venus, do it now. And don't forget, do not eat or drink anything given to you in this house. If you've been poisoned, you specifically have been targeted, no one else."

Venus pulled away. "It's very difficult. Thank you, Dillon, Sherlock, for coming." She walked with them to the door. "I'll get the list to you as soon as I'm able.

Now, though, I have to get to a board meeting at the office. Life must go on."

Sherlock said, "Tell your driver, MacPherson, to be extra careful, all right? Have him escort you in and out of the building. And don't worry, we'll figure this all out."

"Yes, of course you will. I feel better now that you know. MacPherson will love playing my protector. He's been complaining he has too little to do. This should keep him occupied."

7

Sherlock laid her hand over Savich's as he was firing up the Porsche's magnificent engine. "I'm so glad we came, Dillon. How do you want to handle looking into Rob? There's got to be something new happening between him and Venus, some reason she still seems to be protecting him."

"Which might be a mistake. First thing I'm going to do is find him, call him in for an interview." He'd pulled away from the curb when Carrie Underwood sang out *Two Black Cadillacs*. It was Ollie with additional crime scene photos of the murders in Bar Harbor, Maine, he wanted Savich to look at right away. He pulled the Porsche over again as he went over them with Ollie. He'd just slipped his cell phone back into his pocket when three fast shots rang out from behind them. From the Rasmussen mansion.

He slammed the Porsche into reverse and skidded to a stop in front of the house. He and Sherlock were

out in a flash and headed for the garage on the far
side of the house, Glocks drawn. They heard a fourth
shot.

They saw MacPherson in the Bentley first, saw
him floor the car straight back toward a man who
was standing next to the garage, a gun raised, aimed
toward him. The man leaped out of the Bentley's path
and fired twice more at MacPherson. MacPherson, no
fool, was scrunched down low in the driver's seat. The
man had shot out the back window of the Bentley and
now the driver's window shattered. Where was Venus?
Had he hit her?

"FBI! Drop the gun, now!" The shooter jerked
around to face them, fired two wild shots, then jumped
through the ornamental gate that led to the gardens in
the rear of the house, and out the service entrance to
the alley.

"Sherlock, stop him from getting to the service
road. I'll follow him." He stopped a moment next to
the Bentley. "MacPherson, are you all right? Is Venus
all right?"

"Yes, we're both okay. Mrs. Rasmussen is down on
the floor in the back."

Venus popped up, shouted, "Dillon, go get him!"

"Stay with her. Call 911." Savich jumped the garden gate and ran down the winding path bordered by
cascading jasmine and trellised roses, past a beautiful
Italian fountain and several stone benches. He stopped
near the service gate and listened, heard the man
still running, in the alley now. Had Sherlock made

it around to the service road? He yelled, "Drop your weapon! FBI!"

The shooter didn't drop his gun, he whirled around and fired twice, wildly, then ran, bending over. Savich raised his Glock and fired back at him. He heard the sound of garbage cans flying, and a curse. He crouched low as he went through the open gate, heard two bullets hit the garden wall behind him, two feet above his head.

Savich fired again toward the garbage cans. He heard a loud ping, then silence. He looked around the gate, but saw no one, not the shooter, not Sherlock. He couldn't fire again, couldn't take the chance of hitting her.

He stepped out into the service alley, heard Sherlock yell, "Stop right there, it's over! You try to shoot again and I'll blow off both your ears."

He saw the shooter now, crouched behind the garbage cans, looking back toward Sherlock, and he moved forward, his Glock center mass on the shooter. "You heard her, drop your weapon!" His voice brought the shooter's attention back toward him, but the shooter rolled and came up, running, his gun raised, and fired off two shots at Sherlock. Savich's heart was beating madly as he ran toward them. He heard another gunshot and his heart stopped. When he came around the alley into the service road, he saw Sherlock standing over the shooter, rocking back and forth on his knees, moaning, holding his right wrist, Sherlock standing over him. His gun—it looked like a .45 Chief's Special—lay on the ground beside him. Sherlock kicked the gun away, looked up and grinned at Savich. He slipped his Glock back into his waist holster as Sherlock planted a knee in the middle of the shooter's back, pulled out her handcuffs, jerked back his left wrist and snapped a cuff on. She hesitated. She couldn't very well handcuff his other hand, not with his wrist shot up. "All right, stay down—" The shooter grabbed her knee, threw her off, rolled and pulled a knife out of his jacket with his left hand. He was panting with pain, and fury, jabbing the knife at her as she jumped to her feet, her Glock aimed at him. He cursed, and took off down the service road.

"Not smart, you moron!" she yelled after him. "Don't make me shoot you again."

She started after him, but Savich ran past her. He was on the man fast. He stopped, reared back on his left leg, and kicked out at the shooter's left arm. He heard the bone break above the elbow, watched the knife go flying. The shooter screamed and fell to his knees, both his arms at his sides, his right wrist gushing blood, the handcuff dangling off his left.

They looked down at the groaning man who was now in the fetal position. "A real tough guy," Savich said. "You okay, Sherlock?"

"Yes, but this dude isn't."

Savich knelt down by the shooter, pulled out a handkerchief and wrapped it around his bleeding right wrist. "I suggest you press hard to stop the bleeding." The bleeding wasn't that bad now, but thinking about it might focus his brain and keep him quiet. He ran his hands over the guy's legs and belt, no more weapons.

The shooter looked up at him, eyes glazed with pain and shock. Then he looked over at Sherlock. Savich saw rage in his dark eyes, and he wanted to kick him again. "Now both your arms will be out of service for a while. I doubt you'll lose either of them, although you deserve to for being so stupid."

Sherlock said, "I'm giving Ollie a big kiss. If he hadn't called with those crime scene photos, we wouldn't have been here." She went down on her knees. "We've got help coming. You want to tell us your name?"

The man whispered between groans of pain, "You bitch."

"Well, that's a unique name."

He whispered *bitch* again, turned his head away, and said nothing more. She imagined the pain had to be over the top. Then he whispered, his voice blurred with shock. "I can't believe you're FBI, I mean, driving that fancy Porsche? I watched you talk, talk, talk to the old biddy, and then I heard you rev that engine and leave."

They heard sirens.

Savich leaned over him. "And then Mrs. Rasmussen stepped out of the house and into her car and you decided it was your chance. You didn't count on her driver protecting her, did you? He nearly drove right over you. Who paid you to kill Venus Rasmussen?"

The shooter could hardly focus, his eyes rolling in his head. "I saw you leave. You were gone."

Four Metro cops came running down the narrow service road toward them, guns drawn. Savich and Sherlock put their Glocks on the ground, rose, and held their creds above their heads. They shouted together, "FBI!"

8

Vincent Willig was in surgery for more than two hours to repair the shattered bones in his wrist and fix a rod in his broken left arm. He would mend, the orthopedic surgeon told them, didn't even mind the feds talking to his patient right away, once he found out what the man had done. He gave them a salute and wished them good luck.

Willig had no ID on him, but there was no problem identifying him, his prints had popped up in minutes. Willig, Vincent Carl, born in Brammerton, Massachusetts, thirty-four years ago. He had an impressive sheet that included armed robbery and an attempted murder charge in New York that had sent him to Attica on his twenty-first birthday for a thirteen-year term. He was something of a hard-ass in prison, but managed to keep out of trouble enough to be released only weeks before.

Detective Ben Raven's captain at Metro let Sherlock and Savich take the lead, even though it hadn't been declared a federal case. Ben stood beside them as they looked through the window at Willig. Both his arms were thickly bandaged, immobilized and propped up on pillows, his IV line tethered to his chest. Before they stepped into the room, Ben said, "Mr. Willig isn't up to making a break for it anytime soon. But the person who hired him might be concerned enough to try to kill him, so we'll keep a guard on him while he's here. Hope that morphine he's on helps you guys."

Sherlock said, "He threw me off him and pulled a knife on me. That was humiliating, but it might help us, since I saw how much he dislikes women. I'll rile him up in no time what with me being the bitch who shot him. It's unlikely, but I'm hoping, like you, Ben, that the morphine takes enough of an edge off that we can get him singing *Kumbaya* before he realizes it."

The three of them surrounded the hospital bed and looked down at Willig, who was lying still as a stone, his eyes closed. His face was a bit sunburned, and Sherlock thought that was odd, until she realized he'd been in jail for a decade, had probably come out pasty-white, and headed straight for a beach or a tanning bed.

Willig's eyes flew open and stared up at Sherlock. His gray eyes were light as scattered smoke. Then they turned opaque and empty, and Sherlock would swear she could feel the black behind them. She knew all of them had seen eyes like that before. Willig was a seriously bad man.

Savich leaned over his bed, said quietly, "Your surgeon says your arm will heal. Your wrist will, too, assuming you get proper physical therapy, that is. If not, you'll be as helpless as a toothless dog."

Willig's voice was low, scratchy with the effort of talking. "You. Feel safe, don't you, since I'm all bandaged up? I'll use my arms again, you'll see, and come for you. I'll kill you, kill you hard." He looked toward Sherlock. "As for you, bitch, I'll have even more fun killing you."

Sherlock said, "Yeah, yeah, blah, blah. Hey, nice tats. Would you look at your left wrist—the one I didn't shoot. I like the snake wrapped around the man's neck, quite a statement.

"I have to wonder though, Mr. Willig, how much physical therapy you'll get in prison. You any good with your left hand?"

He didn't react, only stared up at her, his eyes filled with mean. "Wait a minute. I recognize you. You're that FBI agent who brought down that big-shot English terrorist. You think that makes you some kind of hero, don't you?"

She leaned close. "He was harder to take down than you, Mr. Willig. But I'd give you the nod for being more stupid. Whoever hired you to murder Venus Rasmussen didn't know how incompetent you are. Or was it because you came that cheap?"

Willig tried to jerk up but fell back, breathing hard, trying not to groan. "I'm not stupid. You and this bozo shouldn't have even been there."

She leaned in close. "Personally, I don't think it would have mattered. Ms. Rasmussen's driver nearly ran you down. Like I said, you're incompetent."

Willig didn't move, but his eyes were hot now, with rage at her and his own helplessness. "If I'd had you at Attica—"

"You just proved my point. I mean, trying to murder Ms. Rasmussen in her car, in the driveway, with two FBI agents twenty feet away and a smart driver in the car who laid it on the line for her. Do you see the idiot in this picture? Now, tell me about the other idiot, the one who hired you."

Willig tried to curse but it was swallowed on a moan of pain.

Savich laid his hand on Sherlock's arm, drew her back. "Mr. Willig, we'll see you get more morphine if you give us the name of the person who hired you to kill Ms. Rasmussen. We can also see to it you don't go back to state prison for the rest of your life. We'll talk to the prosecutor, get him to cut you a deal, but only if you tell us the name. Otherwise, you're going back for the rest of your life."

Willig sneered, or tried to, and turned his head away from Savich.

Sherlock elbowed Savich out of the way, leaned close again. "You're thirty-four and you're supposedly tough, or at least you know how to act tough. Maybe you'd last into your seventies, even in a place like Attica. You've already been there long enough to see the young bucks coming in. How long before you can't keep them off you? You'll be one of those older guys who survive as their personal slaves. Or maybe you'll get lucky and they'll shove a bar of soap down your throat in the shower."

Even though the pain had to be riding him hard, Willig didn't react. There was no give in him at all, certainly no mercy, and he didn't expect any in return. Sherlock was impressed despite herself—clearly Attica had taught him well. The only way to survive there was to keep your mouth shut. But this wasn't Attica.

Savich said, "Mr. Willig, tell us which Rasmussen hired you and we can make a deal."

Willig whispered, "I want a lawyer."

Ben stepped in. "Mr. Willig, do you really want to go away for life for the idiot who hired you? And you will, there's no chance of you getting out of this. We have the .45 Chief's Special you stole from Mr. James Wyndham's house in Baltimore, not three days after you were released from Attica. We have the motorcycle you parked behind those bushes two blocks away from the house and the lockbox you had strapped to the back, with your backup ammunition. We have ballistics, eyewitnesses. You're nailed, going down for the rest of your life. Tell us who paid you and like Agent Savich said, we'll cut you a deal."

"What kind of deal?"

Well, that was a start. Savich said, "I told you, we'll speak to the prosecutor, maybe he could see his way to reducing your sentence to ten years."

"Which is much better than a life sentence," Sherlock added.

"I want full immunity."

"That's not going to happen in this universe, and you know it," Sherlock said. "See, there's another example of your not thinking straight. Look, you've danced at this hoedown before, and you know what happens now. You either go down forever, or you make the deal with us. Last chance."

"I want full immunity," he said again.

Savich said, "Save yourself, Mr. Willig. How much did Rasmussen pay you?"

There wasn't a flicker of knowledge in his cold, dark eyes. "I want a lawyer."

The Rasmussen bait hadn't worked. Savich didn't hold out much hope, but he took a last parting shot. "We'll find him ourselves soon enough. He had to have paid you some of the money by now. Will we find it scattered in some bank accounts? Or will we find it all stashed under your mattress at your apartment?"

Willig was hurting, but when he spoke again, his voice was cold and hard. "I don't own any motorcycle. I want some morphine and I want a lawyer."

"Judges don't like thugs who try to kill cops," Sherlock said, her voice as hard as his. "And you know what else? You won't even be able to pay your lawyer, because all that lovely money will be in our evidence locker."

Ben said, "Very well. Shall I call the public defender?"

"I got money. I want my own lawyer."

"You mean Rasmussen's money, don't you?" Sherlock said. "Is Alexander Rasmussen your lawyer?"

"Nah, he sounds stuck-up and prissy. My lawyer is Big Mort Kendrick."

Ben Raven knew Kendrick well. He'd made a career out of defending lowlifes like Willig for twenty years. "Fine," he said. "Without an arm to use, you can't call him yourself. You want me to get him on the line?"

"Yeah, do it now."

Willig watched him dial up Kendrick on his cell. When Ben punched off, he said to Willig, "You heard him, said he couldn't talk right now, but he'll be here in an hour." Ben laughed. "I wonder what he'll say when he hears you tried your pitiful best to murder three people."

9

They heard Willig yelling for more morphine as they walked to the elevator. Ben asked, "Are you guys really looking at Alexander Rasmussen trying to murder his own grandmother? Or was that a ploy to get Willig talking?"

"A ploy that didn't work. But it's possible."

Ben gave Savich an assessing look. "A shame Willig didn't bite. You've got quite a mess on your hands, with the Rasmussen name such a huge deal here in Washington. It's like our own royalty was attacked. I know you're not surprised that my wife left me a text asking for something she could use no one else could find out quickly. She usually knows better, with all her years in the business, but that's how excited she is. I told her not to tell her editor, since he's a powerhouse at the *Washington Post* and would be after her to do whatever necessary to get a story."

Savich said, "Can't blame Callie for trying, Ben.

But she has to know the media's already all over this, gunshots at the Rasmussen mansion in the middle of the afternoon. Everyone who's tuned in on the news knows about the shooting by now. I've told Venus to tell her family to avoid the press entirely, or if cornered keep saying, *No comment.* Now if Callie can see her way to planting some information we might want someone to know, give me a call."

Ben said, "I will. Thank the powers above I know how to bribe her." He grinned. "I'll wash her hair for her in the shower. She really likes that. Always works."

Ten minutes later Sherlock and Savich walked out of the hospital lobby to the crowded parking lot.

Savich leaned down, gave her a quick kiss. "I wonder if Ben scrubs her scalp. You really like that."

"Oh my, yes."

"Actually, I'll bet Ben throws in a lot of things." He cupped her face in his palms, arched a dark eyebrow. "Speaking of showers, you threatened Willig with a bar of soap?"

She gave him a big grin. "Pretty cool visual, don't you think? A pity it didn't shake him loose."

"I wouldn't be surprised if Willig himself executed another inmate in that manner." They were getting into the Porsche when Savich's cell blasted out Lynyrd Skynyrd's *Free Bird.* It was Dr. Amick at the forensics lab. Savich listened, thanked him and punched off. "There was arsenic in her blood. They're still running the tests on her hair to see how long it's been building up in her system, but I won't be surprised if the poisoning started three weeks ago, that first time she was ill. So Venus was right."

Sherlock blew out a breath. "You never doubted her, and neither did I."

Savich said, "Some of his forensics team is still at the house. He wanted to examine Venus himself, but she insisted on her own doctor, Dr. Filbert, who cleared her after the medics left. She's still at home."

"I don't understand, Dillon," Sherlock said as the Porsche sped up through a yellow light. "A hit man—no other way to describe Willig—comes right to Venus's house—in broad daylight—to kill her? It doesn't make sense to me. How do you go from administering small doses of arsenic, enough to maybe still get away with killing an old lady without drawing attention, to an open assassination attempt? At her home, putting it all over the news? Alerting the cops? Is someone getting desperate?"

Savich nodded. "I'm thinking maybe Willig was only there to case out the place, and saw a prime chance to get it done."

"And he failed big-time," Sherlock said. "Or maybe," she continued, "someone is afraid that something that's now covered up will come uncovered if Venus isn't dead. And another thing. Let's say it was Alexander, or maybe even Guthrie, since they ate with her on all three occasions. How could they, or any other Rasmussen for that matter, find someone like Willig?"

"I don't doubt Alexander could find a hit man hiding in a monastery."

"Okay, having known Alexander over the years, I'll agree with that. Don't forget he's sly, manipulative, insulting—"

"All true, plus I imagine he's got a lot of contacts, not only in Washington, but in New York. As for the rest of the Rasmussens finding someone like Willig, you know as well as I do that the Rasmussen money could buy almost anything."

Sherlock said, "Also, one of Venus's staff could have managed it. And there's Veronica. Understandable that Venus didn't want her around today when she met with us, but she and Veronica are close; she spends most of her time with Venus, doesn't she?"

"Yes, for fifteen years now. They're so close Venus might even forget to mention her as a person of interest here. We need to check Venus's will and trusts she's made to her staff as well as to the family, look into each of their finances. We need to see who desperately needs money—not in five years, but immediately, right this minute.

"And there's Rob, of course, the long-lost grandson. I don't believe she suspects him, but every other Rasmussen finger will be pointing at him. No wonder Venus wants to protect him."

"What about that accountant, Zapp, who was with her that first time at the Ambassador Club?"

"Ruth ran a check on him, couldn't find anything. She told me he had a solid alibi for the second and third times Venus was poisoned."

"You know what I think? It's all too neat, too tidy.

Everything points to either Guthrie or Alexander."
Sherlock sighed. "It's like someone is handing us the
answer on a silver platter.

"Dillon, whoever is behind this had to know Venus
would figure it out and call the cops, or us, so he was
ready with Willig. Immediately."

Savich's phone sang out *Free Bird* again. It was Alexander Rasmussen—speak of the devil—at the mansion with Venus, playing the man in charge, demanding
to know what the FBI was doing to protect his grandmother, wanting to know how a shooting like that
could have happened and in the middle of the day.
Savich held his temper, there was no use goading Alexander, not yet. He; his father, Guthrie; his aunt, Hildi;
and her daughter, Glynis, were all at the house, gathered around the matriarch, probably fussing over her,
driving her a bit mad, knowing Venus. Still it was good
the family had come together, good for her and good
for the investigation. He wondered if they'd yet gotten
to the stage of accusing one another. Savich made a date
to meet them all at the house that evening and made
no comment when Alexander said he was hiring private
security since the FBI couldn't seem to protect her.

He punched off. "Alexander, playing lord of the
manor. We'll see the lot of them this evening. Let's stop
at Willig's apartment, give it a look over. He's not in a
great neighborhood; it's near the warehouse district."
When he turned the Porsche onto West Elmstead
Street, they entered a neighborhood that hadn't seen
any federal aid in decades, if ever. It was slowly col-

lapsing in on itself, overgrown with weeds surrounding low-rent buildings, some of the yards littered with abandoned cars. Savich stopped the Porsche in front of a building that should have been boarded up years ago. "He's on the third floor."

They saw three teenagers gaping at the Porsche and a half dozen older men and women sitting on the stoops, paying them no attention at all. Savich stopped on the steps and yelled out, "Anyone touches my ride gets five years in lockup. We're cops." He shifted his jacket to the side and let everyone get a look at the Glock, clipped to his belt. "I really like my ride."

They climbed stained creaking stairs, grateful there was enough light to see where to put their feet. On the third floor, they turned down a dark corridor, past an old man smoking marijuana in an open doorway, staring at them, uncaring and silent. Sherlock hoped that in his mind, he was someplace else, someplace nicer. Willig's door was locked, but Sherlock had her pick set with her. They were inside Willig's nest in under a minute.

It was one room with a single filthy window covered with thumbtacked newspaper, an ancient bathroom at its far end. There was a small fridge and a hot plate on the floor with empty pizza boxes piled up next to it, a single mattress and nothing else. They found two thousand dollars stuffed into the mattress, about the only place to look. When they left, the old man was still sitting on the floor, his back against the wall, humming and pulling bits of paper from his lip.

Sherlock knelt next to him, gave him her sunny smile. "Have you seen the man who lives in that apartment, sir? Or has anyone come by looking for him?"

The man stared right through her, his eyes vacant. He continued humming under his breath until Sherlock stood up and followed Savich out of the building.

They were glad to see the Porsche hadn't been touched. The teenagers were gone, and everyone else sat exactly where they'd been. It was eerily quiet.

"Two thousand dollars—that isn't very much for murdering someone, even as a down payment," Sherlock said as Savich drove back to the Hoover Building. "He either stashed the rest of it, maybe buried it, or Willig really is an idiot."

Savich flipped from station to station on the radio, listening to what the news had to say about the attempted murder of Venus Rasmussen, the CEO and chairman of the board of Rasmussen Industries. Her age—eighty-six—seemed to be the biggest news, as if it was astonishing someone would try to murder an old lady who could die at any time. He was glad to hear there was no comment from any of the family, and no formal statement yet from Metro. Savich knew the FBI's role would leak out soon enough and the tabloids would flock to the story with screaming headlines, FAMILY MEMBER OR BUSINESS RIVAL?

Yet again, he wondered how was it done? *Evil always finds a way*, he remembered his father saying.

10

At eight thirty that evening, Savich and Sherlock showed their creds to the single Metro police officer still on duty in front of the Rasmussen mansion. They saw the bright yellow crime scene tape still blocked the driveway. Behind it stood the stately black Bentley, its shattered glass scattered over the driveway, gleaming like diamond shards under the moonlight. The last of the news crews had left, thankfully, at least for the night.

When Isabel showed them into the living room, they saw a tableau of the entire Rasmussen family huddled around Venus, except for Glynis, who sat quietly opposite the sofa in a delicate Louis XVI chair, seemingly fascinated by her designer shoes. Only Hildi was in motion, hugging her mother tightly, nearly burying her in her substantial bosom, murmuring her outrage and relief.

Veronica sat a bit apart from the family, and Guthrie sat on Venus's other side, his hands dangling between his knees, looking like he wanted a drink. Alexander stood behind the sofa, at Venus's back, resting his hand lightly on her shoulder. Savich looked back and forth between father and son. *Were one or both of you feeding Venus arsenic? But if so, why would you be so stupid as to be the only ones present?*

Alexander looked up and stiffened. His handsome face hardened, he straightened to his full height and sneered. "So you're finally here. Are you going to tell us what you're going to do about this?"

Savich smiled. "Good evening, everyone. Venus, how are you feeling tonight?"

She looked relieved when she saw them and pulled away from Hildi. "I'll survive, Dillon, but the Bentley's going to be in the shop awhile." She looked a bit pale but solid, like she'd weighed what had happened, tucked it away, and faced forward. She was wearing a lovely black silk blouse that flowed loose over black slacks, her French pedicure on display in her open-toe gold sandals. Amazing. Try to kill her and you get a fashion plate. She was a formidable woman.

Venus waved them forward. "I'm so glad you're both here. If you want to speak to MacPherson, he's in the kitchen having his dinner. Mr. Paul grilled him a porterhouse steak, MacPherson's favorite, as a thank-you for his saving my old hide. Poor MacPherson—I'll bet he's having to listen to Mr. Paul complain about a team of federal techs coming into his kitchen to look for poison. Poison! He was quite incensed, but I don't doubt he was relieved when they left. He assured me they wouldn't have found anything.

"As you see, everyone is here, waiting for you. Everyone is eager to hear your ideas on who's behind this. Now, please sit down. I expect everyone will gird their loins and cooperate." Her words were bright and strong, but Savich saw the tension lurking in her eyes. He knew her well enough to see she was drawn tight as a bowstring after the wild shootout, and without knowing if anyone here was responsible. But she was playing the matriarch and, even more than that, the corporate executive, always in charge, always in control, even with her life on the line. Did the family resent her for being able to do that, or admire her strength? Or a bit of both?

Savich and Sherlock greeted every Rasmussen present, turning last to Alexander, who met them with his habitual sneer, and finally, Veronica, who gave them a wobbly smile. After they'd sat down on a love seat facing Venus and accepted coffee and tea from Isabel, Venus cleared her throat to draw everyone's attention and said in a firm, matter-of-fact voice, "I've explained to the family that your FBI lab confirmed what I thought. Someone has been slowly poisoning me with arsenic over the past month. Apparently the poison wasn't working fast enough, and so they launched the direct attack this afternoon. I survived only because MacPherson was a hero, nearly ran the attacker down with the Bentley." Venus's eyes glittered as she looked at each of them in turn. "I'm very thankful Dillon and Sherlock were still outside and actually caught the man."

Alexander said, "Grandmother told us his name is Vincent Willig and he will survive."

"Yes, he will," Savich said.

"So, has he agreed to tell you who paid him to kill Grandmother?"

Venus said, "Not as yet, Alexander, but I have some ideas about that," and she gave Savich a smile, her chin up.

Veronica leaned forward. "Yes, thank you both very much for catching that horrible man. Maybe now this nightmare will stop."

Hildi said, "How can it stop, Veronica? This Willig criminal isn't the one who was trying to poison Mother."

Glynis looked up. "Mother and I could move in."

"Yes, we could," Hildi said, and once again hugged Venus. Venus managed to pull back enough to pat Hildi's face. "You're very kind, my dear, and you, too, Glynis, but no, that won't be necessary. Veronica will protect me. She has for fifteen years."

Veronica said to Savich, "I failed her this time, I know, but you can take this to the bank, Dillon. I will not let Venus out of my sight."

Alexander flicked a piece of lint off his gray Italian cashmere blazer. "But we're still left with a killer who won't talk."

Venus, well used to Alexander, said, "Not yet, true. Now, Dillon, we know his name is Vincent Willig. Tell me more about him."

Savich set down his china cup. "He's thirty-four years old, a lifelong criminal, until recently an inmate at Attica for attempted murder. We spoke to him, offered him a deal if he would tell us who hired him. I'd wager he'll open up soon enough." He watched their faces as he spoke, hoping for an unguarded expression. He saw nothing except a look of relief from Hildi, a look of disbelief from Alexander. As for Guthrie, he looked miserable. Worry for his mother? Or did he still want a drink? Both Glynis and Veronica looked frankly worried. All of which told him exactly nothing. He didn't expect this to be easy. It could be none of them was involved. Maybe it was a business associate, someone covering up a crime, or who stood to profit. Venus had sent him a preliminary list that afternoon and he'd asked Dane to help Ruth start the process of checking everyone on the list, looking for financial motives.

Sherlock added, "We doubt Mr. Willig will want to be shipped back to prison for life. He knows that's what will happen if he doesn't tell us who hired him."

Alexander said, "It's possible this Willig has no idea who hired him. Or he could toss out any name he wanted to. Trust me, testimony from a convicted felon isn't worth much in court."

Thank you, lawyer Rasmussen. Savich gave Alexander a cool look. "Is that what you think happened? He took two thousand dollars as a down payment from someone who emailed him instructions, or wrote him a note? That he has no clue who his employer is?"

Sherlock saw the pulse pounding in Alexander's throat at Dillon's questioning his opinion. *Are you the one trying to murder your grandmother?* She said, "He's a career criminal, Alex, so there's no way he wouldn't do his due diligence—my bet is he knows exactly who hired him. And tomorrow morning, we may very well find out." She cracked her knuckles and smiled.

Did Alexander look alarmed? Or angry because she'd had the nerve to call him Alex and not Alexander?

Venus dropped her bombshell. "You know, Dillon, I would very much like to meet the man who tried to shoot me. It may help if he knows who he's dealing with. And there's a great deal I could offer him that the FBI can't. I'd like to be there with you tomorrow."

"Mother, no! You with this horrible criminal? No, you can't possibly want to do that."

Veronica said, "I agree. Venus, that isn't a good idea."

Venus patted Hildi's hand, smiled at Veronica. "You know, a lot's happened today that I've never done before. I never considered that I'd actually fit in that small space between the front and backseat of the Bentley, for instance, but when MacPherson yelled for me to get down, I did. Meeting Willig should be a walk in the park compared to all that." Her tone brooked no room for argument. Savich imagined she used the same tone to shut up opposition. The Rasmussen had spoken, and that was that.

"Good." Savich looked at each Rasmussen in turn.

"Guthrie, Hildi, Glynis, Veronica, Agent Lucy Carlyle and Agent Davis Sullivan will be speaking to you individually tomorrow morning. Please make yourselves available."

"What about me?" Alexander moved from behind the sofa to stand in front of the fireplace, his arms crossed, stiff as a soldier.

"I'll call you when you need to come to the Hoover Building," Savich said. "Keep your schedule open tomorrow morning."

"As if I have nothing better to do than wait for a cop to call."

Sherlock gave him her patented sunny smile. "I sure hope it's important enough for you, Alex, since someone is trying to kill your grandmother. Trust me, you'll find the interview room quite comfortable."

"What I want to know," Glynis said as she walked to the sideboard to pour herself a glass of water, "is who in our family could possibly want to kill Grandmother?"

11

Guthrie poured himself a glass of gin, drank it down without pause, felt it steady him. "Savich suspects either my son Alexander or me, Glynis. And for good reason. Alexander and I were with Mother all three times before she became ill, no one else." He turned to Savich. "You're not really going to look anywhere else, are you? The obvious road for you *is* to try to nail one of us. Or both."

Alexander's voice snapped out sharp and impatient. "And that would be ridiculous, Father. Neither of us have any reason to harm Grandmother. There are, naturally, other answers, including the truth. There are hundreds of people, major companies, that might think they could benefit from attacking Grandmother, our family, like this. Multimillion-dollar contracts, mergers, share prices might be at stake." He shot a look at Savich. "But looking at all of them would be difficult. And these two would need to have the intelligence and resources to look *in the* right place, and of course that is a big problem with law enforcement today."

Hildi was wringing her hands. "It's got to be an outsider, someone who hates Mother because she took over their company, fired them, or something. I know this family, and none of us would ever do anything like this, never. Dillon, both Guthrie and I have always loved our mother, and of course Alexander and Glynis love their grandmother. This—evil plot isn't us; it can't be us."

A moment of hot silence, then Glynis laughed. "Wouldn't that be something? One of us sneaking around, putting a pinch of arsenic in Grandmother's coffee without anyone seeing us? Without anyone knowing we were hiding behind the curtains?"

"The first two times, the arsenic was probably in my champagne," Venus said coolly, eyeing her granddaughter. "At a restaurant."

"Better yet," Glynis said. "The murderer disguised as a waiter."

The phone rang.

Veronica, sitting nearest to the phone, rose, lifted the receiver, listened, snapped out, "No comment," and hung up. "Another reporter. At least there are no more of their vans camped outside the house. The neighbors wouldn't allow that. They called the police and three squad cars came and shooed them away.

"I was sorry to see them go. With everyone leaving, I don't think there's enough protection for Venus."

Alexander said, "I understand from the officer outside that a squad car will remain here overnight, then our own private security will arrive in the morning. Grandmother will be amply protected. The guards will stick with her around the clock."

Venus nodded her thanks to Alexander, who stood shoulders squared against the fireplace. She looked at Hildi, her artist-hippie daughter wearing her habitual tie-dyed long skirt and peasant blouse, those ridiculous pearls, so many strands, and Birkenstocks on her long narrow feet, Venus's own feet, she realized. Hildi's dark hair hung long and straight down her back, mixed now with strands of white that looked like an amateur attempt at highlights. Hildi had only her art and her daughter to tether her to this earth ever since her worthless husband, Elliott DeFoe, had stepped willingly out of her life years before. An abandonment that Venus, admittedly, had orchestrated, but she'd never expected her daughter to remain unattached for the decades following. It made her sad sometimes to think of Hildi alone. And then there was Glynis, in her designer clothes from head to toe, looking like a beauty queen next to a bag lady. She was divorced now, too, and adrift.

Venus smiled at each of them and said, her voice thoughtful, "Each of you is so different, but that's what makes all of you so very interesting. I've loved all of you forever, tried to make you happy, tried to stay out of your lives. And I have to ask myself: Does one of you hate me enough to want me dead? Couldn't that person wait until I drop over myself?" Venus swallowed, then to Savich's surprise, she lowered her head in her hands and began to cry quietly.

Everyone but Hildi stayed frozen in place. "Mother!" Hildi pulled Venus to her, patting her back, stroking her hair, cooing like a dove in her ear.

Sherlock watched every face react to Venus's breakdown. She saw consternation on Guthrie's face, a bit of contempt on Alexander's, and Glynis's face was a study in embarrassment. Veronica had already jumped to her feet but stopped when she saw Venus pressed against Hildi. She sank back into her chair, her expression angry and worried.

Savich and Sherlock waited, watching Hildi fuss, watching Isabel silently press a fresh cup of tea into Venus's hand. Was it all a performance?

Venus took the cup of tea and slowly raised her head. Sherlock saw her eyes were bright with the sheen of tears. Then the weeping old lady became the boardroom queen again. Venus said, "I apologize for that. Now, listen. We have to face the facts as they are, children. Someone who lives or works in this house is very likely responsible for trying to kill me, someone close enough and clever enough to poison me. Whoever that is, whether they are in this room or not, I want them to know I will not let my family be destroyed.

"I do recognize that I'm old. But you know what? I do not want to depart this earth until I'm good and ready." She looked at each of them in turn. "Every one of you has enough money for two lifetimes. If one of you is in trouble and you see your inheritance as your only way out, you need to come to me now, and we will work it out. I will forgive you, and I promise I will do my best to fix your problems. Please, come to me before Agent Savich shows up at your door." Venus turned her laser-beam gaze onto Alexander. "And if any of you think you're smarter than Dillon and Sherlock, you are dead wrong."

Savich turned to Venus. "Have you told the family about finding Rob?"

Savich heard a quick intake of breath from Guthrie, who stared at his mother, stunned. "What? You tracked down Rob, Mother? Is he all right? Where is he?"

Venus gave Savich a long look and slowly nodded. "Of course he's all right, Guthrie, and if you had cared, you could easily have found your son yourself. He's been living in Peterborough, Maryland, for the past three years. He owns a construction company that, I might add, is running in the black this year. And he has a girlfriend. Her name is Marsia Gay, and believe it or not, she's an artist, and very successful. Evidently Marsia worships your grandmother's work, Dillon, which predisposes me to like her.

"As for finding him, I simply googled his name, but before I could contact him, Rob emailed me, wonderful coincidence. We met for lunch at *Primavera* in Chevy Chase, neutral ground."

"How long has this been going on?" Alexander asked, his voice strained.

"About three months. Alexander, your brother is thirty-one, he's matured, and, I might add, he is stable and has his life together. He told me how much he's missed all of us. He'd like to see everyone again."

Alexander said, both his face and his voice expressionless, "Don't you think it's more than possible that Rob is the one trying to poison you, Grandmother? Unlike any of us, he's actually come into contact with low-life criminals like this Willig."

Venus arched a perfect eyebrow. "Then your brother would have to be a magician, would he not? He'd have to have slipped into two different restaurants unnoticed, and then the third time, into this house, and somehow put arsenic into my food or drink.

"Yes, I can see from your faces that you're wondering why I wanted to contact Rob. That's easy enough—he's my grandson and I'm getting older, and I wanted to see what sort of man he'd become. Then his email arrived and I decided fate had taken a hand."

Alexander shrugged. "Like fate would care about my worthless brother. I'll bet old Rob leaped at the chance to ingratiate himself to you, didn't he, Grandmother? He always was bad news, you know that, all of us do. People like Rob don't change. Have you forgotten what he did? He should have gone to jail. I hope you won't encourage him further. I, for one, have no interest in seeing him again. You shouldn't either, Father." Guthrie stared down at his Italian loafers. "He's a criminal and a loser." Alexander shot a look at Savich. "And he should be your top-running suspect."

Venus's voice was like a soothing oil. "I knew you'd hardly approve, Alexander. But as I said, Rob has made quite a transformation. You'll be surprised."

"I've actually heard of his girlfriend," Hildi said. "Marsia Gay. She works in metals, very modern sculptures, mostly human figures. She's considered something of a wunderkind, being so young."

Venus said, "I haven't met her yet, but it seems it's serious. And I haven't had a granddaughter-in-law since you and Belinda divorced, Alexander." She smiled over at Hildi. "It might be nice to have another artist in the family."

Hildi beamed back at her. "I always liked Rob. Such a vibrant boy, so full of promise. Such a shame what happened."

Glynis said, "I can't wait to see Rob again. Do you know he kissed me once? We were seventeen, I remember, and even though I didn't want to, I had to tell him to cut it out, we were first cousins, and kissing was against the law, or something. I know better now. Imagine, Rob's not in jail or dead. That's wonderful."

"You can tell Rob that yourself, Glynis," Venus said. "I've invited him and his girlfriend to dinner tomorrow night. I expect all of you to be here and to welcome him home."

There was steel in her voice again. Savich had no doubt every single Rasmussen would be present. As for welcoming Rob home—who knew?

12

Sheriff Dreyfus Murray had been notified by Special Agent Morgan, Criminal Division Unit chief, that one of Morgan's people was coming from Washington to assist in the Serial case. Assist them, now that was a joke. A Fed was coming to take over the case, more like. He hadn't been told a name. He spotted her the second she walked through the door. He could tell from twenty feet away that she was a looker, tall and fit, striding like she owned the world, and looking like she could outrun him when he'd been twenty. She was wearing dark blue pants, a tucked-in white shirt, a red blazer to cover her Glock, and black banged-up boots with a high shine.

Then Dreyfus Murray did a double take.

"Cammie, is that you, girl?"

A smile bloomed. "Dreyfus! How lovely to see you."

He hugged her, then set her back, shaking his head. "Of course I knew you'd gone into the FBI, but—look at you, here you are, the bigfoot Fed sticking your nose in my business. What's it been, three years since I last saw you?"

Cam smiled. "Nah, I'm no bigfoot, my feet are princess-size. Well, maybe a nine isn't all that small, but still, even my toes have no intention of wriggling under your tent. Yeah, about three years, it was Mom's birthday and you brought her balloons and cupcakes. Speaking of Mom, after I told her I was coming, she laughed, said I should surprise you, and that's why I didn't call."

"Lisabeth's a real joker, always having fun, always getting such a kick out of life, even though she didn't marry me." He sighed. "Everything turned out for the best. I finally had to admit your dad is an okay guy. He's never strayed, unusual for an actor, right? Even my wife likes your mom, but not enough to invite her to dinner more than once a year."

"No, Dad and Mom are a rarity in LaLa Land— happily married for longer than I've been alive. Must have something to do with them staying outside Hollywood's rarified A-list. How's Suzanne? And the boys?" Cam asked.

Murray shook his head. "Can you believe none of them wanted to be cops? Engineers, the four of them, two of them partners in a company they started up, Murray Engineering, and they're populating Southern California. We're up to ten grandkids now." He turned to his dispatcher. "Hey, Al, a couple of coffees for me and the lady Fed. Still drinking it like a girl—half milk?"

She laughed. "No coffee for me, thank you."

Murray ushered her into his office, sat her down. "Now, you tell your mom to keep out of this. I know she and your dad knew Constance Morrissey, lived what—eight houses down from them in the Colony? They're to steer clear, all right? I don't want them taking any chances, and you know your mom, she wouldn't hesitate."

"I'm not even staying with them, Dreyfus. They'll have their ideas about Constance Morrissey, I'm sure, but they won't be knocking on doors and questioning people." She paused. "Well, more than they already have. I'll tell them again to stay away from all this mess."

"Well, that's something. Are you sure they'll listen?"

"Not really."

"Don't know why I asked in the first place. Okay, Cammie, if you're ready to meet my detective who's lead on this case, let me take you to Daniel Montoya. He was here for a week when Constance Morrissey was murdered. May 3rd. He's the one who figured out we had a Serial on our hands." He sounded like a proud papa, so Cam didn't bother to tell him she'd already found out everything there was to know about Montoya and she'd read his murder book cover to cover. He'd done all the right things, and more, put the two other murders from different sheriffs' jurisdictions together himself, and spotted the Serial.

"I'll be glad to meet him. We've got lots to do today. First thing, I want to visit the house where Connie

Morrissey was murdered, maybe stop by my parents' house. Then Detective Montoya and I will head to the new Parker Center for a meeting I've arranged with detectives from all four of the jurisdictions the Serial has struck. I'm hoping it will help us all get on the same page, get us working together."

"It's occurred to us the Serial may have killed in different jurisdictions to confuse matters, to slow us down. Not only that, three of the murders were in sheriffs' areas, not LAPD jurisdictions."

"Could be. Don't know."

"You'll find out. It sounds like quite a big-dog meeting, a real free-for-all." He eyed her pretty face, her short blond hair as wavy as her mom's. "I hope you survive."

She gave him a big grin. "Have some faith, Dreyfus. I intend to herd all those territorial egos into the same holding pen as sweetly as I can, use my branding iron only if they get too frisky. I understand Montoya's ex–Army Intelligence. I saw from his murder book he knows his way around a computer, has a good brain. I imagine he isn't particularly happy to have the FBI here in his face, messing with his case. I hope you told him to play nice."

"Daniel's not an idiot, he'll cooperate." He looked at a younger version of her mother, Lisabeth, the woman he almost married. Cammie had her mother's face and her wide infectious smile, not to mention the dimple identical to her mother's, adorable when she was seven years old. "But I'll tell you, Cammie, when he gets a look at your face and that smile of yours, only the good Lord knows what he'll have to say."

Cam knew a smile got a woman FBI agent only so far. It didn't help with perps taking her seriously, or with some male agents and law enforcement, for that matter. She could but try. "Please, Dreyfus, it'd help if you called me Cam. Not Cammie—sounds like I'm still seven and smearing birthday cake all over my face."

"Cam. Sounds good." Sheriff Murray led her into the bullpen, not all that large a room, with maybe twelve desks, half occupied, buzzing with low voices. The men and women detectives were on their cells or typing on their computers, one talking with a perp or a victim as he leafed through a file. She smelled bitter coffee, like every other cop shop she'd ever been in. It felt like home, down to the doughnut crumbs and the half, lone bear claw lying on the table next to the pot of coffee, probably strong enough to corrode stomach lining.

"There he is, over there, the guy with the Mac laptop, the cell crunched between his shoulder and his ear, and the bagel in his hand."

Cam eyed Detective Montoya, then turned when Dreyfus said, "I'll let you introduce yourself. Keep me in the loop, Cam," and left her to it.

Cam walked over to Montoya's ancient banged-up cop desk, stood quietly beside him as he spoke in a slow comforting voice on his cell, maybe talking to a witness or a victim. If he saw her, he didn't acknowledge her. She watched him take a bite of his bagel, end up with some cream cheese on his upper lip. As he listened, he typed on his laptop with two fingers. He finally looked up at her, jerked his head toward the chair.

She sat down and looked around, fully aware the other detectives in the room were eyeing her, knowing who she was, because there were no secrets in a police or sheriff's station. Montoya said thank you and punched off his cell. He took the final bite of his bagel, wiped his hands on a paper napkin, and continued to type on his laptop. The dab of cream cheese was still on his lip.

Cam said, "I admire a multitasker. You nearly have that email to your mom finished?"

He didn't look up. "Been a busy morning, lots to tell her."

"It's only eight thirty in the morning, Detective Montoya. You sure don't look Latin to me. Where'd you get the Spanish name?"

"You could ask where I get the gringo first name—Daniel."

"Nah, Daniel's biblical, way back before Latin America was invented. He got tossed into a lions' den and lived to brag about it. I bet you've never even seen a lion."

"Yes, I have. I was six years old, down in the San Diego Zoo."

"Are you through?"

"Just one more sentence to Mom, telling her how I miss her chicken pot pie—two crusts. There. All done." He closed the laptop and slowly rose, eyed her up and down when she stood to face him. "You're the Fed?" Incredulous voice. Then, under his breath, but not quite low enough, "Oh, joy."

Cam was closing in on five foot ten in her boots, but came only to the middle of this guy's nose. "Yeah, I'm the Fed. Big dude, aren't you?"

"You ain't no midget yourself." He stuck out his hand. "I'm Detective Daniel Montoya, as you already know."

"I'm Special Agent Cam Wittier."

They shook hands. He looked pissed for a moment, then she watched his face change as he reminded himself to accept the inevitable and settled on resigned. "Okay, the sheriff told me you were coming to take over the case."

"True. But right now, I'm here to meet you, see what you think."

"And then kiss me off because I'm a worthless yahoo without a sentient brain?"

"Depends on the ideas you have about this Serial. Then I'll assess if you're worthless. Or not."

13

Daniel looked at her short wavy blond hair and into her blue-gray eyes, no, there was hazel in there as well—and a jaw that looked more stubborn than his older sister's, and that was saying something. She was a looker and wasn't that a kick in the gut? He had to laugh. Of course he'd been expecting a dark suit, skinny tie, wing tips, a stone-cold face, and a sense of humor like a stick. "I'll try, Agent Wittier, to make myself both worthy and useful."

"Hey, that's the recipe for a decent husband. Well, that and a flat stomach. I was going to buy you breakfast, but you already chowed down on that bagel. You've still got some cream cheese on your lip." She watched him dab the rest of his breakfast away. "There, all presentable again. Like a real grown-up. You ready to talk?"

"We can do that while I drive you to the Morrissey crime scene. What about all the other crime scenes?"

"We'll begin with Constance Morrissey."

He nodded. "If we're going to spend some time there and make it to the Parker Center on time in the L.A. traffic, we should get started. How about I tell you what I think and you tell me if I pass muster on the way over? By the way, my dad's still got a flat gut."

Daniel guided her out of the bullpen, all eyes following their every step, past Dreyfus's office and outside into the morning sunshine. He led her to a row of Crown Vics parked beside the station, pointed to one that looked as tired as the others. "I haven't been to the crime scene in over a week. But I agree you should see it even though it's cleaned up."

"Forensics came up with nothing?"

"Not a thing, as I'm sure you already know. The killer was careful. All the fingerprints were identified, including the housekeeper's. When I interviewed her, she told me she liked Morrissey, said she was a sweet, clean girl."

"So she was one of those women who clean before the housekeeper arrives?"

"I hope that's what she meant. Most of the fingerprints other than the victim's belonged to the house owner, Theodore Markham, a big-shot Hollywood producer."

"You said in your report you believe Markham was more than the owner of that house, that he and Connie Morrissey were probably lovers."

"That's the working theory."

"You interviewed Markham. I read your report, but

tell me what you thought about him, stuff that isn't in your report."

"I was allowed to speak to Markham one time, his lawyer sitting at his right hand, measuring me for a coffin. The lawyer claimed Mr. Markham was distraught, but Markham reminded me of my grade school principal, Old Stone Face. When the lawyer finally allowed Markham to speak, he insisted he'd picked Morrissey because of her great talent; he'd wanted to nurture her, he said, take away her money worries so she could focus on her career. Markham claimed he wasn't sleeping with Morrissey, no way. He's allegedly happily married to his second wife, has two sons with her, both studying computers at UCLA. He was alibied up to his tonsils, at a party at his house when Morrissey was murdered, with his wife and fifty guests. Toward the end, he looked put out at the inconvenience of having to deal with a lowly cop. As I wrote in the report, he could have snuck out of the party because alcohol was flowing freely and some of the guests were frolicking in the swimming pool. Naturally, everyone who attended the party was sure he'd been there every second."

"From your report I gathered you believe Markham to be a pompous, ruthless jerk. Well, not in those exact terms, but it came through loud and clear. You think he could have killed her?"

"He could have. Say they were lovers and she no longer wanted him—rejection didn't happen to someone of his stature, so in a rage he killed her. But that would make him the Serial, and I can't see that." Daniel shrugged.

"You know, of course the Serial took both her laptop and her cell phone, as he always does. We don't know why yet, but that's made it harder to track down Morrissey's personal information."

Cam nodded. When Montoya turned onto Bleaker Road, she lowered the window and breathed in the soft breeze off the Pacific. "You can smell the ocean from here. I've missed that. Now, as for the big pow-wow at LAPD headquarters, I understand you didn't have a meeting with the LAPD but Supervisor Elman called you and the detectives at the San Dimas Sheriff's Department."

"Yes, he called, even asked for our murder books."

His voice was neutral, at best. She could imagine how the LAPD folk felt about the sheriffs' detectives. She said, "I spoke to Supervisor Elman and he thinks a meeting with all concerned detectives would be fine and dandy. Not his exact words." She grinned at him. "I told him to consider it sort of like an orchestra that's never played together, and I'm the visiting conductor."

"My idea of fun. Hope there won't be too much carnage. Just in case—are you armed?"

Cam laughed. "It's odd, Agent Savich said the same thing."

"Savich? I've heard of him, he's the husband of Agent Sherlock of JFK fame, right?"

She nodded. "That's her. And my Glock's loaded, no worries."

"Always smart to be prepared. You never know what could happen with a Fed in the mix. Couldn't be worse than the navy and the army meeting to plan a mission, could it?" He shot her a look that didn't seem very full of confidence in her abilities.

She only smiled. "Probably not, but I think it's worth a try, whatever happens. Now, tell me more about Constance Morrissey."

Daniel raised an eyebrow, knowing she probably already knew all about her, down to the woman's birthmark behind her left knee. "Her life was ended on May 3rd and I've got nothing, zip, zero. She was twenty-five, divorced going on three years from a real loser—and yes, we checked on the ex-husband, called himself Bravo Morrissey. She kept his name. He was in Chicago on the night she was murdered, playing in an illegal poker game, verified by the seven guys playing with him. She was from Fort Lauderdale, Florida.

"She didn't have a steady boyfriend, lived in the Colony going on a year. She could afford living there because Markham rented it to her, charged her only $200 a month. I was told the going rent would be at least seven thousand a month—if a cottage like that even came up for rent in the Colony. So it makes sense they were more than friends."

"Did any of her friends, relatives, or Markham have any ideas about what was on her laptop or cell?"

Daniel turned onto Pacific Coast Highway, or PCH as the locals called it, not three blocks from the ocean at this point, past a Subway, anchoring a small shopping center. "Nothing of relevance so far. We're coming up on the Colony—it's the hoity-toitiest spot to own a home in Malibu. It's been around—"

"Since the 1920s, when it was called the Malibu Motion Picture Colony. All the early film stars built homes here, like Bing Crosby, Ronald Colman, Gary Cooper, Gloria Swanson, to name an illustrious few. They came to play in privacy." She gave him a fat smile.

"So you read a guidebook on the plane out here?"

"Nah, my folks live in the Colony. They're both actors. I was raised here. After we look through Connie Morrissey's house, we'll drop by, see what they have to tell us, okay? Trust me, they know a lot."

He eyed her, then said slowly, "I wondered why a local FBI Field Office agent wasn't assigned to take over. So, the powers that be in Fed-Land think because you were born into this in-crowd, you'd be the best bet."

"That was second-biggest reason I was sent rather than an agent from the L.A. Field Office."

"What's the biggest reason?"

"I'm that good," she said, and stuck her head out the open window, breathed in deep, and let the ocean wind whip through her hair.

14

Chet Brubaker was a buff twenty-three-year-old surfer dude who manned the kiosk and monitored the cars entering and leaving the Colony. Not that it had done Constance Morrissey any good. Daniel had met him the day after Morrissey's murder.

Cam sang out as they pulled alongside the kiosk window. "Hi, Chet, let us in, okay?"

Chet peered at her, then grinned. "Hey, I remember you, you're Lisabeth's daughter, right? Camilla? Cammie?"

"Plain Cam's good. Yes, and I'm FBI." She flipped open her creds. "You know Detective Montoya?"

"Oh, yes. Hi, Detective. You must be here about Connie, right? Listen, everyone's still torn up about her, still scared, you know, still can't believe it happened here. Everyone's supposed to be safe in the Colony, but they're not. I've told the company they have to completely block access from the state park into the Colony, you know, put in a real fence that goes all the way down under the sand, not that lame excuse for a barrier that's been here since year one. Any yahoo can duck under it easy enough. Maybe they should make it electric, you know?" Chet paused, pushed his long blond hair out of his eyes, beamed at them. "And you know what? They're going to do something, finally. Lots of bureaucratic-state red tape since it's a state park next door, but it might happen now."

"I'd say you did good then, Chet," Montoya said.

Chet saluted him, then stepped back, raised the bar, gave them a little wave.

Cam said as they drove through, "Most residents agree with Chet, including my parents, given the abundance of millionaires and celebrities in this very small area, many of whom could attract the wrong kind of attention. There's the kiosk at the entrance, but no protection from anyone who wants to bend over and walk beneath that fence at the eastern end of the beach. It's been a political football since I can remember."

"And that's why I don't think it's going to happen before my kids graduate college," Daniel said. "Since the Morrissey murder, we've seen more private security, more video cameras. They call you Cammie?"

"Sometimes Cammie, on rare occasion, Camilla."

"You want to know what those two names bring to mind?"

"Yeah. What?"

Daniel gave her a sideways look as he drove slowly down Malibu Colony Road. "I'd say Cammie braids her hair and wears patent leather shoes. Camilla lies on a chaise longue in a flowing robe and holds a flower on her chest."

She laughed. "Good enough. And Cam?"

"That one wears boots, has an attitude, and carries a Glock."

That sounded good to Cam. She waved her hand. "It seems frozen in time, only a remodeled house now and then."

Malibu Colony Road took them down to the ocean and swept past a long line of houses on both sides, ranging from palatial glass mansions to small wooden cottages, some dating back to the forties.

Daniel said, "It's ahead of us, a small bungalow, about halfway down, very nicely remodeled five years ago when Markham bought it as a weekend getaway place. Not waterside. The neighbors who'd met Connie said she seemed like a levelheaded, friendly young woman. Never saw her behave like Markham's mistresses, but who knew? I can show you the layout, but like I said, all the evidence we have was collected and processed weeks ago."

"That's for later. I want to see it for myself, get the feel of it. Do you see that house we just passed? That's my folks' house, where I grew up."

The Wittier house was on the ocean side, not palatial, but not a small bungalow like Morrissey's, either. It was an older, well-maintained two-story house. If not for its exclusive location, it would have solid middle-class standing. A big bruiser of a palm tree sprawled in the front yard, its giant fronds stretching to the road.

Daniel said, "That's a really nice house. The Colony's wildly expensive."

"My folks say the prices zoom higher every year. Back in the day, Mom and Dad managed to score some really good roles at the same time, enough to afford a good deal they found here in the Colony. They plunked down the cash, moved in, and had me. I think they paid off the mortgage three years ago."

"No siblings?"

"They tell me they had their hands so full with me they didn't have the time or energy to make any more kids."

"That's what my dad thought, but Mom kept getting pregnant. It always seemed to surprise my dad. Go figure."

"How many siblings?"

"Four, I'm the oldest. There's Morrissey's bungalow. Hey, what's this? I didn't expect these guys."

A dark green moving van with bright white stars all over it, the signature of the Starving Actors moving company was parked out front, a large buff man in dungarees looking at them from a ramp at its rear.

"Well, it has been six weeks since Morrissey's murder," Daniel said. "The D.A.'s office must have given Markham full access. We'll let these guys have a break, and I'll show you around. I wonder if Markham sold the cottage or rented it out to some other actresses in need of nurturing. Let's see if the starving actors know."

"Hang on a second," Cam said, and punched a number on her cell. "Mom, hi. Yes, that was me and

Detective Montoya driving by. We'll come back in a little while. A question. Do you know who's moving into Constance Morrissey's house?" A couple of seconds passed, some more questions, more hmms, then, "Okay, thanks." She looked over. "Theo Markham was evidently so broken up by Connie's murder that he sold the bungalow to a special-effects software guy from Seattle last week. It went for just under three mil, Dad said. He heard the family was moving in next month, but they must be moving in some of the furniture early."

Daniel was impressed. "Three mil for that little bungalow?"

"Don't forget, it was remodeled." She gave him a grin. "That room on the left? That's where the master bedroom is, biggest room in the house, but of course you know that. Let's go check it out. There was a security system?"

Daniel said, "Yeah, it was a good system, but naturally not foolproof, if you know how to disarm it. The Serial knew to cut the wires."

A hunk named Lance, who didn't look much like he was starving, met them at the door. He didn't seem surprised when they told him who they were. "Really a bummer, that poor girl getting killed like that," he said, shaking his head. "I didn't know her." He waved a hand over his shoulder. "Bart and Jules didn't, either. You want us out of here for a half an hour? Fine by me, we'll take a break and have a swim while you look around." He waved the other two starving actors over.

Cam and Daniel watched the young eye candy jog down the road together toward the state park. By the time they reached the end of the road, they were wearing only cutoffs.

Cam stepped through the open front door, painted a bright red lacquer, into a small Mexican-tiled foyer. To her right was a small living room, modern furniture piled in the middle and boxes stacked high against the walls. She walked into the room and looked around, easily picturing the Connie Morrissey she knew from her photos enjoying this lovely airy house, all windows and light. The walls were painted a pale yellow, and the oak floors were buffed to a high shine. She followed Daniel down the short hallway to the master bedroom, en suite after the remodel. She walked slowly into the room and stood quietly, surrounded by boxes and light rattan furniture. She closed her eyes, pictured where the bed had been, the bloody violence, Connie's surge of fear, if she'd had time to even realize she was going to die, hoping it would bring her closer to what had happened and why. Two years ago at a murder scene, she'd stood over the chalk outline of the victim, an older man who'd been stabbed in the heart, and felt a sort of wrinkling in the air itself and a numbing coldness that had scared her to her toes. Then she'd felt the same coldness pouring off the great-nephew and known she'd met the killer. But she hadn't found the proof to nail him, and what she believed, what she was sure about, wasn't enough. It still burned.

But here, now, in Constance Morrissey's lovely

bedroom, its pale blue walls and pavers accented with Mexican tiles, she felt nothing like that, only sadness. There was nothing of Connie here anymore, only an empty room with cardboard boxes stacked against the walls.

The bathroom was very large, no expense spared, evidently, the countertops a lovely pale Italian marble, the double washbasins painted with Spanish scenes. Big shower, Jacuzzi. There was a roll of toilet paper on the countertop. There was no trace of Connie here, either.

Daniel touched her arm, made her jump. "Sorry, didn't mean to startle you. Let me take you through it." He led her to the second bedroom, this one smaller, its walls a mellow pale green. He pointed to the window. "After the Serial disabled the alarm, he broke that window and walked down the hall to her bedroom. This was something new for him. He usually breaks in through the kitchen door, but here it's too exposed. Everything else was the same. He walked quietly to the bed, grabbed her by the hair and sliced her throat. The medical examiner said it happened so fast she never knew she was dead. And doesn't that sound comforting?

"He took her cell phone off its charger by her bed and the computer from the second bedroom, where the router is, and left the same way he came in, through the broken window. He could have been back in the state park in just a couple of minutes."

She nodded. "Your report said there was a party

on the state park side that night, lots of music, lots of dancing, beer and lots of pot, too, I bet. Not the kind of party where everyone knows everyone else. He picked a good night for killing her."

Daniel said, "I went back every night for a week and talked to anyone who showed up. A couple of nights I even took a six-pack of beer to get them to believe I wasn't there to bust them. But nothing."

They walked back outside into the bright sunlight, Cam mourning the young, vibrant life, violently ended with no perpetrator in sight. There was no sign of Lance and the other two starving actors.

15

"Camilla DuBois! My darling!"

Daniel turned to Cam. "I know about Camilla, but who's DuBois?"

"Don't go there." A big smile bloomed on Cam's face. "Speaking of key local informants, there's one of them—my mom, Lisabeth Wittier. Come on, Daniel, let's go talk to my folks."

Cam jogged down the road to meet the woman walking toward them. She hugged her and waved back at Daniel. Daniel drove the Crown Vic, parked it, and stepped out, watching them. Her mom was talking nonstop, laughing and patting Cam's face, her shoulder, her hair, whatever part she could reach, since Cam topped her by a good eight inches. An older man tall enough to be a forward for the Warriors back in the day came loping out of the house behind them. Both of them were handsome, fit and full of life, probably knockouts when they were younger. Daniel recognized them from a few movies and TV shows.

He was introduced, his hand pumped enthusiastically. "Call me Lisabeth, please, Detective Montoya, otherwise I'll feel like your mother, and believe me, one adult child is enough."

Cam's dad gave him an appraising look and a firm no-nonsense handshake. "And I'd like you to call me Joel, otherwise I'll feel like my dad, who made all six of us boys call him Mr. Wittier. Makes me shudder to think of it. I recognize you from the time of Constance's murder, Detective Montoya. You were here so often, I wanted to offer you a bed. I bet some of the neighbors did, too. It's a pity the killer hasn't been caught. We know it was you who identified him as a serial killer, that there were two other women he'd killed before Constance. It's still hard to accept that something like this could happen here in the Colony."

"Or anywhere at all, Joel," Daniel said. "I'm sure you're glad your daughter's here to help us now."

"You'll see soon enough she's got a very good mix of our two brains, makes her unstoppable." Joel paused a moment. "It would have made her a great actress, but never mind that."

Lisabeth said, "Cammie, we've got iced tea and sugar cookies ready for you, made with Splenda of course, on the back porch. Come in, come in. You can take the time, can't you? We can fill you and Detective Montoya in on everything going on here."

"Do call me Daniel."

Lisabeth beamed at him. "A very good name, solid and trustworthy."

Cam took her mother's arm. "Come on, guys, you're not going to try to quarterback this whole business, are you? Dreyfus already told me he'd ordered you to keep out of it."

"Of course not, dear, but your father and I see things here, of course, how could we not? We hear things, too, and we love to talk to people. I guess I never should have told Dreyfus that Joel slept out under the palm tree the night after Connie's murder, hoping the killer would return to the scene of the crime. He had a prop Beretta."

Cam's blood froze. "Mom, Dad, this isn't the silver screen with a scripted ending, this is real, and this guy—this serial killer—he's a cold-blooded murderer. So keep out of it. No more sleep-outs. Okay? Don't listen, don't see, don't talk. If I have a question, I'll ask you."

"Dear, you know your dad and I are always careful. But Connie's murder was a huge shock here, and all our neighbors want to talk about it, trade theories, you know how it goes."

Lisabeth looked at Daniel for support. He started to open his mouth, and closed it. Better to let Cam deal with her parents.

"We've only got a few minutes, Mom, then it's off to LAPD headquarters to meet with the detectives involved with the four cases here in California."

"Sure wish I could be there with you, princess," Joel said. "I've had roles playing LAPD before, but can you imagine what I'd pick up at a meeting like that?

Have you thought about how you're going to handle those detectives who are focused on throwing you off a cliff? I mean, a Fed prying into their business. You sure Detective Montoya is going to have your back? Is he on your side?"

She turned to Daniel. "Are you on my side?"

He grinned back at her. "Depends on whether you've decided I'm not a worthless yahoo."

Good shot, Montoya. Cam said, "It's still a little soon, but I've got to say I'm leaning in your direction."

Lisabeth said, her beautiful mouth curving up to show a dimple, "Not to worry, that means she likes you, Daniel. Cammie—no, Cam—I think Detective Montoya will make an excellent guard for you. I'm right, aren't I, Daniel?" Lisabeth Wittier cracked her knuckles.

"Ah, okay, sure. I'll guard her back."

Daniel wasn't about to admit he still wished she was anywhere but here, in his face, in his business. But you didn't argue with someone's parents. It was rude, possibly dangerous.

The Wittiers' house was open, as inviting and colorful as they were—with a few theatrical distractions, like a five-foot-tall giraffe standing by a window. His name was Oslo, and he'd appeared in *Bumper Shute*, a movie they'd made fifteen years ago, Lisabeth told him over iced tea and sugar cookies made with Splenda. Daniel listened to Cam's parents volleying their neighbors' opinions and ideas back and forth, bringing Cam up to date with them, and he soon realized Cam was right—they seemed to know most everything about most everyone who lived in the Colony. He remembered the two other officers assigned to interview the neighbors he hadn't had time to do himself, and they'd reported nothing of any help. How could that be? He was learning as much about the victim as he had in several weeks of investigating her murder.

The most interesting tidbit came from Joel as they were preparing to leave. "I remember Connie telling me she had an audition coming up. She was hoping to score the role, believed that particular role could shoot her to the top." Joel shook his head. "She was killed the night before the audition."

Why hadn't Daniel known that? The producer Theo Markham hadn't said anything about a promising role.

The question was, why not?

16

Half an hour later, Daniel and Cam were back in Daniel's Crown Vic headed for the Parker Center, each carrying a sugar cookie folded in a napkin.

Before turning off PCH into Santa Monica, Daniel shot a look toward *Paco's*, just a block up from the Santa Monica Pier. "Too bad we don't have time for some of Mrs. Luther's tacos."

"I'm glad Mrs. Luther's still here. I was a glutton at *Paco's* at least once a week growing up. Maybe we can do a late lunch." Cam looked at her Waze app. "Or a very late lunch. I'd forgotten how bad the traffic can get."

"Yeah, it gets worse every year. I know a couple of shortcuts, but this time of day they'll be backed up worse than this, so it's traffic all the way, 110 to 101. It'll take about an hour."

Daniel talked more about Constance Morrissey as he drove, how something about the murder scene had felt like a Serial to him, and he'd looked into other recent unsolved murders in Southern California—a sliced throat in bed in the middle of the night, a missing laptop and cell phone. He found both the Melodie Anders murder and the Davina Morgan murder and called Supervisor David Elman of the Homicide Special Section. Elman already knew about the Davina Morgan murder in Van Nuys, agreed it fit a pattern. He hadn't known about the second victim, Melodie Anders, in San Dimas.

"I have to admit I was surprised when the LAPD didn't kiss me off. Supervisor Elman even called me after the murder in North Hollywood, said he was going to contact all the sheriffs' departments, but I'd already done that.

"After the LAPD agreed we had a Serial, I convinced them to tell the press and they agreed. I suppose we thought it would make a difference, get everyone on the same page, get his next possible victims warned. The media was all over it, one of the tabloids even came up with his moniker, the Starlet Slasher. Every young actress in L.A. had to know he was out there." Daniel sighed. "But it didn't help. The fourth victim, Heather Burnside, was killed in North Hollywood on June 2nd, after we spent weeks investigating and getting nowhere. I hated that, Cam, really hated it."

She did, too. "That had to be tough. We'll have more resources now, with all of us working together. We'll get him, Daniel, no doubt in my mind."

At 11:50, Daniel turned onto First Street, drove a short distance to the LAPD staff-only garage, and stopped at the guard window. Cam gave the guard their names and showed him their shields. The guard meticulously checked their names against his computer, studied their creds, and finally let them through with a stingy smile. He even went so far as to nod toward a visitor's slot not far from the garage booth.

Cam had visited the old Parker Center a handful of times over the years, but never the new headquarters. She paused on the sidewalk to look up at the incredible architecture of the building. Its glass and white concrete blended over the front of the building like a large white curtain. There were so many angles to the facade, it was like a puzzle in geometry. Palm trees added a bit of Southern California dash, as did the warmth and sunshine, and the loud, constant background noise from the heavy traffic on the nearby 101.

They were met in the lobby by the supervisor of the Homicide Special Section himself, David Elman. He looked like a seasoned veteran, in his late forties, tall, broad-shouldered, balding rapidly. His smart dark eyes went immediately to Daniel, then, with something like regret, he turned to her.

Par for the course.

17

Cam stepped forward and stuck out her hand. "I've heard so much about you, Supervisor Elman. It's a pleasure to finally meet you, sir. I'm Special Agent Cam Wittier, FBI."

He shook her hand, straightened, cleared his throat, and said in a butter-rich baritone actor's voice, "A pleasure, Agent Wittier." He turned his smart eyes to Daniel, shook his hand. "Detective Montoya, it's a pleasure to finally meet you in person. Come with me, the whole group is waiting for us."

Daniel nodded but didn't smile. He focused on looking competent. He knew they would both have to prove themselves in that room full of LAPD detectives.

Elman pressed the elevator button, turned back to Cam. "As I told you over the phone, Agent, the fact that the Serial wasn't identified until the third murder is regrettable, but understandable, given the second murder was in an outlying sheriff's jurisdiction. Since

Detective Montoya called me, we've all been focused on identifying this killer."

The elevator pinged, the doors opened to three exiting cops. Cam gave them a hundred-watt smile, a smile Daniel had no doubt would have gotten her elected prom queen in high school. The cops didn't know who she was, and they smiled back. He wasn't surprised when one of them turned back to say something to her, saw Elman, and continued on his way.

Elman punched the fifth-floor button, turned to Cam. "We'll be meeting in the conference room we use for our quarterly meetings of all our divisions to discuss cases, trends, coordination. Our group today will also include the detective from the San Dimas Sheriff's Department, as well as reps from Chief Crowder's office. And Detective Montoya, of course."

"Thank you for making all the arrangements," Cam said, and gave him her full-monty smile. It was Lisabeth's smile, Daniel realized.

They walked down a long noisy hall, with people ducking in and out of offices, talking while they walked, bits of conversations floating out of rooms on either side. Cam heard a lot of male voices talking even before Elman waved them into room 315. The moment they stepped inside the big utilitarian conference room, voices began to drop off, and all eyes locked onto her and Daniel. Cam took in ten or so men, one woman, all seasoned cops by the looks of them. She easily recognized the police chief's representatives, two young men, conservatively dressed, looking vaguely bored, sitting away from all the detectives. She also easily spotted the single detective from the San Dimas Sheriff's Department, off by himself at the end of the table. Many eyes moved quickly from her to Daniel, assuming he was the Fed, weighing him, assessing him, planning how to deal with him.

Elman stepped to the head of the table, leaned his elbows on the podium and spoke in his deep rich voice into the microphone. "People, I'd like you to meet Special Agent Cam Wittier from FBI headquarters in Washington and Detective Daniel Montoya from the Lost Hills Sheriff's Department, who first identified the killer as a Serial.

"As you all know, the Serial murdered another young actress, Molly Harbinger, in Las Vegas over the weekend, and that brought the FBI into this case. Agent Wittier will be leading the investigation." He nodded toward Cam and she took her place behind the podium.

She said nothing until Daniel had sat down at the middle of the table, bridging the sheriff's detective and the LAPD, and remained silent until every eye was focused on her. She knew local distrust ran deep because still, more often than not, when the FBI showed up, local cops were relegated to gofers.

She saw some sneers on a couple of male faces, a smile from the only female detective. But mainly, she saw wary, stone faces. Back in the beginning, when she'd faced whole rooms of cops who believed she would be getting them coffee and taking notes, she'd felt acid burning her gut. But not anymore, not in a long time.

She said, "I've read all of your murder books, seen the hard work you've done." A hand shot up into the air. "Yes, Detective Jagger? You're out of Van Nuys. You handled the first murder of Davina Morgan, on February 26th."

A flash of surprise in the older cop's pale eyes. "Yeah, that's me. I googled you, Agent Wittier. Your folks are actors, live in Malibu, live in the la-di-da Colony. Is that why the FBI sent you here instead of using the L.A. Field Office? Because they think since you're connected, you'll find out the truth faster than we can?"

She honestly couldn't tell if he was shooting off his mouth or he was asking a serious question.

Corinne Hill, Jagger's partner, called out, "Stick a sock in it, Morley, let's hear what she's got to say."

Cam never changed expression. One shot was okay. She wondered which one of those two drove the bus. She'd bet on Corinne Hill, based on that exchange. She didn't put up with any guff. Cam said, "The fact that both my folks and all the victims are in the business certainly went into the FBI's decision to send me out here, which means, contrary to some local opinion, there are some live brains at work in Washington."

That tried-and-true chestnut gained her a couple of laughs. Cam paused again, studied their faces, leaned forward. "After Detective Montoya connected the first two murders to the murder of actress Constance Morrissey in the Colony in Malibu on May 3rd, he realized we had a Serial at work and notified Supervisor Elman. I know you've been geared up ever since. With the fourth murder of Heather Burnside in North Hollywood on June 2nd, you've brought even more resources to bear on catching this man—I say man because statistically most serial killers are male. We hope to verify this when the witness in Las Vegas is found and brought in." She briefed them on the killing in Las Vegas and the burglar who'd seen him. "I've been in touch with Agent Aaron Poker at the Field Office in Las Vegas, and will continue to be. The details of his investigation will be available on a daily basis to each of you. Am I correct in assuming each of you has studied all the other murder books and familiarized yourselves with the details of all the other murders?"

Cam heard sounds of assent, saw some shrugs. Glen Hoffman, the youngest of the detectives, something of a hotshot, she'd thought when she'd first read his bio, called out, "Hoffman, North Hollywood. People in this room have worked cases like this before. Sure, there's an obvious group of victims, and an M.O., but he hasn't left a single actionable clue. We've processed some suspects, but none of them turned out to be viable.

"Look, there are hundreds of Serials busy at work in the U.S. as we speak, and now we've spotted one of them here. He's obviously had lots of practice, so catching him might not happen no matter how hard we bust our chops and read profiles issued by your FBI buddies. What are you going to do to help us?"

Daniel's first inclination was to haul the jackass outside and bust his chops himself, but he knew Cam would deal with him. Odd, but after only a couple of hours with her he was sure of it.

Cam said, "We're bringing all the resources of the FBI, Detective Hoffman, and we're going to catch him by working together. Until we find the clue that will bury him, we will use the nature of his crimes themselves to find him. He's been remarkably consistent, picking young actresses, using the same large single-edged knife, and taking their laptops and cell phones. Let's start with that. Why does he take them? What does he do with them? Why do you think, Detective Hoffman, that the Serial takes only those two items?"

Hoffman stared at her a moment. "I don't think they're souvenirs. I don't believe this guy is that crazy. I believe there's something on the laptops or tablets and cell phones that could tie him to the victims, or maybe leads him to other victims."

Hoffman's partner, Detective Frank Alworth, world-weary, and not far from retirement, added, "That's the problem, Glen, too many possibilities. They're all young actresses, beautiful. It doesn't take a lot of imagination to think he uses the laptops and cell phones to look at their pictures and posts after he's killed them. But he could see a lot of that on their Facebook fan pages, almost all these young actresses have them now, or look at their Twitter accounts, or their YouTube videos, for that matter. He has to be taking them for something that's not available on social media."

Cam said, "Agreed. And there's not a lot he could cover up by taking those laptops and cells. There are few secrets today that can't be traced through the Internet. I know you've been looking through the victims' emails and text messages, their activity on social media. What else could it be?"

Detective Allard Hayes of the San Dimas Sheriff's Department spoke up next. "Daniel and I got together, tried to think outside the box, explore what isn't obvious. Maybe it's part of his ritual, part of how he kills them, over and over again. The laptops and cell phones represent their ties to life itself and he takes those ties, as he takes their lives. That sounds new age dippy, but we have to consider the Serial's brain isn't necessarily running on the rails."

Daniel said, "We know this guy is into control. He thinks, he plans, he acts carefully, nearly always the same. Is he playing out a fantasy? Again and again?"

Jagger, Van Nuys, said, "What do you think, Montoya, he's killing the same person over and over again, maybe someone he once knew and now hates?"

Corinne leaned forward, chin on her clasped hands. "Or maybe he's terrorizing someone in his own life with these murders, using the murders to threaten someone, to control them. I thought of that after I read the FBI profile."

One of Chief Crowder's reps said, voice tentative,

"Maybe the guy got turned down by one of the actresses, killed her, and turned it into a blood sport."

Glen Hoffman, North Hollywood, said, "Or maybe the guy's so crazy he doesn't know why he's doing any of it. Doesn't know why he takes the laptops and cell phones. God tells him to take them and stash them in a locker at a train station."

Cam waited, but the room remained quiet. "Let's step back for a second. The Serial has those laptops and cell phones, for whatever reason. He's been smart enough not to use the cell phones, so we can't track by GPS. So what do we have left to work with?"

18

She paused, let the question sink in. She leaned forward, rested her elbows on the podium. She didn't need the microphone. She had her mom's voice, it could carry from Malibu to the freeway. "There's a good hundred years of experience sitting in this room, well versed in every violent thing one person can do to another, with every motive imaginable. So use it, people."

Frank Alworth, North Hollywood, said, "One motive we can discount is robbery. Heather Burnside owned a very expensive Rolex watch. The Serial could have taken it, but he didn't."

His partner, Glen Hoffman, said, "We didn't think he'd be that stupid, but we checked the local pawnshops, fences, wherever the Serial might have sold the laptops and cell phones. We got nothing. Same with the rest of you. We also tagged Heather Burnside's bank accounts and credit cards, but there's been nothing there, either."

Allard Hayes from San Dimas said, "We all have our theories, but I think there's something we're missing, something that's driving this guy that we haven't nailed. The talk about his fantasies, it just doesn't ring true for me, not any longer."

"Me, either," said Jagger from Van Nuys. "He might be crazy, but he's still got a reason for picking out and killing these young actresses."

Cam realized Detective Alworth out of North Hollywood was holding back. He was older, and he was smart, the alpha dog in this group. She said, "Detective Alworth, what do you think?"

Frank was aware all eyes were on him. He said slowly, "If you know the why, you will find the who. If you don't know the why, you've got to look elsewhere. How is the Serial finding and picking out these women? It's unlikely he knew them all. He breaks in, they don't let him in. And if he's contacted them all beforehand somehow, he's done a good job disguising himself on their emails, their fan pages. We haven't heard any of them felt threatened. So how, Morley? Tell us how."

He looked over at Jagger, sitting slouched back in his chair, looking bored as a lizard on a sunny rook, making it obvious he didn't hold out any hope that the blonde from Washington could move anything forward.

Cam waited. She saw him shoot Alworth a don't-you-force-me-to-play-with-this-girl-from-Washington look, but Alworth didn't let him off the hook. "Come on, Morley, can you help us out or not?"

At that, Cam saw a growing spark of interest in Jagger's eyes. He sat forward, clasped his big hands in front of him on the table. "I got to thinking about a murder case I was on fifteen years ago. A corporate lawyer was shot in the head at close range, and the only thing stolen was his computer, big old honker, like all of them were back in the day. We finally tracked down a land developer under a layer of fake corporations and proved he was the killer. The motive? The vic was no saint—he was blackmailing the killer, had him nailed for big-time land fraud. The proof was on the computer."

Daniel said, "So you think all five victims had something on their computers? Some sort of file that existed only there? And he followed Molly Harbinger all the way to Las Vegas to get it?" He paused a moment, shook his head, looked around the room. "I think that sounds too cerebral, too easy. I think these killings are personal."

Hoffman, Van Nuys, said, "The motive is personal, with five different actresses? There was nobody who dated all of them. But I don't think it's random, either. Maybe it's personal to him in some other way, and that opens up a whole other can of possibilities."

Cam nodded. "It's still possible they all knew one specific person we haven't found yet. Their families, friends, agents, showbiz contacts—someone might know if any of them kept things on their laptops or cell phones that isn't easily found elsewhere."

Frank Alworth clasped his hands, sat forward. "I think the chance of there being some sort of magical tie-in with a single guy's name on all the laptops and tablets, not to mention the cell phones, is off-the-planet unlikely. Agent Wittier, I think we need to dial that idea back. I'm thinking we've got ourselves a sicko Serial, with no fancy motive except a hard-on for pretty actresses. Maybe he dated one of them once, got dumped, and is killing them off as payback to the lot of them. Maybe we're talking a garden-variety fruitcake here." He shrugged.

"Detective Montoya believes the Serial is obsessed, with control," Cam said. "I agree with that. He certainly showed how important it is to him in Las Vegas this past Saturday night. After he killed Molly Harbinger, he chased a burglar from the house, but he still went back and took her laptop and cell phone with him anyway."

Corinne said, "Maybe our best shot at getting him right now is to find that eyewitness in Las Vegas. You know, people, Serials aren't Einsteins. So far I'd say our guy has just lucked out."

Cam nodded to Corinne. "Agent Poker and the Las Vegas police are using all their resources, scouring the area for him, but so far no luck.

"I know that all of you hate it that five young lives

have wantonly been snuffed out, that all of you want to catch this monster as much as I do. I know each of you is involved up to your eyeballs in your own cases, but now you're going to be part of all of them, because there's only one case now—our case.

"The FBI has set up a private, encrypted server for our use. On the back of these cards I'm going to give you, you'll see how to access it and the log-in procedures. We've already uploaded your murder books. This site is for all of us to use as our shared worksite. After today, I'd like you to use it for all your records in this case. Tell us what you're doing, all your ongoing efforts, what you've managed to eliminate, whatever you're thinking that the rest of us might use.

"I know you feel like you're swimming in mud right now, since the possibilities seem endless. That's why we need each other. Call me day or night, folks. And talk to each other. I'll be working directly with Detective Montoya out of Calabasas. Even though I only met him this morning, he's told me he's got my back." And she sent Daniel a big grin.

There were some smiles.

"Okay, let's get this bastard."

She pulled out a handful of business cards, walked over to each of the detectives at the table, addressed each by name, and gave them a card. She knew every single name, a show of respect, except for Chief Crowder's people, and she introduced herself to them, gave them each a card as well. It was obvious she'd surprised them.

She returned to the front of the conference table, looked out at the detectives one final time. Some stares of approval, some lingering wariness. Some open and willing, some not as much. At least she had no doubt Allard Hayes from San Dimas would now have no problem interacting with the LAPD detectives, and Daniel had already made an impact. She gave a curt nod and turned on her heel to exit the room, Daniel following behind her.

Elman escorted them back downstairs. "I thought that went very well, Agent Wittier. You handled some of those crocodiles better than I expected." Cam wished he'd sounded more hopeful.

He gave her a smart salute in the lobby, and disappeared back into the elevator.

When they stepped out into the bright L.A. sun, Daniel shot her a look while he slipped on his aviator sunglasses. "That group didn't sound like a bunch of pea-brained local yahoos to me."

She tapped his arm. "Your words, not mine. Tell me, Detective, how many federal agents have you worked with?"

"Three."

"Okay, I guess it happens. I kind of like Agent Dillon Savich's working philosophy—'Always play nice with locals, you never know when you might need a volunteer for a firing squad.'"

Daniel spurted out a laugh. "He really said that?"

"Nah, he said something nice, like one of the locals might throw a touchdown pass."

"Sounds like a guy I'd like to get to know." Daniel clicked open the doors of the Crown Vic, already looking forward to the blast of the AC in the dry heat. "Next stop, *Paco's*."

19

Savich took a bite of his Cheerios as he listened to Sean describe every detail of the muscle shirt he'd seen online on his iPad. This was a new one. What, Savich wondered, was a five-year-old doing shopping on the Internet? He shook his head at himself. He shouldn't have expected Sean to stick to the zillion games and puzzles and books they'd put on his iPad. Sean had cottoned to what Wi-Fi was and what it meant. But a muscle shirt? What was that all about?

"A muscle shirt, Sean?" Sherlock asked as she sliced a bit of banana onto his cereal. "To impress Marty?"

Sean looked up at his mom. "It would make my muscles look bigger, that's what Marty says. She told me if we put our allowances together, we could buy one on eBay, but the only one we found is nineteen dollars. So far we've got eleven dollars and thirty-five cents." Sean took a bite of Cheerios, spooned up a banana, shoved it in, and frowned. "I think the one we found is too big for me."

"A muscle shirt needs to fit nice and tight, don't you think?"

"Yeah, that's what I thought. Marty said when we get enough money, we should buy it for you instead, Papa. I told her we could save the money by Christmas. I think she's trying to kiss up to you because she wants to marry me."

Savich, who'd been thinking about Venus and the family meeting the previous night, tried to look solemn, since it wouldn't do to laugh. He studied Sean's serious little face, his intense dark eyes, and he marveled at how his boy could bring him back instantly to the real world.

But Sherlock didn't hold back—she spurted out a laugh, grinning like a bandit at Savich. "Hey, big boy, how would you feel about that?"

"Which?" Savich asked. "The muscle shirt or Marty being our daughter-in-law?"

"Marty's already a given, so the muscle shirt. I suggest black, Sean, that'd be good. I could show your papa off at the gym."

Sean looked confused, then his face scrunched up. "I just don't know, Papa, maybe I should tell Emma about the muscle shirt, too." He fell silent, stirring his soggy Cheerios around, then grinned, his eyes shining. "Emma gets a really big allowance, so she could put in more money, so maybe we could get it before Christmas." Then he sighed. "But Marty might get mad, and then I couldn't play *Flying Monks* with her." Again, that intense look. "What would you do, Papa?"

Savich looked thoughtfully into his cereal bowl, then at his son. "You want me to be honest, Sean?"

Sean nodded, all his attention on his father, as was Sherlock's.

"I'd wait for a girl just like your mama. Then I'd beg her to marry me and stay with me forever. And the best thing? I'd only have to worry about one wife. We'd have plenty of time for *Flying Monks*."

Sean turned his father's dark eyes to his mother's face, and slowly nodded. "Maybe that'd be okay. You're pretty nice, Mama."

"Thank you, Sean," Sherlock said. She felt such a burst of love she thought she'd float to the kitchen ceiling.

Savich's cell rang out *It's Time* by Imagine Dragons. "Savich." For Sean's benefit, he walked into the hall to take it, and when he returned, he drew a deep breath, and said in as emotionless a voice as he could manage, "That was Venus. Reporters are camped out in front of the mansion again and the neighbors are screaming at the police for not doing anything. Venus's number is ringing off the hook.

"She also said the shooting yesterday is front and center in the *National Enquirer*, not a big deal in itself, since everyone else is already covering it, but the *Enquirer* got every single juicy detail, the arsenic poisoning, our names, our meeting with the family last night. Everything."

"But how?"

"Venus's driver, MacPherson, left her a letter, apologizing but saying they paid him a great deal of money for his story and he has a sick kid to take care of. He resigned. They put his picture on the front page, along with Venus's."

Sherlock paused a moment. "Venus must be disappointed, but it doesn't change the fact that MacPherson saved her life yesterday. I suppose a father afraid for his child will do what he thinks he has to. What's wrong with MacPherson's child?"

"She didn't know. She said MacPherson had never brought it up and his letter didn't say."

"But does it really matter? I mean bits and pieces of what happened are all over the news. You don't suppose she might offer him his job back, do you?"

He shrugged. "She might consider it too big a betrayal. If she asks my opinion, I'll tell her what MacPherson did might keep the story in the news longer, but not much more than that.

"It's up to her. We'll see."

Sherlock saw Sean was all ears, and said quickly, "Sean, it's chilly this morning, so go get your jacket. Gabriella will be here soon and you want to be ready for school."

When she heard his footsteps on the stairs, she said, "You were working on MAX late last night. What were you doing?"

"Researching arsenic, and how someone might get access to it. There's a great deal of information, but it wasn't much help. You order arsenic online or by mail order from dozens of chemical-supply companies that in turn have hundreds of customers in more industries than you can name, from gold mining to semiconductors to insecticide manufacturers. Access is restricted, but any intelligent person could get hold of enough to poison someone.

"Still, it's rarely used as a poison, not in this country. It's too easy to detect, produces too many symptoms. It wasn't any smarter a choice than hiring Willig."

Sherlock said, "I'm thinking it was used since Venus is so old, and if the arsenic killed her, it wouldn't necessarily be suspicious."

He nodded. She had a point.

Sherlock sighed. "Poor Venus. It's got to be hard on her, thinking someone she loves might be willing to trade her life for money."

"You know she's tough enough to get through it, Sherlock. While Sean's getting his jacket, I'll call Mr. Maitland, keep him in the loop." He thought of Callie, Detective Ben Raven's journalist wife. There wouldn't be an exclusive news story for her after all, no possibility of one now that MacPherson had spilled it all himself to the *Enquirer*, and no chance for her to plant information on their behalf, now that the real story was already out in the open. Savich hoped he had a solid down payment on a future favor.

20

Savich smiled as he and Sherlock approached the tall good-looking man chatting with Agent Griffin Hammersmith in the interview room, using his hands to make a point. Griffin wanted to laugh, Savich saw it, but he managed to keep his expression flat. It was hard for Savich to look at Rob Rasmussen and think *suspect*. They'd been friends once, so long ago, a decade. But a suspect he was, and Savich knew he couldn't forget that. He was a man now, not the boy Savich had known, too wild and ungoverned for his own good, but loyal to his toes, someone you'd want at your back if trouble came knocking. He looked older and more settled, too, more content, as if life was working in his favor now. He had the Rasmussen good looks—green eyes, dark hair and naturally lean body. Rob looked over, saw him, and broke into a big matching grin.

"Savich! Hey, Agent Hammersmith tells me you're the big honcho here. I told him I wasn't surprised." And he was up and around the interview table, pumping

Savich's hand, patting his shoulder, still grinning. "I'm not in prison, isn't that great? Unexpected, maybe?"

"Nah, you take after Venus, way too smart to end up in the slammer. It's good to see you, Rob. Venus tells me you live in Maryland now, own a construction business. She's bursting with pride. Let me introduce you to my wife, Agent Sherlock."

Rob Rasmussen met Sherlock's eyes, leaned in close. "You've got eyes as blue as a June sky. How ever did this mongrel get you to marry him?"

Sherlock studied the good-looking, smiling face of the Rasmussen black sheep. She imagined Dillon was going to have a hard time keeping their interview cop and suspect, since they were old friends. She said coolly, but with a smile, "He needs me, so I had no choice." She shook his hand, and if he held her palm a bit longer than he should have, it felt like a friendly gesture. "It's a pleasure to finally meet you, Mr. Rasmussen. Dillon's told me all about you. Ten years is a long time to stay away. What have you been doing all this time?"

Rob placed a hand over his heart. "It begins already? The grilling?"

Sherlock said, "It's our job, Mr. Rasmussen. Please, sit down. Tell us, do you expect a warm welcome tonight from your father and brother?"

"Grandmother clued me in they won't be welcoming me with open arms, but I'll have Marsia with me for protection. My girlfriend—Marsia Gay—I've told her a lot about my family. She's good with people so

I'm thinking there's a chance she'll be good with them as well." He paused, gave them a crooked grin. "My dad should go nuts over her. She might even charm Alexander. Stranger things have happened, though I can't think of any off the top of my head at the moment." He sat forward, his face now deadly serious. "Grandmother called me this morning, told me about everything that's happened. This is bad, Savich, it shouldn't be happening to her. It's not like she's going to be around even another decade. She should have all the years allotted her to enjoy herself, exit the planet on her own terms.

"I know Dad and Alexander were the only ones with her, she told me that, but I can't buy it being either of them. Why would they want to kill her? Both of them are loaded, so money can't be the motive. One of her staff? Isabel has been with her forever, and so has Veronica. Maybe a Rasmussen employee who blames her for something?" He shook his head. "But no, not Dad, not Alexander. Grandmother told me Alexander isn't happy with her for forcing him to lawyer for the Smithsonian, but unhappy enough to feed her arsenic? Trust me on this—that would be too low-class for him. And my dad? Grandmother told me 'give him a woman and a bottle of gin—even leave out the woman—and he's happy.'"

Savich said, "I've checked through your finances, Rob, also part of my job, and it appears you've been near the bitter edge until this past year. Unlike the other family members, you aren't loaded, but you are finally in the black. Congratulations. But you're going to be wanting to expand, and to do that, you'll need a healthy amount of capital. Did you and Venus discuss money at all? A loan, a gift, an investment?"

"No, I wouldn't have done that. I've stayed away from approaching her for years, exactly because I wanted to make it on my own."

"Did she discuss her will or trusts with you? Do you know if you're named?"

"I know Grandmother set a trust up for me, but I don't know how much. The principal comes to me when I turn thirty-five. I'm thirty-one and I'm doing fine, just fine. I don't need her money, or the trust, not that I won't enjoy it when it hits my bank account."

"This is important, Rob. Did anyone else in the family, or on the staff—Isabel or Veronica—know you and Venus had been communicating, that the two of you had met, were continuing to meet?"

"She said she wanted to keep it a secret until she felt the time was right. She didn't even tell Veronica. But the attempts on her life have forced her hand, she told me. Her driver, MacPherson, knew. He drove her to our meets, of course, but I never met him, she just mentioned him a few times."

"Okay, we need to go through the three nights Venus got sick, Rob. Three weeks ago, Wednesday night, she was having dinner with Alexander and your father at the Ambassador Club. The 4th of June. Do you remember what you were doing?"

Rob Rasmussen didn't change expression. He pulled

a small black notebook out of his shirt pocket, thumbed through the pages. "Grandmother told me you'd have to know about my alibis, so I wrote them all down. The first time, June 4th, I was with my girlfriend—Marsia—at a restaurant. I have the receipt, and it's dated. The second time, I was on a job. I have all the particulars for you. Last night, I was watching the Nationals get trounced, burying my pain with bean dip and beer. Lots of witnesses." He paused. "I'm not the guy you want here." He handed Savich his black book.

Sherlock asked, "What made you first decide to email Venus after all this time, Rob?"

He grinned big, showing fine white teeth. "Because I finally had something to show her. My business. I'm proud of that. And I missed my family, well, Grandmother, mainly. I realized she was getting up there in age and I didn't want her to die without knowing how grateful I am she saved me from going to jail ten years ago. I wanted to see her, tell her how much she means to me. I gotta say, though, I was scared. I mean, she could have told me to stay out of her life. I finally got up the nerve, but only after I'd proved that I'm not a loser, that I could make money myself—not through Rasmussen Industries like the rest of them. My accountant shouted last quarter's numbers to me on the phone he was so pleased." Again, that big white smile. "Not bad for a loser."

He sat forward. "Look, it's not as if I turned my back on the lot of them over the years. I've kept track of Grandmother especially, running this, sponsoring that, making those deals with the government bigwigs, throwing benefits for some of her charities. She is amazing, always has been. I thought it was finally time. Marsia agreed with me, maybe even pushed me a little to do it. I tried the same email address Grandmother used ten years ago, having no clue if she'd even answer me, but she did."

Rob paused. "When I heard back from her, she told me she'd been about to call me. Can you imagine that? We had lunch and talked and caught up. She was really pleased to see me. She hasn't changed.

"Do I have expansion plans? Sure, I'd like to push onward, but that will come. I have lots of time to take over the world. And my plans for the business had nothing to do with my contacting Grandmother—she can tell you that herself."

Savich pulled out his cell, pressed a couple of buttons, brought up a photo, and handed it to Rob. "Do you know this man?"

21

Rob studied the photo of Vincent Willig, his eyes drugged and vague, fresh out of surgery. He frowned, cocked his head to the side, a mannerism Savich had seen Venus do when she was curious or worrying a problem. "Is this the guy who tried to kill Grandmother yesterday?"

"Yes."

"I think he looks familiar." Rob tapped his forefinger on the phone. "But I can't remember from where."

Savich said, "His name is Vincent Carl Willig and he has an impressive rap sheet—spent ten years in Attica. He got out six months ago. Think about where you could have seen him, Rob. It's important."

Rob nodded. "I'm not sure I have, but I'll think about it. What about employees? Would Veronica have any reason to want to poison Grandmother?"

Sherlock said, "Veronica has been with Venus fifteen years. Her finances are sound, since Venus invests most of her pretty substantial income for her. And she has free room and board in a mansion. She's dependent on Venus for her livelihood. I can't see a reason for her to want to do away with her meal ticket."

"She must be nearly forty now, isn't she?"

"She's thirty-six," Savich said. "Only five years older than you."

"Grandmother speaks highly of her, says Veronica makes her laugh. And she's always been completely loyal to her."

"Were you in love with her when you were a teenager?" Sherlock asked.

"Sure, she was a young guy's wet dream, blond, beautiful, a superb body. Is Alexander sleeping with her?"

Savich said, "Evidently not."

Rob laughed, shook his head. "I doubt it, too—Alexander wouldn't ever dip his quill in company ink. He always used to preach to me to keep away from the Help, always said it with a capital letter. He actually used those words—the Help. Veronica never liked him anyway."

Savich said as he rose, "That would sure make things neat, now wouldn't it? Not a Rasmussen behind this. Only the Help." He added more formally, "Sherlock and I will see you this evening, Rob. Thank you for coming in. I'll call if we have more questions."

Rob splayed his palms on the table, leaned toward them. "I'm not only angry, Savich, I'm scared. I just found Grandmother again and I don't want to lose her. That shooting yesterday, if you guys hadn't been there, if MacPherson hadn't been there—she'd be dead. Please find out who's doing this."

"We will." Savich turned to Griffin. "Let's show Mr. Rasmussen to the elevator."

"You know, Savich, both my dad and Alexander wrote me off years ago—Alexander ever since I stole his new Mustang and took it for a spin. A pity I wrecked it."

"You were thirteen, Rob," Savich said, as the group of four walked together down the wild hallway.

"And a spoiled little idiot. I remember Alexander had just turned eighteen, the Mustang was his graduation present from Father. A fine car, that Mustang. Then after I nearly killed that guy in the bar fight, Alexander wanted me sent away forever."

Sherlock knew all about the bar fight, but she wanted to hear what he would say about it. "What happened?"

"I hate to own up to it, even now, but I was treating my girlfriend like dirt because I was drunk and I'd heard she cheated on me, and this older guy—around twenty-five—took exception. We got into it and I hurt him, ended up in jail. Then my girlfriend hauled off and whacked me in the jaw. I was lucky, she didn't break it, even though I deserved it.

"Venus arranged the army option, she has friends everywhere who've helped me out more than once."

"There were other times?" Sherlock asked.

He cleared his throat. "Well, I did a bit of shoplifting when I was a kid, a bit of pot when I was in high school, some speeding, well, okay, a couple of DUIs when I was old enough to know better. But beating up that guy, that was the biggie. His name is Billy Cronin, he's married and has three kids, lives up in Philly. I, ah, check on him every couple of years."

When they reached the elevator, Savich pushed the button. The doors opened almost immediately and out stepped Agent Hammersmith's sister, Delsey Freestone, singing a twangy western song Savich didn't recognize, thought she'd probably written it herself. Two agents on the elevator stood behind her, obviously enjoying themselves.

She broke off, mid-verse, turning to the agents behind her. "I'll catch you guys later, thanks. Dillon! How nice to see you. I'm here to take Griffin to lunch. Hi, Sherlock." She stopped cold, blinked at Rob. "Who are you?"

Griffin laughed behind Savich. "Delsey, what's that song you're singing?"

Delsey sang a couple of bars, never taking her eyes off Rob Rasmussen. "I call it 'Lamebrain at the Hoedown,' classic country and western, all the way down to the twang and the head in the toilet the morning after. I'm hoping you'll sing it at the Bonhommie Club, Dillon."

Savich saw that Rob stood staring back at Delsey, his eyes a bit unfocused, looking shell-shocked. *Tell me this isn't happening.* Savich didn't want to, but he had no choice. "Delsey, this is Rob Rasmussen."

Delsey looked up at him, and slowly, she smiled. "Have you had lunch yet?"

Rob shook his head, ran his tongue over his suddenly dry lips. "Well, no, and I'm starved. But what about your brother?"

"Who? Oh, Griffin, I'll bet he's going to take Savich and Sherlock to lunch, right, Griffin?"

Griffin looked from Rob Rasmussen to his sister. He was no match for her blazing smile. "Sure, Dels, right."

"Let's go see what we can find," Rob said, and offered Delsey his arm. "Savich, Sherlock, please keep me in the loop. Please find out who's doing this. Agent Hammersmith, it was very nice to meet you." He gave Savich a little salute. "See you tonight."

Savich watched the elevator doors close behind Rob and Delsey, neither of them speaking, only smiling at each other like loons. "Well, Griffin, it looks like you've been kissed off."

Sherlock shook her head. "Let's just hope Rob has nothing to do with the attempts on his grandmother's life."

22

Half an hour later, Agent Ruth Noble stuck her head into Savich's office. "I brought Alexander Rasmussen up, put him in the interview room. Ah, Dillon, he's not a happy camper. Not that he wasn't civil when I fetched him from downstairs, but he's pissed off at your demanding he come here to our house. Said he was a very busy man and this was nonsense. Can I sit in?"

Savich swallowed the last bite of his veggie wrap. "Sure, come on."

Savich, Sherlock, and Ruth walked back into the interview room recently vacated by Alexander's brother, Rob.

"Alexander," Savich said as he walked in, closing the door behind him. "Thank you for coming. You've met Agent Noble."

Alexander stood up from his chair. "You insisted I come." He didn't spare either Ruth or Sherlock a glance. "Listen, you know I have a lot of demands on my time, Savich, so what do you want that's so important you dragged me here?"

"Sit down, Alexander."

He sat down, stiff and angry. "Well?"

"It's obvious you're here because you are one of the people who may be trying to murder your grandmother."

As an opener, this one scored big with Alexander. He went pale, lurched back in his chair, then flushed red with outrage. "*What?* You believe I would ever harm a hair on Grandmother's head? You're a disgrace, incompetent, the lot of you! If you think you can frame me, railroad me into prison, you're dead wrong."

Savich's voice remained calm. "You and your father were the only people with her all three times she got ill from arsenic poisoning."

"Use your brain for a change—anyone could have gotten to her food. Her own flesh and blood trying to kill her? That's absurd. You and I have never gotten along, Savich. It's natural you would feel jealous of what I have and who I am, and I don't hold that against you, but you need to get over yourself. I have no motive, nor does my father.

"Now, you've said what you wanted to say and I've responded to it. Over and done. There was no reason for you to demand I come here."

"You say you have no motive?" Savich raised a finger. "You're very angry at your grandmother for forcing you to work at the Smithsonian—with those bureaucratic morons I believe you called them. You consider it a rank insult." He raised a second finger. "Two years ago you embezzled from Rathstone, Grace and Ward, and your grandmother made you pay back the money, convinced them not to prosecute, and I can only imagine how much you resented that." A third finger went up. "Since she's brought you into Rasmussen Industries, she's kept a close eye on you, looks over your shoulder at everything you do to make sure you don't fall back into old habits. How you must hate being on that short leash, under that constant supervision, of her belittling you in that way." He raised a fourth finger. "You've disappointed her, Alexander, and that scares you because she could cut you off whenever she wishes. You want her position, you want to run the show, and you don't want to risk losing that, but you don't want to wait any longer. A prosecutor would have no trouble supplying a motive, Alexander, and you know it."

Alexander rose straight out of his chair, leaned toward Savich, his hands splayed on the tabletop. "How dare you, you no-talent suck-up! The only reason Grandmother pays you any attention at all is because your grandmother was Sarah Elliott. She keeps you around because of her childhood friend, nothing more. And your talent? You whittle! You're an embarrassment, a low-life cop."

Sherlock smiled at the man she was tempted to cold-cock. "Dillon is an artist, he carves beautiful pieces, many of them at the Raleigh Gallery. And guess what? Dillon isn't the only one with talent in our low-life cop family. I play classical piano. You should come hear me play sometime." And Sherlock cracked her knuckles.

Alexander lasered her with a look, but Savich raised his hand, cut him off. "I think that's quite enough. We're not here to talk about us, Alexander, or what you think of us. If you have nothing to hide, I suggest you check your insults and answer our questions."

"I don't have anything to say."

Savich said easily, "I hope you do, Alexander, because more than your father, more than anyone else in your family, you're the only one who stands to benefit if your grandmother dies."

"I am not the one doing this! Listen, it's got to be a competitor. The business world is a ruthless place. We've had to cut out the guts of more than one company in a merger or sale. That breeds resentment, even hatred.

"Anyone could have hired one of the staff to put poison in her food. That's where you need to look, not at me, not at my father."

"You believe Isabel could be poisoning Venus? That she's being paid by a disgruntled business associate?"

"Why not? And there's Veronica. I never trusted her, always sucking up to Grandmother, always agreeing with her. Why? She's not family, she has no reason to be loyal to Grandmother. Question her. And there's Aunt Hildi, Grandmother paid off her husband to leave her, and that had to burn."

Off the rails. But interesting that Alexander had thrown his aunt Hildi under the bus.

Savich said quietly, "Do you know why Venus bailed you out of those charges at the Rathstone law firm?"

"She didn't want her name blasted in the tabloids. She was afraid it would negatively affect Rasmussen stock. She was afraid for her own reputation."

Sherlock said, "She saved you, Alexander, because you're family. She loves you. It's that simple."

Alexander looked at them like they were mutts beneath his notice. He pulled his mesmerizing lawyer's voice out of his hat. "Of course she does, and I love her. You want the facts about Rathstone, Grace and Ward? I had a disagreement with the partners about using my influence with Grandmother to bring them more business. I refused. They threatened they would let me go if I didn't agree. I refused to. They came up with this malfeasance nonsense, threatened to report it to the bar. That is when Venus stepped in and made her own threats. Malfeasance? She never believed it for an instant."

Savich said, "Specifically, it was a matter of siphoning off a client's funds, actually two very wealthy clients whose finances the firm handles. Well, make that past tense—handled—because they left the firm. Venus must have been very disappointed in you."

Alexander stared at him. There was a bead of sweat on his forehead. Savich said, "Venus kept quiet about what you did, but that doesn't mean I wouldn't find out about it. I know everything you did, every person's name you did it to. Tread carefully, Alexander."

Alexander swiped his hand over his forehead. He

managed to kick in his lawyer's voice again. "I will say this once and only once. This is idiotic. Neither I nor my father were poisoning Venus. As for that fool who tried to murder her outside our home yesterday, I know nothing about him." He rose, shot his cuffs, and looked down at Savich. "I came believing that perhaps you would wish to have my help. Instead, you accuse me of wanting my grandmother dead. If I'd known the two of you were going to speak to me in this manner, I would have brought Rasmussen lawyers. Next time, I will. Don't think I won't tell Venus what happened here." He stepped around the table, made a beeline for the door.

Savich let him go. He looked from Sherlock to Ruth, raised an eyebrow.

"I say we hang him up by his thumbs," Ruth said, "and let him dangle above the floor for a couple of days. Come on, boss, let me do it."

Savich said slowly, "It's a lovely thought, Ruth."

Ruth gave him a cocky grin. "Do you think we could run it by Mr. Maitland?"

23

Cam picked two big bottles of ketchup off the shelf in *Ralph's Organics*, really only a grocery store with inflated prices. Should she buy a third bottle? Heinz was a must-have for the cookout her parents had planned that evening. Her father had shooed her out of the house, along with an order for more beer and chips.

"Cammie! Cammie Wittier! Goodness, is it really you?"

Cam turned to see an incredibly beautiful young woman wearing chic ripped cut-offs, a tight tank top, and a perfect tan topped off with a head of glorious blond hair, streaked and full. And then she recognized her. Mary Ann Duff, a high school classmate she hadn't seen since she'd left for college. She looked amazing, no longer carrying twenty extra pounds, and she'd lost the glasses and the dull, brown hair. She'd always been pretty, but now, she was flat-out glamorous. Cam remembered she was smart, too, and a good writer, the two of them thick as thieves on the high school newspaper their senior year.

"Mary Ann? You look stunning! Goodness, all that incredible hair—I swear, if I were a guy, I'd jump you." The two women laughed and hugged.

"I'm so glad you recognized me. I mean, I was such a dog in high school." She paused, fluffed her hair. "I'm Missy Devereaux now, have been for nearly eight years. A guy I met in a bar in Santa Monica, Anthony Margoulis, suggested it. He turned out to be a jerk, but he changed my life. But enough about him. Think you can call me Missy?"

"Sure, not a problem, and call me just plain Cam."

"You here to visit your parents? Do they still live in the Colony?"

"No and yes," Cam said. "Actually I'm an FBI agent now, on assignment from Washington."

"I guess I'm not surprised. You had your heart set on that for as long as I've known you. Cammie— Cam, you're so pretty, how do you get all the guys you work with to stop staring and listen to you? I mean, you're the spitting image of your mom, and I've seen guys do a double take when she walks down the street here in Malibu. I even saw Ben Affleck stop once to stare after her. You said you were here on assignment. Can you tell me what it is?"

"I'm in charge of the serial killer case—the murdered actresses."

"Oh my goodness, you mean the *Starlet Slasher*?"

Cam rolled her eyes. "Trust the media to come up

with something alliterative that makes you want to throw up."

Missy shuddered. "Whatever, it's scary. This monster is all my friends can talk about. Cam, I was there! In a show with Molly Harbinger at the Mandalay. To die like that, Cam—it's horrible."

"Yes, it is. Wait a minute—Missy, you're an actress? I never even knew you wanted to act."

"That's because I never told anybody back in high school. Fact is, Cam, I really was a dog, and I was too insecure, afraid I'd be mocked, but yes, I always wanted to act, even as a little girl. I'm not exactly a success yet, but maybe, in time. Who knows when some fairy dust will fall on my head? I'm working on and off, small roles in TV shows and commercials mostly, but it's steady enough I can support myself." She paused a moment. "I guess I brought both the killer and my stalker with me to Las Vegas."

"What? You have a stalker? What's that about?"

Missy gave her a huge grin, showing even white teeth. "You'd have been proud of me. I ran him down, I caught that loser myself in Las Vegas last weekend. And then—I couldn't believe this—the cops let the jerk go."

"He followed you to Las Vegas?"

"Yes. I saw his reflection in a store window on the Strip last Saturday, and I just snapped. I'd bought myself a Ka-Bar, you know, one of those big, scary military knives—"

"Yes, I know them."

"Of course you'd know. I was so mad I was spitting, and so I took off after him, ran him down in the Wynn hotel garage. The cops came; the stalker said he didn't do anything, that he'd never seen the crazy woman chasing him with a knife before, never in his life. Then the creep said he wouldn't press charges because he realized I was upset, but I'd made a mistake; he wasn't a stalker. Can you believe that? Then that night Molly was murdered. She was a longtime dancer in the Beatles show I'd just snagged a role in. People called her Legs— yep, she had legs all the way to her tonsils. I met her only once in Vegas, to say hello. She was nice, Cam, and she wanted to make it so bad, just like I do, like all of us do."

Missy's eyes filmed with tears. "And that idiot stalker. I'd just gotten to Vegas and there he was. It was too much. I broke my contract with the Mandalay and came back home." She dabbed her eyes with a careful fingertip. "Sorry, but it was really bad. And that reminds me, Cam, I need to check in again with the police in Calabasas. The older detective I originally talked to isn't there anymore. He retired. Not that he did much of anything before I left for Vegas. There's a new guy, and I have a name to give him, so that's something. I'll get a restraining order on him." Missy stopped, shook her head. "Sorry, I'm a motormouth. I'm so excited to see you, Cam. I'm glad you're here. If anyone can catch this psycho who killed Molly and the others, it's you."

"Did you know any of the other murdered actresses, Missy?"

Missy swallowed convulsively, nodded. "I knew Connie Morrissey. I didn't know Melodie Anders but she lived up in San Dimas. I couldn't believe it when I heard she was killed, in early April. I heard she was a good actress, really committed, always out there pounding the pavement when she wasn't working, but she visited her older parents most weekends in San Diego.

"Connie Morrissey lived right here in Malibu, in the Colony, but I bet you already know that. I'd see her at auditions, go out for coffee after, or margaritas and nachos at *El Pablo* in Santa Monica some Friday nights. She was nice, Cam, and talented.

"Melodie was twenty-six, and Connie was only twenty-five. So hopeful, so filled with dreams, just like me. And now they're gone—just gone."

Cam squeezed Missy's shoulder. "I'm very sorry. You know I'll do my best to catch him."

"Yes, I know." Missy cocked her head. "I remember a basketball game in high school against the Calabasas Bears. We were down eleven points, but we never folded because you kept whipping us up, and sure enough, we ended up winning by two points."

Cam remembered that game as clearly as Missy did. She could still hear her parents yelling down at them. She also remembered she and her team, and her parents, had ridden the joy wave for a solid week.

"Can you tell me what's going on now that you're here?"

"I can't tell you much, Missy. I'm sorry, but I would like you to tell me more about Connie Morrissey. Okay?"

"Sure, anything to help."

"Missy, are you living alone right now?"

"Yes. My great-aunt Mary died last year and left me this cute little cottage on Malibu Road, not far from the Colony. Bless her, that's why I don't have to work an extra job to keep body and soul together."

Cam lightly laid her hands on Missy's shoulders. "I don't want to scare you any more than you already are, but please, Missy, have someone move in with you until we catch this killer."

Missy stared at Cam. "You really think the Starlet Slasher could come after me?"

"No, but it would be smart if you weren't alone until we catch him."

"Cam, are you staying with your folks?"

"Nope, the Pinkerton Inn."

A big smile bloomed. "How about you move in with me? I've got two bathrooms."

24

Venus Rasmussen was looking elegant as usual in a dark blue Dior suit, a white silk blouse, and low black pumps, her hair a shiny salt-and-pepper bob. She looked, Sherlock thought, and not for the first time, like the older Barbara Stanwyck, an indomitable will, indisputably in charge. She'd been driven by an assistant directly from her office atop Rasmussen headquarters, a modern spear of smoked glass and steel outside of Alexandria, to the hospital. Even if she weren't recognized, the hospital staff still straightened when she walked through. She had that effect on people.

Sherlock remembered once when she and Dillon had visited Venus in her top-floor corner office, guarded by three assistants. The incredible space with its two walls of floor-to-ceiling windows, wasn't, however, sleekly modern like the rest of Rasmussen headquarters. No, Venus had created an oasis of elegance and grace, soft grays and pale blues to showcase very fine English eighteenth-century antiques. Sherlock also remembered two senators waiting to meet with Venus, discussions Venus had mentioned in passing, about new defense legislation they wanted her to consider. And now this mess. She knew Mr. Maitland had a direct line to the vice president with instructions to keep him updated on the situation.

Venus grinned when Sherlock told her how beautiful she looked, patted her arm, and said, "A little face work does wonders, my dear, wonders. Give it some thought in fifty or so years." She was flanked by Savich, Sherlock, and Veronica now. They paused outside Vincent Willig's room while Savich showed Officer Lane Gregson his creds. "Anyone come around?"

"No, Agent Savich. All quiet. Well, a lot of complaining from Willig when he's awake. Makes me feel good to hear it."

Savich grinned. "Keep an eye out, Lane. He's certainly not up to try an escape, but you know the guy who hired him might come by to silence him."

Officer Gregson patted the Beretta on his hip. "I'll be ready for him, Agent."

They saw Willig was alone, no nurses, no techs, no doctors. He seemed to be asleep, an IV line tethered to his left wrist, his breathing slow and even.

Venus said, "Looks like he's down and out. I thought you only shot him in the wrist and broke his arm."

Savich said, "The surgery on his wrist was more complicated than they thought going in. The bullet nicked an artery. And now he's developed an infection. He'll be here for another couple of days."

Venus said, "As old as I am, the truth is I haven't had many dealings with anyone like this man, Dillon. I do hope he doesn't try to throttle me."

"You could take him, easy."

Venus grinned, showing lovely white teeth, her own, Savich knew. She did look well south of eighty, fit and healthy. "I know you don't approve of my coming here, but I appreciate your being here with me."

They both knew the truth was he'd hardly had a choice, except maybe to bar her physically, something he didn't much want to do. It was one of the perks of being Venus.

Savich looked back at Veronica, who stood a couple of steps behind them, ready to leap forward to protect Venus, all her attention focused on Willig. She'd told Savich she wished Venus hadn't insisted on seeing Willig, but like him, she hadn't made any headway with Venus.

Savich said, "I'll go in and get his attention, Venus, then ask you to come in. Veronica, stick close to her."

Venus touched her hand to Veronica's arm to keep her silent. "Dillon, I'm the one he tried to kill; I'm the one who should get him to pry his eyes open." Without any hesitating, Venus strode into the sterile hospital room with its single bed and single nightstand, her heels clicking on the linoleum floor.

Savich watched Vincent Willig slowly open his eyes as Venus walked brisk and confident toward him. He saw Savich behind her and flinched. Good, Savich thought, he remembered, knew Savich could cause him a load of pain.

"Who are you and what do you want?" Willig's voice was low and scratchy and filled with mean.

"And good day to you, too, Mr. Willig. I'm the person you tried to murder yesterday, but of course you know that."

"Why would I want to kill an ancient old broad like you? You look nearly ready to topple over without any help from me. I didn't try to murder anybody yesterday. You're thinking of somebody else. What are you doing here?"

Venus stepped close and stared down at him. "I was hoping you're not completely brainless."

"I'm not brainless, you old bat."

"Of course you are. You couldn't even manage to kill someone who's twice your age. From reading about you, I know you've never done anything worthwhile in your miserable life. You've got no morals, no center. Offer you a buck and you'll happily do whatever is asked."

"You're three times my age, at least. Hey, I see you're not alone. You're kind of pretty, you back there. You the old bag's granddaughter? Maybe you can come back later and we can have some tapioca together? No, I guess not, given that frown on your face. And you've brought those FBI guys with you, too. He's the one who tried to kill me, him and that broad with all the red hair. What, is he afraid I'll wrap my IV lines around your scrawny neck?"

"My neck is in fine shape, Mr. Willig, so maybe that means your eyesight isn't good, either, like the rest of you. As for your attacking me? What a joke—you can't even pee on your own."

Willig looked ready to spit. He looked from Venus to Savich. "I was thinking you brought the old broad in here to soften me up. Well, all she's done is insult me."

"I brought her because she insisted. She wants to make you an offer."

"That's right," Venus said. "Listen, Mr. Willig, I'm not here to trade insults with you but to show you that you're clearly on the wrong side. If indeed you are not brainless, you know the FBI will find out who paid you, with or without your help. You also know your telling us would speed things along. To that end I am willing to use my influence with the prosecutor, urge him to lessen the charges against you for what you tried to do to me, and I will pay you a great deal of money if you give us the name of the person who hired you. We want that name right now, Mr. Willig."

Venus paused a moment, leaned down. "I will pay you ten thousand dollars if you give me the name of the person who hired you to kill me."

"Ten big ones? You gotta be kidding me. That's nothing to you, you're richer than Rockefeller and maybe even richer than that Russian guy who doesn't wear a shirt. How about a mil?"

"Pay attention, Mr. Willig. You're not worth a million dollars. I'll give you a hundred thousand, not a

penny more. It should be more than enough to pay off
your lawyer."

Willig wheezed out a laugh. "A hundred grand for
a name? All right, I'll give you the name—it was you,
you crazy old bat, you hired me to make all those lazy
relatives of yours sit up and take notice. Are you going
to pay me now?"

"Very amusing, you idiot." Venus leaned down and
smacked his face. Willig moaned, tried to raise his
hand to shove her away, but the IV line held him down.

"You hit me again I'll have you arrested."

Willig's lawyer, Big Mort Kendrick, came roaring
into the room—exactly on time. Savich smiled. It had
taken only one well-timed phone call. He'd looked
forward to Big Mort making a grand entrance, yelling, threatening, and bless his heart, here he was. Mort
yelled, "Lady, I saw you hit him! You can't do that.
That's physical torture. I'll sue you from here to Sunday. You'll be a bag lady before I'm through with you!"

Venus turned and stared at Kendrick like he'd just
slithered from beneath a rock. "I beg your pardon?"

Kendrick stared at her, froze. He swallowed, looked
ready to choke. "Ah, oh, it—it's you, Mrs. Rasmussen—" He stopped dead, flushed red to his eyebrows,
realizing he was standing not three feet from the biggest financial gun he'd ever speak to in his lifetime. "Ah,
ma'am—Mrs. Rasmussen—you really shouldn't hurt
Mr. Willig. He's already hurt."

Venus waved a graceful hand toward Willig. "Of

course he is. He should probably be dead for what he tried to do. Who are you?"

"I'm Mr. Willig's lawyer, ma'am, Morton James Kendrick." He didn't want to be intimidated by one of the most powerful women in America, but he was, and knew he sounded like a prisoner being sentenced by the hanging judge.

Savich wanted to laugh, it was everything he'd hoped for. He looked at Sherlock, knowing she was having trouble keeping her face straight. Veronica had her hand over her mouth to keep in a laugh as well. The three of them watched Venus eye Kendrick slowly up and down. "It seems to me, Mr. Kendrick, that you have a great deal to talk about with your client. You can represent him until he runs out of the small bit of money he has to pay you for defending him against a charge of attempted murder, or you can convince him to tell us who hired him and accept one hundred thousand dollars from me, as well as my promise to intercede with the prosecutor to keep his sentence as short as possible. What do you have to say to Mr. Willig?"

Savich saw Kendrick swallow, could practically see him counting zeroes in his head, saw the you'd-better-take-the-bucks look he gave to Willig.

As for Willig, he was staring up at Venus as if mesmerized. Finally, he nodded, and whispered, "All right. I'll tell you everything I know. It was that good-looking broad over there who's acting all righteous, like she'd fling herself in front of a bus for you."

Veronica opened her mouth, hissed, but Savich said over her, "You don't even know her name, do you?"

Venus fisted her hand, but she didn't smack him again. She really wanted to, very much, for that rank bit of idiocy, but she didn't. She sighed and shook her head in disappointment, her eyes never leaving his face. Then she turned to Kendrick. "I will leave it to you, Mr. Kendrick, to talk Mr. Willig into accepting one hundred thousand dollars in exchange for the truth. And you will tell him he will give us the proof we need to be certain it is the truth, since his word isn't worth much, now is it? Don't stand there like blubber fallen off a whale, make your brain-dead client own up."

Savich had to say that Big Mort looked ready to shoot Willig if he didn't cooperate. His cut would be what? Thirty thousand dollars? Savich watched him clear his throat and boom out, "Yes, very well. Vincent, tell her the truth. I will get it in writing that Mrs. Rasmussen will pay you one hundred thousand dollars for the name of the person who allegedly hired you."

Willig yelled, "I want more than the money. I want to walk, no jail time. I want that in writing, too."

Savich said, "Mr. Willig, I've already spoken to the federal prosecutor. If you are ready to tell the truth, to cooperate fully, he's willing to sit down and talk with you. But you will serve some time, no way around it."

Willig gave him a cunning look. "How much time would I be looking at?"

"Your attorney can work that out with the prosecutor."

"You think I'd trust a lawyer? Only fools trust lawyers." Willig stared over at Big Mort. "How much would you take of my one hundred thousand?"

"Thirty percent," Big Mort said.

"See that? Thirty percent for doing exactly nothing. Tell you what, I'll think about it. Get me some pain meds."

Savich said, "You have twenty-four hours. I suggest you consider the alternative, Mr. Willig, namely spending the rest of your life in Attica."

25

Venus's face lit up when Rob strolled into the living room that evening and smiled broadly at his family. Ten years had passed and now a man stood in front of them, not a boy. His father, Guthrie, inhaled sharply and smiled. His voice was scarce above a whisper. "Robbie, it's really you?"

"Yes, Father, I'm home."

Savich thought for a moment Guthrie would leap out of his chair and embrace his son, but there was too much reticence on both sides, too much uncertainty. But no one could be blind to the hunger in both men's eyes. It was like a beacon for all to see, including Alexander, who stood motionless by the fireplace, allowing no expression at all on his face. Rob looked at his brother from a distance of fifteen feet. "Alexander."

Alexander said nothing, merely nodded to him.

Venus rose, her beautiful Rasmussen green eyes lit to a hundred watts, and when Rob leaned down and kissed her cheek, she hugged him close, a look of sheer joy on her face. Savich saw how gently Rob held her, so very carefully, until she turned away toward his girl-friend, shook her hand, and lightly patted her cheek. "You're Marsia, I presume?"

"Yes, ma'am."

Marsia Gay was tall and model thin, her dark hair cut in a wedge that came to two sharp points at her jawline. She had remarkable dark purple eyes. Sher-lock felt the pull of her when Marsia held out her white artist's hand and beautiful long fingers to Venus. "At last," Venus said, smiling at her. "Rob has told me so much about you, particularly your amazing sculp-tures. It is a pleasure to finally meet you. Welcome to our home."

"The pleasure is mine, Mrs. Rasmussen."

"I believe you are younger than I expected."

Rob gave them a silly grin. "Perhaps Marsia looks so much younger, Grandmother, because she never had the threat of jail hanging over her head like one of us here."

There was a bit of laughter, and all eyes fixed on him.

Rob looked back over his shoulder. "The two guards you have posted outside were so thorough I expected to be strip-searched. I'm relieved they're here, Grand-mother."

"I am as well. They will remain until this matter is resolved. Now, let Marsia meet everyone." She made the introductions with an unspoken yet very real threat in her voice that the entire family seemed to heed. Even Alexander stayed civil, though he eyed his brother with wariness and barely veiled contempt.

Savich and Sherlock watched with interest as silence fell, as when the curtain first rises on a play. Then Hildi was quickly at Rob's side, touching his face and hugging him, leaning forward to have him kiss her cheek. She stood back and looked up at him. "My beautiful boy, how I've missed you. You must let me paint you, as I did your mother. There's so much I'd like to capture, that special light in your eyes, the way you tilt your head, just like your father." She smiled at Marsia. "I fear even you, my dear, couldn't capture those qualities in your metal sculptures."

"No," Marsia said, "you're quite right." She stood quietly at Rob's side, a fixed smile on her face. Rob had probably warned her that pretty much anything could come floating out of Aunt Hildi's mouth. If anything, she looked mildly amused.

When Venus introduced Marsia to Veronica, Veronica stepped forward, took Marsia's hand. "I've read all about you, seen your sculptures at the Mianecki Gallery in Baltimore. Your work is amazing. I remember in particular a large piece named *Hercules,* copper and steel, I believe. I could feel the power you gave him, the bold spirit. A pleasure to meet you, Ms. Gay."

"Thank you," Marsia said. "He spoke to me," she added. "Call me Marsia, please."

Veronica gave her a beautiful smile. "Call me Veronica."

Veronica turned to Rob. "Rob, I remember you as a teenage boy, all swagger and fun. I also remember you were always kind to me. Welcome home." She smiled up at him, not all that far since she was tall. Rob lightly kissed her cheek. "Thank you, Veronica." He said against her ear, "I've got to say you're as beautiful as ever. I was telling Savich and Sherlock that you were a very sweet fantasy from my misspent youth."

Veronica pulled back, laughed up at him. "I remember, too, how you liked to tease me, always telling me how hot I was, and that always made me perk right up."

Rob nodded. "I remember how close you were to Grandmother, even back before I left a decade ago. She tells me you do everything to keep her safe except sleep next to her."

Veronica sent a smile toward Venus. "I asked her if I could move a bed into her room but she refused. You've grown up well, Rob. Venus knew you would; she never doubted you, only thought you'd gotten lost along the way, that you'd find your way back. And you did."

Marsia turned to Savich. "Rob told me Sarah Elliott was your grandmother." She nodded to the painting above the fireplace. "I want you to know she was a great inspiration to me. Did you inherit any of her incredible talent?"

Sherlock said, "Dillon whittles, beautiful pieces out

of rosewood, maple. Some are exhibited at the Raleigh Gallery in Georgetown."

"I should like to see them," Marsia said. "I noticed the fine scar lines on your fingers and wondered." She held up her own hands. Fine white scars scored her palms. "Working with metal has its dangers, as does working with a knife and wood."

Glynis sashayed up to Rob, past the woman at his side, took his face between her hands, and kissed him, with tongue. Rob gently set her away and lightly touched his knuckles to her smooth cheek. "Good to see you again, too, Glynis." She tried to kiss him again, but Rob was fast and took a quick step sideways, held her hands in front of him.

Marsia gave Glynis a friendly smile, said without rancor, "It's a good thing I've got Rob nailed down because you've got quite a technique there."

Glynis nodded, chin up. "Rob didn't kiss me back this time, not like he did when I was seventeen," and Glynis gave her a smile with teeth.

Venus clapped her hands. "Let's not forget that no one is seventeen now." She gave Alexander a speculative look. "You've been unusually quiet. Are you pleased to see your brother again?"

Alexander was still at his post against the fireplace mantel, a martini in his right hand, like he'd stepped off a page of *GQ*. He recognized an unspoken order when he heard it. "I'm in favor of anything that pleases you, Grandmother." He turned to Marsia, spoke in a smooth, emotionless voice. "Your name is interesting, Ms. Gay. Are you hoping to change it to Rasmussen?"

"My name has quite a history, Mr. Rasmussen, as I'm sure yours does as well. It's a distinctive history, one I will tell you about if you're interested." She gave him a long look. "I would like all of you to know that Rob has never traded on his name. He built his construction business on his own hard work, and on the trust he's earned. That's how I met him, through his business."

Rob said, his voice easy, "I remodeled her kitchen. I did a great job because I hoped I'd be cooking Marsia dinners one day on that Wolf range I talked her into. Don't look surprised, everyone, I like to cook. I'm good at it, too."

"Part of your army training?" Alexander said, sneer at full bloom. "Pork 'n' beans in the mess hall?"

Rob appeared to give this serious consideration. "No training as a cook directly, but I'll say the army helped me grow up. By the way, add the right hot sauce and some onion to the pork 'n' beans, and they're not bad."

He turned back to his family, looked at each of them in turn as he had when he'd come in. "I know this is difficult for you, here I've turned up out of the blue, and now we're suddenly together, thanks to Grandmother, but I've got to say I'm really grateful to get to see all of you again. I've missed you. I hope you'll forgive me for all my young man's stupidities. I am sorry for them." He looked straight at his brother.

"What's important now is that we all work together to help Savich and Sherlock find out who's trying to kill Grandmother."

Alexander put a bit more wattage in his sneer. "Indeed we should, little brother. The trouble is that some of us—you, for example, have a, ah, troubled past. I might add you have your fortune tied up with this family. The income from your construction business is nothing compared to Rasmussen Industries. Isn't it true you have no access to your trust fund while Grandmother is alive or until you're thirty-five?"

Rob said matter-of-factly, "Yes, we all know that's true. That has helped me to focus my life in the meantime, on what's really important to me. Do you know what I found out? I discovered I could make it on my own. Have you ever wondered whether you could, Alexander?"

Alexander flicked a piece of lint off his beautifully tailored sleeve. "Do you doubt I could, brother? But that is not the point. Like the rest of the family I'm worried for Grandmother. Someone is trying to kill her." He paused a moment. "And here you are, the returned prodigal, turned up out of the blue."

Venus said, her voice cool, "Not so out of the blue, Alexander, we've been in touch for six months, and that's hardly damning. Rob is not some new card in the deck, he's my grandson, and I won't have you casting around suspicions on anyone in this room. We're here to have dinner, as a family. Let me add that civility,

Alexander, is a major requirement to run a company the size of Rasmussen."

Isabel appeared in the doorway, as if on cue. "Ms. Venus, the *Pied Piper* has delivered your dinner. We are ready for you in the dining room. Mr. Paul has outdone himself." She smiled warmly.

No matter the provocation, both Savich and Sherlock doubted Venus would allow any more fireworks tonight. A pity.

26

Cam marveled at her parents. They'd arranged an impromptu barbecue for as many of the detectives she'd met that day as would brave the traffic, all within a matter of hours. Some of the Calabasas sheriff's deputies they knew as friends, and the sheriff himself, Dreyfus Murray, and his wife, Suzanne, made up the group on the back deck. Some of the neighbors they knew would remember Cam had been invited as well, to leaven the pot and cut down on complaints about all the cars clogging the street. She smiled when she heard Corinne Hill laugh at something her partner, Morley Jagger, said. She suspected they'd come out of curiosity. She saw Allard Hayes of San Dimas lean close to hear something Supervisor David Elman was saying. Whatever discomfort so mixed a group felt on arriving, it was fast gone when they were chowing down ribs and burgers with all the fixings—potato salad, baked beans, bags of chips, and Joel's famous salsa, with enough beer to float the *Queen Mary*.

And plenty of Heinz, courtesy of Cam's earlier trip to *Ralph's Organics*.

Cam overheard her mom telling Hill and Jagger, "You may well ask why Cam never followed in our footsteps."

Her dad chimed in. "Nah, not Cam. For Christmas we wanted to get her a toy Oscar, maybe a tiara, a script to read, but she wouldn't have it. She wanted a toy gun. That fired."

She heard Hill and Jagger laughing. Would that help give her a rep of a badass? She looked over to her mom, who had moved on to introduce Supervisor Elman to Dreyfus and eased back, watching the two men eye each other. Then Dreyfus laughed, told him to take a bite of his hamburger. "You'll tell me you've died and gone to heaven. Best burgers north of Santa Monica. I've always envied Joel's way with hamburgers cooked on a grill."

Lisabeth and Suzanne both laughed. "This was a great idea, Lisabeth, you and Joel pulled it off so fast," Suzanne said. "And would you look at Cam, she's smiling, working the room like a pro. She learned it from you."

Joel Wittier came up, kissed his wife's neck. "Look at Detective Jagger hanging on to every word out of Betsy Gilman's mouth. Who'd have thought he's a fan? Everyone's enjoying themselves, I'm pleased to say, and my Cammie is the recipient of all the goodwill."

Toward ten o'clock, when everyone was well oiled, stuffed to the gills with Suzanne Murray's homemade strawberry ice cream, and most of the neighbors had floated off to their homes, Cam walked out to stand on the wide wooden deck, resting her elbows on the railing. Daniel joined her. She said, not looking away from the bright half-moon sparkling the water like diamonds, "When I think of home, this is what I picture in my mind." She breathed in, pointed at the gentle waves fanning like lace onto the sand. "It's so perfect, always there, the water, so beautiful, no matter its mood. You feel at once blessed and grateful to be alive to see it."

Daniel said, "I grew up in Truckee, California, deep in the Sierras. I always believed there was no more beautiful place in the world. This"—he waved his hand at the endless stretch of ocean—"still seems alien to me. But this does seem timeless, too, like the Sierras, always there at your back." He turned to face her. He saw her clearly in the moonlight—no makeup, her hair tousled from the light breeze off the water.

He leaned back, his elbows on the wooden railing. "Cam, your parents are amazing, pulling this cookout off in what? Under six hours? You did as much as you could today to get everybody thinking on the same page, as a task force. And this cookout might just seal the deal. We'll see what happens. Oh yeah, when I thanked your folks, your mom kissed my cheek."

"Huzzah, I say."

"For your mom's kiss or for the task force?"

Cam punched his arm. "Both, of course. You weenie."

27

Officer Chas Golinowski yawned, took another sip of his lukewarm coffee, checked his watch. Only five minutes had passed. It was 3:00 a.m. on the dot. He had to keep it together for another four hours until Lane Gregson relieved him. It was so quiet on this floor. He preferred the insanity of the ER, remembered the nights over the years he'd brought in people with broken bones, heart attacks, bullet wounds, you name it. He looked up and down the empty long hallway, as he did every few minutes. Nothing. He looked toward the nurses' station twenty feet down the hall. Only two nurses were behind the desk, putting pills in those little cups when they weren't working on the computer or answering patients' calls. He wondered how his little girl was doing with her bad cold. He knew she was tucked in bed, her mother hovering. He wished he could be there, but he'd pulled guard duty over a guy who was about to get his butt hauled back to state prison for the rest of his miserable life. He'd heard talk about how he'd tried to kill Mrs. Venus Rasmussen herself, the stupid bozo, and that's how he'd earned a round-the-clock crew to guard him.

Chas's head was swimming with boredom and the urge to sleep, so he got to his feet and walked up and down the length of the hallway several times. He looked into Vincent Willig's room, where he stood quietly a moment, listening to Willig's even breathing. He was deeply asleep. Chas went back to his chair, stretched, tried to get some kinks out, and sat back down against the wall. He picked up the novel he'd brought with him, decided against trying to read it. He dropped it to the floor and closed his eyes. When he looked up again, he saw a tech wheeling a cart toward him. He could never figure out why they simply didn't let the patients sleep through the night. Wasn't sleep the great healer? The tech was dressed in a long white lab coat, a mask and a cap over his head. He didn't recognize him.

"Willig's sound asleep," he said.

"Good," the tech said in a low gritty voice, probably a smoker's voice, the fool. "I won't have to chat with that jackass." He jerked his head toward the open door of Willig's room. "You know what he did, don't you? It's all over the hospital."

"Yeah. Show me your ID and you can go in and torture him."

The tech leaned toward him as he reached into a pocket. In the next instant Chas felt the sharp stab of a needle slid into his neck, above his collar. He opened his mouth and went for his Beretta, but his arms didn't work. He felt an instant of terror, then nothing.

The tech gently eased him back so he would stay upright. If anyone noticed him, they'd believe he was asleep.

After a look toward the nurses' station, the tech walked into Willig's room.

Vincent was dreaming. He was lying on one of those fancy chaises, on a beach, maybe Fiji, someplace like that, and he had so much money he couldn't spend it all. There were drinks all around, and beautiful young native girls were hovering around him, laughing and teasing him, a kiss here and there, and he was happy, so very happy. They all wore bikinis, tiny little swatches of cloth. One girl leaned down over him, her breasts nearly in his face, whispering something.

The dream cut off like a spigot and Vincent came awake. Something was wrong, very wrong. He felt a tremendous pain in his arm and he wanted to scream but he couldn't move. He realized his heart was pounding out of his chest, fast, hard, and he couldn't catch a breath, couldn't suck in air. In that instant, Vincent knew he was dying, and he thought about his soul. He stared up at a shadowy face. "Wha—?"

"Goodbye, Vinnie."

28

Savich and Sherlock stood over Vincent Willig's body. Detective Ben Raven, Metro, said, "It's a hell of a thing. Whoever took Chas down was good." Ben sighed. "I have a team standing by. I wanted you guys to see Willig before I let them in."

It was a hell of a thing, Sherlock thought, as she leaned down and studied Vincent Willig's face. She felt a stab of pity, said a brief prayer. *Sorry, Vincent, you shouldn't be dead*. "He looks surprised," she said. "His eyes are open, his mouth is open, like he wants to speak." She cocked her head to one side, a move Savich recognized. She was reconstructing what had happened. "Our killer injects a drug into Officer Golinowski's neck, walks in, sees Vincent sound asleep, injects a lethal dose of a drug into his IV tubing. Vincent jerked away, you can see that on his face, Dillon. Look at his eyes. I think it's more than surprise. I'd say it was shock when he realized who was killing him. And he was feeling pain, probably couldn't breathe. Maybe potassium chloride, and then he's dead."

Ben was staring at Sherlock. "You see it that clearly?"

She shrugged. "I do wonder if he had time to say anything."

Savich said, "Ben, you said a nurse found Officer Chas Golinowski slumped unconscious in his chair. Is he awake yet?"

"He woke up by himself, but he was pretty confused. They decided not to give him any reversal agents, at least until his bloodwork's done and they see what the killer gave him. They're monitoring him, letting him sleep it off. The doctor spotted the needle mark on his neck, like I told you. It isn't clear where the killer got the drugs yet. We're checking the pharmacy, the crash carts. Maybe the killer brought them into the hospital. The nurses didn't see anybody. I haven't looked at the security tapes yet. You guys done in here? Let's go to the security office, see what we've got."

They didn't have much. They saw a tech of indeterminate sex wheeling an IV cart with all the expected paraphernalia, vials and tubing and syringes. The tech was covered head to toe with hospital garb, under a white lab coat.

"No more of this tech?" Savich asked Security Chief Doug Cummings.

"Just a backward view. Fast forward, Lonnie."

The security assistant fast-forwarded, hit pause. "Here he or she comes to the stairwell at the end of the hall. The camera catches his or her back. Leaves the tray and is gone. If someone is careful, they can avoid the cameras in the stairwells, and he or she did. Sorry, guys, that's it."

Cummings said, "I've already fielded two calls from reporters. This is going to burst wide open, and very soon now. The man who attempted to kill Venus Rasmussen is himself murdered, with a police guard outside his door. You've got a mess on your hands."

An understatement, Savich thought as they walked to the ER, where Officer Chas Golinowski lay sleeping in cubicle four.

Ben said, "I've alerted our media liaison. We're going to take a big hit for this. No excuses, but the killer was good." He sighed. "I hope Golinowski has something to say that's helpful."

Officer Chas Golinowski didn't have anything to say. He was still sleeping peacefully, snoring.

Savich and Sherlock spoke to the nurses, the orderlies, anyone who could have possibly seen the killer. No luck. Savich called Mr. Maitland, then Venus.

She was silent a long time, then, "Whoever it was worked very fast, Dillon. Terrifyingly fast. I only made the offer yesterday. Do you think it was a man or a woman?"

"I've studied the security tape, saw a tech garbed in hospital white. It's impossible to tell." He paused, then added, "Venus, it doesn't mean that it has to be one of the family. The one behind this had to know Willig was here, but that was all over the news."

"Will the police officer be all right?"

"He's stable. They're letting him sleep."

Venus said, "You know, Dillon, you ask anyone where they were in the middle of the night and who's going to say they were anywhere but in bed, sleeping with the angels?"

No one, Savich thought, no one at all.

29

Cam showered in Missy's second bathroom, pulled on boxers and a T-shirt and snuggled down on the soft mattress Missy had replaced when she moved in, along with the old green wall-to-wall carpet. "I love my shiny new oak floor," she'd said to Cam as she'd showed her around. "A new kitchen when I snag a good role. The fifty-year-old fridge and the green kitchen cabinets will be the first to go."

It was a nice house, cozy, comfortable, and the mattress was heaven. Cam was tired and hyped up at the same time, but the beer and soaping up in a shower old enough to be on an *I Love Lucy* episode mellowed her enough to nod off.

She came awake at 7:00 a.m. at the loud horse-racing bugle ringtone of her cell. For a second, she didn't know where she was, then remembered. "Wittier here."

It was Supervisor David Elman, LAPD.

"Our Serial struck again, call came in twenty minutes ago, in Santa Monica. Another actress, Deborah Connelly, aged twenty-six. Fits the profile exactly. She was killed in her bed last night, her laptop and cell phone missing, according to her boyfriend, who found her."

Cam closed her eyes, let it sink in. Another murder, and on her watch. It was a punch to the gut.

"Thank you for calling me so fast. I'll be there in thirty-five minutes. Don't let them touch anything, okay? We need a pristine crime scene."

He was huffy about that, for good reason, but Cam didn't care. She called Daniel, got an out-of-breath voice. "Yeah?"

"Cam here. Another murder." And she gave him the address in Santa Monica. "I'll see you there. Fast as you can, Daniel."

———

She parked her rented Toyota at the sidewalk at Deborah Connelly's condo thirty-one minutes later, Daniel pulling in right behind her. There were two patrol cars and two Crown Vics crowded in the driveway and at the curb.

When he joined her, Cam asked, "You were out of breath when I called. What were you doing?"

"I'd just come in from my morning run."

He didn't look like he was hungover from too much beer, and he'd gotten up early to run? He looked sharp in gray chinos, a blue blazer, and white shirt, boots on his big feet. She wanted to slug him.

"Do you know any of the people in the Santa Monica station?"

"Arturo Loomis, on the force for twelve years and counting, so lots of experience, and pretty smart. Your only problem with him is that he was married to a DEA agent who screwed him over big-time in their divorce. Maybe you'll luck out and someone else took the call."

She didn't luck out.

30

Cam spotted Loomis immediately, center stage, surrounded by three other officers, two men and a woman, listening to him talk. They fell instantly silent when they saw her.

Detective Arturo Loomis was a big man, midthirties, fit, and in charge. She couldn't see him ever taking crap from anybody. He wore aviator glasses over sharp, intelligent eyes and didn't acknowledge her. He looked toward Daniel, nodded.

Daniel said, "Arturo, let me introduce you to the case lead, FBI Special Agent Cam Wittier. Agent Wittier, this is Detective Arturo Loomis, Santa Monica."

She saw rage on his face. That was good, it meant he cared. Unless the rage was directed toward her.

"Agent." A clipped, hard voice.

"Detective Loomis." She stuck out her hand. Slowly, unwillingly, Loomis shook it.

"How long have you been on-site?"

"I was called in forty minutes ago. My lieutenant told me not to process the scene because it's an FBI case. So we've all been standing around with our thumbs in our mouths waiting for the Feds to show up."

"The Fed is here now. I understand Ms. Connelly's boyfriend found her?"

He nodded. "The boyfriend, yes. He called 911, then the housekeeper showed up. Boyfriend's in the kitchen. He's a mess. So far we can't get anything useful out of him. As of a few minutes ago, he was still Froot Loops. His name's Mark Richards. The housekeeper, Pepita Gonzalez, is in the living room and she won't shut up. Detective Turley"—he nodded toward a tall, no-nonsense woman in her thirties—"she speaks Spanish, almost as well as you do, Daniel. Ms. Gonzalez told her the boyfriend and the vic were moving into a new place together. Ms. Gonzalez usually comes every other week, but she came today to help pack boxes. She didn't see any strangers, only the boyfriend's car in the driveway.

"As I said, nobody touched the scene or the vic, order of Supervisor Elman."

Cam knew she should let it go, but she couldn't. "We can at least give her the dignity of using her name, Detective Loomis. She was Deborah Connelly."

Loomis stared at her, surprised, then dismissive. "Yeah, I thought you already knew that."

They walked together to the entrance hall, stacked high with neatly labeled boxes. Deborah Connelly had nearly finished moving out. Would she still be alive if she'd left a night earlier? No, not if the Serial had targeted her. He would have followed her.

Cam said, "I'd appreciate your calling your forensics team in, Detective Loomis, if you haven't already. I'll look in on the crime scene, then I'd like to speak to Mr. Richards."

Detective Loomis shrugged. "Knock yourself out. Our forensics team is already here. I knew we'd be covering that, from my buddy in Van Nuys—"

Cam turned back. "Detective Jagger?"

He blinked, obviously surprised she knew his name, shook his head. "No, Detective Corinne Hill. Nice to know you trust us to investigate a crime." He gave her a long look, added, "Corinne said even Frank was coming around after that bash your showbiz folks threw last night in the Colony. Too bad the vic—ah, excuse me, Deborah Connelly—didn't buy it a day earlier, I could have rubbed elbows with the rich and famous, too."

"That's enough, Arturo," Daniel said. "Cut her a break."

If not for the fact that Daniel had told Cam Loomis's wife had really burned him bad she'd have taken him apart. Her hand fisted, but she only nodded and left them, hoping Daniel would get him in line. She calmed as she walked down the oddly silent hallway, steeling herself for what she was about to see. She walked past the master bedroom and continued down the short hallway to the rear of the house, and into a room she saw immediately had become an office. On top of a desk were neat stacks of papers, piled high and ready to be stacked into boxes standing open nearby. Deborah Connelly had been neat, orderly. There was no laptop, no cell phone.

She stood in the center of the empty room. She smelled jasmine. Deborah had spent a lot of time in here. Cam could see her getting halfway down the pile of papers stacked in the center of her desk, wishing she could get another box or two packed before going to bed but hanging it up for the night. Was she already showered, wearing her nightgown? Cam picked a sheet of paper off the top of one of the piles. It was a notice of an audition for a part in the last *Mission: Impossible*. Printed in neat black ink across the bottom: *Yeah! Now I can pay the rent. Tom Cruise was very nice to me.*

It was dated nearly a year ago. Cam leafed through the rest of the pile. More auditions, some won, some lost, all with notations of what had succeeded, what had gone wrong. Records of a life, too short a life.

The window was open, broken glass on the floor. She looked for footprints outside the window, but the Serial had been careful to walk on grass. He hadn't used the back door. Had he changed the pattern, or as with Molly Harbinger, had there been someone too close, possibly watching, and so he'd chosen the window?

She traced his path to Deborah's bedroom. Down the narrow hall, and into a lovely light-filled room. Two uniformed policemen were standing over a double bed, looking down at Deborah Connelly's body, their faces set. It felt to Cam like the air itself was thick with anger. When they saw her, they looked at each other and stepped aside. Cam nodded to each of them and looked down at a young woman who'd been beautiful in life. But not now. Her face was gray and slack, her eyes closed. She was wearing a lime-green nightgown, a sheet pulled to her waist, both soaked with blood. There was blood spray on the wall beside the bed, on the ceiling. Her neck was cut so deeply her head hung to the side, her long black hair stiff with blood. So much blood. Her mouth was open, not in terror, but in surprise. She hadn't had time to register what he was going to do before he'd slit her throat. That at least was a blessing.

Cam felt a noxious mix of anger, sadness, and regret, saw her hands were trembling. She forced herself to focus on what was in front of her. She said quietly, "He broke the window in the other room, her office, and climbed in. He was wearing soft-soled sneakers that made no noise, probably the same ones he's worn five times before. He came into this bedroom, stood over the bed, looked down at her. What was the monster thinking? What was he feeling? Anticipation, elation? Did he know her?"

She felt the cops staring at her, but she kept her focus on Deborah Connelly's face. She moved a few inches to her right, closer, and leaned down. "This was exactly where he stood." She felt a punch of cold, then a light scent of jasmine. *We would have liked each other, Deborah. Or were you Deb? I'm so sorry. I promise you, we'll catch the monster who did this to you.*

31

Cam looked up to see a young officer standing in the doorway. "Agent, ma'am? The boyfriend, Mark Richards, he's waiting in the kitchen. Detective Loomis told me to get you." She wondered what else Loomis had suggested the officer tell her. Whatever it was, he'd been smart enough to keep it to himself.

Cam walked back down the skinny hallway with its pale blue–painted walls to the kitchen, past techs moving purposefully through the house, skirting boxes. The medical examiner walked past her, toward the bedroom, all brisk and impatient, not even giving her a nod. He would add no dignity to her death, her body now a job to him, a mystery to solve. She paused outside the kitchen door, closed her eyes a moment, and said a prayer for Deborah Connelly. Again, she smelled jasmine. It calmed her, helped her focus. Daniel was probably interviewing Pepita Gonzalez. She hadn't known he spoke Spanish. She hoped he'd got something useful from her.

She walked into a small ancient kitchen to see a man sitting alone, still as a stone at a small table, his face in his hands. Loomis had said he was hysterical, but now, he was utterly silent. No, not quite. He was whispering something over and over, *"I'm going to find you, you son of a bitch,"* the same words, nothing else, sounding singsong. She knew it was his way of keeping hold of himself, of keeping him from flying to pieces.

She lightly laid her hand on his shoulder. "Mr. Richards."

He slowly raised his face and Cam saw he was a tanned and buffed man in his early thirties with long dishwater-blond hair to his shoulders whipped back in a braid, lovely thick hair. He was wearing a white T-shirt and cutoff jeans, sandals on his big tanned feet. She saw a small diamond stud winking in his left earlobe. He looked up at her out of dazed eyes. She saw a pair of glasses on the table near his hand. "Who are you?" His voice was hoarse, blurred with tears.

"I'm Agent Wittier, FBI. You're Mark Richards?"

"Yes. People call me Doc." He sounded exhausted.

He looked like a surfer dude to her. "Doc?"

"Yes, I'm a neurosurgery fellow at Children's Hospital in Santa Monica, only a half mile away, as if that matters. That's why I wasn't here. It's all my fault, I as good as killed her."

"Why do you say that, Doc?"

He looked up at her with blind eyes. "She shouldn't

even have been here. Deb and I were moving in together. You saw all the boxes and crap in the hallway and living room? It was all her stuff. We were all set to move her into our new place yesterday, but—" He swallowed. "I was treating a four-year-old with an ependymoma—a kind of brain tumor—and his parents were a mess and he wasn't doing well, so we moved up the surgery to yesterday.

"I let Deb down, I wasn't here. If I hadn't put off moving her out of here, she'd still be alive. The house would have been empty, I'd have been sleeping next to her in our new apartment across the street from the hospital. That bastard wouldn't have found her here, alone.

"I know I shouldn't have touched her, but I couldn't help it. I closed her eyes. She had the prettiest blue eyes. She was staring up at me, but she wasn't seeing me any longer. I wondered if she was thinking about me when she died, how I should have been here with her." He hunched his shoulders, put his face in his hands again, and sobbed.

Cam wondered if that guilt would gnaw at him for as long as he lived. She laid her hand on his shoulder, lightly shook him. "Listen to me. You know as a doctor you can only do the best you can. This was not in your control. You are not responsible." She said nothing more, to give him a moment to process what she'd said, to get himself together. Slowly, he quieted. Cam said, "Doc, tell me about Deborah."

His eyes glazed and his mouth worked, but nothing

came out. He shuddered. Cam pulled him against her and held him. She said against soft hair that smelled like lemons the same thing she'd promised Deborah. "I swear to you we'll catch this monster. Do you understand? And you can help us, all right?" She paused a moment, listening to his breath stutter and catch. "How did the child's surgery go? On the brain tumor?"

That snapped him back. He raised his face. "His name is Phoenix Taylor and we clipped that sucker right out. I think we got it all. He'll need some radiation treatment, but he has a chance at a life now. Deborah even came by after the surgery and took a photo of Phoenix and his parents—you can see the relief on their faces, big smiles. I guess it was still on her cell phone. One of the policemen told me it was stolen. Sorry, of course you know that.

"Phoenix had a bit of a setback with his intracranial pressure that I had to manage, and that's why I wasn't here last night. I couldn't, I needed to be close, just in case.

"This morning, Phoenix was fine, even gave me a little smile through his missing front tooth. So I was able to leave the hospital early this morning—this would have been our moving day." He lowered his head to his hands but didn't make a sound.

Cam waited. He raised his head, looked at her blindly. "She was only twenty-six. Last Sunday was her birthday. We spent the day anchored off the coast, kicking back and drinking beer, eating chips and salsa, talking about how we were going to furnish our new place." He ran out of words and sat there, motionless and silent. He reached for his glasses with small circular lenses and put them on. "Thank you, for caring about her. Of course I'll help, any way I can."

Twenty minutes later, Cam met Detective Loomis in the hallway. "The M.E. estimates the Serial killed her about midnight, but that's not definite yet. He'll let us know if anything we don't expect turns up at autopsy. Did you learn anything from the boyfriend?"

Cam said, "Her boyfriend is a doctor, but he seems to know a lot about her career, maybe because she spent so much time recording it all. We may have caught a break with that, actually. Deborah was a record keeper. There are piles of documents in her office that she was going through before packing for the move. They've got to be filled with the names of people she worked with—actors, agents, producers— probably anyone with any clout at all that she'd met. He told me practically Deborah's whole life is on her laptop that's missing—it's a Toshiba Satellite—every part and audition, every personality. Maybe with all those paper records and Dr. Richards's help, we can reconstruct a lot of it. It's more than we had in the other cases.

"I asked him to reconstruct as much of her activities this past week. I believe too this will help him, keep him focused on something other than his grief and guilt for not spending the night with her."

Loomis sighed. "It's something. The Serial's killed twice now, in under a week. He's escalating, and that scares me spitless."

She nodded. "The profilers don't like it, either. It's something they didn't expect."

"So even Olympus isn't always in control of the facts?"

"Alas, no. Where'd you get the name Arturo?"

Again, the look of surprise, then he eased. "Arturo's my second name actually, after a big flamenco dancer in the thirties in Barcelona. My wife—a DEA Fed—didn't like it, called me Lou. Lousy name."

"I think Arturo is cool." Cam gave him her card, explained the FBI website to him. "I'm going to visit the lady across the street Doc told me about, Mrs. Buffet. Doc said she knew everyone in the neighborhood, said it sometimes drove him crazy, since she always seemed to know what Deborah was doing before he did. He said Deborah treated her like her grandmother, was always over there, checking on her, drinking her lemonade, just hanging out whenever she had a chance."

Loomis nodded. "The housekeeper and Daniel still have their heads together. I hope she has something helpful to tell him."

"If she knows anything, I bet Daniel will get it out of her. Tell your people get all chatty with the neighbors, use their shock and surprise to their advantage—"

"Thanks for the hint, they were wondering what to do."

"Yeah, that was heavy-handed, sorry."

Loomis's mouth fell open.

She smiled. "Please tell Daniel I'll hook up with him when I'm through speaking to Mrs. Buffet."

32

Mrs. Buffet's 1940s stucco bungalow was directly across the street from Deborah Connelly's house. It was painted a blinding bright pink that fit right in with the other rainbow colors of the neighborhood. The window frames were painted white, with built-in window boxes filled with impatiens and marigolds, adding color to a yard covered with gravel and cacti. An ancient pale blue Chevy Impala sat in the driveway.

Cam breathed in the soft morning air, still too early to be hot, and knocked on the door. Oddly, there was no doorbell.

A good two minutes later, she heard shuffling, like slippers sliding over a wood floor. The door opened and she looked down at a very slight lady, at least ninety, maybe older, wearing a pink jogging suit, pink UGG slippers on her tiny feet. Her hair was all over her head, tossed around like she'd been in a stiff wind, and sprayed to within an inch of its life. Her faded blue eyes were red with crying.

Cam introduced herself, presented her creds. Mrs. Buffet waved them away. "I don't have my glasses, but even in a blur, they look official and so do you. Come in, young lady, I know why you're here. I'm surprised it took you so long. Come with me in here, it's more comfortable." She led Cam into a living room that looked as ancient as she did, the pale green sofa from the forties, at least, with springs that dug into Cam's bottom. Yellowed doilies covered the backs of every chair, knickknacks and old hardcovers filled the shelves of a weathered bookshelf. The rugs were old and faded, but still, it was a very cozy and comfortable room. The first thing out of Mrs. Buffet's mouth was "I hope you don't want tea, because it would take me a long time to make it, and my feet hurt."

"My feet hurt, too, Mrs. Buffet. And I'm fine, thank you. I'm here about Deborah."

Mrs. Buffet's eyes filled with tears. "I can't believe she's gone. Just yesterday, my Deborah was telling me how it didn't matter she was moving, she'd come back to visit me at least three times a week and tell me everything she was doing. But now I'll never see her again." Mrs. Buffet picked at an old blue afghan and began smoothing her hands over the soft material, silent now, without words, her grief palpable, just like Doc's.

Cam leaned forward, relieving the pressure of the springs. "I'm very sorry, Mrs. Buffet. Please, tell me about Deborah."

She gave Cam a small smile. "My sweet Deborah, she was always happy, always up, that girl, always singing. She had a great voice, a big voice, like Judy Garland, and she loved to sing. She'd come over and I'd give her lemonade and my famous sugar cookies and she'd sing me all my favorites. What's the world coming to when someone would kill a girl like that?"

"It was a terrible thing, Mrs. Buffet, for all of us."

"Not just terrible, no, it's an evil thing. In all my years I've never found an answer to evil." Mrs. Buffet turned her head away to blot her eyes, then looked back at Cam. "Maybe you can do something, who knows? I'll tell you what I saw last night. It might help you catch that monster."

Cam felt her heart kick up a beat.

"Unlike you, young lady, I'm old, so I don't need much sleep, a good thing, since it gives me more time awake to appreciate that I'm still alive and kicking." She nodded toward the lacy white curtains hanging still, since there was no breeze coming in through the open window. "Last night I was standing just there, looking out at the stars, once everyone's lights were turned off for the night.

"It was around midnight, calm and quiet, and so I heard what sounded like glass breaking, but really muffled so I couldn't be sure. I thought some of those wild teenagers from one block over had busted a car window again, but to be honest, I didn't think much more about it." She huffed. "Where are their parents? I'd like to know."

Cam smoothly steered her back. "You didn't call 911 to check it out?"

"No, not then. Everything was quiet again. It was maybe ten minutes later when I saw a shadow coming around the side of Deborah's house, and then a man. He was carrying something in his right hand. He walked away from the house, didn't hurry, could have been the middle of the day to him. I thought he'd come out from the house behind Deborah's—taking a shortcut. I watched him walk away down the street, never hurrying, just walking. Do you think it was him, that monster who murdered poor Deborah?"

"It's likely, ma'am. Can you describe him to me?"

"Young." Mrs. Buffet laughed, but it sounded more like a grunt. "Well, anyone south of eighty is young to me. But I mean he moved easy, not like he had a stiff knee or sore joints. Smooth. He was wearing a short coat, maybe black or dark blue, I think, and a cap. He looked pretty ordinary, common."

"Could you see if there was any lettering on the cap? The color?"

"Hmmm, maybe the cap was green, with letters, like a John Deere, but it was so dark I can't be sure."

"That's good, Mrs. Buffet. Did you get an idea of how tall he was?"

"Let me think about that. Everybody's tall compared to me. I shrink an inch every single year, that's what my doctor says, and he laughs and pats my hand, says by the time I'm one hundred, I'll only be three feet high!" She beamed at Cam, then shook her head. "Maybe he was about as tall as Doc, not fat, but I really can't be sure because he was wearing that dark coat. I thought that was odd, since it was very warm last night. You think he was wearing it to hide the knife he used to kill my poor Deborah?"

And to hide her laptop and cell phone.

"It's possible. Mrs. Buffet, could you make out his hair color?"

"He didn't have any hair. He was bald as an eagle's egg. I wouldn't have been able to tell you that, but he stopped up against that big oak tree three doors up and lifted off his ball cap—and then the weirdest thing—he rubbed his hand over his head, looked at his hand, and rubbed it on his pant leg. Then he put his ball cap back on and began walking again. Maybe a little faster that time."

Mrs. Buffet cocked her head. "I think something came off on his hand when he rubbed his head?"

Blood splatter, but Cam didn't say it. "Is it possible he wasn't bald, that he was wearing something on his head to cover his hair, like a skull cap?"

"Of course it's possible, dear. This is Hollywood."

Nothing was ever easy. "Why didn't you call 911, Mrs. Buffet? After you saw that man?"

"I did. A man and a lady officer came around, asked me what the problem was. And I told them what I told you, and they took flashlights and walked around the neighborhood. They came back maybe ten minutes later, said everything was all right. One of them even patted my shoulder and told me to go back to bed. So I drank a dram or two of my husband's favorite single malt, rest his soul, and slept until I heard all the commotion at Deborah's house."

So the officers hadn't seen the broken window or the broken glass. Would it have mattered if Deborah had been discovered last night rather than this morning? It could have, but probably not. She'd check the officers' log-in for the exact time they were here.

Mrs. Buffet said, "How is Doc dealing with all this?"

Cam said simply, "I believe he's torn to pieces."

"I would hope so. It's not that Doc hasn't been nice to me, because he's always nice, and I hear he's a good doctor. But I told Deborah more than once that she was making a mistake, moving in with him, maybe even eventually marrying him. He was always trying to push her out of acting, into something that would bring her a regular paycheck. She admitted that to me one day when she was mad at him and came over. Can you imagine? The girl was a born actress and I told her so. I know she would have made it, and soon.

"But with Doc, it was always his patients who came first, never Deborah. And would you look at him—he dresses like a bum. I told her he wouldn't look good on her arm when she showed up for her Oscar. She laughed, said she'd clean him up herself if the day came. *When* the day came, I told her." Mrs. Buffet looked back down at the afghan, began pulling on a loose thread. When she looked up again, her eyes were sheened with tears. "I always told Deborah she should have been my great-granddaughter. And she'd say maybe I needed to put another *great* in there. I'm ninety-one years old, she'd just turned twenty-six, barely born, and now she's dead. I gave her a bottle of her favorite chardonnay for her birthday." Tears ran rivulets in the deep seams on her face. Mrs. Buffet made a disgusted sound, pulled a pink handkerchief from her pocket, and gently daubed her eyes. "Gotta be careful. At my age, my eyes might pop out if I rub too hard." She swallowed.

Cam took Mrs. Buffet's hand when she thanked her. She sat in her Toyota a moment to enter the man's description on the FBI website, then texted Daniel to meet her at Missy's cottage. She called Special Agent Aaron Poker in Las Vegas. She wanted to know if he'd caught up with their eyewitness from the Molly Harbinger murder, the would-be thief.

Did Aaron Poker ever have good news for her.

33

Daniel's Crown Vic pulled in right behind Cam's Toyota in Missy's driveway. Cam jumped out of the car. "Daniel, good timing. Wait until you hear what I got from Agent Poker in Las Vegas. We have an ID on our eyewitness—they got a DNA match on his blood on CODIS. He lives in Las Vegas, name is Marty Sallas, thirty-eight, with a rap sheet up to his elbow, so it makes sense he wouldn't want to come forward, but he's not violent, no guns or assaults. Aaron emailed me his photo."

She grabbed his hands and began dancing with him on the driveway. "We've got him, Daniel, we've got our eyewitness. And he didn't see some guy in a ball cap off in the distance, he was in the house with him. Aaron's got the local cops looking all over for him now. It's only a matter of time before they find him."

Daniel grinned down at her, and stopped dancing. "Show me."

She punched up her cell phone, showed him a mug

shot of Marty Sallas, being booked for petty theft. "We never would have identified him from the grainy video at Valley ER."

Daniel said, "I'll bet he was bleeding too much to drive out of Las Vegas, a mistake. No matter how bad my hand was cut, I'd drive to Canada I'd be so afraid the Serial would find me."

She nodded. "Aaron said he'd bet his next paycheck Sallas is hunkered down, still in Nevada, trying to get himself together and figure out what to do, nursing that hand, cursing his luck. Aaron has already sent the local TV stations Sallas's picture, asking them to make an appeal. He thinks he could get reward money because the casinos don't want this sort of publicity. Do you think Sallas would call it in?"

"Probably not, too risky for him. But this could be exactly what we need, Wittier, if the cops find him. Now you want to tell me why you texted me to come over here?"

"This cottage belongs to Missy Devereaux. We're friends from high school. I ran into her at the market and she invited me to stay with her. I didn't want her to be alone because she's young and an actress, and she knew a couple of the victims. I was thinking it might be a good idea if the two of us talked to her, tried to find out more about the circles these women travel in. Could give us a lead."

They looked up to see Missy dash outside, her blond ponytail bouncing up and down. Her face was clean of makeup. She was wearing shorts and a tube top, showing a tanned flat belly, and Skechers on her small feet, no socks. She was gorgeous. Had Deborah been this beautiful? This full of life?

Missy yelled, "Cam, why are you just standing out here?" Then she paused. "Hey, who are you?"

Daniel stepped up, introduced himself.

She looked him over, then met his eyes. "A pleasure to finally meet you, Detective Montoya. I didn't know you'd be coming over, but I'm glad you're here. Come on in, Cam, I was out running, and heard talk about Deborah—it's true? It's really true? That monster killed Deborah Connelly?"

"Yes, I'm sorry."

Missy shook her head, looking shaken. "It's horrible, horrible. Poor Doc. He and Deborah were going to get married—sometime in the misty future, Deb'd say, and Doc would kiss her hard and say, Not so misty."

Cam couldn't believe it. "You knew Deborah Connelly, Missy?"

"Yes, I do. I did. I mean we weren't BFFs, but I knew her well enough. We had the occasional drink to commiserate when we didn't get a part, you know? Shopped for shoes several times on Rodeo Drive. Like I did with Connie." Missy broke off, her eyes tearing up. She grabbed Cam's arm. "My friends are dying, Cam. You've got to do something."

"We are. We've got a pretty good description of the guy and we've identified a man in Las Vegas who was an eyewitness to Molly Harbinger's murder. Keep that under your hat, Missy, okay?"

"Yes, of course, but Deborah—"

Daniel said to Missy, "Could we go inside?"

"Yes, sure. But Detective Montoya— Oh, you're here about the restraining order, aren't you?"

"No, I'm here because I'm working with Agent Wittier, but I do have your restraining order ready for you at the Lost Hills station against John Bayley, identified as your stalker. It's in effect for ninety days, then you'll have to renew it."

"Good. Come with me, I'll make us some tea." As Missy led them to the kitchen, she said to Daniel, "I know his name, it's Blinker, the putz. And yes, legally, it's John Bayley, like you said."

"Where'd he get the nickname?"

"Good question," Missy said, eyeing him. "You know he's some sort of bond trader, lives just down the PCH in Santa Monica. He swore to the Las Vegas cops that he didn't even know who I was, just this crazy girl who chased him down with a Ka-Bar. The lying little jerkface. I couldn't believe it, but they said they had to let him go."

Daniel, who knew all this, let her tell her story, then said to this exquisite girl who came to his chin, "Now if Mr. Bayley comes close enough for you to see him, take a photo of him, with a date stamp, and call me. I'll personally throw his butt in one of our cozy cells. I gotta say, you sure picked the right person to invite to stay with you."

Cam grinned at Missy, and they high-fived each other.

Cam said, "Missy, I'm going to tell you something that's been kept out of the media and you need to keep secret, okay?"

Missy cocked her head to one side, sending her hair cascading over her shoulder. "Yes, I can do that, Cam."

"The killer took all the victims' computers and cell phones—and nothing else. He's done that every time. I'm hoping you can help us figure out why."

"He took Deborah's Toshiba? She was practically attached at the hip to that thing. She bought it with royalties from *Mission: Impossible*. I remember she was so proud. But I know that Doc was always making fun of her about how she documented her life on that freaking laptop, and only he and her parents cared. And she'd punch him and laugh. Oh, Cam!" And she threw herself against Cam, nearly sending her over backward.

Cam held her, rubbed her back. And she waited. Missy shook her head, swiped her hands over her eyes. "Sorry, sorry, it's just such a shock. And Connie was killed only six weeks ago."

"I know. Listen now, Missy, the police working the other murders haven't been able to connect the victims through anything on their laptops. You knew both Connie Morrissey and Deborah Connelly personally. And you'd met Molly Harbinger in Las Vegas. And you didn't know any of the other actresses who were killed?" Cam repeated their names. "Davina Morgan, Melodie Anders, Heather Burnside?"

Missy shook her head. "No. Isn't it strange, though,

that I knew three of them? There are so many of us trying to break into this business, thousands of us, I imagine, and we all sit around and talk and worry about how we're doing. How we could improve our chances, who could help us and how, who got a part at an audition, who didn't, and why we didn't, at least why we think we didn't win a part we wanted. Stuff like that."

Cam felt a spark. "Show us what you have on your laptop, Missy."

34

"My laptop's right here in the kitchen. Let me put on some tea and show you what I've got."

Once the kettle was on, they leaned over her as Missy booted up her laptop. "Lots of actresses use their cell phones, but I find the bigger screen is easier." Missy's screen filled with shortcuts, organized by type, in columns and rows.

"Creative Artists Agency is right on top. That's your agency, Missy?"

"Yes, my agent's with them. Dick North's his name. They're one of the largest."

"Heather Burnside was with them, too. Was Deborah?"

"No, Deborah was with Abrams. And Connie was with a smaller agency, I don't remember which one."

"It was Gush," Daniel said. "A William Burley was her agent, for nearly three years, before her murder."

Missy nodded. "Yes, that's it. Burley has a rep for a mover and shaker. She was lucky to have him."

Cam said, "SAG-AFTRA, what is that?"

"That's the new name of the Screen Actors Guild since they merged. You know, they represent actors, but just about everybody else, too—newswriters, dancers, DJs, voiceover people, everybody."

"Do you spend a lot of time on that site?"

"Not really. I occasionally go on for some industry news. I think a lot of us spend more time on *Backstage*. They focus on casting, job opportunities, career advice. And the *Hollywood Reporter*."

Daniel said, "I see a lot of these shortcuts are to shopping sites, magazines. Do you post on any blogs, or on online forums?"

"The only place I blog is on my Facebook fan page. I'm trying to build a fan base, so I go on and blog every couple of days and answer when people have comments. Anytime I win a part, I post it, along with any new photos to build up name and face recognition."

Cam said, "I see a file labeled Auditions. You keep records?"

"Sure, I can't imagine not keeping good records of who liked me, who didn't and why, what roles I've won, what roles I didn't win, my impressions of why I may have lost a role, plus lots more stuff, like the actresses who beat me out, and why I think they did. You think that's important?"

"Maybe, yes."

Missy opened the Auditions file. They saw subfiles for movies, TV, and commercials going back for the past four years. Missy pressed a key. "This is for the first six months of this year."

She scrolled slowly down, showing them how she'd formatted it all, with each comments section completely filled in. It was a history of Missy's triumphs and failures for the past six months, more than seventy auditions. "The files are less useful after about three years because there's so much turnover. I've streamlined it pretty well, though. All the information is spot-on, and easy to find. Mostly I use it to make me think about how I could do better. It's really helpful with a repeat, say a producer I've already dealt with, and the impressions I had the first time around."

Daniel thought the detail was amazing. "Do you know if both Connie and Deborah kept this good of audition records?"

"Oh yes. Deborah was even more detailed and particular than I am. I remember she told me about her experience with an advertising agency—they were pigs, as in sexists, and wanted sex for parts. I have that information in my file.

"Connie had everything on her smartphone. She had what she called a suck-up list, people she had to be nice to no matter how obnoxious they were. Wait a second—I forgot the tea."

Missy took the whistling green teakettle off the flame, fetched three cups from a cupboard painted the same pale green, and handed Daniel some napkins and spoons.

Missy poured the boiling water over tea bags, added a dollop of nonfat milk into her tea, took a sip, nodded to herself. "I don't know if Doc told you, Cam, but Deborah had a good part in a movie—a period piece called *The Crown Prince*. Most of it was filmed in Italy. They came back maybe two weeks ago, to wind it up at the studio." Her voice caught. She stared into her cup, swishing the tea around, as if there were answers to be found amid the steam and the swirling water. "But now she won't get to finish it. She was really excited about that role. She even hoped it might get her an Oscar nomination." She paused. "Cam, all of those murdered girls, they were all so keen to make it, they worked hard, dreamed, dealt with their lives as best as they could, even when they weren't sure how to pay their rent. And now they're gone, just gone." She looked up. "Now none of them will ever have a chance to get her Oscar."

Daniel said after a moment, "*The Crown Prince*— what will they do now that Deborah's dead? Will they simply go down their list and select the next actress they'd considered for the role?"

Missy stared up at him. "You're thinking another actress would have gone around the bend and killed Deborah for that part?"

Daniel shrugged.

"Plus five others? Listen, even if you killed an actress who won a role you wanted, who's to say they'd give it to you? They'd have to find an actress who looks enough like Deborah to cut in smoothly, and the second actress in line probably wouldn't fit the bill. Given that, they'd probably give the role to someone who'd never auditioned for the role before."

"One step at a time, Miss Devereaux. Also, according to our eyewitness who saw the killer leave Deborah's house, the killer is a man. Oh, yes, keep that to yourself as well, all right?"

"Of course. Oh, for goodness' sake, Detective, call me Missy." She gave him a long look, smiled, showing beautiful white teeth. "And that makes you Daniel."

Daniel slowly nodded, never looking away from her. "Yes," he said, "it does."

Cam cleared her throat as she swished the tea bag around in the hot water. "I'm wondering—what if the murders do indeed have to do with the roles these actresses have won, and played? What if it has to do with their rivals? Maybe there's an actress who lost out to all of them, maybe even more than once, and did have a mental break. Or maybe she complained about it to, say, a husband or boyfriend, and he was the one with the mental break? How would we begin to even find these actresses?"

Daniel was shaking his head.

Cam raised her hand, sighed. "I know, all the task force has already spoken to all the agents, tried to compile lists. There are far too many names to get them all together, find unique connections."

Missy nodded. "There have to be hundreds of actresses who go to every audition they can, and that's thousands of auditions. Fact is, everyone can win, and everyone loses out, at least once in a while."

Cam said, "Then let's simplify. Both you and Doc said Deborah kept very complete records. Plus, Doc seems to know a good deal about her career, her friends. So let's start by looking through your contacts, and hers. I've asked Agent Aaron Poker to review the flight manifests between Las Vegas and L.A. this past week. Maybe the Serial flew commercial. Maybe we'll find him on one of your lists. Missy, you keep a list of contacts on your computer, right? Including actresses you know?"

"Oh yes," Missy said, and punched a key and pulled up a file labeled Friendly Enemies. There were about twenty names. "Several of us were hanging out on the beach one day, came up with that file name. We all use it. These are the people I sometimes hang out with. I met some of them at auditions, actually, and sometimes, afterward, we'd go shopping, drink beer, complain and whine, trash guys. Many times at Ivy's at the shore." She paused. "I met Connie there."

"I'd like to copy that list, Missy. In fact, I'm going to copy all of your contacts. I want to make sure every actress you know gets a call telling her she might have a connection to these murders, that she should never be alone, and emphasize she should take this seriously.

"I'd also like a copy of your auditions files. I want to compare it with whatever I can find at Deborah's place, or find out from Doc. Now, tell me about Connie. You said you met her at Ivy's?"

Missy nodded. "Connie was nice and I liked her. She talked a lot about this great guy she was seeing—Theo Markham—he's a really important producer who believed in her so much he even rented her his house in the Colony for peanuts so she could quit selling shoes at Saks and concentrate full-time on her career. She was so excited, said he was lining up roles for her. Of course all of us were thinking he rented her the house because she was sleeping with him, and it was convenient for him. She laughed about it, said she knew what we were thinking, but she wasn't having sex with Mr. Theo—that's what Connie always called him. No one cared, but I thought it was strange she'd deny it, but maybe he asked her to deny it because he's married.

"But hey, maybe he really did think she was a big talent." She saluted them with her teacup. "It would make me wonder if Mr. Theo isn't an alien—I mean, a bigwig in show business, in Hollywood, not screwing around on his wife? Wouldn't that be a first?"

Daniel asked, "Did you ever meet Theo Markham?"

"Once. I chatted him up for about two minutes. He was pleasant, but he had this sort of 'knowing' look in his eyes, smug, like he knew he could crook his finger and most young wanna-be actresses, like me, would come running. He's older, well into his forties, but a man's age doesn't mean much in Hollywood as long as there's Viagra. He wasn't bad-looking, nice thick head of hair."

Daniel was taking notes. He said, "Missy, I already told Cam that I spoke to Markham after Connie's murder, how his slick lawyers shut me down. He had to be acquainted with Deborah, since he's producing *The Crown Prince*. At least he had to know who she was."

Cam said, "Yes, indeed, and that gives us the perfect reason to interview him again. Missy, you said you had a suck-up list. I imagine Theo Markham would be on everyone's list?"

"Sure he would. I've met a lot of these guys. I'm usually just another pretty face to them, although they might jot down my name for a possible part or for possible sex, who knows? I wish there were more women's names on lists like that."

"My mom says the same thing," Cam said. "It makes her so mad she sputters. Daniel, I want to go see Theodore Markham, now. This time, let's just show up, that way maybe we can escape his herd of lawyers."

Cam's cell rang. She looked down at the name, then walked out of the kitchen. When she came back, she looked shell-shocked, but her voice was easy. "Missy, I brought a thumb drive along, could you use it to copy those files we talked about?"

"Sure, Cam. Is something wrong?"

Cam shook her head. "Daniel, I need to speak to you while Missy's copying those files."

Daniel merely arched a dark eyebrow at her, followed her out of the kitchen. Cam leaned close. "That was Dr. Eli Umbricht, a pathologist from the local field office. I asked him to be on hand at Deborah Connelly's autopsy. Here's the thing. He compared her wounds to the previous autopsy reports and they don't exactly match. He said the cut on her throat is from right to left, but all the others were left to right. And the neck wound that killed her wasn't as deep as the others. He's not saying it was necessarily the work of a different killer, maybe he's ambidextrous or he hurt his right hand, and so used his left, but it does raise questions."

Daniel said, "If it wasn't a different killer, maybe the killer was startled by something, or he had to improvise for some reason?"

"Yes. And I noticed the bedcover had been smoothed around her waist, not left in disarray like the others were. Dr. Umbricht won't say it's a copycat but admitted he isn't certain either way."

Daniel said, "So he won't commit himself. Here's a question for you. The killer took Deborah Connelly's computer and cell phone. If it's a copycat, how did he know to do that?"

35

Marty Sallas felt like crap. He'd doubled up on the pain meds the clinic had given him because his hand hurt so bad, and he'd run out last night. He'd been popping aspirin like candy ever since, but it didn't touch the pain. He remembered his last girlfriend, Lila, calling him a baby for taking four aspirin for a headache, but what did she know?

Marty moaned and cursed the stitches that dug through his hand. It itched and burned, felt like it was on fire. But there were no red lines running up his arm, no particular swelling, so that was good. Still, he cursed as he pulled himself out of bed, cursed again as he stood there, cupping his bandaged hand, and staggered to the bathroom to brush his teeth. The pain pills had made his mouth taste like a bad hangover, and even after twelve hours, it still tasted like a toilet, go figure that.

He stood under the shower, his arm stuck outside the curtain to keep the bandage dry, and did the best

he could with the stingy sliver of soap left stuck in the
rusted soap holder. The stream of hot water splashing
on his face helped, took his mind off the pain. But not
off his fear. He'd about lost it when he saw his name
and face all over the local news that morning. The cops
were calling him an eyewitness to a murder by a serial
killer and asking him to contact them. Did the cops
think he was stupid? That he would walk in there and
admit to breaking and entering into Molly's house, let
them charge him and put him away again? Not without an arrest warrant they wouldn't, and they'd have
to catch him first. But thanks to those cops on TV the
killer could be after him already. Maybe he was standing across the street, watching and plotting how to kill
Marty when he came out of the motel.

He was losing it. How could that lunatic know
where he was? He wasn't smarter than the cops, didn't
have their resources. Besides, Marty was always careful. He'd learned long ago not to make it too easy to
find him. He moved around, never gave his real name
when he booked a room. The cops hadn't gotten near
him since his two-year stay at Pilson. He was safe, for
another day at least.

His biggest problem was he was nearly broke, and
that meant he had to leave this room, put himself out
in the world. Staying anywhere near Las Vegas wasn't
an option, not with the cops and maybe the killer
looking for him.

What had happened to the bracelet—*his* bracelet—the one Moneybags had bought for his beauti-

ful princess? One of the cops probably had slipped it off her wrist or snatched it out of her jewelry box to give to his girlfriend. It wasn't fair; it wasn't right. The pain in his hand spiked again, and nausea swam in his throat. He knew it was because he was afraid.

Marty got out of the shower, managed to get himself dry with one good hand and one mangy towel. The small bathroom was steaming hot, making him sweat again, but he knew it wasn't any hotter than it was outside. It didn't matter where you set your feet in Nevada, it was always hot. Maybe there was no humidity like they told the tourists who complained, but to Marty, hot was hot.

He brushed his teeth again, looked in the mirror, and his belly twisted. He saw not his own reflection, but Molly's, looking out at him from the steamed-up glass, her eyes wide and dead, her neck sliced open, her blood everywhere, on the walls, on the covers, on the floor, and on that lunatic. He remembered the man jerking around toward him, that knife raised, still dripping blood. Marty's heart drummed in his chest. He wiped off the glass with the damp towel, to wipe Molly's face away, until only his own pale face now stared back at him.

Sure, he was a criminal and he was good at it, but there was a big difference between him and the crazy who'd murdered his princess. Marty had never killed someone for the sport of it, not like the man he'd surprised standing over Molly. That man was sick or evil, Marty didn't know which was worse. Evil, probably, no rhyme or reason with evil, that's what his pa would say when his head was in a bourbon bottle.

His fingers went to his throat. He had to get away from here today. He wouldn't be on TV outside of Nevada. He'd drive up to Seattle, lots of rich folk up there. He had a few contacts there, but nothing like the network he'd built in Las Vegas. He'd have to start over, and that would mean small jobs with quick and easy payoffs, enough to keep body and soul together.

Didn't matter, he knew his business. It wouldn't be the first time he'd had to start over.

It was better than being dead. He would stop on the way at a Walmart, buy whatever he needed, maybe change into something nicer in the men's room. It wouldn't be a problem.

As he slowly pulled on his seedy clothes, he turned on the television again. They were talking about another actress the lunatic had killed, in Los Angeles. Her name was Deborah Connelly and she'd lived in Santa Monica, this followed by another plea for him to come forward. He was safe, then—the lunatic had gone back to his old hunting grounds. They even gave the name of the lead agent in L.A.—Special Agent Cam Wittier. Should he call her, get the FBI off his back? Talk about a bad joke, as if that would ever happen.

When he walked out of his motel room, he saw a man getting off a motorcycle, like the one he'd seen that night at Molly's house. He flattened himself against the dirty stucco wall. Even though his brain knew it couldn't be the killer, he was still, breath held, and watched until the man walked into the Coyote Diner. His breath whooshed out. He had to get a grip, that lunatic was nowhere close. He was safe. Soon he'd be driving across the border into California and get himself lost in the Sierras by nightfall, maybe in Tahoe City.

Again, he saw Molly front and center in his mind's eye, first smiling, then dancing in her outrageous costume, and then as she looked when she was dead, gone, the slash in her throat open wide, like a bloody mouth.

His hand throbbed. He dry-swallowed two more aspirin, cursed and held his stitched hand close to his chest, worried it, and found he simply couldn't let it go. Then he knew what he was going to do. Maybe he could help avenge Molly, help get that lunatic who killed her without ending up in jail. Get the FBI off his back, too.

He pulled out his cell and punched in Reggie Nash's number. Reggie owed him a favor.

36

ON THE WAY TO MILLSTOCK, MARYLAND
WEDNESDAY AFTERNOON

Savich turned the Porsche onto I-95, heading north to Millstock, Maryland, to interview Ms. Marsia Gay in her studio. "I know, we could have asked her to come to the Hoover Building, but—"

"But she's an artist, you're an artist, and you want to see where and how she works."

"I'm not really an— Well, yeah, you might be partially right."

Sherlock sat back and closed her eyes.

Savich sighed. "It's been a long day and what do we have to show for it? Another actress murdered in Santa Monica, and our prime weasel dead. Officer Golinowski didn't remember anything at all, thanks to all the propofol and ketamine the killer put in that syringe."

"It's the middle of the night, he's trying to stay awake, sees the tech coming, asks for ID, and the killer gets close enough to stick the needle in his jugular vein before he can react. He must have been out fast."

"At least the killer didn't murder Golinowski, too," Savich said. "Ben is pretty steamed at him. I bet he won't like the write-up he gets in his file."

"He deserves it," Sherlock said. "Now we've got no possible ace in the hole. It's depressing."

"Let it go for now, Sherlock. We've got Marsia Gay to think about."

"I've got to admit I'm curious about her metal sculpting. She seemed straightforward and very nice last night at the mansion, dealt well with Venus and the family. I liked her. I found it interesting she knew about your grandmother, worshipped her, in fact, even noticed the scars on your fingers. Do you think she did her research on your grandmother to suck up, or was her appreciation for real?"

"If she'd wanted to suck up, she would have checked me out," Savich said, and grinned at her. "But why? It's Venus she should care about."

"And she appeared to. She's good-looking, talented, probably makes a lot of money. She certainly seems to think highly of Rob."

But what did Rob think about her, Savich wondered, clearly remembering the stunned look on his face when he'd seen Delsey Freestone. He said, "Now we'll see how she behaves in her own environment."

Sherlock looked over at a lime-green car with a teenager singing at the top of his lungs, fingers tapping on the steering wheel.

Savich maneuvered the Porsche around an SUV filled with small children, all of them laughing and yelling like hyenas, felt a moment of sympathy for the woman driving. As he went past her, she gave him a smile, with dimples. So she liked chaos, did she? He said, "It'd be simple if it was Alexander who was behind Willig's killing, but you know, I don't think it is. If I've learned anything over the years, it's that you've got to work to really know another person, what ignites them, what enrages them, to figure out what they're really like at their core."

"I know your core, Dillon. It's solid. Maybe even awesome."

He laughed. "Same goes for yours, sweetheart. But what do we know about Alexander? He can behave like a self-absorbed egotist, all me me me. But is there maybe a spark of decency? A bit of love for someone other than himself? And Veronica, does she really love Venus as much as it appears she does, as much as she says she does?"

"I really like Veronica, always have. I do hope she's for real. As for Alexander, after our interview with him, I'm inclined to say what you see is what you get—a selfish man."

Sherlock felt the familiar g-force when Dillon pulled out around a white Impala and gave the Porsche the go-ahead. The Impala driver, a natty-looking octogenarian, looked pissed until he saw the Porsche, then he gave them a thumbs-up and a smile lit up by big white false teeth.

Savich gave the Impala driver a nod. "Maybe it could be Alexander, except for the shooting. That still makes no sense to me. I know our killer realized the jig was up with the arsenic, but why would Alexander up the ante by hiring Willig to shoot Venus in broad daylight?"

"Don't forget Willig could have gotten away with it if we hadn't delayed leaving. So maybe it was reckless, but not all that stupid. On the other hand, he failed, and it signed his death warrant."

Savich sighed. "Yeah, there is that."

37

Savich turned off I-95 at the Millstock exit. Neither he nor Sherlock had ever visited this bedroom community. They saw quickly enough that it was a hub with a tangle of crossing and crisscrossing concrete highways curving off in every direction. They heard horns honking before they saw a long line of stopped cars. Rush-hour traffic? No, something else, probably an accident. Savich smelled frustration and impatience thick in the air. Sure enough there was a pileup maybe a quarter of a mile ahead. Everyone was blocked.

Sherlock said, "Take that right, Dillon, let's see if we can go around."

Savich pulled the Porsche off onto Buckley Street, and continued on side streets until they came to a small warehouse district. A good dozen warehouses faced one another in a long line. They weren't abandoned and decrepit like some of their counterparts in Washington, D.C., with homeless people and drug addicts huddled in doorways. These warehouses looked like they'd been taken over by yuppies and the artist crowd for many years now, and gentrified.

Savich stopped the Porsche in front of the very last warehouse on the right. Unlike its neighbors, this warehouse exterior was stained aluminum siding, looked old enough to be condemned. Until they stepped inside and beheld a miracle—modern and shiny white walls, two art deco boxes containing palm trees, happy as could be, given the broad light coming in from the high windows. There was a brand-new elevator, mailboxes by the door, and three mirrors reflecting a big expanse of tile floor.

"Why do they keep the outside looking so derelict?" Sherlock wondered as they stepped onto the elevator and punched the third, and top, floor.

"Maybe it's as simple as running out of money. Or maybe they want to keep the salesmen away."

She laughed. "Or the management company. If they haven't bothered to check out the interior, the rent might stay low."

Savich thought she might be right. The elevator took them swiftly to the third floor and its three suites, the end one, 666—wasn't that a kick—Marsia Gay's studio. They heard a hammer pound in rhythmic time, then the low buzz of a welder.

Sherlock knocked, but the welder kept buzzing. He tried the door. Not locked. He and Sherlock walked into a large space filled with light from four enormous windows. At least a dozen metal sculptures of what could possibly be representations of men and women, in various stages of construction, stood like contorted and twisted sentinels along the walls. The sculptures looked oddly graceful, and drew the eye.

They saw Marsia Gay surrounded by machinery and a table of tools in the far corner wearing a welding apron, a welding mask, and thick gloves. She was welding together two pieces of metal that looked like copper and aluminum, but Savich couldn't be sure. It would have been stifling in the room were it not for several large fans that churned the air and dissipated the heat, making a huge noise. Marsia Gay still hadn't seen or heard them.

Savich saw she was using an arc welder, the metal she was working on held by a clamp handle at the positive lead. Sparks flew around her. She was steady-handed, completely focused on what she was doing. They said nothing, only walked around the studio, studying her work. The smell of burned metal was strong, and bits of metal detritus hung in the sunlit air. The large room was ruthlessly organized. They saw bins filled with various sizes and shapes of scrap metal, each labeled: steel, brass and bronze, carbide, aluminum, and copper. Larger pieces of scrap metal, likewise labeled, stood in large bins against the wall.

Sherlock stopped to stare up at an eight-foot-tall figure with muscles of raw steel and prominent pecs, almost like breasts, long muscled steel legs at twisted angles, and a protruding tangle of bulging thick copper pipes banding the middle. "A pregnant man?"

"Actually, it's a figure spun in a dream, and the

dreamer is visualizing fecundity." Marsia stepped forward and lightly touched her hand to the sculpture's steel arm. "Her name is Helen—*A Dream Vision*. She was quite a challenge. For example, those copper ribs? I had to weld them to steel, but because the two metals aren't mutually soluble, I used nickel as an intermediary metal. That way I could weld them and end up with a strong joint."

Marsia pulled off her welding mask and set it carefully onto a countertop covered with tools and more even smaller containers of scrap metal. She ran her hands through her hair, smiled at them, took off her welding apron to show a long white artist shirt over black leggings. She wore Doc Martens on her long narrow feet. "Helen is going to be the focal point in the lobby of a fertility clinic in Baltimore." She stripped off her welding gloves as she spoke, laid them beside the mask. They shook hands. Hers were strong, her fingers and palms callused.

She said, "Agent Savich, I have to admit, I visited the Raleigh Gallery in Georgetown this morning to see your pieces. I guess I wanted to see if you had really inherited some of your grandmother's talent. It's obvious you did. I particularly like the dolphin you whittled in rosewood. It's marvelous really, so fluid you can almost see the dolphin moving.

"Mr. Raleigh also told me about your sister, Lily Russo. I realized soon enough that I read her in the *Washington Post* every Sunday. Her political cartoon featuring No Wrinkles Remus—he's quite a personage, always has me laughing and shaking my head. Both of you are quite accomplished. Ah, I see that makes you uncomfortable. And you, Agent Sherlock, Mr. Raleigh told me you're an accomplished pianist."

Sherlock shook her head. "Not so much anymore, since I don't practice enough. Now I tend to cruise the keys for pleasure."

"I would enjoy hearing you play. Come have a cold drink and you can tell me what I can do for you. Sorry it's so hot in here, but it'll cool down quickly with the welder shut off. I'll turn off a couple of fans so we can hear each other without shouting."

Marsia turned off two of the four fans. Sherlock said, "Yes, that's better. You have quite a setup here, Ms. Gay. All those bins—so many different metals."

"Yes, most of it scrap metal. Sometimes I think the folk who sell scrap metal online make more money than I do. They scrounge through dump sites, carry away tossed-out washers, TVs, toasters, whatever—and strip them down for scrap metal to sell. Come, sit down."

Savich and Sherlock were soon sitting on an old love seat beneath one of the large windows, glasses of water in their hands. Marsia sat on the floor facing them, her knees drawn up to her chin.

Sherlock said, "Ms. Gay, how long after you met Rob Rasmussen did you realize who he was? Or did you find out who he was and that's why you hired him?"

38

Marsia's head snapped back. "You come out of the gate fast, don't you, Agent Sherlock? Let me think. I didn't realize his grandmother is *the* Venus Rasmussen until after he had lunch with her. I remember asking him why he'd broken our date and he told me about seeing his grandmother for the first time in ten years. Then he told me his history, the severed relationships with his family, how it turned out both he and his grandmother wanted to see each other again at nearly the same time. A quite wonderful story, really. As you know, I met her for the first time last night. She's a grand old lady. I've got to say she has quite a flare. I loved her Dior suit."

Savich said, "When Rob told you about her, you knew who she was?"

"Of course I knew who she was. I'm not deaf or blind. I occasionally watch the news, read the paper. The woman is practically an institution. What amazes me, though, is that someone is trying to kill her. Why?

She's getting up there, maybe another five years at most before she passes the reins to one in her family."

Savich said, "Alexander is being groomed, yes, but I can see Venus driving the bus for more than just another five years. I think she'll know when it's time to hand over the reins."

"That's what Rob says. You know, if it is Alexander who is trying to poison his grandmother, I can't see what his motive would be. So he'd have to wait a bit longer until she stepped down. Why would he care so much? Ah, forgive me, talking about the family as if I'm intimate with them. I'm certainly not."

She brought her legs into the lotus position. "All of them were very kind to me last night. And I was there to make a good impression. You were there to observe, weren't you? To see how everyone reacted to the black sheep—namely Rob—and to me, his girlfriend?"

Again Savich remembered Rob and Delsey Freestone when they'd first seen each other the day before, by the elevator at the Hoover Building. Instant chemistry. Maybe Rob wouldn't follow up with Delsey. Maybe he was in love with Marsia, maybe he was loyal. Savich wanted to believe it. But from the look on Delsey's face, and Rob's, they seemed ready to leap right into the fire.

"And what were your impressions, Ms. Gay?"

"Please call me Marsia, sort of a weird name, I know, but my mom is very—whimsical. If it had been up to my dad, I'd have been a Jane or an Ann."

Savich nodded. "Marsia, what did you think of the

family? I assume you googled all of them, learned about them?"

"Yes, of course, and Rob told me a lot about them as well. A lot of his information was a decade out of date, though." She shrugged. "But people are people, and they don't change unless something happens to them and they're forced to, so they were pretty much what I expected. I wanted to make a good impression. I wanted them to like me. I trust they did, at least they didn't seem to want to throw me out the window.

"I've got to say, though, that Glynis surprised me, with that lip-lock she put on Rob. You see, he'd never said anything about her, probably because she was a teenager when he left. I was struck by her beauty, and how bone-deep mean she is."

Sherlock cocked her head at Marsia.

"I have a feeling she wouldn't hesitate to do anything at all to get what she wants." She paused a moment. "I got the impression last night that just maybe she wants to have Rob."

"Nah," Sherlock said. "Glynis wanted to rub your nose in it, that's all. You're basically her age and you're very accomplished, successful in your own right. Glynis is rich, sure, but not by her own hands. I think you made her feel inferior and Glynis retaliated the only way she knows how. She'd find it amusing to take Rob away from you, I think, to prove herself better than you, but she's not going to try that hard. Too much work. If I were you I'd watch my back with her, though."

Marsia nodded. "I will."

Savich's phone vibrated. He pulled it out and read the text, slipped his phone back into his jacket pocket. He said, "Ms. Gay, ten years ago both your parents died in an airplane accident. You were a teenager. It must have been difficult for you."

Marsia froze. She picked up a glass of water and drank it down. Slowly, she turned back and gave Savich a slight smile. "That question threw me right back to when the headmistress of my school called me out of class to see my parents' lawyer. Mom and Dad were flying to Granada, Spain, and crashed in the foothills of the Sierra Nevada. Because my parents were very nearly divorced, the irony of their dying together slaps you in the face." She paused a moment, drank more water. "I quickly learned the two of them were deeply in debt and there was no money. My relatives didn't know me and didn't want me, so that meant foster care for me until I graduated high school. I had three different fosters—they were all okay, no problems, except for one son, and I broke his finger. There's nothing more, really."

"I should say there is a lot more, Ms. Gay," Sherlock said. She saw the sheen of tears in her eyes. "You worked two waitressing jobs to put yourself through art school. Two years ago, you made your first big sale. And now you're considered an artist on the rise. That shows me you didn't need your parents' money, you had grit and talent. What you've accomplished is admirable, Ms. Gay."

Marsia shook her head, wiped her eyes with her fist. "You're very kind. I'll tell you, it feels good to know that you're not going to be out on the street." She paused, looked around at the big airy space. "Do you know what? I was able to buy this whole building three weeks ago—it was a real steal."

Sherlock smiled. "Will you make improvements to the outside?"

"Oh no, given the way it looks, everyone but my renters steers clear of my building. I intend to keep all its original patina."

Savich said, "The man who tried to kill Mrs. Rasmussen on Monday, Vincent Willig, was murdered early this morning in George Washington University Hospital."

Marsia stared at them. "He what? Murdered? But why?"

"Because," Sherlock said, "he was ready to take Venus Rasmussen's offer of one hundred thousand dollars to give up the name of the person who hired him. Where were you last night, Ms. Gay, after you left the Rasmussens'?"

Marsia reared back as if she'd been slapped. "Fun time is over, I see. You want to know where I was? But I have nothing to do with anything."

"Yes, you do," Savich said. "You are currently seeing Rob Rasmussen. Like everyone else near Mrs. Rasmussen, he is a person of interest. And now so are you. Please tell us where you were, Ms. Gay."

"Here, I was here, sleeping, all night. And yes, I was alone. Rob dropped me off, said he had work to do and couldn't stay. But I assure you, once I was here, I never left."

Savich said, "Is your relationship with Rob serious? Are you planning to marry him?"

Marsia took a deep breath, settled herself. "You certainly got down and dirty. I was beginning to think we were friends." She shook her head. "No, that's stupid. You're here to interview me, see if I have a motive for killing Mrs. Rasmussen, for killing this Mr. Willig. Is that his name?"

"Yes, it is," Sherlock said. "Did you know him, Ms. Gay?"

"Goodness, no, how could I? And now he's dead, murdered. You have no idea who did this? Tried to kill Mrs. Rasmussen and now Mr. Willig?"

"We will, soon," Savich said. "You didn't answer my question, Ms. Gay. Your relationship with Rob Rasmussen—what are your intentions?"

"I've thought about it, certainly, asked myself if Rob and I have a future. Marriage, kids, the whole works. To be honest, I haven't made up my mind. As for Rob, I just don't know." She smiled. "Like many men, Rob doesn't like to discuss the future. He's a here-and-now kind of guy."

Savich gave Ms. Marsia Gay one last look. Talent, looks, brains, all in one neat package. He hoped she was what she seemed. After a long beat of silence he stood, Sherlock following him. "Thank you for show-ing us your studio and answering our questions. We'll be in touch." He and Sherlock left the studio.

"Who texted you?" Sherlock asked once they were back in the Porsche.

Savich had just fastened his seat belt and was pulling away from the warehouse. "That was Cam. Agent Poker called her from Las Vegas. There was an anonymous sketch left in their field office lobby of Molly Harbin-ger's murder scene. The Serial is there front and center, just as that burglar, Sallas, would have seen him. They think Sallas left it there, or had someone do it for him, to get the cops and the media off his back. There's been no other sign of him. He's disappeared."

"Is the sketch good enough for Aaron to use it to identify the Serial?"

"Sorry, sweetheart, the man in the sketch is wearing blood-splattered goggles and a watch cap."

Sherlock slammed her fist against the dash, then lightly patted it, apologizing to the Porsche. "Wait, Dillon. Maybe there's enough of a jawline, or a head shape, or a nose and mouth, to help them find him on facial recognition?"

"I doubt it, but it's worth a try. Cam emailed me the sketch after she texted." He pulled his cell out of his pocket and handed it to her. "Take a look."

It was a surprisingly well-detailed drawing, obvi-ously done by a pro. She felt a punch of toxic rage at the spray of blood on the goggles. "What does Cam think?"

"She said a neighbor saw this man who looked like this leaving Deborah Connelly's house. As you can see, he's tall and thin. He took off his watch cap to rub blood off his bald head. Cam pointed out it could be a skull cap."

"Did Aaron identify the artist?"

He pulled the Porsche onto I-95. "Good question. Call him, Sherlock."

She did, but after she asked Aaron that same question she listened for a moment and then hung up, shaking her head. "Aaron said the artist wasn't nice enough to sign the sketch, so it's a dead end."

39

The Culver Building, in Century City, soared up twenty-two glass-encircled stories, the tenants' joke being the L.A. smog wasn't too bad if you could see them all.

Cam and Daniel were shown into the huge corner office of Mr. Theodore Markham by his personal assistant Ms. Brandi Mikels. She looked like she would be as comfortable wearing wings for Victoria's Secret as wearing a slick black suit.

"Special Agent Wittier and Detective Montoya, sir."

"Thank you, Brandi. Agent, Detective, you've given me no warning, and I'm busy, a meeting, in fact, in twenty minutes. But I'm certain Brandi told you that and you simply pulled rank?"

Close enough. "Thank you for seeing us, Mr. Markham," Cam said.

He rose slowly and watched them walk across the expanse of thick pale gray carpet to his desk. It was all polished glass and bubinga wood, a dark reddish brown with purple streaks so stunning Daniel wondered if it belonged on an endangered list. Markham took her offered creds and Daniel's badge, gave them a cursory look-see, and handed them back. "I've already spoken to you, Detective Montoya. I remember you and I had a conversation in my office at Universal Studios after Constance was killed. I, of course, had nothing to do with her death, and naturally, you verified that. For whatever reason I cannot begin to fathom, you are back again—I assume it was because Deborah Connelly was killed last night? I heard about her murder this morning with great sadness. Her death—it was like poor Connie's, from what I heard on the news. That maniac struck again.

"Is that why you're here, to interrogate me? I rather think you two should be looking for the killer instead, or all over her damned boyfriend." As he spoke, his hand reached for his phone.

"Mr. Markham," Cam said quickly, not wanting him to call in his lawyers, "we're here because you've been personally affected, twice now. You're an important person in show business in L.A. and you could be of great assistance to us. We would like to hear your ideas on how and why a serial killer would target these particular young actresses. There have been six young women now, brutally murdered."

His hand hovered, then backed away. He waved the same hand at them. "Sit down. As I said, I have a meeting, but I'll tell you what I know, what I think."

They sat. His chair was higher than theirs, a bit on the obvious side, Cam thought, but she only smiled at him. As Missy had said, Markham was tall, fashionably thin, his dark hair receding just a bit but still thick and full. He had a bit of white at his temples, carefully brushed on by an expert hand. His jaw was honed and firm, probably the work of another expert hand. In short, Mr. Markham looked exactly as he wanted to look, an important Hollywood big shot. Cam saw a framed photo of a lovely woman about his age, mid-forties, she guessed, flanked by two boys, both college-age. Mr. Markham was standing on the other side of his sons, his arm around them.

She smiled at the photo. "Your sons, how old are they, sir?"

"What? Oh, both are at UCLA, both computer majors, something their mother applauds." He shrugged.

"And you don't?"

He shrugged again. "They'll make a decent living, I have no doubt, but it won't be an exciting life."

"Not like yours, you mean?" Cam said.

He smiled at that, and Cam saw the charm in this smile, easy and prepackaged. "Thing is I don't know anyone who could help them, then again perhaps they'll want to join a start-up. At least I could be an investor. We'll see."

Daniel said, "Most people have to make it on their own. It builds character, I'm told."

"They have too much character as it is," Markham said, shaking his head. "As I said, I have a meeting. You want to know why I think anyone would target these particular young women. Naturally, I've given this a lot of thought. I've come to realize I have no special insights or brilliant theories about that. I wish I did. I will tell you, though, that in Deborah's murder, you should look closely at her boyfriend—he's a doctor and goes by the name of Doc, but I don't remember his name. Talk about a dark cloud hovering over Deborah. He could even be your serial killer." He looked down at his Rolex.

"We still have a little time, sir. We'll certainly be looking at everyone, Dr. Mark Richards included. At the time of her murder, Deborah Connelly had a meaty role in one of your movies—*The Crown Prince*. What are your plans now that she's dead?"

Markham picked up a Montblanc pen and began weaving it through his fingers. "You'll find this hard to believe, but the director has already been on the phone to me, told me he's tracking down an actress who looks enough like Deborah to fill in for her. Once they have her made up, he'll shoot the remaining scenes without any close-ups and no one will know the difference. If you didn't know, *The Crown Prince* is a remake of *Mayerling*—the suicides of thirty-year-old Crown Prince Rudolf of Austria and his seventeen-year-old mistress, in 1889. The costumes are voluminous, the bonnets wide-brimmed.

He'll manage. The director also pointed out that with Ms. Connelly's murder the movie would get some free press. Yes, I know, that's fairly disturbing, but unfortunately, that's the way of the world. Ms. Connelly will be missed, but the film will remain on schedule."

Cam said, "Do you think this movie could have been a springboard for Ms. Connelly? To bigger and better roles?"

"I review the rushes each day, of course. She was very good. The casting director selected her from an audition of at least sixty young women. I reviewed her audition, approved it. After that, I had very little to do with her."

Cam said, "Ms. Connelly kept extensive records about her career—all sorts of impressions, insights, gossip about other cast members, directors, producers. According to her boyfriend, she knew a great deal about you, sir."

That question got her a raised dark eyebrow. "I see. So is this why you are really here? If this is an interrogation I will call my lawyers."

"Oh, no, sir, certainly not," Cam said. "Had you met her before her role in *The Crown Prince*?"

"Yes, at a party, maybe six months ago."

"Can you tell us about that party? Tell us your impressions of her?"

He gave her a stingy smile that still managed to charm, and slowly nodded. He paid no attention at all to Daniel. "You look familiar, Agent Wittier. Wait, are you related to Joel and Lisabeth Wittier?"

Cam nodded. "Yes, they're my parents. But like your sons, I didn't choose to follow them into Hollywood, I chose law enforcement. Now, the party, sir, where you first met Deborah Connelly."

40

"It was your basic drunk free-for-all party at Willard Lambeth's house up in the Hollywood Hills. He's a longtime producer, very successful, been around nearly as long as Technicolor. I escorted Connie."

"Was she your girlfriend, sir?" Daniel asked.

Markham stiffened, then shook his head. "Certainly not. I rented her my house in the Colony in Malibu because she had great talent and I was able to lift some of her financial burden. That night I escorted her to Willard's party because I wanted to let her rub shoulders with people she should know.

"An assistant director introduced Ms. Connelly to me. Of course, like all the young actresses and actors at Willard's party, she was eager to meet people who could help her career. I remember she brought her boyfriend—this Doc character. I only remember him because he wasn't what anyone would call an asset to her. I wondered why she didn't have the sense to leave him at home. He was very possessive of her, didn't let her out of his sight, like a jealous dog guarding a bone. It was obvious he didn't want to be there, didn't want her to be there, either. I remember thinking he looked at us like we were a pack of perverts out to despoil his girlfriend."

Markham shrugged. "I'm a very visual man, Agent Wittier, and I have an excellent memory for faces, expressions, body language. I remember clearly how sullen he was, not even trying to disguise his contempt. I wondered if he might snap and do something stupid, maybe even dangerous. Even Connie said Doc was acting like a real jerk. She asked me to introduce Deborah to some important people, and tried to pull Doc away.

"I remember Connie telling me she was getting fed up with Doc, because he was always belittling Deborah and her work. Yes, Connie and Deborah knew each other, how well, I couldn't say. This business runs on contacts, and everyone wants to know everybody else. They say only nepotism counts in Hollywood, and to a large extent, that's true, but it's there in every walk of life.

"I did introduce Ms. Connelly to a couple of producers. Her biggest hit was with Willard.

"All the while, this Doc character stood against the wall, drinking quite a lot of Will's excellent vodka, staring at Ms. Connelly. Connie was doing her best to keep his attention.

"I can add that although I found Deborah beautiful, that isn't what struck me about her, or struck Willard.

She was smart, fast on her feet, and charming. She was witty, but not malicious.

"I spoke to her once more, caught her when she was on her way to the bathroom, told her she should have left her dog in the kennel, nodded toward her boyfriend, who wasn't further than three feet away, looking ready to froth at the mouth. She laughed, said wasn't that the truth, but I could tell she was pissed off. I wondered if she was afraid of him, a jealous, possessive man like that.

"There was probably more, but I've forgotten. It was over six months ago. Then I saw her audition and approved her for the role.

"I did see her on the set of *The Crown Prince* now and then when I flew to Tuscany, and I was pleased I'd had the wit to cast her." He rose. "And that is what I know of Ms. Connelly. My meeting begins in four minutes. I bid you good day."

"One more question, sir," Cam said, rising. "You were acquainted with two of the six murdered actresses. If you would, you could be of great assistance to us. You were good friends with Constance Morrissey. Were you asked to reconstruct any information that might have been on her laptop and her cell phone?"

"I don't understand, Agent. Weren't Deborah's computer and cell phone taken by the killer, as Connie's was?"

"I'm not at liberty to say, sir."

"I see. I understand that you wish to keep the stolen laptops and cell phones out of the media. However, I don't believe you will be able to keep that under wraps much longer. I quickly found out from Connie's friends and her parents who'd been asked to reconstruct any information, so it was obvious they were taken. However, Detective Montoya didn't ask me. Even if he had asked, I wouldn't have been of any use. Oh, she kept me informed about her auditions, how she felt it all went, but to recall them now? No. And there was nothing else I knew of that could be helpful."

"But I was told you were of great assistance to her, Mr. Markham. Yet you can't remember any of her business dealings?"

"No. I was her most important business contact. Is there anything else?"

"Do you believe the serial killer targeted Deborah Connelly for some specific reason?"

"How could I possibly know why this madman targeted any of these young women?"

Cam said, "Do you think your very good friend Connie was targeted specifically?"

Daniel saw it—pain and rage, a heady brew, passing over Markham's face. Only a slight pause, then, "Yes, I do."

"Why is that, sir?"

"Because Connie was going to make it in this crazy business. She would have been a star, maybe even without the help I gave her. It was only a matter of getting the right parts, and she was getting them."

As he spoke, he gathered papers and slid them neatly into an exquisite Malmo briefcase.

Cam waited until he clicked the briefcase closed and looked back at her. "Sir, what if I told you the serial killer may not have been the one who killed Deborah?"

He jerked up, stared at her, shook his head back and forth. "Well, if you're not lying for shock value, then that settles it for me: go arrest that psycho boyfriend of hers." He punched the buzzer. "Brandi, please show the agent and detective out."

He gave them a dismissive smile and strode past them, out of his own office, past beautiful Brandi, whose smile was gracious and lasted until they were gone from her sight.

Cam said to Daniel as they rode the elevator to the lobby, "Mr. Markham has an excellent memory, doesn't he?"

"For what happened at a party six months ago? I'll say. He's sure got some hate in him about Doc. He even tied Doc to Constance Morrissey. Why so much animosity toward a man he only met at a party six months ago?"

Cam said, "I don't know. Did he want Deborah for himself, now that Connie is dead? As for Doc killing Deborah—I spoke to him. His wild grief was real. He was drowning in guilt because he hadn't moved her to their new place yesterday and she'd been alone there last night. I know, out of great love can come great hate. But it wasn't Doc. He didn't kill Deborah."

"Doc—Mark Richards—told you he was at the hospital all night, taking care of that boy he'd operated on?"

"Yes. Detective Loomis has probably already spoken to all his coworkers. But let me check." Cam texted Loomis, asking him to call her.

Daniel said, "It may be impossible to prove he was there the whole time, every single minute. Hospitals can be a madhouse."

"It wasn't Doc," Cam said again. She pressed down the window and stuck her head out. The wind tore through her hair, teared her eyes, salted her skin. She breathed in the ocean air and wondered why she lived in Washington. The smell of the Atlantic wasn't at all the same—the water looked cold, opaque, hiding deadly secrets that shifted and roiled beneath the surface. As for the Pacific, ah, the water smelled oddly sweet. It was welcoming, somehow promised magic when you swam beneath those waves.

She pulled her head back in. "Hey, Daniel, isn't *Paco's* up ahead? I need brain food and that means Mrs. Luther's chips and salsa, round two."

41

When Daniel and Cam walked into Missy's living room it was to see her and Doc sitting on the sofa, their heads together, laptops on the coffee table in front of them.

"Did you know he'd be here?" Daniel asked quietly as he set down a big cardboard box with papers from Deborah's house in the doorway.

"No, but it's just as well, saves us time." Cam studied Mark Richards's haggard face. He looked almost terminally ill, needing only a little push into the hereafter. When he took off his glasses and looked over at her, she saw something else. Intense eyes, even fierce, and she knew despite his grief he had a mission now, to find Deborah's killer.

They stepped forward. "Hi, Missy. Dr. Richards, I'm glad you're here. I've brought a box of Deborah's papers to go over with you."

Missy pulled a long hank of hair off her cheek and

tucked it back into her ponytail. She gave Daniel a blinding smile. "Hi."

He nodded to her, smiling. "Hi, yourself."

Missy turned to Cam. "Doc called me to tell me about Deborah and we got to talking and I invited him over. I hope it's all right, Cam, I told him we were concentrating on Deborah's auditions. What's in the box?"

"Deborah's paper records. A lot of them. They probably include all her auditions for several years. Whatever you can tell us about these will help us, Doc."

Missy laid her palm lightly on Doc's shoulder, a show of support and comfort. "Good. We were just beginning to go over my own auditions and those contacts I gave you. We know a lot of the same people, which makes sense, of course. It's too bad we don't have her cell to help us. Doc pointed out you could get those contacts through the phone company."

Doc finally raised his head, nodded to them. "Agent Wittier." He looked at Daniel. "Who are you?"

Missy said, "Sorry, that's Detective Daniel Montoya, from the Lost Hills station. He and Cam are working together. And they're letting me help them." She sounded like a proud mama.

Cam said, "Doc, as Missy said, we're focusing on the idea that Deborah's death, all the killings, might relate to professional rivalry in some way. The fact that Deborah was a record keeper will be a great help."

"And I'll do anything I can to help you," Doc said,

and then broke off, as if speaking more words were beyond him.

To give him time to get himself together, Cam and Daniel looked down at the list Missy was making on her tablet. Daniel said, "So these are actresses you remember Deborah beating out in auditions. I see they go back to last year. Let's go through the box, see if we can narrow the time frame."

Cam said, "We'll also narrow the list by importance. For example, I don't think an audition for a mouth-wash commercial would be relevant. What we're look-ing for are TV or movie roles."

She saw that Doc had gotten himself together, and handed him a sheet of paper dated three months before, Deborah's record of an audition for a role in a TV comedy. He looked at her neat handwriting and swallowed hard.

"Do you remember this audition, Doc? It looks like a meaty role, for *Comfort Zone*, a TV comedy, casting for a fall pilot. Do you know if she won that, or turned the role down for something else?"

He slowly shook his head. "I would know if she won a role like that. She'd have taken it, I'm sure. Wait, I think I remember her talking about that one, but then again, she was always talking about her auditions, worrying about them. It went on and on, there were so many." He swallowed. "Sorry, I'm not making much sense. Please, give me more of her records, maybe one will stand out. It's tough to think about the auditions, it seems so trivial now." He looked at her helplessly.

"Tell us about Deborah winning the role in *The Crown Prince*."

"How do you know about that?"

Cam smiled. "We do a lot of interviews, Doc. We know she was in Italy filming for two weeks."

He nodded. "Yes, and she'd been back home for about two weeks. The rest of the filming was set to take place at the studio. It's all she could talk about when she got that role. I didn't want her to take it, not with her having to be in Italy for two weeks. But you want to know who she beat out for it? You think there's some sort of crazed actress or boyfriend out there?"

"It's a theory," Daniel said.

"I'm sorry, I don't know. She didn't include who she beat out in her records."

Daniel looked through a folder with huge red stars drawn all over it. *The Crown Prince* was the top sheet. He scanned it, shook his head. "It doesn't say. We'll have to get those names from casting."

Doc was staring down at his hands, clasped between his knees. "We drank champagne, not that night, because I had to be at the hospital. But the next night, we drank a whole bottle and she ate a burger. A big double-decker with all the fixings, just as she liked it. I remember Deb told me it was her last splurge. She had to lose five pounds before filming started. She had to keep herself so thin, it pissed me off." He paused, swallowed again. "Look at all the red stars. She loved her red stars. She even put them on bills she'd paid off."

He looked down at the sheet of paper. "She had two weeks to prepare before she went to Italy for the actual filming." He met their eyes. "This role meant everything to her."

Missy looked like she wanted to say something, but Cam shook her head.

"So she went to Italy," Cam asked.

"Yes, I knew it meant as much to her as practicing medicine does to me. I knew she'd come back to me, but it was two whole weeks, too long apart." He stopped, put his head down, and Cam saw his hands were balled into fists.

Missy said, "There are so many parts, they tend to run together, but I just realized I didn't tell you about a part I lost to Connie, sometime this past March, shortly before she was killed. They called me to offer the role. I have the exact date on my laptop."

Cam said, "Did you take the part?"

"I couldn't. I was already booked and couldn't get out of it. But I was sorry I missed out."

Daniel asked, "Missy, do you remember what the part was?"

"Sure, it was a small but juicy role as the younger, uptight sister of this biker chick in *The Gravy Train*. The movie's out sometime this fall."

"Doc, do you remember if Deborah was offered that role?"

He raised his head. "Sorry, Agent, I don't recall her even auditioning for that one. I do remember Deborah getting offered jobs when other actresses couldn't take them, for whatever reason. It happens all the time." He looked blindly past Cam. "If there's a reason you're focusing on Deborah's auditions, I can't see it."

"Do you remember a party about six months ago at a producer's house in the Hollywood Hills? You took Deborah because she wanted to mix with the L.A. movers and shakers? Like Theodore Markham?"

Doc's pale face flushed with contempt and anger. "Oh yes, I remember. All those pompous arrogant snobs, feasting on those gorgeous young women. It was like a smorgasbord for them—like a bunch of degenerate sheiks looking over the latest crop of harem girls. I was disgusted, couldn't wait to get Deborah out of there. I remember Connie Morrissey was there. I didn't know her well, but she and Deborah were—well, acquaintances. I remember Connie tried to pull me away so this pervert producer could ogle Deborah, probably tell her he could make her a star, all the while hoping he could use his position to get in her pants. Since we're looking for a murderer, any one of those debauchers would be high on my list."

"Do you remember Theodore Markham?" Daniel asked him.

"Yeah, he was one of the worst, I could tell by looking at him. He was hanging all over Connie. I remember Deborah said she didn't know if Connie was sleeping with him, but all I had to do was take one look at him and know he was just the sort to take advantage.

He's probably sleeping with some other young actress now that Connie's gone."

Missy said, "Wait a minute, Doc, I remember that party. Sure some of the guys in the business were on the make, and the deeper they're into the booze the heavier it gets. It's a professional hazard. None of us like it, but most of us learn to handle it."

"Obviously she didn't handle it. Do you know she blamed me? Me! All I wanted to do was protect her from those smug perverts, and she called me a dog in the manger, said she'd never take me with her again. It was all about making contacts, networking, and I was being a nut-job. I should open my eyes because the same thing happens everywhere, including the hospital—haven't I seen male doctors trying to get the nurses in the sack?" He snorted. "As if there's any time for that. Or any energy, we're always exhausted." Doc rubbed his forehead, and suddenly, tears filmed his eyes. "Yes, we fought about it, but we'll never fight about it again. Deborah won't go to any more Hollywood parties, with or without me." He locked eyes with Cam. "She's dead. She won't ever do anything again."

42

Delsey Freestone had felt like this about a man only once before, so focused and excited about meeting him, simply nothing else in the world mattered. Her palms were damp and her stomach roiled. It didn't help she remembered the first time she felt this way was about her criminal ex-husband.

She checked her watch for the umpteenth time. Five o'clock on the nose, exactly the time she'd set to meet Rob Rasmussen after their impromptu lunch date the day before that had ended abruptly when Rob had gotten an emergency call from a job site and had to leave. She couldn't remember what they'd said to each other, it simply didn't matter.

She had to be careful here, had to be. She wasn't a stupid kid any longer. She herself had picked the Cadillac Bar and Grill. They would have a beer and talk quietly, see if this insane attraction was real, if it made sense. They would get to know each other a bit, see if they were compatible. She shook her head at herself, wondered what exactly it was about him that made her feel like this.

Delsey stopped in her tracks in the doorway, stared at the herd of government staffers, fresh out of the office, already hootin' and hollerin', nearly all of them under thirty and happy, making huge noise. They had to be celebrating a win, maybe a contentious bill had passed.

She saw him seated in a side booth, alone, rolling a bottle of Brau pale ale, her favorite, between his hands. Her heart skittered seeing him now. This was over-the-top crazy, but it didn't matter; she knew she was a goner.

Rob looked up and saw her. His eyes locked on hers, his lovely smile bloomed big. He rose so fast he nearly knocked over his ale, and stepped out of the booth. Getting to her was hard, so many happy folk in the way.

Then he was standing in front of her, still smiling big, his green eyes bright and hot, she couldn't miss that. He was incredible, tall, lean and fit, splendid, yes, that's what he was, simply splendid.

"Hi." She couldn't seem to get any spit in her mouth.

"Hi, yourself," Rob said, and took her hand. "Let's see if I can't navigate you safely through this government horde. No wonder the politicos hire them young in Washington. They're worked like dogs and party like college frat kids, burn out at thirty."

Delsey didn't care if they were puppies freed from the pound.

The jukebox cranked up and Delsey's brain kicked in. She tugged on his hand. "Listen, they're playing one of my songs—no, not a favorite, I mean, one I wrote myself, for a friend."

"You wrote it?"

"Yes. The title's *Bongo Beat*. Do you like it?"

"Like it? My feet are already tapping. Too bad it's too early to dance. You a good dancer?"

She grinned up at him. "Oh, yeah. You?"

"My moves are legendary."

He led her laughing to his table, ordered her a bottle of the pale ale from a harried waiter, who rolled his eyes at government staffers blocking his way.

Rob had only to look at her face and his words came pouring out. "At lunch yesterday I sort of hoped it was an aberration or a weird temporary hallucination, but it isn't. You're incredible, Delsey, incredible. You're beautiful; you're smart; you're funny. And your talent? You blow me away." He stopped talking and stared at her glowing face, her dilated eyes.

"Thank you. My brother thinks I'm an idiot. All I could talk about was you."

He reached out his hand, a beautiful hand with long strong fingers, and short buffed nails, like his. She didn't hesitate, put her hand into his. He said, "I hate this place. I want to leave, I want you—us—alone, all right?"

"Yes, all right."

He threw a twenty down on the table, and pulled her through the laughing crowd to the sidewalk outside the Grill. He pulled her against him, leaned down, and kissed her. People parted to walk around them.

There was a whistle, then a woman's voice saying, "I'm jealous, go home."

"Nah," a guy said. "Go find a room."

Delsey pulled back, saw the woman grinning at her and grinned back. She looked up at Rob. "A good idea," she said, nothing more.

"The Gibson Hotel, it's on the next block."

They walked hand in hand to the hotel, and Delsey stepped away from him while he went to register in the small ultramodern lobby. People flowed around her, all of them talking, but she didn't really see them or hear them. All of her was focused on him, only him, and what she was going to do to him and with him.

He was with her again, holding a key card. He took her hand and they nearly ran to the elevator. Two older couples got on the elevator with them, the two women talking up a storm, so many shopping bags in their hands, and in their husbands' hands. They'd obviously had fun. But she knew she was about to have lots more.

Once inside the dim-lit room, Rob grabbed her, lifted her, and laid her on her back on the big king-size bed. He was over her, kissing her, and she kissed him back, her hands on his back, in his hair. He whispered, "You're sure?"

She looked at him straight-on. "I probably shouldn't be, but yes, I'm more than sure. If you don't kiss me again, I'll hurt you."

He laughed, kissed her, and lay on top of her, and that was only the beginning.

The early-evening turndown maid stopped outside the door, her hand raised to knock. She heard moans and laughter, some words she couldn't understand. She smiled. She left a dozen pillow chocolates outside the door, sitting on top of two towels.

Delsey lay on her back, her legs sprawled, her hair tangled about her head, half her clothes still on. Rob lay beside her, both of them breathing hard, his hand clutching hers. She felt deliriously content and happy. She felt sated. "I don't want any more time to pass. I want it to stop, right here, right now."

"That'd be good," he said, his voice low and scratchy. "What's your middle name?"

"Faith. What's yours?"

"North, after an uncle back in the Rasmussen family tree. The old dude left my dad a bundle of money, not two days before I was born. Your brother's name is Hammersmith. Why is yours different?"

"I was married once, for about thirty minutes. He was a criminal, but I really liked his name, so I kept it." She grinned, turning to balance on her elbow above him. "I'm a mess."

He raised a hand, ran it through her hair, pulling out some of the tangles. "I didn't know you existed before yesterday. And now I never want you out of my sight. I've been pathetic, all I could do was think about you and grin like a fool, when I should have been working. My guys knew, the bastards. I couldn't wait to see you. I wanted to call you an hour after you left but I didn't know your cell number or where you were. I wasn't about to call Savich or your brother. They might have shot me."

He leaned down, kissed her, and began unbuttoning her blouse. "I don't know how I could have left you half dressed. It's like eating only half a slice of cake." He looked down at her long bare legs. His fingers slowed. "Delsey, I don't want you to think I do this all the time, you know, take a woman to bed the minute I meet her. I don't. I haven't wanted to, and that's the truth. But you're different, and I know this is different for you, too. Your eyes are green, like mine, only they're darker, more beautiful."

Everything was slow and sweet after that. Everything was right.

Delsey fell asleep, her head on his shoulder, her palm on his belly. They'd talk, but later, much later.

43

Cam was scrolling through page after page of auditions from hundreds of film companies on a purple laptop. Some were highlighted in red and dozens were redacted, marked through in black so she couldn't read them. She heard her mother's voice telling her she needed those entries covered in black ink, otherwise how could she find the killer? Some of the red letters started to bleed, covering the screen, then fountaining down, sending ribbons of blood dripping over the purple keyboard. She knew that was the key audition, the one that would give her the big clue, but she couldn't read it now, there was so much blood. Her mother was talking behind her, telling her she'd ruined it now. The bloody page must have flown free because she heard it striking softly against the glass in the window, but then she knew it wasn't the paper, it was something else. Someone was outside, trying to get in.

She jerked awake, her heart pounding, her breathing too fast, too hard. She started to fling off the sheet and jump to her feet when her training kicked in. She lay still and listened. She heard it again, something brushing up against the bedroom window. She'd left it cracked open to let in the warm night air and someone was looking in. He could easily push the window up and climb in. To kill her? *No, not me. Missy. He was here.*

The Serial was outside.

Slowly, quietly, she reached over and pulled the knob on the bedside table drawer, eased it open. She slipped her hand in, felt the comforting steel of her Glock. *Easy, easy*—she lifted it out of the drawer. She didn't need to rack the slide, she kept a bullet in the chamber.

She breathed low and quiet, completely focused, and eased off the side of the bed. There was a quarter moon tonight, its light streaming in through the window. She'd see him clearly if he crawled in. She listened for the sound of the window coming up higher.

She heard him breathing, heard his sneakers thunk lightly outside the window. He thought the room was empty. Did he have his knife in his hand, his goggles already on so when he sliced Missy's throat he wouldn't be blinded by her blood?

If Missy were alone in the cottage, sleeping in the master bedroom, she'd never have heard a thing. Until it was too late and she was about to die.

The bastard. She was ready.

Come on, come on.

But he didn't climb in. He stood at the window for

several minutes, looking into the room, and then he turned away.

Cam came smoothly up, aimed her Glock through the window at the man's chest. "FBI. You move and you're dead."

His eyes flew to her face. "What, who are you? You're not Missy. FBI?" He jerked around and started to run, tripped and landed headfirst into the thick bougainvillea bushes. He cried out as he rolled away onto the ground. She didn't fire because she knew she could catch him. She was out the window on the ground as he pulled himself to his knees to take off again.

She kicked him in the back before he got to the street, sending him onto his belly against the ground, not two inches from a cactus. She dropped down on top of him, laid her Glock against his neck. "Don't you even think of moving. It's over."

He wasn't wearing goggles and she didn't find a knife when she patted him down. He twisted, managed to kick his legs against her back, knocking her sideways, and slammed his elbow against her jaw. She saw bursts of white but she held tight to her Glock, no way would she let it go.

She caught his arm, jerked him around, and chopped her hand against his throat. He lurched back, gagging, his hands clutching his throat, wheezing for breath.

She kicked his legs out from under him, slammed down on top of him, and stuck her Glock into his ear. She leaned close. "That's enough. Feel that? You want me to shoot you in the ear, splat your brains all over the ground? Calm down now, there's a lot you and I have to talk about."

He tried again to throw her off, but Cam grabbed him around his neck in the crook of her elbow and jerked back so he was looking up at her. "Listen, you moron, if you move again, you're dead, you got that? I can shoot you or I can break your neck. Where's your knife? Where are your goggles?"

"Knife? I don't have a knife. Why would I wear any fricking goggles?"

She smacked the back of his head, slammed him down on his stomach. "So you were coming into my room to serenade me?"

"Cam! You've got him?" And there Missy was, leaning out the window, in boxers and a short filmy top, a Ka-Bar in her hand.

"Yes. It's okay, Missy."

He froze at the sound of Missy's voice. Cam dug her Glock into his ear. "Don't you think about moving. There's your seventh victim, but she doesn't look all that helpless, does she? She would have carved you up. You're lucky I got you first." She thrummed with rage, felt it burning deep in her throat. She felt her fingers tighten around the trigger. She could kill the monster right now, in this very second, and it would all be over. She felt Missy's hand on her shoulder. "Cam? Are you okay?"

Missy's voice drew her back from the chasm.

"Yes, I'm okay, Missy. Here's our Serial. We got him. It's over."

He heaved and twisted, but Cam kept him down. "No," he yelled, trying to turn his face to look up at Missy. "I'm not the Starlet Slasher, I'm not."

Cam slowly rose. "Stay flat on your face or you're a dead man."

He was stammering, panting. "Y-you have to listen to me. I don't know what you're talking about. I wasn't here to kill you, I wanted to see Missy, ask her to go to the movies with me, I—"

"Shut up!"

Missy stood over him, her gorgeous hair blowing in the breeze. "He looks so skinny, Cam. Without his knife, he looks like nothing at all. I want to see his face. I want to see what a serial killer looks like."

She kicked his leg with her bare foot. "Turn over or I'll stick my Ka-Bar in your eye." Slowly, he turned over onto his back, his hands still rubbing his throat, and stared up at her.

Missy's brain went blank. "Oh no."

"Missy, what's wrong?"

"Cam, he isn't the serial killer. He's my stalker. It's Blinker."

And that's why he doesn't have a knife or goggles. Cam wanted to yell and curse and weep. She'd been so close to killing him, and he wasn't the Serial. She stared at him a moment in the dim moonlight—he was pale and skinny, his light-colored hair already thin on top. He looked terrified. "If you weren't sneaking into the window to kill Missy, what were you planning to do?"

He blinked. "I told you, I wanted to see her one

more time, it's been so long. There's a movie playing down the street I knew she'd like. Maybe she'd like to have dinner after at *Mama Mia* in Santa Monica."

Missy hissed. "Go to the movies with you? Are you nuts? Let me cut out his tongue, Cam."

"Just a moment, Missy. Your name is Bayley, right?"

"Yes, my friends call me Blinker, but my clients call me John, John Bayley. I'm a bond trader."

"Mr. Bayley, you violated your restraining order, you were breaking and entering, you assaulted a federal officer. Apart from those charges that could put you away for a decade, I could have easily shot you."

He licked his tongue over his lips. "Don't let her stick me with that knife or I'll sue both of you. Why didn't the cops take that knife away from you?"

"They did. I bought another one."

A bubble of laughter rose in Cam's throat, nearly burst out of her mouth. Amazing. She'd gone from believing she'd caught the serial killer to dealing with this lame idiot. "Sue her? Highly doubtful since you'd be in jail."

He looked up at the two women, one with a gun, and Missy with her knife, long bare legs on both of them. He wheezed out, "Look, there's no reason to make a big deal out of this. There was no harm done. I'm a respectable bond trader, as I told you. Everyone knows me. I have trouble sleeping and I usually go out and walk. I liked the looks of this house. I thought it was vacant."

Missy kicked him again. "So now you coming into

my house is a misunderstanding? There's a freaking car parked in the driveway, how could you think it was vacant? You came to ogle me, you pathetic putz."

Cam said, "I guess you forgot about the restraining order."

He was still rubbing his throat. Cam let him sit up, both women standing over him. "Look, Agent, ma'am, Missy, I've got money. I can make it worth your while if you'll let this go."

Cam leaned close to his face. "So now you're saying if you pay us money Missy should let you stare at her?"

"Well, not really, but if I had managed to get a look at her, well, why not? Maybe she'd wake up and like what she saw and we could go to the movies, like I said. Agent, ma'am, can't we let this go?"

"I strongly suggest you shut up now, Mr. Bayley, or I'll let Missy carve you up."

He looked up at Missy and stopped talking.

"Missy, please get me my handcuffs. They're in my jeans pocket, in the closet. And my cell is on the table beside the bed. We'll let Daniel deal with Blinker. He's got jail cells that smell like sweaty underwear."

When Missy walked back out the front door with Cam's handcuffs and cell, Cam rolled Blinker onto his stomach, jerked his hands back and handcuffed him. "Sit up and stay there, don't move."

Neither woman helped him. Finally, panting, he managed to pull himself up.

Cam punched in Daniel's number. Two rings, then, "Cam? What's wrong? Are you all right?"

"Both Missy and I are fine."

He said, his voice sharp, "Missy's okay, you're sure?"

"Yes, Daniel, she's fine."

"That's good. Okay. You woke me up from a wonderful dream. I just won the Daytona. There were so many cheers, and I was about to be crowned— Okay, what happened exactly?"

"Detective Montoya. Missy, who's fine as am I— and thank you for asking—will give you a big congratulatory kiss if you come over to her cottage. We have a surprise for you."

"At two o'clock in the frigging morning?"

"Don't whine, Daniel," Missy called out. "Get your very fine butt over here. Cam's got my stalker for you."

44

Griffin waited until the waiter left and Delsey had eaten three bites of her spaghetti bolognese, smothered in Parmesan cheese. He watched a moment, knew her brain was elsewhere and imagined he knew very well where. "Dels, listen to me. I need you to turn your brain back on and pay attention. I don't enjoy telling you this, but it has to be said. I saw the look on your face when you met Rob Rasmussen Tuesday at the Hoover Building. And I know you saw him again yesterday. I really don't want to know exactly what happened." But it was easy to tell exactly what had happened. She glowed, and he knew why. "You didn't get home until very late, I might add."

Delsey blinked at him. "How do you know about yesterday?"

"A neighbor saw you, wondered who the guy was who dropped you off, described him to me. This could be a problem for you, Dels."

"I can't imagine why it could be. I might add that it's none of your business, Griffin."

"Don't be obtuse, Dels. Rob Rasmussen is a suspect in the murder attempts on his grandmother's life. You knew this, yet you had lunch with him Tuesday and saw him again Wednesday afternoon and evening."

Delsey wiped her napkin over her mouth. "Listen, Griffin, Rob's a suspect only because he happened to have come into Mrs. Rasmussen's life at the wrong time. Rob, a suspect? That's nuts and you know it. He loves his grandmother. He told me about how he'd missed her for the ten years they hadn't seen each other, how much she did for him when he screwed up. He loves her; no way would he try to kill her.

"Don't give me that understanding-older-brother look. I know my history. So I sometimes pick the wrong guys, but not this time, Griffin. Rob is open and honest. He's special. He has nothing to do with this. There's no reason to warn me off him."

"Savich has known Rob Rasmussen nearly all his life. He likes him, too. But here's the deal, Dels. Forget he's a suspect for a moment. Savich told me he and Sherlock met Rob's girlfriend at the Rasmussen mansion Tuesday night. He said Rob and Marsia were tight. He and Sherlock interviewed her at her studio in Maryland yesterday while you were out with her boyfriend. It doesn't sound to me like he's all that honest and open. I'm sorry, Delsey, but it's clear he's a hound dog."

Delsey's face was utterly blank. Was history repeating itself? Could Griffin be right? Could her luck in men be that sucky? Was she that much of a pushover? "You said Dillon and Sherlock met his girlfriend Tuesday night? There's got to be a mistake here, Griffin. They mistook things. They had to."

"Marsia Gay lives in Millstock, Maryland. She's a successful sculptor, or getting there. Savich said he and Sherlock asked her about her intentions toward Rob, if she was serious, if she was thinking about marriage. She said she hadn't made up her mind. But they were tight, and he introduced her to his family as practically his fiancée."

Delsey stared down her spaghetti, very carefully laid her fork on the table. She looked sick, leached of color. "There has to be an explanation."

"I just gave it to you, straight from Savich's mouth. You think either he or Sherlock would say that if it wasn't true?"

"He didn't mention her, not at all."

"I'm really sorry, Delsey. Do you want me to bust him up?"

She hunched in on herself, shook her head. The man who'd loved her the whole afternoon and evening, shared all of himself with her, told her he'd never felt the same about another woman in his life. She'd believed him because she felt the same way. They'd sat cross-legged on the rumpled bed, room service sandwiches, potato chips, and a bottle of wine between them, talking and laughing, and touching, always touching, kissing between bites. He'd spoken so freely, with such enthusiasm, such openness, she had no doubt he'd meant it. She remembered her ex-husband's golden tongue, how she'd believed everything out of his mouth until she'd nearly drowned in his lies. "Griffin, am I doomed to always fall for the wrong guys?"

"Stop looking pitiful, the moron's not worth it." He eyed her, watched her pick up a roll, look at it as if she didn't know what it was, set it back down on her plate.

"I thought he was the one, Griffin, finally, the perfect guy for me. I never thought to ask him if he was unattached. I mean, of course he had to be or he wouldn't have come on to me, he wouldn't have wanted to have—" Her voice wobbled. She wet her lips. "And now you're telling me he was cheating on his girlfriend?"

Griffin, always more cynical than his sister, said, "At least you found out before things went any further. You need to step back right now, Dels. I don't have to bust him up, but I could have a chat with him, set him straight."

"No, I'll do it," Delsey said. She looked down at her congealed spaghetti and wondered what would happen if she threw it against the wall.

"A week in Paris might be just the thing for you. You've still got plenty of time before your grad classes start up again at Stanislaus."

"Yeah, it sounds lovely. All alone staring up at the Eiffel Tower."

"There would be advantages. The Eiffel Tower's got a great view from the top. If you happened to spot a single good-looking guy, you wouldn't be able to get back down fast enough to catch up with him."

———————

Rob called her on her way out of the restaurant to ask her if he could make dinner for her that night at his apartment.

"I was thinking sushi. Do you like sushi? I miss you, Delsey, you can't imagine how much I miss you, how much I want to see you again."

It hurt so bad to form the words, to open her mouth. Then she thought of his girlfriend and felt a clean spray of anger. "You should invite Marsia Gay, not me."

She heard him groan. "How did you find out about Marsia? Oh, I see, Savich told you about her. Delsey, it isn't what it seems. I know that sounds lame. But listen, I was planning on clearing things up with her this weekend. Really, Delsey, she's been more than a friend, I'll admit that, but there's always been something missing. It won't go any further. Now it can't. I only took her to my grandmother's mansion Tuesday night so I wouldn't have to face the family alone. She helped me by running interference. You and I, it happened so quickly, I haven't had time to speak to her, but I will."

She said clearly, "I'm not going to start another relationship with someone who lies to me, Rob. I don't want to hear from you again." She punched off her cell. Sometimes, she thought as she walked the three miles back to Griffin's condo, life smacks you in the head.

45

Cam and Daniel sat across a scarred table from John Bayley, aka Blinker, in the only interview room at the Lost Hills station, Chief Dreyfus Murray watching and listening behind a two-way mirror. Daniel had processed Blinker at 3:00 a.m. into one of Sheriff Murray's jail cells, and they'd all gone home for a few hours' sleep.

Blinker looked pathetic this morning, his chinos and shirt wrinkled and dirty from his face-plant in Missy's yard. It was obvious he hadn't slept, and he looked scared, his eyes darting back and forth between them. It was odd, but he looked even scrawnier this morning than he had lying in Missy's yard.

Daniel said, "Mr. Bayley, you've had ample time to think of a better story than the lame one you told last night. So tell us exactly why you were at Missy Devereaux's house after dark, well after midnight in fact, when it was obvious she'd be asleep?"

"I told you when you were shoving me into a cell

last night, Detective Montoya, that I occasionally have insomnia and I've found that walking around helps. I like Malibu at night, it's quiet and smells nice, you know? And all the movie stars are sound asleep and I can picture how it must feel to live like that." He shot Cam a look. "Don't you ever wonder what the movie stars look like without makeup?"

"No," Cam said.

"Okay, okay, just a little joke. Listen, I thought the house was empty and I liked it. My lease is coming due and I've been thinking about maybe renting something in Malibu. I didn't know it was her house, I didn't. It's a weird coincidence." Blinker fanned his hands in front of him and went hopefully silent.

Cam said, "But you didn't walk far, did you? We found your car parked a block from Ms. Devereaux's house."

"I live in Santa Monica—you know that. It's way too far to walk, so I drove to Malibu, then I began walking."

"So you decided to climb in through a window to see if you'd like to rent this house?"

"No, no, you know I never went inside. Yeah, I did look inside, maybe, but that's all. I just wanted to get a feel for the house, you know? I was ready to leave because I didn't want to disturb anyone when you jumped out the window in your underwear and attacked me. You started pounding on me and I was only trying to defend myself, and then this blonde jumped out and attacked me, too. I couldn't believe it—it was the same woman in Las Vegas, the one who accused me of stalking her. She even got a restraining order. That's the truth. Look, I was a gentleman in Las Vegas. I agreed not to sue her for attacking me with a knife."

Cam said, "You really want us to believe you didn't know it was Missy Devereaux's house?"

"Of course I didn't know! I told you, I never break the law, I believe in the law. Sure, the restraining order is humiliating, but I wouldn't have gone near that house if I'd known it was hers."

Daniel said, "Apart from being ridiculous, what you're saying doesn't matter, Mr. Bayley. You violated the restraining order whether you knew it or not, and you assaulted a federal agent. I'm wondering how you could be so stupid as to show up at Missy Devereaux's house in the middle of the night? Did you forget there's a serial killer out there? And Missy Devereaux is a young actress? And just maybe you're the serial killer."

"Me? No, that's crazy! That's nuts!"

"Mr. Bayley," Cam said, "we know you were in Las Vegas last Saturday, and that night Molly Harbinger was murdered. You've already admitted to the little dustup with Missy Devereaux in the Wynn hotel garage."

"No, no, I flew home to L.A. that afternoon. You can check with Sunset Airlines, my plane left McCarran airport at five in the afternoon. I wasn't there!"

Daniel sat forward, pinned Blinker. "And where were you Tuesday night, Blinker?"

"Tuesday night? Why? Okay, I was at the movies, over in Century City. I saw Scarlett Johansson in something, I don't remember the name of the movie. Wait, wait, I still have the ticket stub," and he shoved his hand into his empty pockets. "You took all my stuff away from me last night. The stub has to be with my stuff. You have to look."

Daniel left the interview room. He was back shortly with Blinker's envelope in his hand. He poured his personal effects onto the table. And there was the ticket stub, for Tuesday night, the late show.

Given time of death, it was very unlikely Blinker could have driven to Santa Monica to Deborah Connelly's house to kill her. He wasn't the Serial, although neither Cam nor Daniel had ever seriously believed he could be. At least now he could be formally eliminated.

Blinker sat forward, his hands clasped, his look earnest. "I couldn't hurt anybody, really. I'm a bond trader. I'm responsible, except this morning. I need to call my supervisor." At their stony looks, he cleared his throat, straightened. "I want a lawyer."

"Very well." Daniel shoved his cell phone over to him, and he and Cam left the interview room.

Chief Murray met them outside the interview room. "He might get the Nitwit of the Year Award, but he isn't the Serial, not that either of you thought he was."

"No, he isn't," Cam said. "He doesn't fit the body type and there wasn't a knife or goggles."

Dreyfus patted her arm. "Still, we've got him on

trespassing, maybe breaking and entering, violating the restraining order, and attacking a federal agent."

Cam said, "He didn't really enter, only break." She sighed. "I really did attack him, Dreyfus, jumped right out the window and took him down."

"Doesn't matter, too bad for him. If he gets himself a good lawyer, he could plea-bargain down to maybe three months, and out on bail until his hearing."

Missy, who'd been pacing up and down the bullpen with every male eye following her progress, overheard Sheriff Murray. She grabbed Cam's sleeve. "He'll get three months or maybe nothing? And he'll be out on bail? I'm going to go break his arm, Cam, he deserves it. He was going to come into your bedroom, you know it."

"But he didn't, Missy," Cam said.

"He would have. And what if you hadn't been there, Cam? What was he going to do? Sneak to my bedroom and try to kiss me? Lick me? Rape me? Then when the schmuck gets out of jail, if he ever even goes in, he can come after me again? Sheriff Murray, can't we get him committed to a loony bin?"

Daniel took her hand. "Calm down, Missy. He wasn't at your house to kill you. He worships you, he's obsessed with you, and that's got to stop. We're all on edge because of the serial killer, but it isn't Blinker. Do you know he doesn't have a mark on his record, even a speeding ticket? He's a putz, that's about it. I'll see to it he has a psych evaluation. Don't worry."

Missy said, "Maybe he did have a knife and goggles, maybe you just didn't find them. I'll go back and search, see—"

Cam interrupted her. "Missy, I just called Sunset Airlines. Sure enough, Mr. Bayley flew back on their flight 415 to L.A. early last Saturday evening. Also, none of the murdered actresses reported a stalker. He's got the wrong build, too, and his features aren't remotely close to the sketch we have of the killer. He's just a putz, like Daniel said. We'll see what the psychiatrist says after his evaluation. Stop your worrying, all right?"

"Easy enough for you to say," Missy said, and began pacing again, much to the pleasure of the men in the bullpen.

Daniel looked after her, talking to herself, her hands waving to make a point, pacing in her skinny jeans and her 49ers sweatshirt. He said to Cam, "What with that Ka-Bar of hers, I'd be willing to bet she'd cut off some of Blinker's prized real estate if he tried anything again. I think he knows that, but before he leaves, I'll tell him I'll hold him down for her if he ever gets near her again."

Cam smiled at him. "I know you would. Missy told me she wants Blinker sent to prison in Antarctica." Her cell beeped and she excused herself. When she strode back into the bullpen a couple minutes later, she looked upset.

Daniel said, "So who's the fool who pissed you off?"

"No, I'm not pissed off. Confused is more like

it. That was David Elman, the LAPD supervisor of Homicide Special Section. The administrator at Children's Hospital in Santa Monica called to tell him there was a private investigator asking questions about the surgical staff's working hours and schedules on Tuesday night, when Deborah was killed. Elman said it was Gus Hampton, a P.I. with a good rep for being thorough and very expensive. When Elman had Loomis confront him about it, Hampton freely admitted he was working for Theo Markham. Hampton said Markham believes Doc killed Deborah and that we—the cops—wouldn't take him seriously. He used my name, as lead investigator, and that Doc had fooled me with his grief routine, had us believing his alibi about being in the hospital all night. He said Mr. Markham doesn't think the cops will ever take him seriously unless Hampton proves him right."

Missy called out, "I'm sorry, but I heard you. I don't care what Markham thinks. You know it can't be Doc, Cam. I mean, he saves lives, he's a surgeon. It's not possible. Listen, I talked to him, held him while he cried. Doc was nuts about Deborah. You've met him, you've talked to him, you know he's devastated. Deb meant everything to him. I never heard a word about her dumping him or being afraid of him. Afraid of Doc? That's stupid. Markham's got this all wrong."

Murray said slowly, "Why would Markham care enough about Deborah Connelly's murder to hire an expensive P.I.? He barely knew her from what he told you and Daniel. Where does that interest of his come from? And why focus on her boyfriend, this Doc? It's obvious Markham hates him. My question is why?"

"Good questions, Murray," Cam said. "I don't know the answers, but could he be that upset because Deborah couldn't finish her role in his movie? That sounds lame to me. I'm going to try to find out. Do you think I'm wrong about Doc, Daniel?"

"No, you can't be," Missy said when Daniel remained silent. "Listen, I can ask around, see who else spent time with him and Deb together."

Daniel got in her face. "No way you're going to ask anybody anything, Missy. You're already too involved in this."

Missy cocked her head at him. "But I'm already in the case, Daniel, Cam asked me to be. It won't hurt to ask. What could happen?"

"No," Daniel said.

Sheriff Murray said, "Ms. Devereaux, Daniel's right. You're a civilian, you should keep out of this."

Cam was shaking her head. "I still have a hard time picturing Doc planning to slit Deborah's throat, covering his tracks. I saw him, I spoke to him, saw his grief. Like Missy, I'd swear to my last breath it was real. He was raw with pain."

Daniel said, "Unless he's the one who's the fine actor. I'll call Arturo, tell him to dig deeper at the hospital, put him on the hook—he's got to prove or disprove Doc's whereabouts on Tuesday night. Definitively. The last thing he wants is to have a private cop find out things he didn't. Arturo doesn't deal well with civilians sticking their noses in his business. This will fire up his burners."

46

It was a beautiful day in Washington, not too hot, perfect for another walk she really didn't want to take, but Delsey had no sooner gotten back to Griffin's condo than he'd called her, told her he knew if she stayed inside she'd only brood. Take a taxi back into the middle of Washington, get out and walk, look at all the monuments, enjoy all the people, and while she was walking he suggested her best payback was to write a song about how rotten Rob Rasmussen was.

So here she was, on K Street, walking with hordes of tourists and government employees, humming a few bars of her new song, spinning words and notes in the back of her mind, her step lagging now and then as she let her mind worry the line about a two-timing dog.

When she stopped at the corner for a red light, a dozen people quickly filled in behind her. There was a lot of traffic, but it was moving right along. Her eyes were on her silver sandals—she needed a new coat of polish on her toenails. Maybe a deep purple?—when something hit her hard in her back, hurling her into the path of an oncoming black limo.

Delsey saw her mother's face clear as day as the big car bore down on her. She heard screams and shouts, felt strong hands under her armpits literally jerking her off the ground and backward. The big car's brakes screamed like a banshee, and the front end spun into the oncoming traffic as it slid past her. There was a tremendous crash and the sound of metal rending as several cars slammed into one another. People were yelling, horns blaring. It was pandemonium.

She stared up into Rob Rasmussen's face. "Delsey, are you all right?"

Was she all right? When she'd nearly met her maker? Had he saved her? "I'm not dead," Delsey said, "so that's something." She couldn't quite grasp what had happened. She knew she couldn't stand on her own yet, so she let him hold her up. People crowded in beside them, some asking if she was okay, others seeing if people were all right in the crashed cars. Someone called 911, not for her, but for the mad jumble of cars smacked together in the middle of K Street. Drivers were getting out of their wrecked cars, some of them angry, screaming for the cops, others dazed, wondering what had happened. It seemed like only a second had passed when she heard sirens.

Rob said, "You're white as a ghost. Are you sure you're okay?"

She tried to pull herself free, but her legs wouldn't hold her. She sagged against him. "What happened?"

"You fell into the street, right in front of a black limo."

An older guy wearing cowboy boots called out, "I'll bet she can't walk a straight line!"

That straightened her back and her legs. She pulled away from Rob and rounded on the man. "I'm not drunk. Someone pushed me. Did anyone see who it was?"

There was a punch of shocked silence, then voices, talking over one another so she couldn't make out what they were saying.

She felt light-headed, and, admittedly, a bit crazed as she looked at the faces around her, wondering which of them had pushed her. More than likely that person was long gone now. She'd nearly died. Someone had tried to kill her. The shouts from the wrecked cars in the street stopped when a cop car arrived on scene. An officer leaped out, called for quiet and calm.

No one had seen anything. And that's what everyone told Metro officer George Mankins, all at once when he pushed through. He listened, then raised his hand. He looked at Delsey, saw her dilated eyes, her pallor, the dirt on her hands, the streak of grime on her cheek. "You okay?"

She nodded. She waved toward the insane wreckage in the street. "I'm not responsible, really, Officer. Someone pushed me."

Mankins eyed her. He'd just finished a double shift,

thankful to be on his way home when the call came in. He'd been only one block away, so he couldn't ignore it. What was this about someone pushing her? "You sure you don't need the hospital?"

"No, honestly, I'm okay. My brother's an FBI agent. Please take me to him. He's in the Hoover Building."

"No can do. I've got to take you to the station, let you tell a detective what you told me. Who are you, sir? You know her?"

"He's Rob Rasmussen. He was my boyfriend for a day until I found out today he was a liar. But he did save my life, pulled me back just in time."

Or maybe, Officer Mankins thought, the lying ex-boyfriend had pushed her, then regretted it just in time to save her.

47

Griffin, Savich, and Sherlock were met by Detective Ben Raven in the lobby of the Daly Building. He led them through security and up to the third floor to his captain's office.

Captain Juan Ramirez, built like a fireplug and stronger than most of the officers under him, looked up when three people appeared in his doorway. He nodded to Ben, rose. "Savich, Sherlock, good to see you. Ben said her brother was coming. That you?"

"Yes, Special Agent Griffin Hammersmith."

He looked back at Savich. "What are you guys doing here?"

Savich shook Ramirez's outstretched hand. "Good to see you, Juan. Griffin Hammersmith is in my unit. Griffin, this is Captain Ramirez." Griffin stepped forward, stuck out his hand. He turned immediately to Delsey, pale as a death shroud, sitting on the edge of the captain's ratty houndstooth sofa, looking straight ahead, as if studying the captain's desk would keep her safe. Rob Rasmussen stood in the corner, staring at her.

"Delsey, sweetheart—"

Delsey blinked at Griffin's voice, jumped up and ran into his arms, squeezed him tightly. "Someone shoved me into the street, right in front of a black limo, Griffin. It wasn't people pushing in behind, you know how that is— No, it was a hard shove, square in my back, hard enough to push me into the street. Rob said he didn't see anyone shove me, simply saw me flying into the street and he managed to grab me and pull me back." She gave Rob a brief nod.

Griffin continued to hold her as he looked over at Rob Rasmussen. He opened his mouth, but Sherlock beat him to it. "Were you with Delsey, Mr. Rasmussen?"

Rob looked at her, then fast down at his sneakered feet. "Well, no, not yet. I was trying to catch up to her. I called her but she hung up on me. I drove to Agent Hammersmith's condo, saw her get into a taxi and followed. I wasn't stalking her, really, I only wanted to talk to her, tell her that I wasn't—"

"A lying jerk?" Delsey said, turning toward him, never leaving Griffin's arms.

"I'm not, Delsey, I swear I'm not."

Savich slashed his hand through the air. "Rob, this isn't the time. We all know you were with Delsey all afternoon yesterday while Sherlock and I were interviewing your girlfriend."

"Yeah, I know, but—"

Savich cut him off. "Right now you need to focus. Think back, Rob. Picture the scene in your mind. Picture each person. Can you describe the man or woman directly behind Delsey?"

Rob gave Delsey one last look, then said to Savich, "Okay, there were lots of people, at least a dozen, maybe more, both men and women. Delsey was on the curb, first to go, waiting for the light to change. A man and a woman were directly behind her, crowding close, and then a second later, I saw Delsey flying into the street. I pushed through the crowd and managed to pull her back." He swallowed convulsively. "It was close, too close."

"Did anyone look familiar to you?"

"I don't know, I wasn't paying attention, only looking at Delsey. Even when I shoved through people to get to her, I didn't notice their faces."

Detective Ben Raven said, "Officer Mankins and three other patrol officers corralled some of the people who were behind Ms. Freestone. They took their names so we can question them. But many of our fine upstanding citizens couldn't wait to get away. Our best shot at seeing the person who shoved Delsey might be the traffic cams at that intersection. We'll have the footage within the hour. We'll also check the cameras on all the buildings within a block radius. I'm hopeful we'll nail our perp in living black and white."

But Griffin wasn't hopeful, not if the person who'd shoved Delsey was savvy about the cameras plastered all over Washington, almost as many as in London. He saw Delsey was looking wobbly and led her to the sofa and sat down beside her, never letting go of her hand. He saw she was looking at Rob Rasmussen, who still stood behind a utilitarian office chair, not moving, looking back at her.

She licked her dry lips. What would have happened if he hadn't followed her to try to talk her around? "Griffin, why would someone want to kill me? I mean, I don't know many people in Washington. I haven't had the time or the opportunity to make a serious enemy. Even your doorman likes me. Could this have something to do with someone trying to kill Mrs. Rasmussen?"

Captain Ramirez came to attention. "What's this? Wait a minute—Rob Rasmussen. You're related?"

Sherlock said, "Rob is Mrs. Rasmussen's grandson."

Rob said to Captain Ramirez, "I had nothing to do with the attempts on her life and Delsey hasn't even met her. What happened today couldn't have anything to do with that mess."

Savich said slowly, "It could have something to do with a woman's anger at a rival. Rob, how would Marsia know you spent hours with Delsey yesterday?"

Rob never looked away from Delsey. "I went to see her last night. Before I could speak to her about Delsey, she told me about your visit at her studio and said she hoped she'd passed with flying colors. Then she eyed me, and finally asked me about my day. I told her I'd had lunch with a new friend in Washington." His eyes fell to his sneakers. "Not much more. I wanted to wait until the weekend to break it off with her, but I did tell her I'd met someone I really liked, and I told her your name, Delsey. She smiled at me, asked if you were an artist like she was, and I told her you wrote music. She said she'd like to meet you. She didn't seem disturbed at all. She said it was nice to meet new people that I liked. I started to get into it then, explain everything to her, but I got a call from one of my people about an emergency at one of our job sites. I had to go see to it. I told myself I had enough time. This weekend, I'd get everything clear with her.

"But listen, Savich, I'm not making it up. Marsia wasn't at all upset when I told her about Delsey. She was understanding, agreeable, sweet, like always."

And did you come back after your house emergency and sleep with her, Rob? Aloud, Delsey said, "Yeah, a nice new friend, that's me."

"Well, you are, plus you're a whole lot more than that, and you know it." He saw Captain Ramirez rolling his eyes at him and said quickly, "Savich, you can't believe Marsia would do something like this. She's a sculptor, an artist, for heaven's sake. As I told you, she wasn't jealous or upset. No, she wouldn't do anything like this, it's absurd. I know her."

Savich said, "How serious do you think Ms. Gay is about you, Rob? Does she expect a marriage proposal?"

Rob froze like a deer in the headlights. "A marriage proposal? Neither of us have ever said a word about marriage, never. We've been really good friends, well, maybe there was more, but that's all changed." He looked at Delsey dead-on. "Everything changed when I met Delsey."

Sherlock said matter-of-factly, "Rob, I know you believe what you said to Ms. Gay didn't give her a big clue that your feelings for her had shifted to another woman. However, the fact that she remained calm and sweet to you doesn't mean she wasn't threatened or furious or jealous. We'll confirm where Ms. Gay was this afternoon. Of course, even if she spent the day snug in her studio, she's smart enough to have hired someone. Maybe we'll clear this up quickly with the camera footage. Now, if you think of anything else, please call Dillon or me. Ben, Captain Ramirez, thank you for taking care of Ms. Freestone. We'll be in touch."

Rob Rasmussen took a step toward Delsey, only to have Griffin get in his face. "No, Mr. Rasmussen. Not now. Thank you for saving her, but I'm taking her home."

Delsey stood beside her brother, her hand on his arm. "I told you, Rob, I don't want to speak to you ever again and I meant it. From now on I'm avoiding men altogether. No more making bad decisions for me. Yes, Griffin, let's go home. Thank you, Detective Raven, Captain Ramirez."

They left Rob Rasmussen standing in the hall outside Captain Ramirez's office, staring after Delsey.

48

Savich and Sherlock sat across from Alexander in the same interview room they'd been in Tuesday, only two days before, but it seemed a lifetime ago. Alexander sat down, shot his cuffs, and said, "I don't wish to begin until my lawyer arrives." He looked down at his watch. "He said he was on his way. It appears he'd been waiting for Grandmother's call."

They waited in silence until R. D. Gardener, a formidable criminal attorney, strode into the room five minutes later. He stopped short, recognizing Savich. "Agent Savich, it's been a while. May I ask why you have brought my client to the Hoover Building tonight? It couldn't wait until tomorrow, this questioning he told me you demanded to conduct? You threatened to arrest him?"

"Hello, Mr. Gardener, let me introduce you to Agent Sherlock. I don't believe you two have met."

Gardener nodded at her, then his eyes widened. "Like most of America, I know your wife. The heroine of JFK. A pleasure, Agent Sherlock. Now, Agent Savich, you will tell me what evidence you have to support bringing my client in at this ungodly hour on a Thursday night."

"Please sit down, Mr. Gardener, and I'll lay it out for you and Alexander. On Monday, Venus gave us permission to search the house, after the attempt on her life. It required several days for the forensics team to process all they took from the mansion. They found nothing suspicious, except for traces of arsenic in your medicine cabinet, Alexander." Savich added to Gardener, "As you may know, Mrs. Rasmussen was being systematically poisoned with arsenic. Why would you have traces of arsenic in your medicine cabinet, Alexander?"

Before Alexander could open his mouth, Gardener said, "You're telling me you brought Mr. Rasmussen down here because of some traces of a substance in his medicine cabinet? Are you that desperate, Agent Savich?"

Savich continued, "I would certainly like to hear Alexander's explanation for the arsenic."

Gardener said, "You searched Mr. Rasmussen's suite of rooms without his permission? Without a warrant?"

"As I said, Mrs. Rasmussen gave us permission and it is her house."

"But his rooms are his alone. Your evidence will be inadmissible in court, Agent."

Savich said, "I'm sure you will argue that point very well if we come to that, Mr. Gardener. Alexander, do you have an explanation?"

"No, I do not. Obviously anyone in the house could have put it there. Do you honestly believe I'm so stupid as to leave arsenic in my bathroom, Savich?"

"That remains to be seen, Alexander, but it's only one of the reasons you are here. We found calls to a burner phone sold to Mr. Willig made from your cell phone, calls made on Sunday, one day before Willig tried to murder your grandmother on Monday afternoon. You said you didn't know Vincent Willig. If that is true, then why did you call him?"

Alexander rose out of his chair, leaned close to Savich. "I don't know the man, I told you that. I did not call him."

"Doesn't this all look highly suspicious to you, Agent Savich? As my client has said, how stupid would he have to be to not only leave traces of arsenic in his medicine cabinet but also to make calls that could be traced to the man he was hiring to kill his grandmother? I understand the man was a convicted felon who was murdered last night while in your custody?" He shook his head. "Unfortunate, and very prejudicial to any case you might wish to make."

Alexander gave a sharp ugly laugh. "Excellent police work. Do you have anything else to ask me?"

Before Savich could answer, Mr. Gardener said, "Look, Agent Savich, the phone calls and the traces of arsenic—hardly enough to get an indictment, I'm sure you'll agree. Anyone could have planted the arsenic, and I'm sure Mr. Rasmussen doesn't keep his cell phone on his person all the time. Again, anyone could have tampered with his cell phone."

"Alexander," Sherlock said, "where were you early Wednesday morning?"

"Oh, come on, Agent—"

"Where were you, Alexander?"

"I was at home asleep. Alone. Where do you think? At some nightclub drinking my brains out? I certainly wasn't at the hospital disarming a guard and killing Willig. I'm sure there are cameras at the hospital. Look at them. You won't see me." He paused. "But you've already looked, haven't you?"

"Yes, we looked, and no, we didn't see you," Savich said.

Alexander rose. "I want to go home."

"Where were you this afternoon about four o'clock?"

"Why?" Gardener asked.

"Tell us where you were, Alexander," Savich said.

"I was in my office at the Smithsonian, finishing the paperwork for the acquisition of one of Johnny Cash's guitars. Would you like my secretary's number?"

"Yes, thank you."

Alexander recited the number. "What happened this afternoon?"

Savich stood. "A crime that might be related. You can go now, Alexander. Venus asked me to tell you that she believes it best for both of you if you stay at a hotel until this is cleared up. She's booked you a suite at the Dupont Circle Hotel. Isabel is sending clothes over. You're to call her if you need anything else."

There was an instant of hot silence. Alexander half rose, leaning again toward Savich, this time nearly snarling. "You and I both know this banishment from my home is your doing, Savich. I won't forget it."

Gardener laid his hand on Alexander's shoulder. "Let's go, Alexander."

Savich said, his voice matter-of-fact, even gentle, "Agent Hamish will escort both of you out of the building. Thank you for coming."

Savich and Sherlock watched them walk down the long hall to the elevator. Sherlock said, "That went about as expected. He didn't do it, Dillon. He's perfect for it, from his supercilious nose down to his Gucci tassels. Makes you want to run with the evidence and try to nail him to the wall. But he's not a moron. It's all too pat, too convenient, and wheeled right up to our doorstep and dumped so we'd have to step in it. Makes me nuts."

Savich cursed, nothing really nasty, but still, it surprised her. He was upset. "And someone went to a great deal of trouble to make us believe he's guilty. So here we are, twisting in the wind. Sorry, sweetheart, I lost it."

She hugged him. "I think I heard Sean say something like that under his breath just the other day. No worries."

Savich lightly ran his fingertips down her cheek. "My heroine of JFK. It has a nice ring to it."

"I sort of like it, too, but one has to be modest, you know?" She kissed him. "There are too many threads dangling to deal with tonight. Tomorrow morning we'll have the videos. Maybe we'll see who pushed Delsey into traffic."

"If Delsey's smart, she'll go back to Stanislaus and put all of this behind her."

Sherlock didn't think she would and knew Dillon didn't think so, either. The heart wants what the heart wants. All too true. She'd watched Delsey and Rob in Captain Ramirez's office. Even though Delsey was furious with Rob, there was still something between them, something deep and urgent, maybe even something lasting. She said, "You know Sean's over at Lily and Simon's house for a sleepover. I always think the house feels different without him. I know I'll keep listening for him—those little snorts he makes in his sleep, his bare feet padding to the bathroom."

"Tonight, Lily and Simon will hear the little snorts and the padding feet." He pulled her against him, brought her close. Since they were alone, she leaned up and nibbled on his chin, then kissed him, whispered in his mouth, "Let's go home, Dillon, and make everything right again with the world."

He looked down at her beloved face. "What a nice idea," he said.

49

Gloria Swanson knew if she ever got famous enough to write a memoir, this day would rank right up there with winning her first Oscar.

She'd been called back that morning for a second audition for the role of Detective Belle DeWitt in *Hard Line*, a new HBO cop series, slated for release in January. It was the part she'd been waiting for since she'd moved to L.A. two years ago, and she knew she'd nailed it. She kept staring at her cell phone, willing it to ring. Euphoria didn't come close to how she felt, until she took that call from Detective Arturo Loomis of the Santa Monica police warning her she was on a list and could be the Starlet Slasher's next victim. He told her the smart thing to do was to leave town for a while. Like that would ever happen, not when the gold ring was nearly on her finger. Besides, she wasn't the kind to run away.

She cursed herself for not getting a gun when she'd first arrived in L.A., but thanks to Detective Loomis, she'd get one now. She drove her Toyota to East L.A. and bought a .22 revolver from a street kid who'd knocked a hundred bucks off the price for the butt-ugly little gun because she was so beautiful.

One of her long-ago boyfriends in Toledo, a bad boy her parents knew nothing about, had taught her how to ride a hog, roll a joint, and how to aim and shoot a pistol. No way was she going to be number seven on that madman's hit list.

She'd known Deborah Connelly, sure, she lived only two streets away, but not much more than to say hello. She hadn't particularly liked Deborah, a holier-than-thou sort of girl, playing the good girl in a town where it paid to know when to accept an offer and to know who was doing the offering. She had to admit she'd been surprised when Deborah got her role in *The Crown Prince*. Well, she hadn't finished it, had she? Gloria felt a stab of guilt and said a prayer for Deborah. It was too bad no one had warned her.

Her cell played the theme from *Happy Days*. It was her agent, Austin DeLone. Casting had called to offer her the part. He was as euphoric as she was, as her parents would be when she called them with the news. She bought a bottle of good champagne, opened it in her living room, drank deeply, and let emotion wash over her. She turned on some music and drank as she danced, right out of the bottle.

Finally, she was on her way to being a star. The part of Detective Belle DeWitt was perfect for her. She was hot and smart and street savvy. So what if Gloria was sleeping with the producer? He was easy enough to please, the old horndog. And he hadn't been toying with her, he'd gotten her the audition, probably thrown in a good word for her. It was the way of the show-business world, something her parents couldn't begin to understand or accept. Her agent hadn't believed they'd even let her in the door, but they'd ushered her in, openly admired what they saw—a caramel-skinned, six-foot gorgeous Amazon with perfect white teeth, thanks to her dentist mom.

It was her first big break. Sure, she'd scored some small roles, mainly because she was so striking, but nothing that put her in the lights. She got a waitressing job at *Burgundy's*, the current "in" café in Beverly Hills, fully aware that every important producer dropped in for lunch at one time or another. She was careful about who she went out with, who she slept with. She was sure the men realized she was using them as much as they were using her. It didn't matter, everyone was happy, especially Gloria, especially now. She was about to be Detective Belle DeWitt, a badass cop in Baltimore. Was Belle short for something else? She'd have to ask.

Would Detective Belle DeWitt be her breakout role? They'd even asked her if she liked her character's name when she'd done her second audition, and that had made her glow.

An old geezer on the showrunner's team, a genius with a camera, she'd been told, claimed he'd filmed the original Gloria Swanson when she'd roared through

Hollywood back in the day. He asked if she was related, since she looked so much like her, and he'd laughed and laughed at his own joke.

She drank more champagne from the bottle, rubbed her mouth. She wasn't hungry, her stomach was too jumpy.

She thought again of Deborah and wondered if she should make an appearance at her funeral. It meant she'd have to be nice to Doc, that boring stick-in-the-mud doctor Deborah had been practically engaged to, who'd hated that Deborah was an actress. If he had such a burr up his butt about it, why had he wanted to marry her? Yes, she'd go. She owed Deborah that.

She was pretty buzzed when she started her nightly ritual. She closed all the draperies, checked every window, dead-bolted the door, and set the burglar alarm, installed thanks to her parents.

When she was finally in bed, the AC set on high and her new .22 beside her on the bedside table, she settled in and picked up the latest copy of *Vanity Fair* and tried to concentrate, but all she could see was a future photo of herself, proudly holding up her Baltimore PD badge. Looking hot, of course.

It was a quarter to one in the morning when she finally closed her eyes.

WAKE UP, GLORIA.

Her eyes flew open and she was fully alert. Her heart was pounding, the covers tangled around her legs. That voice, it was loud and clear. It was Deborah's voice shouting at her to wake up, but Gloria knew that wasn't possible. She shook her head. A dream? Sure, she'd been thinking about Deborah and she'd dreamed about her, that made sense, but she was wide-awake now, her champagne buzz gone, and she was scared. She looked at her bedside clock. 1:59.

She grabbed her .22 off the bedside table, felt the cold steel against her fingers, her palm. And waited, listening for all she was worth. She heard something. No, her brain was playing tricks on her because she was scared. She hadn't heard anything, it wasn't possible. But she clutched the gun to her chest, not moving. *You have a gun; he can't kill you. Don't make a sound, just breathe, listen, focus.*

And then she heard it, the sound of the window slowly sliding up in her second bedroom, nearly noiseless, but she knew the sound. Why hadn't her state-of-the-art alarm gone off?

She hadn't actually believed the serial killer would come, even after Detective Loomis's call. How many hundreds of wannabe young actresses were there in L.A.? And how could she have gotten on that madman's hit parade? At least she wasn't asleep, and she had a gun. No way was he going to slash her throat, no way was she going to be his seventh victim.

Gloria slipped out of bed, molded her pillows into her shape and covered them with lots of blankets, and that made sense since the room was cold from the full blast of the air-conditioning. She backed away and slipped down to her knees behind her ancient red velvet chair, a present her grandmother had given her for luck in LaLa Land. She concentrated on stilling her breathing, slowing the wild pounding of her heart. She was used to doing that each time she performed, but this was real and it wasn't the same. She realized she'd forgotten her cell and ran on bare feet to the bedside table, pulled her cell out of its charger, fell to her knees and crawled back behind the big chair. She fumbled, finally managed to press 911. She heard the operator's calm voice asking what was her emergency and she whispered, "The Starlet Slasher is in my house. Hurry, please hurry." She punched off, not wanting him to hear her, knowing her address would show up on the operator's screen.

Would the cops get there before he walked into her bedroom? Her heart was still beating so loud she wondered if he'd hear it as he came closer. She heard a board creak. He was in the hallway, outside the bathroom. Would he hear her breathing? Would he smell her fear and know she was awake? He could have a gun as well as a knife. Would the lump in her bed fool him at all or would he start shooting?

He was outside her bedroom door. She heard his breathing, slow and easy, as he pushed on the partly opened door. She felt the air change as the door swung inward, though she hardly saw it because it was very dark. She knew he was looking into her bedroom, toward her bed. He stepped into the room. She saw the brief flicker of a small flashlight, aimed directly at her bed, at the lump beneath the covers, then it was dark again. He didn't want to take the chance of waking her up.

Gloria kept swallowing bile she was so scared. She could barely see him in the narrow shaft of moonlight coming in through the small opening in the drapes. He was tall and thin, but that was all she could see. He was wearing a cap pulled down low and something covered his face. Goggles? To hide his face? That wasn't in any of the news reports. And then she realized it was to keep from being blinded by blood. Her blood.

He walked very quietly toward the bed. If she'd been asleep, she'd never have heard him. When he stood beside the bed, he bent forward, reached out his left hand toward the pillow where her head would be, and he raised his knife, ready to slice it across her throat.

Sirens shrieked in the distance. Her breath whooshed out. She jumped to her feet and fired, and she kept firing, staring right at him, focused, as she'd been taught, pulling the trigger slowly, steadily, though she was nearly blind now with fear and shaking from the adrenaline pumping through her. She fired until the revolver was empty, and she kept firing, and the small .22 clicked and clicked.

50

"I'm Detective Arturo Loomis, Santa Monica Police Department. I called you today to warn you about the killer and to suggest you might want to leave town for a while." He showed her his badge.

Gloria looked up at a scruffy-looking man in tight jeans and a Lakers T-shirt faded from too many washes, wearing ancient sneakers with no socks on his big feet. "Yeah, I remember you. I couldn't leave town, but your call sent me right out to buy a .22. You and the gun saved my life." Arturo heard only a slight tremor in her voice. She was trying to keep it together.

He straddled a kitchen chair, crossed his arms over the back, and scooted it close to her. He studied her a moment. She was gorgeous, young, and she looked exhausted, crashing from the adrenaline high, but she was trying to be tough, and Arturo liked that. "I like cats," he said, and nodded at her red-and-white cat-covered pj's.

She blinked, swallowed, and he saw a ghost of a

smile. "I do, too. I had to leave Lola at home with my parents."

"My tabby's a bruiser named Hank, jumps on my chest when he wants me to get up."

She stared at him. "His name's Hank?"

Arturo smiled, studied her amazing face. "Hank and I live only a quarter of a mile away, that's how I got here so fast. When you're ready, tell me what happened."

She'd rehearsed it, he realized, like a part, and so her recounting was straightforward and precise. "It seemed like he was standing over my bed forever, but I knew it had to be only a couple of seconds. It was the weirdest thing, but I was frozen, couldn't move. Then we both heard the sirens and he jerked up and everything inside me broke open, and I emptied my gun at him. A minute later I heard two officers banging on the front door, yelling at the top of their lungs, to scare him, I guess, if he was still here. But he wasn't. I told them he'd probably jumped out the window. I might have shot him, I don't know. They immediately went after him, but I guess they never saw him, and then you were here."

Arturo waited a moment, but she said nothing more. He saw her swallow, fist her hands. He said calmly, "There are a lot of us here now, looking for him. They'll be speaking to neighbors, checking garages, any empty houses. If he's still around, they'll find him." He pulled her empty .22 out of his jacket pocket.

"You'd have to be really lucky if you hit him. This is a crap gun."

She raised dark brown eyes to his face, her pupils still dilated. "I know, but it's all I could get. I thought I was a good shot. I really did my best to hit him."

She sounded disappointed. Excellent, more power to her. He watched her walk to the sink to get a glass of water, noticed her long legs that probably brought her height to his forehead. She filled a glass, looked at it and set it on the counter. He said to her back, "Even I couldn't have hit him with this sorry excuse for a gun unless I was nearly on top of him. You were scared, too, and the adrenaline rush makes you shake. How far away was he when you shot at him?"

"I was behind my big velvet chair, and he was standing by the bed, maybe ten, fifteen feet." She walked to the fridge and pulled out a nearly empty bottle of champagne, pulled the cork out with her teeth and chugged the last of it down. He couldn't help the grin when she swiped her hand across her face. "What chance is there you're going to catch this guy, Detective?"

"Depends on whether you hit him, and whether he's still anywhere near. Not much champagne left. What happened to the rest?"

She tossed the champagne bottle in the trash can beneath the sink and came back over and sat down. She gave him a huge smile and told him the role she'd won as Detective Belle DeWitt. "So I was a little buzzed when I went to bed, thanks to the rest of the champagne. I read *Vanity Fair* for a while, then fell asleep." She stopped cold, swallowed.

"What?"

"I don't know whether to tell you this because it sounds so unbelievable, but I heard a voice yelling at me to wake up." Her voice fell away and she searched his face. "You think I'm nuts, don't you?"

"Did you recognize the voice?"

"Look, I know it had to be a dream, no other explanation, but the voice was Deborah's. Deborah Connelly's." Her chin went up, daring him to call her crazy, but Arturo said, "It was only a matter of seconds before you heard him coming in the window in the second bedroom, right?"

He watched her push a hank of hair behind her ear. "Yes. You don't think I'm crazy, do you?"

"Nah, you're not the least bit crazy." Arturo stood up. "You did good. You're alive."

She cursed, full-bodied curses, then, "You don't think I hit him, do you?"

Arturo was charmed. He hadn't heard a fine ripe curse from a woman since his ex-wife. "They haven't found blood anywhere yet, no blood trail. Maybe they'll have more luck in the morning. So you knew Deborah Connelly?"

"Yes, and Doc. Not all that well, but well enough." She ran her tongue over her lips. "I didn't want to die like she did."

He rose, lightly laid his hand on her shoulder. "Ms. Swanson, I don't think I'll arrest you for firing an illegally obtained firearm. Your .22 will have to go in my report and into evidence, but I don't think you'll be hearing from the D.A."

She rose and shook his hand. "In that case, you can call me Gloria."

A black eyebrow went up. "Gloria. Gloria Swanson."

"The new and updated version. One of these days I'm going to be famous and you'll tell everyone how you met me."

Arturo turned at the sound of voices to see Cam and Daniel in the kitchen doorway. "Come in, guys, and let me introduce you to Gloria Swanson."

Cam shook Gloria's hand. "Ms. Swanson, I'm delighted to meet you. You're alive and well and that pleases me more than you know. I know you've already been talking to Detective Loomis, but we need to hear it all, too. Arturo, if you could stay, break in if you think of more questions?"

Arturo raised his hand in the middle of her second recital of what had occurred. "I'm not clear about something. When did you call 911?"

"Sorry, I forgot. I'd practiced each step I'd take if he broke in, but then I forgot my cell. I crawled back to my night table to get it, and called 911." She swallowed. "It was only a couple of minutes before he opened the bedroom door."

Daniel said, "One more time. Can you describe him?"

"It was really dark, but from what I could make out, he wasn't that young, like in his twenties, more like he was thirties or forties. I couldn't see his face with his goggles, and I can't tell you his hair color because the watch cap was pulled low. It was dark, too, like his clothes. He was on the tall side, at least six feet, I'd say, and lean. As soon as I started firing, he ran, fast."

Cam said, "Gloria, we've been searching for a connection among the women the Serial has chosen to attack. As you know they've all been actresses about your age. Have you been offered any important roles lately? Or competed in any auditions?"

Gloria grinned hugely at Arturo. "Yes, I won a huge role just today. I told Detective Loomis about it."

"And she's been celebrating with champagne," Arturo added.

When Gloria had told her and Daniel all about the role of Detective Belle DeWitt in *Hard Line*, Cam said, "Congratulations. Gloria, I know it takes a lot of talent and grit and luck to score a part like that. I'm sure you agree it often helps if you know people in the business, people who are willing to use their influence on your behalf. Did anyone in the business help you score that role in *Hard Line*?"

"Yes," Gloria said readily, "I know one of the producers of the show."

"What's his name?" Daniel asked.

"Theo Markham, he's big-time TV and movies. Strange, but he was helping Connie Morrissey before she was killed." Gloria shrugged. "I'm sure there were other girls he's helped. And there'll be girls after me. And who knows? Maybe there are more right now. Theo's a busy guy."

How long did he wait before he went scouting for Connie's replacement? "How did you meet Markham?" Daniel asked.

"I'm a waitress at *Burgundy's* in Beverly Hills, well, not anymore. I'm giving my notice tomorrow. I knew who he was when he came in for lunch one day and made certain he sat at one of my tables. I gave him great service, made sure he noticed me." She shrugged. "He called me two days later and we had dinner."

"How long ago was that?"

Gloria cocked her head at him. "Maybe three weeks."

"Did he ever talk about Connie Morrissey?"

"No. I've got to tell you, I was glad of it."

Cam said matter-of-factly, "You're sleeping with him?"

She gave them a smile. "He wouldn't want me to say. Truth is, I owe him big-time. He's changed my life."

Sex, Daniel thought, the currency in Hollywood.

All of them realized the well was dry. Cam said, "Where does your family live, Gloria?"

"In Toledo, Ohio. But I don't want them to know about this, not yet. They'd want to come out here or beg me to come home and stay with them. No, not yet."

"For now," Cam continued, "the press will know only that there was a break-in with shots fired, and no one hurt. You'll have a little time to tell your parents yourself, but not much. This is going to be a very big story when it breaks. Maybe going to visit your parents isn't such a bad idea."

Gloria was shaking her head. "Really, I can't. You don't know my relatives."

"You know your condo is now a crime scene. You can't stay here tonight."

"I've got some friends who'll put me up."

"No, that might be dangerous," Arturo said. "We don't know who the Serial is or where he is, or why he picked you this time, or whether he'll try again. He's never failed before. Hey, you could stay at the police station, in one of the holding cells."

Gloria gave him a look. "If there's no attached bathroom, you can hang that one up, Detective. But you can give me back my .22."

Before Arturo could offer his own house for her to stay at, Cam said, "Tell you what, you and I still have a lot to talk about. I'm staying with a friend of mine, Missy Devereaux, in Malibu, not far from the Colony. She's an actress, too. I'll check with her, but I'm sure she won't mind. Go ahead and pack a bag, and don't forget to bring your laptop and your cell phone. We can put you up until we get a better handle on this."

"I wish you'd said until you caught him."

Cam smiled. "I'll say it now. Come stay with Missy and me until we catch him."

Gloria smiled back and headed for her bedroom. "Missy Devereaux," she called back to the group in the kitchen. "I think I've lost a couple of auditions to her."

51

Missy stood in the kitchen doorway, hands on her hips, wearing shorts, a tight orange tank top, and sneakers on her bare feet. Her hair was tousled all over her head and she looked about eighteen. Daniel swallowed.

"Gloria's already over at Cam's parents' place. When Cam told her who they were Gloria nearly frothed at the mouth she was so excited to meet them."

She poured Daniel a glass of orange juice. "You look tired. Drink up, it'll make you feel better." When he set the empty glass on the counter, Missy said, "What Gloria must have gone through—" She shuddered, then straightened, took a wide-legged stance and tried to look tough. "I wouldn't have fallen apart, either. Maybe I should get a gun like Gloria did."

Over my dead body. But Daniel wasn't stupid. "There are now three of you in the house, and that includes an FBI agent. You're safe."

Missy said, "Yeah, I know, you're afraid I'd shoot Blinker if he showed up again."

That isn't such a bad idea, but he said, "Another reason you shouldn't have one."

But Missy had moved on. "None of us could go back to sleep when Cam brought Gloria over, so the three of us went over Gloria's emails and I showed her my records, and we studied hers. You want to know what I think? The connections to Markham have got to mean something. I got to thinking I'd be pretty good at this gathering evidence thing, using my deductive reasoning on the facts I've gathered, and nailing a perp. That's what you call the criminal, right? The perp?"

"That's what they call the criminal on TV," Daniel said, watching her pick up the coffeepot, examine the remains, and set about to make a fresh pot.

She got the coffee going, turned back. "It's too bad I can't be a cop like you, Daniel, but seeing as how I like acting and I'm going to be a rich and famous star, it's not to be."

Daniel raised his eyes to the kitchen ceiling and moved his lips.

"What are you saying?"

"I'm thanking the power above that all is as it should be. The thought of you roaming the streets toting a gun and looking gorgeous makes my heart seize. Rich sounds good, though."

"You really think I'm gorgeous?"

Daniel slowly lowered his coffee cup to the table. "Well, yeah, you're okay, sure you are."

"Hmm. Why would your heart seize?"

"It's a condition of the men in our family. We see a woman with a gun and we're goners." He saluted her with his dinosaur mug. He heard Cam in the living room speaking on her cell. Good, she was here, he had some news for her.

He breathed in the smell of Missy's delicious coffee. "Has Blinker stayed away since Thursday morning?"

"I saw the bozo yesterday at the library, pretending to read a book. I caught a glimpse, it was *Pride and Prejudice*." She shook her head. "Isn't that a joke? That moron a Jane Austen fan? He acted all surprised to see me and I ignored him. He followed me out, but he did keep his distance."

"You're messing with my heart again, Missy. You've got Cam here and Gloria." He saw immediately it was the wrong thing to say. "If I were Blinker I'd already be afraid of you."

She preened. "He should be, the little putz. Isn't there anything more you can do, Daniel?"

Yeah, I could tell him I'll beat the crap out of him if he doesn't stay a hundred miles away from you. "Let me think about it. And let me know if you see him again." He looked toward Cam, who stood frowning in the kitchen doorway.

"That was LAPD forensics on the phone. Six bullet holes and a broken window, but no blood anywhere, no tracks."

Daniel saluted her with his mug. "Come on, Wittier, all is not lost. Let me cheer you up. Remember your parents mentioned how excited Connie Morrissey was about an audition she was scheduled for right before her murder? I phoned her agent, William Burley, at Gush. He remembered the role—are you ready for this? It was the female lead in *The Crown Prince*."

Missy said, "And Theo Markham is the producer."

"Correct," Daniel said. "Burley said Markham's assistant called him, told him the audition was a formality. The role was Connie's."

"Same role Deborah had when she was killed. Now that can't be a coincidence." Missy danced to Daniel, threw her arms around him and gave him a loud smacking kiss. She pulled back, grinning. "Well done, Kemosabe. Isn't he something, Cam?"

Cam was staring at Daniel. "I wonder why Mr. Markham didn't mention that nugget when we talked with him? Why would he not want us to know? I mean, why would we think he'd be involved in killing off actresses after giving them roles in his own movies? It makes no sense."

Daniel said, "What if Connie threatened to kiss him off if he didn't give her the role? What if she infuriated him somehow and he killed her, using the other murders as cover?"

Cam took a drink of coffee, frowned and stuck it in the microwave, punched in thirty seconds.

"Cam? That's Daniel's coffee. Let me pour some for you, in your Princess Elsa mug."

"What? Oh, I'm sorry, Daniel."

"Not a problem, you're warming it up for me."

Missy said, "It's disgusting that Theo Markham is

already sleeping with another actress. But, Daniel, I don't think he murdered Connie. He paid her rent, introduced her to producers, and the way she talked about him, I think she really cared about him, and he cared about her. She wouldn't have threatened to leave him if he didn't give her a role." She paused, then said, "You don't think he tried to murder Gloria, too, do you, guys? I simply can't see Mr. Markham creeping around at midnight killing actresses in their sleep. That'd make him a psychopath, seriously over-the-edge crazy."

Daniel said, "We can't exclude him, Missy. He has alibis for four of the six killings, but the four have huge holes in them. Even though there's no record of his flying to Las Vegas to kill Molly Harbinger, commercial or private, he could have easily driven."

"Before you go," Missy said, "I forgot to tell you that Doc called a few minutes before Daniel got here. He wanted to discuss Deborah's funeral arrangements. He wanted me to ask you when the medical examiner will release her"—Missy swallowed—"her body."

"You can tell him Monday. They have more tests, and the M.E. wants to go over the autopsy findings again."

Missy said, "Poor Doc, it's so hard on him. He's such a mess."

There was a knock on Missy's door. Daniel's hand automatically went to his Beretta, but he smiled when Arturo's voice sounded out. "Hey, anybody home?"

"Come on in," Missy called back.

When Arturo strolled into the living room, Daniel

said, "I expected you to be at the station or at the hospital. What brings you here?"

"I have something for you, but first, where's Gloria? I wanted to see if she remembers more about last night. Is she around?" He looked at Missy. "Are you Missy Devereaux?"

Missy stepped up, shook his hand. "Yes, I am, and, I might add, a future star. You're Detective Loomis?" At his nod, she continued, "Gloria's not here, she's at Cam's parents' house in the Colony."

Cam said, "She was having such a good time with them, I left her there for the morning. We can all go over there later, maybe have some lunch."

Missy shook her head. "Bummer. I have an audition for a buttermilk commercial. Actually, I have to go get ready. Good luck, guys." She padded out of the kitchen.

Daniel said, "Arturo, you have something for us?"

"Come, sit down," Cam said.

Once seated, Arturo said, "It's about Dr. Mark Richards's alibi for Tuesday night, the night Deborah was murdered. He claimed he'd stayed at the hospital all night. We thought we'd interviewed everyone who could verify he'd been there, but it turns out we missed someone because she'd switched to day shift. I found her, spoke to her. She thought Dr. Richards was in the doctor's on-call room, sleeping, but she needed him, and when he didn't answer his page, she checked. He wasn't there. She wondered where he was, but then got busy and forgot it. She says she did see him coming out of the on-call room later, like he just woke up. But there was a sizable gap, and he wasn't where he said he was.

"Remember he's a runner, so he could have run to Deborah's place, killed her, and run back. I timed it, twenty-eight minutes. He could have easily avoided the cameras in the hospital. That late, who would even notice a guy out running?"

Cam said more to herself than to anyone else, "No, I can't be that wrong about somebody."

Daniel patted her arm. "Maybe you're not wrong, but I've got to wonder why Theo Markham is so convinced Doc murdered Deborah. What reason could he have?"

Cam said slowly, "It seems to me it's got to have something to do with Connie Morrissey. But what?"

Arturo said, "Or maybe Doc did kill Deborah, and Markham found out about it."

Cam looked around. "If that's the case, just shoot me."

Daniel said, "Let's not be hasty, Wittier. Look, Gloria's a good reason to talk to Markham again, that and why he didn't bother to tell us he was about to give *The Crown Prince* role to Connie before she was murdered and then the role went to Deborah. We might get more out of him if we go tell him about Gloria before he finds out from the media."

Cam nodded, stood up. "Arturo, why don't you talk to Gloria at my parents' house while we're gone? We'll hook up with you there later."

52

Savich knew he was being perverse for not wanting to crate Alexander Rasmussen up and ship him to Attica, but his gut simply wouldn't allow it. Alexander was probably Venus's smartest progeny. He was also too sly, too willing to torpedo ethics when it suited him, as he had when he embezzled money from his New York law firm. But if Alexander had decided on a head-on battle with his grandmother, to unseat her from her throne at Rasmussen Industries before she wanted to retire, and he'd decided on murder, he would have gotten away with it, no doubt in Savich's mind. Nor could he see Alexander hiring Willig—he was more the type to sink into the shadows and wait until the timing was perfect. Nor would he ever leave evidence behind. That wasn't Alexander. He was many things, but Sherlock was right, he wasn't stupid. He hadn't tried to murder his grandmother. And that left the big question—who was framing him?

It had to be someone close, very close, most likely another family member. But who? Glynis, as shrewd and ruthless as Alexander, but less driven? Less ruthless? Besides, she'd simply ask for more money, and probably get it, not plot her own grandmother's murder. Hildi? Did she hate her mother for paying off her husband and getting him out of her life? A hippie artist, was Hildi capable of that? And faithful Veronica, fiercely loyal and protective of Venus, with her for fifteen years? Had Veronica been the one to fabricate evidence to bury Alexander, to cover her own guilt? She certainly had all the opportunity she could want. But why?

His cell belted out Little Big Town's *Tornado*.

It was Cam, calling from Malibu. His brain happily switched gears. "Hi, Cam. Thanks for the heads-up about the actress Gloria Swanson. You've got something new now?"

"Not a lot, Dillon. We're back to making sure Doc—Dr. Mark Richards, Deborah Connelly's boyfriend—didn't kill her. One of the LAPD detectives, Arturo Loomis, found out he couldn't account for over forty minutes around the time of her murder. Doc claimed he was asleep in the break room."

"What about security tapes?"

"There aren't any in the doctors' break room, and there's only one security camera in the stairwell beside the room, but easily spotted, easily avoided."

"What about the cameras in the parking lot?"

"His car never moved. But Deborah's house is only about a half mile away from the hospital, and he's a runner. He knows the area, so he could have avoided all the cameras. But we don't even have a good focus on the motive yet, Dillon. The Serial could be a complete stranger, someone completely off our radar."

"But you don't think so. You're looking at Markham."

She paused, and Savich waited.

"We've been looking for whatever connects all the victims, for a single motive, though of course a Serial might not have anything like a motive we'd recognize. But unless something falls into our laps, it's our best approach. And it's turning my brain into mush. One path suggests another, and those lead to dead ends. I'm being sucked under for the third time, Dillon. Maybe you should send out another agent to lead the case. I'm clearly incompetent."

Savich smiled. "I know the feeling well."

"You said in a class at Quantico that when you can't see the forest through the trees, get an ax."

He laughed. "Yes, simplify. Seems to me your cases may not be connected in a straightforward way, Cam. It's even possible you're looking for more than one murderer given what our M.E. said. I suggest you focus on Deborah Connelly's murder. Dump everything else out of your brain, the auditions, all the obvious connections among the actresses. When you solve her case, you'll see what connects all the murders, and everything will fall into place."

Cam paused again. He heard her draw a deep breath. "Good advice, Dillon, all my focus is now on Deborah Connelly. Thank you."

"Trust your gut, Cam. At the end of the day it's all you've got."

He rang off, thinking about what he'd just told Cam. Simplify. Back to basics. Time to take his own advice. Savich woke MAX out of sleep mode again. Even clever people left more trails in the Cloud than they even dreamed existed. MAX was his bloodhound in cyberspace. Maitland had told him once he didn't ever want to know where Savich took MAX to mine all his data. He was certain Maitland wouldn't want to know this time either.

He scrolled through his preliminary information about Veronica again, all of it expected, pedestrian, really, except for the bust for marijuana back in the day, and that was only a point of interest. A short bitter marriage to an army major, no children. He looked up when Sherlock stuck her head in the door.

"Dillon, we've finished studying every bit of footage from retailers' security cameras and traffic cams near K Street. Griffin spotted a guy standing very close to Delsey at the intersection just before she was pushed into traffic. But the guy's in a crowd, and he's wearing a hoodie and sunglasses, showing a bit of jaw and that's it. Griffin wants you to have a look at it."

Savich nodded. "Let me see it."

"The reason I came in, though—and this is a surprise—Veronica is here. She says it's important."

Savich glanced down at MAX's screen, a summary of Veronica's grades at Smith, mainly Bs and As, psychology major. He punched several keys, and MAX's screen went black. "Let's see what she's got to say."

53

Savich found Veronica seated next to Shirley's desk, laughing at the photo of Shirley's Pomeranian enthusiastically licking her face. "His name is Barker," Shirley was saying, "after the old show host. He's a yapper, particularly when he sees me eating bacon, which is way too often." She looked at Savich. "You've told me Barker is Astro's cousin when it comes to bacon."

"Only difference is Astro prefers turkey bacon. Come, Veronica, let's talk." Savich touched Veronica's hand, nodded to the CAU conference room. Sherlock joined them.

Once she was seated, Veronica said without preamble, "I had to insist on taking Venus to see Dr. Pruitt this morning. What happened between her and Alexander last night, your insisting he move out of the house, on top of that horrible man Willig trying to shoot her, it's all having a very bad effect on her, though she's trying to hide it. Her blood pressure was way up this morning, and she didn't look well. Dr. Pruitt told her all the stress she's been living under would be too much for a twenty-year-old, but a twenty-year-old didn't have to worry about a heart attack and she did. He told her she had to face the fact that she wasn't a spring chicken any longer and she simply wasn't up to all this nonsense. He said at her age a heart attack could kill her, and that's why I'm here. She needs answers, Dillon. Can you tell me anything I can pass along to her? Or could you speak to her yourself?"

"Is she home resting?"

"Ha! Not a chance. You know Venus, she's at Rasmussen Industries, in her big corner office, running things as she always is. She says if her heart goes, it goes, but she isn't going to lie around with her feet up, waiting for it to happen. She's got work to do."

Sherlock said, "In other words, she insists on living her life until she drops."

"Yes, that's it exactly."

"What did Venus say to you about Alexander, Veronica?"

"I hate this, Dillon, I really do. Venus asked me what I thought. When I didn't answer right away, she bowed her head, didn't say another word. I should have reassured her, I know that now, but—"

Sherlock said, "So you believe Alexander is guilty?"

"Venus told me about the evidence you found against him—the arsenic in his medicine cabinet, those phone calls to Willig. Honestly, I can't imagine it, but—" She shrugged her shoulders.

"Veronica," Savich said, "are you currently having,

or have you ever had, an intimate relationship with Alexander?"

Veronica jerked back in her chair. "Me and Alexander? Goodness, no, Dillon, of course not. He's never been interested in me that way, nor I him, I might add."

"Why?" Sherlock asked. "He's good-looking, smart, successful."

"Let me say that Alexander's always very polite to me, scrupulously so, for the fifteen years I've been with Venus. But I've always been aware he regards me as a kind of servant, not deserving of his attention, a very upstairs/downstairs mentality."

"One other quick question," Savich said. "Venus goes to her office every day, has for years. I've wondered why she believed she needed a companion fifteen years ago."

Veronica smiled. "One week before she hired me, Venus had a real scare. She had the flu, and maybe it affected her heart rhythm, but she passed out. If Isabel hadn't happened to come in her room that morning, she might have died. Venus decided she wanted someone who would always be there, making sure she put her feet on the floor in the morning. She never had that particular health problem again, but Venus and I really hit it off and she asked me not to leave.

"To tell you the truth, I chafed at first. I mean, the pay was good, but what was I to do with myself? I could read only so many books, walk so many miles since I never accompanied her to work. It was Venus who told me I was free as a bird during the day, so why not spread my wings? Why not decide what I most wanted and do it. I did."

"And what was that?" Savich asked her.

"I started a small retail website for women's clothing, as a reseller. It's called Classic Threads." She smiled. "Actually, it's made what to me is a bundle over the years. I put a lot back into the business, since Venus sees to it that I don't have to worry about money day to day. Nowadays, I'm up against big-time competition, but my reputation is well established, my prices are competitive, and I've got a huge reach geographically. Plus I've established some great relationships with my suppliers."

Sherlock said, "Classic Threads, good website name. I'll look you up. Venus must be really proud. Veronica, do you know if Venus is going to be at her office until this evening?"

"No. She promised me she'd be home by four this afternoon. But what about Alexander? Are you going to arrest him? Is he going to be able to live at home again?"

Savich sat forward. "This is difficult, I know, for you, for everyone in the family. About Alexander, we'll have to see. In the meantime, I'm sure you'll keep your eye on Venus, help her in any way you can. Tell her we'll be speaking to her, and soon. Thank you for coming."

As they escorted Veronica out of the conference room, Sherlock said, "Have you seen Rob Rasmussen since Tuesday night at the mansion?"

"No, why?"

"Just curious. What did you think of him?"

"Well, I have to say I have fond memories of the boy, but I don't know the man yet. He's got those unmistakable Rasmussen good looks. From what Venus tells me, he's turned into a model citizen, a good businessman. But I think he'll have to convince the rest of them, though. Tuesday night he was obviously on his best behavior, wanting everybody happy he was back." She sighed. "He's not at all like Alexander, thank goodness."

Veronica paused, looked up at Savich. "I know you and Alexander don't get along, but do you think he's guilty of trying to murder his own grandmother?"

He only smiled. "Thanks again for coming, Veronica."

54

When they stepped off the elevator at the Culver Building an hour and a half later, Markham's assistant showed them into his office without a word. Markham rose slowly from behind his desk. He said something to a man seated in front of his desk and the man left quickly, not meeting their eyes.

"Forgive Bobby, he doesn't like cops. I find accountants rarely do. His brother's in prison for embezzlement." He eyed them. "So why are you here again? I've already cooperated with answering your questions, more than I needed to. So why am I still in your loop?" He laid his fist against the top of his desk.

Cam said, "We're here to tell you that Gloria Swanson was attacked last night in her home in Santa Monica."

Markham looked like he'd been shot. He stared at them, not speaking, obviously shaken.

"She's all right," Daniel said. "She saved herself. One of our people called some of the actresses we were worried might be possible targets. Gloria bought a gun and when the Serial came, she shot at him but didn't hit him. Unfortunately, he's still at large."

Cam stepped forward. "Mr. Markham, are you all right? Would you like a glass of water?"

"No, no, thank you. She's really all right?"

"Yes, she's quite safe," Daniel said. "Can you tell us where you were last night, say around one a.m.?"

Markham stared blankly at Daniel as if he'd spoken in a foreign language. He moistened his mouth with his tongue. "You think I could have— You're crazy. I was at home, asleep, with my wife, in our bed. I left the house at eight o'clock this morning."

Cam said, "You never mentioned the lead role in *The Crown Prince* was about to go to Connie Morrissey before she was murdered. The same role you then gave to Deborah Connelly. The role she was playing when she was murdered on Tuesday night. You didn't think that fact would interest us? You didn't think our knowing that was important?"

He stared at Cam. "What? No, of course that was true, but I was in shock about Deborah's death and I didn't think of it." He looked back and forth between them, both of them hard-faced with not a bit of give. "Really, it didn't occur to me at the time. I'm not lying and besides, what difference does it make?"

"Where were you Tuesday night, sir?"

"Tuesday night?"

"The night Deborah was murdered."

"I was at the studio, studying rushes from *The*

Crown Prince. We ran really late that night. Then I went home."

"How long after Connie was murdered did you offer Deborah her role in *The Crown Prince*?"

"I don't remember, the auditions for the role were perhaps a week later, I don't know. Deborah won the part—I've told you this, told you that's why that madman Doc murdered her. I'm sure he fought her tooth and nail about it. Maybe she had enough and wanted to leave him. I know she was over-the-top happy when she was by herself filming in Italy those two weeks. I'll bet seeing him again, listening to him grill her, accuse her of sleeping with other actors—"

He ground down, shut his mouth.

Cam said immediately, "You're sleeping with Gloria and that's why you helped her get the lead in *Hard Line*, right?"

He stiffened. "This Gloria Swanson will be as famous as the first one and that role will be her springboard. She's as talented as Connie was. She deserves the role in *Hard Line*. She'll be excellent. Sleeping with her has nothing to do with it."

"But it didn't hurt she was sleeping with you, right? Like Connie Morrissey was sleeping with you? And now Gloria was almost murdered like Connie was, if she hadn't been smart. Help us out here, Mr. Markham. Make us understand. What does that say to you?"

"I don't know! Do you hear me, I don't understand any of this. You should do your job instead of badgering me—" He broke off and licked his lips again. "Did Gloria tell you we were sleeping together?"

"No, she didn't," Cam said. "As I recall, she said you would prefer she didn't say. But of course you were, just as you were sleeping with Connie."

"I have a family and I don't want my wife involved in any of this. We have an understanding, but that includes keeping our private lives out of the press. It would ruin things for me."

Cam wanted to punch him, but she steamed ahead, ignoring his last remark. "Did you have another secret? Like sleeping with Deborah? Is that why you gave her Connie's role in *The Crown Prince*?"

"No!" He fidgeted with a pen on his desk, then said, his voice sullen, "I saw her audition, realized she was born to play the role. Look, I didn't pay people to give roles to Connie or Gloria. The truth is, I did get Gloria the audition for the detective role on *Hard Line* because I know she's gutsy, savvy, and I know she'll nail the part, give the show more depth, more complexity. It was in my best interest. She shined at the audition, as I knew she would. She earned that role."

"And how about the actress who will replace Deborah Connelly in *The Crown Prince*? Is she currently on standby?"

"Of course not. That's insulting."

Cam leaned in. "How many actresses have been special to you, Mr. Markham? Any of the other victims?"

"I appreciate beautiful and talented women. They

appreciate my influence. I wouldn't hurt any of them. It's that Doc character you should be looking at."

Daniel said, "Is that why you hired a private investigator, Gus Hampton, to find proof Dr. Mark Richards murdered Deborah Connelly? Because you didn't believe we would look at him closely? Why are you so convinced Doc murdered Deborah?"

Markham gave them a disgusted look. He opened a desk drawer and pulled out a cigar, clipped it, fondled it between his fingers, and finally lit it. "My hiring Hampton wasn't a secret. I hired him because I concluded that you're fools. I've told you over and over about Doc and what he's like, but you've latched on to me instead."

Daniel said, "Why do you care so much? Why are you spending so much money to prove Dr. Richards guilty of murdering his girlfriend?"

Markham slashed his hand through the air, sending ashes flying from the cigar. "She might have been his girlfriend, but she was starring in my movie, the movie Connie was going to do. He did it, I know he did, because I saw them together and you didn't! Connie and Deborah were friends, I told you that, and Doc couldn't stand Connie because she stood with Deborah against him when he belittled her. He was rabid about her quitting her acting career. I saw it when they were together, and so did Connie." He was panting, beside himself. "I couldn't save either of them. They're both gone because of that monster!"

The room was silent except for his hoarse breathing. Markham drew himself up. "Richards is a monster. There is no doubt in my mind he murdered Deborah. I'll spend whatever it takes to prove it if you don't."

And he turned his back on them.

55

The Santa Monica police station was all modern angles and glass, with a pool and fountain outside, but inside, it was all cop shop, with suspects and victims leaking anger or misery, detectives on their cell phones or computers, their voices in constant conversation. After introducing Cam and Daniel to the police chief, Jacqueline Seabrooks, Arturo stopped by his desk to pick up his laptop, then took them to a conference room on the second floor. They saw through the two-way mirror that the room held a solid new table, a floor of shiny clean linoleum. Even the chairs looked comfortable.

Doc was the only one in the room. He was seated at the middle of the table, staring back at them although they knew he couldn't see them. He was wearing khakis, a short-sleeve Hawaiian shirt, and Tevas on his long tanned feet. His fingers were beating a light tattoo on the tabletop, clearly a habit he didn't even realize he was doing. He looked lost, defeated, still deadened with grief. They watched him drop his head into his hands.

Daniel said, "It looks to me like Doc's at the bottom of a well of grief. I've never known anyone good enough to fake that."

Cam felt the familiar surge of pity for him, closed it down. She fairly itched to run the interview, but remembered Dillon's words about letting local cops take the lead whenever possible. Let them shine when you can, the FBI will make a friend forever. And since Arturo had been the one to break Doc's alibi, she sucked it up. "Arturo, I've dealt with Doc only as a victim, and this has to be hard-edged. You interview him, and Daniel and I will stay outside and watch."

He gave her a surprised look, slowly nodded. "If he killed Deborah Connelly, he might also have tried to kill Gloria last night, would have, too, if she wasn't smarter than he is. Have I ever got a surprise for him. I'll check the recorder's on." Arturo walked slowly into the conference room.

He nodded to Doc, pulled out a chair and sat down. He didn't say a word, only studied him. Doc slowly raised his head, stared at him out of a face that looked sick and pale, that looked a decade older than when Arturo had seen him the day after Deborah had died. He didn't look like he cared about anything around him, didn't care he was sitting in a police station. He was only filling space, waiting. Arturo felt a moment of uncertainty, quashed it. Maybe he was misreading him, maybe what he was seeing was depression and regret for killing Deborah. Facts were facts. The guy had lied, pure and simple, no reason for it unless he'd killed her, sliced her neck open, trying to copy the Serial. He continued to study him.

Finally, Arturo saw a flick of fear on Doc's face at his continued silence. About time. Good, he was ready to go.

Arturo smiled. "Dr. Richards, thank you for coming to the station. You understand that our conversation today will be recorded? It's standard policy, for your protection as well as ours."

Doc waved his hand. There was misery in his voice when he spoke. "Of course, of course, anything to help find Deborah's murderer. That monster is still out there."

"Not for much longer," Arturo said, voice smooth and calm. "Trust me on that." He leaned forward, saw Doc's lips were dry and cracked. "Let's start again with where you were the night Deborah was murdered."

Doc reared back in his chair. "I already told you I was working at the hospital that night. I've told everyone who's asked me. The little boy I operated on earlier that day—Phoenix Taylor—he needed close attention. His parents were sleeping by the bed, they were upset, and so I spoke to them frequently, reassuring them. I had other duties as well, other patients to look in on."

Arturo said easily, "I know what you've told us, Doctor, but I want you to try to remember all the details. You weren't with the Taylor boy all night long, were you? Didn't you take bathroom breaks, get some sleep?"

"Yes, of course I did. Coffee can keep you awake only so long—" He paused, frowned. "You can't really nap on the floor, with all the machines beeping, all the lights and noise, so I remember now, I did go to the doctors' on-call room to catch a nap. I was exhausted, so I excused myself. I was gone for less than an hour. No longer, I know that."

"Sure, I can understand you needed a break, some rest. How do you know you weren't gone for longer than an hour?"

Doc shrugged. "I'm lucky if I get to sleep that long when I'm on duty. But I wasn't officially on call Monday night, so I set an alarm."

"Nice nap, Doctor?"

"Yes. And while I was sleeping . . ." His voice died away. He cleared his throat. "It was only a few hours before I found Deborah."

Arturo said, "Before we go any further, Doctor, there's a video you should see." He punched a key and Nurse Anna Simpson appeared on the screen. "Do you know this woman?"

"Yes, that's Anna. Why are you—"

"Listen to her statement, Doctor." Mrs. Anna Simpson looked square in her forties, a seasoned nurse, her voice firm and no-nonsense. She was asked to give her name, her length of service at the hospital, and to say in her own words what happened that night. "Monday was my final night shift for four weeks. I remember it was a little before midnight, a tough time if some of the patients can't sleep. Not as bad as 2:00 a.m. when—" She stopped, shook her head at herself. "In any case, one of Dr. Richards's patients, Joan Thomas, was asking for a sedative, and she hadn't been scheduled for one, so I needed a doctor to okay it. I knew Dr. Richards was at the hospital that night even though he wasn't on call because he'd operated that afternoon on a young boy, Phoenix Taylor. The parents were upset, not Phoenix—he was doing fine—but Dr. Richards stayed. He's like that, conscientious, always willing to spend time with a patient's parents if they need him to.

"I checked the floor but couldn't find him and he didn't answer his page. One of the nurses said she'd seen him going toward the doctors' on-call room. I checked. There was only one intern in there, Dr. Lyons, snoring like a bull. I'm very sure Dr. Richards wasn't there. I called his cell, but it went to voice mail. I didn't leave a message because Dr. Lyons came around and okayed the patient's sedative.

"It was nearly one o'clock when I saw Dr. Richards at the nurses' station, yawning. I was going to ask him where he'd been, but there was a call from the ER about an admission and things turned hectic. I didn't think much about it until you called and asked me. I'm sure Dr. Richards can explain where he was. There was no harm done."

Arturo turned off the video, sat back in his chair, crossed his arms. "Where were you, Dr. Richards, during that three-quarters of an hour?"

Doc blinked at him, cocked his head to the side. "I remember now. Nurse Simpson was right about Keith's—Dr. Lyons's—snoring being way too loud for me, so I went two floors up to the doctors' break room and slept there for a bit."

"The break room on the sixth floor?"

"That's right."

"Now that's curious, Doctor. There's a security camera right outside the door of the sixth-floor break room. We have video footage from eleven forty-five p.m. to one o'clock a.m. You are not on the footage, either going into the room or coming out." Arturo leaned forward. "It's time for you to tell me the truth. No more lies."

Doc stared at Arturo straight on, and said, his voice eerily calm, "I understand all this now. You think I hurt Deborah. I couldn't ever hurt her. I loved her more than my own life."

Arturo waved that away. "I hear what you're saying, Dr. Richards. But the fact remains you weren't in the hospital. Are you ready to tell me where you were during those missing minutes?"

"Yes, all right. This is the truth, I swear it. I went out to get some air—I needed some time alone to think, it hit me that night that I was moving into a house with Deborah, one step away from marriage. Don't get me wrong, I wanted to marry her. I didn't care if she ever succeeded in her acting career, I only wanted her to be happy. But I started doubting myself because with her role in *The Crown Prince* it looked like she would hit it big and I had to wonder if she'd still want me, want a family with me. How could I measure up to all those hotshot actors she'd be working with? And how would I deal with her fame?

"I jogged down to the beach and sat on the sand. Tuesday night was beautiful out, calm, nearly a full moon overhead. And it all came clear to me. I decided I wouldn't worry if she fell out of love with me, I'd have her for a certain time, and that would be enough. If she wanted to keep acting, I'd stop carping at her about it. I'd support her, completely, no more denigrating the industry. I'd do my best to help her, whatever it took. I wanted her, loved her; I wanted her to be my wife." Tears ran down his cheeks. Arturo said nothing.

Doc swiped his hand over his face. "I'm sorry. I ran back to the hospital. I don't know exactly how long I was gone, but it wasn't even an hour.

"Listen, Detective, I actually forgot about leaving the hospital when you first asked me, and then I realized Deborah was being killed the same time I was gone. I got frightened. I knew you suspected me of killing her, and so I kept quiet. I didn't think anyone had noticed.

"Then early the next morning one of the nurses woke me. I'd fallen asleep at the nurses' station, after all. She told me I had to get moving, it was a big day for me and Deborah. I was happy and I left and went home and found her." He simply stopped talking, stared blindly past Arturo, at her, Cam thought, as if he knew she was behind the two-way mirror, watching him, listening to him, weighing his every word.

"That's quite a story, Doctor. In my experience, innocent people don't generally lie to the police to avoid arousing suspicion. Let me tell you another story, one a jury is more likely to believe." Arturo sat forward, clasped his hands in front of him. "You and Deborah had a huge fight, maybe about that role she was playing in *The Crown Prince*, maybe about what she'd done in Italy for those two weeks she'd been gone filming, who'd she seen, gone out with, maybe slept with. Or maybe you fought about the producer, Theo Markham, the big shot you'd met at that party six months ago. How you despised him, thought he was a lecher, and here he'd hired Deborah to play this role. She'd be with him countless hours, here, in Italy, out of your sight."

"No! None of that's true, none of it!"

"Did you know, Doctor, that Theo Markham, the producer of *The Crown Prince*, Deborah's producer, was sleeping with Connie Morrissey? Did you know he was about to give the role in *The Crown Prince* to her before she was murdered? And then Deborah got offered the role. Surely you had to wonder if she'd betrayed you, if she'd slept with that corrupt debaucher to get the role?

"Or did Deborah break, finally see you as everyone else did—always belittling her, making her career seem unimportant, even immoral, always trying to get her to quit. How long would anyone take that kind of abuse?"

Doc rose straight out of his chair. "No, no! Look, I did have my doubts, yes, but Deborah loved me, she always loved me!"

"Do you know Markham is convinced you murdered Deborah? That he's even hired a private investigator to prove it? This man has a serious hate-on for you. Why? What is he to you, and what are you to him?"

Doc looked puzzled. Arturo would swear it wasn't an act. "Markham? I only met the man that one time. He's nothing at all to me."

"Then why is he convinced you murdered Deborah?"

Doc shook his head. "I don't know, but that's why you came after me, isn't it? Because of what this Markham says?"

"Do you know Deborah's neighbor Mrs. Buffet?"

"What? Mrs. Buffet? The whole neighborhood knows her. She's always watching everyone from her window. Why?"

"She saw the murderer leave Deborah's house, after midnight. Tall and thin, wearing a ball cap, which, she said, he pulled off to rub blood off his bald head."

Doc shuddered, touched his hair. "I'm not bald."

"No, so you wore a cap over your hair to protect you from the blood splatter. And you'd know to protect yourself, Dr. Richards. After all, you're a surgeon, you're used to blood, right?"

Doc shook his head slowly, back and forth, licking his cracked lips. "Why are you saying these things to me? This is all crazy."

Arturo, his voice soft now, leaned forward again. "She'd already cut you loose, hadn't she? Or was about to. You knew it and it burned you, destroyed everything you felt for her. She'd made you feel worthless, like less than nothing, but you held it together. You went to work as usual, but what she'd done festered. You'd given her two years of your life, supported her even though you hated what she was doing. So what if you wanted more for her, you were only being honest, right? That gave her no right to kick you aside. It gnawed at you, deep down, and then you remembered the serial killer who'd just killed again in Las Vegas and how you'd worried about him attacking Deborah. And then it came to you—what better cover was there? You knew he cut their throats. You could do that easily.

"I know you didn't take your car. There are cameras in the parking lot. Your car stayed put, which means you ran back to Deborah's house, not a problem for you. You're an athlete, a surfer, you can run. You gathered everything you needed, waited for your chance to tell everyone you were taking a nap in the on-call room, but you ran home, instead, and broke in like a burglar would, like the serial killer did. Deborah was asleep, as you expected her to be. She must have looked beautiful lying there, but I guess it didn't matter anymore, you hated the faithless bitch's guts."

Arturo leaned close, his voice dropped to a near

whisper. "Tell me, Doctor, how did it feel when you sliced open her throat?"

Doc was shuddering like a palsied man, sobbing, shaking his head back and forth.

"Before you closed her eyes, did you see her confusion, her horror, her terror?"

Doc was no longer shuddering, no longer sobbing. He sat silent, frozen, tears pooling in his eyes, and yet again he started shaking his head. "Why are you saying these things to me? I did nothing to her—I loved her; she loved me. I did close her eyes, I told that agent I did, I couldn't bear looking into her eyes and knowing I'd failed her, I wasn't there to protect her. I did not kill her. If you don't believe me, I don't know what else I can say or do."

"I know what you can do. You can take a lie detector test."

The pain left Doc's eyes, replaced by—what? Fear? Doc said, "I didn't think you were using lie detectors anymore, not accurate enough."

"Maybe not for court, but accurate enough for us. You're in our crosshairs now, Doctor, our prime suspect. You could save yourself and us all a lot of trouble if you take it and pass."

Doc said, "Yes, all right, I will. I did not murder Deborah and I'll prove to you I'm not lying."

"Good choice, Doctor. I'll be back in a few minutes. You want a cup of coffee?"

56

Cam shook Arturo's hand. "Good job getting him to go for the polygraph. I thought he'd be too smart for that."

Arturo gave her a twisted smile. "It's possible he might beat it. He's a doctor, knows how it works, knows the physiology. But if he's hiding something that might not be enough."

"You have someone good?" Daniel asked.

"Yeah, I do. Buzz Quigley, and he's here in the building. I'll bring him back with his machine, set him up in the interview room. I'll need a few minutes, though, to write out some questions he needs to ask."

Cam called after him. "We'll get Doc the coffee, talk to him a bit."

"Have at it," Arturo called back. "The recording equipment's still running."

Cam and Daniel walked in together, said hello to Doc as if nothing unusual was happening. Cam placed a cardboard cup of black coffee in front of Doc. "You like it black, right?"

"Yes, sure." He looked exhausted. He took a wary sip, nodded to himself, and drank more. He paused, seemed to collect himself, and drank again.

Daniel said, "Here at the Santa Monica Police Department, you get to drink Peet's, not the usual bitter burned stuff so popular in cop shops. Enjoy."

"Thank you." Doc looked back and forth between them. "I'm going to take a lie detector test. Of course you already know that. You were standing on the other side of that mirror, watching and listening, right? That's the way you do things."

"Right," Cam said, and pulled out a chair and sat down. "Doc, I know this is a really tough time for you, and I'm sorry we have to ask you these questions. But there's still a killer out there, and you did withhold information from us, so now we have to follow up. You understand?"

"Yeah, sure."

"Tell me, Doc, how well do you know Gloria Swanson?"

A small smile bloomed, briefly, then fell off his face. "Deborah knew her, thought she was a kick, and smart, too, as focused as Deborah is—was. I mean, she kept that name of hers. She was actually going to try to trade on it."

"Wouldn't you?" Daniel said.

Doc drank more coffee. "Sure, I guess. Anyway, she's a nice girl. I'm sure she competed with Deborah for lots of parts. I myself don't know her that well at all."

"Have you seen the news that she barely escaped being the seventh murder victim?"

He gaped at them. "Gloria? When? Is she all right?"

"Last night," Cam said. "And yes, she is."

"So she escaped? Good for her."

"You didn't know?" Daniel asked.

"No, I haven't been watching much news lately. Since Deborah died, I've been on leave from the hospital, at home in my old place, mostly. I haven't paid much attention. I spoke to Deborah's parents this morning, Agent Wittier, about her body being released on Monday. They're making funeral arrangements." He shook his head. "Isn't it odd how your world can come to a dead stop and the world outside keeps on going around you? I'm glad Gloria's okay."

Cam said, "Do you know where Gloria lives?"

Doc frowned, stared down into the cup. "I remember Deborah saying she lived close by, because her parents wanted her to be safe." He laughed, shook his head. "A good area, a safe area. Well, that didn't work. Who saved her?"

Cam said, "She saved herself. She had a gun. Did Deborah like her?"

"Yes, I guess so. I only met her a couple of times. We didn't talk about all that much. She wasn't really a part of our lives, you know? I'd say she and Deborah were like so many of the other young women out here trying to scratch their way into the movies or TV."

"What would 'scratch their way' mean exactly?" Cam asked.

Doc shrugged. "Some of them would probably run their own mothers down to succeed in the business. Was she different? Sorry, I really don't know."

He broke off, became statue still.

"Is that how you thought about Deborah, Doc?" Daniel was lightly tapping his fingers on the table. "When all was said and done, did you believe Deborah was so determined to make it big she'd hurt anyone she believed was an obstacle? Even you?"

"Of course not! Deborah wanted to succeed badly, sure. And she wasn't perfect, I mean, no one is, right? But"—he broke off, tears pooling in his eyes. He swallowed—"for me she glowed. She had this special light that shined on everyone she loved, including me."

Arturo walked into the room with a guy built like a linebacker, massive chest, maybe six five. The lie detector machine looked like a toy in his big hand.

"Everyone, this is Buzz Quigley, our examiner. Buzz, this is Dr. Mark Richards."

Buzz greeted everyone, found an electric outlet for his machine and started unpacking his kit. He asked all of them to witness Doc agreeing to taking the test voluntarily, without any undue pressure, and then he told everyone to leave the room, to watch and listen through the two-way mirror. When they next got a view of the room, Buzz had pulled out some sheets of paper, no doubt including the questions Arturo had prepared for him. As he hooked up the electrodes, Buzz began to tell Doc how everything would work, his voice matter-of-fact.

When Quigley was finished, he looked across the table and said in a calm deep voice, "Is your name Maxwell Mark Richards?"

"Yes."

"Are you thirty-three years old?"

"I am."

"Are you a pediatric surgeon at Children's Hospital here in Santa Monica?"

"Yes, I am, but still a fellow."

"You've been in the program for six years?"

"No, this is my fourth year."

Cam watched the needle, it was steady.

Buzz asked him a series of obvious questions, interspersing truth with fiction, and the needle remained steady. Then he said in the same calm voice, "Did you kill Deborah Connelly?"

Doc reared back in his chair and the needle went crazy for a moment. Slowly, it returned to baseline.

"Did you kill Deborah Connelly?" Buzz asked again.

"No, I did not." No movement at all.

Cam shot a look at Daniel and Arturo. He was telling the truth.

"Do you know who killed her?"

"No, I do not."

"Were you out walking the night Deborah Connelly was murdered?"

"Yes, I was."

"Were you walking on the beach near Santa Monica Pier?"

"Yes, I was." The needle spiked.

Doc couldn't see the spiking needle, but he cleared his throat. "I think I wanted to go down to the beach and sit and think, but looking back, I don't think I made it all the way down there. Sorry, since Deborah's death, I can't seem to think clearly."

The needle returned to baseline.

"Do you know Theodore Markham?"

"I've met him, but no, I don't know him."

The needle jumped, then fell back.

"Do you know why Markham believes you killed Deborah?"

"No, certainly not." The needle jumped.

A lie, but why?

Buzz said, "Did you sleep with any of Deborah's actress friends?"

"No. They did not interest me at all. I was faithful to Deborah."

Needle steady.

"Did you admire Deborah's actress friends?"

"Yes, some of them, but most of them—no." Steady, steady. The truth.

"Have you ever killed anyone, Doctor Richards?"

"Damn it, no!" The machine went haywire. Doc ripped off the tethers, roared to his feet, planted his palms on the desk. "Yes, yes, I have—I'm a surgeon, of course I've lost patients, of course I was responsible, they died under my care—of course I've killed people."

Buzz looked back at them through the mirror and nodded for them to come back into the room. The test was over.

When they filed back in, Doc's face was leached of color. He was huddled in on himself, the picture of misery. "Listen, I can't talk about this anymore, it's— it's too hard. I want to go home."

They cut him loose. They had no grounds to hold him.

57

Savich looked down at the tablet screen. Things didn't look good for Sherlock. "I hate to say this, sweetheart, but I came a lot closer to beating Captain Isbad. It pains me to say you're folding like a two-dollar suitcase. Aren't you even going to put up a decent fight?"

Sherlock looked up, grinned. "Captain Isbad is sly, Dillon, and ruthless. You can't believe a word he says."

"A two-dollar suitcase," Sean repeated. "Okay, I think I get it. Don't fold, Mama. What does *ruthless* mean?"

"It means you'll do almost anything to win," Sherlock said. "Sean, you're going to knock me over the head with that branch hanging down over the water up ahead, aren't you? Keep an eye on me, boyo, I can still make a comeback."

The Nitty Gritty Dirt Band sang out *Fishin' in the Dark*. Savich punched his cell. "Savich here."

He heard Veronica's voice, controlled, but she couldn't hide the worry. "Dillon, I was right about

Venus. She complained of chest pain, said she felt awful, but she refused to go to the hospital. She asked Dr. Pruitt to come over, and I left her with him. She's insisted on summoning the whole family, including Rob and Marsia. And she asked me to call her estate lawyer, Mr. Gilbert Sullivan, have him come over to the house, too. And you and Sherlock. Dillon, I think she's worried she's dying and that's why she wants everyone here."

"Sherlock and I will be over as soon as we can." Savich punched off his cell, pulled Sean against him, hugged him, kissed him. "Captain Isbad will have to wait to beat your mama another night, although from the looks of it, you've already got her on the ropes. We have to go out."

Sean pulled back in his father's arms, studied his face. "Papa, be careful, okay? And take good care of Mama?"

"It's not like that, Sean, but yes, we'll take care of each other. Are you ready, Sherlock?"

"Yes, it's time. I'll tell Gabriella we're leaving."

* * *

Isabel ushered them into the mansion. "The family is upstairs, in the sitting area across the hall from Ms. Venus's bedroom door, arguing, of course, now that Rob and his girlfriend have arrived."

No surprise in that. Savich and Sherlock followed Isabel up the wide staircase. Isabel said over her shoulder, "Mr. Sullivan has arrived as well. Ms. Venus told me to seat him in the living room. She wants to speak to you first, Dillon."

They found Guthrie, Alexander, and Rob grouped together across from Venus's bedroom, Marsia off to the side on a settee, speaking in voices too low to hear until Guthrie said out loud, "Enough is enough. I want to see my mother." He stepped toward the closed bedroom door only to draw up when one of Venus's guards barred his way.

Isabel stepped in, calling out, "Ms. Venus made it clear she doesn't want anyone with her, Mr. Rasmussen, except her doctor and Agent Savich."

Guthrie whirled around to frown at Savich.

Veronica said, "Dillon, come quickly, Dr. Pruitt said he was alarmed at how anxious she is to see you, and to show you in immediately. Let me tell Venus you're here."

"No, Veronica, please stay here with the family." He looked at each face, then at Rob and Marsia Gay, who gave him a tired smile. He nodded to Sherlock.

"Dr. Pruitt insists Grandmother wants to speak to you, but that's absurd. I don't even know why you're here." Savich turned as Alexander took a step toward him. "What could she possibly have to say to you that she can't say to us? What is this about? You're not even a blood relation, much as you may wish to be—instead of a loser cop."

Savich smiled, knowing it would only infuriate

Alexander more. Sherlock said from behind Alexander, "Don't tell Dillon's mother that, Alexander, she might shoot you."

"Well, that would be par for the course, wouldn't it? Guns and violence, that's what you're both about, like my little brother here."

Savich was pleased Rob kept his cool. "We're all here because Grandmother asked us to be, Alexander. I have as much right to be here as you do, as much as you may hate that fact."

"That's enough, both of you." Guthrie laid his hand on Alexander's shoulder. He took one last look at the guard, at Savich. "We will do as Mother wants. Come along now, we'll go downstairs."

Alexander shook off his father's hand. "And what, Dad? Have a drink?"

Guthrie shook his head, gave his eldest son a long look, and walked away.

Savich didn't give anyone time to say anything else, though he heard Rob call out his name. He nodded to Sherlock and slipped into Venus's bedroom, closing the door quietly behind him. As he flipped the lock, he heard Glynis's voice, high and out of breath from running up the stairs, then her mother, Hildi's, voice behind her, panting a bit, begging her to slow down.

He heard Glynis say, "So the gang's all here, I see. And handsome Rob as well. And the girlfriend. What was your name again?" She looked at Marsia but continued before she could speak, "Why all the excitement? Did one of you try to murder Grandmother again?"

Savich heard a babble of indignant, angry voices, Sherlock's calm voice sounding clearly over the lot of them. He turned to see Venus sitting up in bed, looking too pale. Dr. Pruitt was standing near the windows, speaking on his cell phone with someone at the hospital. He looked up, slowly nodded to Savich, and continued his conversation.

"Venus, everyone's here. Sherlock's in charge of crowd control outside your bedroom. How are you?"

Venus waved her hand. "I could hear them all arguing from in here. Of course, Alexander, primarily, accusing Rob of coming back only to murder me and Ms. Gay of being Rob's accomplice, though how that would work, I don't have the faintest idea.

"It always amazes me that Alexander never runs out of vitriol." She sighed. "Of course Alexander would be very happy if you simply disappeared, Dillon." She gave him a grin. "Sherlock is right, your mother would shoot him. I remember Buck, your daddy, what a man he was. Always ready for a joke, yet he could turn on a dime, and you'd see the FBI agent, flat eyes, all cop. I do miss him." She paused a moment, as if garnering her strength. "Come sit by me, Dillon. There's a powerful brew of emotions on the other side of that door. Volatile. All of them are afraid I'm about to pass to the hereafter, worried about what I've left them, hoping they won't be accused of trying to kill me. I do hope Sherlock will keep them apart."

Savich eased down on the bed next to her, took her hand. Her hands revealed her age, thick veins riding high beneath her parchment skin. But her nails were lovely, painted a soft pink. "You've never been a pessimist, Venus, so don't start now. They're all more worried about you than how much money you've left them. They all love you. Regardless of Alexander's antics, he loves you, too."

"Sometimes I wonder, Dillon. I wonder."

"Don't wonder. It's the truth, Venus. You must have heard Guthrie saying he was going downstairs, probably to escape the unpleasantness with a visit to the bourbon bottle."

"Poor Guthrie," Venus said. "He can't face life, any unpleasantness, never could. Angie protected him, but then she died and he dove into the bottle. He simply fell off the earth. It's been downhill for the last twenty years. Even working for Rasmussen didn't change his course."

"Rob's back. We'll see what Guthrie does about his youngest son. It might make a difference. Mr. Sullivan is downstairs in the living room. Are you ready to call him up?"

She sighed. "In a moment. I suppose I'm pleased you don't believe Alexander guilty, at least. He worries me so. I seem to have failed to teach him how to appreciate the people he works with, to value their creativity, help them flourish. He won't succeed unless he learns that, and so far I've failed—oh dear, I should shut up." The hand he held was shaking. "Maybe I should die, or step down, just go away, and let Alexander have whatever he wants. Maybe I should accept that I'm just an old lady causing a lot of trouble."

He rubbed his thumb over her hand to calm her and consulted his Mickey Mouse watch. "That's not the truth, Venus, and hiding from it isn't in your DNA. No one can change what's happened. All we can do is fix it. You've got to hang tough for a little while longer."

He leaned over and kissed her forehead. He looked into her fierce Rasmussen green eyes, still powerful with intelligence, now sheened with tears. He hated her pain. He said quietly, "Thank you for being in my life, Venus. My grandmother thought you were amazing. So do I. So does Sherlock."

He nodded, released her hand, and rose. "When he's a bit older, Sean will think so, too." After a moment Savich nodded to Dr. Pruitt, who was standing now against the draperies, his arms crossed, waiting. "I'll buzz down and ask Isabel to bring Mr. Sullivan up."

Venus nodded, leaned her head back on the pillow, and closed her eyes. "Yes, it's nearly time. Please get the family downstairs and yes, ask Mr. Sullivan to come up. It's time. I want to get this done."

58

Dr. Pruitt faced the family in the living room. "Mrs. Rasmussen is speaking with Mr. Sullivan, then she must rest. She will see each of you later."

"But there might not be a later," Hildi shouted. "Why aren't you with her? Why haven't you called an ambulance?"

Guthrie stood, squared his shoulders as if awaiting a blow. "Is she going to die?"

"You know your mother, Mr. Rasmussen. I would prefer to care for her in the hospital, but she refuses to go. I will return to her immediately." Dr. Pruitt nodded to each of them and left the living room.

Savich remained by the closed door, Sherlock by the windows, studying their faces.

Alexander stood in his favorite spot, by the fireplace, his hands in his pockets, his shock slowly turning to anger. He took a step toward Savich. "You were with her, not her children, her grandchildren—you, an outsider, who never belonged here. What did she say to you? You turned her against me, didn't you?"

Savich said, "Why would I do that?"

"Because you believe I tried to kill her, you tried to convince her—"

"Do be quiet, Alexander," Hildi said. "Please, just be quiet. Mother may be dying, and here you are yelling at Dillon, who, I might add, saved her life."

"Haven't you noticed she's changing her will?" Alexander said, ignoring her. "Sullivan's up there with her right now."

Guthrie looked beaten down, his hands dangling at his sides. "That would be appropriate," he said, "since Rob has returned home. Of course Mother would need to make adjustments."

Looking at him, Savich felt a stab of alarm.

"Adjustments?" Alexander said. "You can't be that dense, Father, and neither is Rob. What, little brother? Are you hoping Savich convinced her to put you in charge? Will you get her shares so you can run Rasmussen Industries yourself?"

Rob held to his temper. "Stop worrying about yourself, Alexander. Grandmother wouldn't think of naming me her successor. She knows I don't have experience running a company the size of Rasmussen Industries. She knows I wouldn't have any idea what to do."

Marsia rose to stand beside him, took his hand between hers. "You can learn if you have to, Rob. Your brother has to know you would learn quickly." Marsia shot Alexander a look of cold dislike.

Alexander ignored her, said to Savich, "You know what she's doing, don't you? Admit it, you know."

He shrugged. "All I know is that her lawyer Mr. Sullivan is with her. I'm sure you will find out everything in due course."

While Savich spoke, he studied Rob's face. He was pale, and he was suffering, Marsia still clutching his hand tight, leaning into him, as if keeping him upright.

Alexander said to Rob, "I see it all now. You came back into her life to ingratiate yourself. You know that's what you want, the big office, all that power."

Rob looked incredulous. "You really believe that, Alexander? You really think I wanted this? Even if that's what Grandmother wants, it shouldn't be happening like this, so fast, too fast. There hasn't been enough time." He shook his head. "I wish none of this was happening."

Alexander flicked a nod toward Marsia. "It's obvious she certainly wants it for you."

Marsia said, "You should look to yourself, Mr. Rasmussen, not blame your brother. He hasn't done anything except reconnect with his grandmother." Rob pulled away from her, stood alone, not looking at his brother now, but staring down at his shoes, misery radiating off him.

Savich studied the faces of the others, wondering if they, like Alexander, were concerned about possible changes Venus would make to her will and how it would affect them. Veronica was seated in a chair away from the family, not making a sound, her hands twisting in her lap, her eyes sheened with tears. Glynis was holding her mother's hand, looking from Rob to Alexander. For as long as Savich had known Glynis, he'd never been able to read her thoughts from her expression or her eyes, and she still remained opaque to him.

Rob whispered, "I don't want her to die. There hasn't been enough time to get to know her again."

"She won't, Rob, she won't." Guthrie walked over to his son and laid his hand on his shoulder. "I haven't been much of a father to you. But I would like to try now, if you'll allow me. I know the business, Rob, inside and out, even if I haven't been involved in decision making these past years. I could be at your side, if it comes to that. You should be there with us, Rob, it's your proper right, it's where you belong."

Alexander looked from his brother's face to his father's. His voice was curiously flat. "So you stand against me, Father? The son who never left, who's spent his entire life working for the good of the family? The son who—"

Veronica interrupted him, her voice gravelly with tears. "None of that matters. Don't you understand? I was supposed to keep her safe, watch over her, and I failed. This is my fault. She couldn't deal with all the stress, and how could she? She's an old lady.

"She didn't even talk to me about her will. Was she afraid I'd break confidence with her? I never have, not in fifteen years, surely she knows that. She's been like a mother to me, she's been my mentor, my biggest supporter." She turned whiplash fast on Alexander. "But you, Alexander, why couldn't you let her spend the rest of her life as she pleased? But no, you somehow found out about Rob, you saw the end coming, and you acted. Damn you, I hope she cuts you out of her will entirely for what you tried to do."

Alexander took a step toward her, stopped cold, fury pumping off him. "You bitch! How dare you accuse me of trying to murder Grandmother. Listen to me, all of you. I did not try to murder my own grandmother!"

Veronica's hands were fists. "All your meanness toward Rob, your spite, your pathetic efforts to discredit him in her eyes. You shoved him out once before, and you weren't about to let him back in to threaten your place in the company. Well, you failed, Dillon stopped you. You killed Willig, too, to keep him quiet before he could tell Venus it was you who hired him."

"That is a damned lie!" Alexander took another step toward her, but again, he stopped. He shook his head, looked around at his family. "Do any of you believe I put arsenic in my bathroom for the forensics team to find? Do any of you actually believe I called that criminal Willig, paid him to murder Grandmother?" He looked around, saw his words met with stone faces. "So all of you stand against me."

He met Savich's eyes from across the living room. "I will say this once again, then I am done. I never tried to kill Grandmother. I love her, even though I have occasionally wanted to strangle her, as I'm sure all of you have, for meddling in my life.

"If Grandmother dies, I will not allow the board of Rasmussen Industries to put you in charge, Rob. I will not watch Rasmussen Industries spiral downward with you and Father at the helm. I will fight you with everything in my power."

Veronica shouted, "If there is justice, you will be in prison for the rest of your miserable life!"

It was time to step in. Savich said, "Rob, everyone knows that Venus is a meddler, but always a well-meaning one. I'm willing to wager she will meddle in your life again."

"What do you mean? How could she meddle in my life?"

"When she is well again, I will tell her what I saw happen between you and Delsey Freestone. I will tell her about how Delsey got off the elevator at the Hoover Building on Tuesday and the two of you looked at each other and no one else existed. I recognized what passed between you because when I first met Sherlock, I had the same experience. As you probably already realize, Delsey's a live-wire in addition to being the sister of one of my FBI agents, and an immensely talented musician.

"When Venus meets Delsey, I think she'll fall in love with her, too. Of course none of you have yet met Delsey, but you will. I find it curious that you and Delsey met on Tuesday, you were together on Wednesday, and someone tried to murder her on Thursday."

59

Marsia slowly rose, looked around at the family, and laughed. "Agent Savich—Dillon—I'm sorry we didn't have more time to get to know each other. I'm hoping Mrs. Rasmussen will come to appreciate and love me as one of her own. I do not understand why you are touting this Delsey woman to Rob. He told me about meeting her on Tuesday at the Hoover Building. When he came over for dinner Wednesday night he said he'd seen her again, but there was nothing more to it, really. If he hadn't had to leave for an emergency at a job site, we would have spoken more about her. I wish we had. I told you on Wednesday when you and Agent Sherlock visited me at my studio that Rob and I haven't made any certain commitments to each other yet." She drew a deep breath, smiled at him, her voice softening. "But Rob knows I love him, and I have for months and months. And I hope that Rob, despite this woman's sudden entrance into our lives, won't change what we have together.

"Rob and I have had no secrets from each other, for a long time now. If he'd fallen head over heels in love with this woman, he would have told me. Wouldn't you, Rob?"

"Yes," Rob said, "I would tell you."

She shook her head. "Look at us. This is hardly the time or the place to discuss our feelings about each other. I would wish that you, Dillon—Agent Savich—would appreciate how deep our feelings for each other are."

Savich said, "I brought up Delsey so the family would understand what happened between her and Rob on Tuesday and to point out that someone tried to murder her on Thursday by shoving her in front of oncoming traffic on K Street. It was Rob who saved her life."

Alexander said, "You're telling us this girl none of us have even met is somehow tied to the attempts on Venus's life?" He turned toward Rob and smirked. "If so, brother, you're right back in the thick of things, aren't you?"

"He's at the very center of things, Alexander, though he doesn't know it yet," Savich said.

Veronica said, "This is ridiculous. It's Alexander who's at the center of things, always has been." She was panting now, beside herself, her eyes on Alexander. "Even though you failed to kill Venus, Alexander, it wasn't for lack of trying. Thank heaven Venus finally realized that. Look at you, repaying her for all she's done for you by wanting her dead. Your own grand-mother?"

Alexander didn't move. He looked at the faces of his family, none of them saying a word to defend him. A great weight seemed to settle on him, cover him, like a shroud. He said, "Listening to you, Veronica, I would have no doubt I tried to kill Venus. So what are you waiting for, Savich? Arrest me."

Savich clapped his hands, once, twice. Everyone in the room turned to stare at him. "What is this, Alexander? You, throwing in the towel? Hurling yourself into the sacrificial fire? This leap from lord of the manor to brave, stoic martyr ready for the auto-da-fé—can't you find a middle ground? It's not you at all."

Alexander shoved away from the fireplace mantel. "Shut up, you bastard! How dare you make fun of me! You don't know what you're talking about."

Savich nodded. "That's better. Sit down, Alexander, and be quiet." He waved a hand around the living room. "No more theatrics from any of you." He turned to Rob. "I imagine you've spent every waking moment wondering who the person was who shoved Delsey Freestone into the path of that oncoming limo. If you hadn't been there to pull her back, she could have been killed."

Rob said simply, "My heart stopped." He did not look at Marsia.

Savich nodded. "And of course you quickly realized there was no one else in the world who could want Delsey Freestone dead and gone more than Marsia."

Rob looked miserably toward Marsia. "No, you've got it wrong, Savich. I'm sorry, Marsia, I was going to tell you all about Delsey this weekend when I'd have enough time to make you understand." He said to Savich, "What I said to her on Wednesday night—it wasn't anything, really. Marsia couldn't have believed it was serious. Believe me, there was no reason for her to want to kill Delsey."

Savich said, "Whatever you said to Marsia, no matter how light your hand, no matter how dismissive you were, no matter how you skated around the truth about Delsey, it was crystal clear to her she was going to lose you, her golden goose.

"Rob, you're not much of a poker player. Despite your intentions, I imagine you couldn't help yourself, you overflowed with Delsey, and it slammed Marsia in the face even though you thought you were being dismissive about her. All of us at the Hoover Building on Tuesday saw both of you light up like Christmas trees when she waltzed off the elevator. Then you spent Wednesday together. Believe me, Marsia understood everything perfectly.

"When Agent Sherlock and I met with you Wednesday afternoon, Marsia, both of us realized you are focused, intelligent, and very talented. We both liked you, admired your work. Until Delsey's near death, I didn't believe you capable of a jealous rage."

Marsia fanned her hands in front of her. "Agent Savich—Dillon—let me assure you, assure Rob, assure all of you, that when Rob happened to tell me about meeting this musician, I didn't consider it of any importance. I ate my spaghetti and took him at his word. I didn't give her another thought.

"Even if I were wrong about Rob and this Delsey, I am not a criminal. I am not a murderer. Allow me to point out that I was not even in Washington yesterday afternoon. I was delivering my sculpture representation of fecundity to the fertility center in Baltimore at the time of Ms. Freestone's accident."

Savich said, "I know exactly where you were." He turned to the group. "You are wondering what the attempted murder of a stranger has to do with Venus. Be patient and you will understand. Sherlock?"

Sherlock walked to stand beside Savich. "The FBI has a sophisticated facial-recognition program. It helps us identify unknown persons involved in a crime. Another agent, Nicholas Drummond, and Dillon, have further refined the program to allow it to identify criminals even from partial or grainy views of their faces. The program analyzes bone structure, relative distances between facial features, the shape of the jaw, you get the idea.

"The person who shoved Delsey Freestone in the back in front of an oncoming limo yesterday was wearing a hoodie, sunglasses, and baggy clothes, all in all, an excellent disguise. On one traffic cam we got a portion of his jaw. We assumed it was a he. From another, we saw the nose. Not enough for us to be certain of who it was, though we had a suspicion. We inputted pictures of everyone connected to this case into the program for comparison.

"The program verified our suspicions. It wasn't you, Marsia. It was you, Veronica."

Veronica reared back, opened her mouth, but Savich overrode her. "Marsia called you, told you Rob had fallen for a woman and he had it bad, he was beyond smitten. He was so transparent, like all men, and of course she could tell. She was worried Rob would break it off with her and she would lose everything.

"But then I imagine Marsia got hold of herself. She had reason to be confident. She's an attractive woman, and she'd been with Rob for months, winning him over, seeing to his every whim. She knew Rob well enough to think she might persuade him to put this Delsey behind him. She'd redouble her efforts to please him, maybe even get pregnant, to force his hand. You knew she didn't care if he slept with Delsey as long as he came back to her. Of course she would forgive him. Marsia probably realized the two of you had no choice but to wait it out. And if talking with you calmed her down, it had the opposite effect on you, Veronica. You saw everything you'd planned falling apart around you, all because of an outsider, and you panicked. You weren't about to let your plan fall apart because of Delsey Freestone."

"That's ridiculous," Veronica shouted, contempt

thick in her voice. "What plan? There is no bloody plan! Rob, a golden goose? That's lunacy—Rob and Marsia love each other. So what?"

Savich looked from Veronica back to Marsia. "The plan the two of you came up with was that Marsia would marry Rob Rasmussen and make both of you wealthy beyond belief. You wanted the gold ring, Veronica, you wanted it all. To you, Delsey Freestone was an obvious threat, and you acted. You followed Delsey from her brother's apartment, saw your chance. She never even gave you a look, another stranger wearing glasses, a hoodie, and she was singing, I'll bet.

"It was easy for you to slip in behind her. One hard shove, and you melted away, your hoodie up, covering your hair and your head. You heard the screams, the screeching cars, the crashes, you must have thought you'd killed her.

"The sunglasses were a good touch, made it more difficult, but the cameras and our program nailed you, Veronica."

Veronica was shaking her head. "Why are you doing this, Dillon? You know me, know my loyalty is to Venus and always has been. Even if I do look something like this person, that's no proof of anything. It could have been anyone."

"You were gone from the house most of yesterday afternoon. You drive a late-model Audi, with a GPS. I've already arranged for a search warrant. I have no doubt the GPS will put you near K Street."

Rob was staring from Veronica to Marsia, a woman

he'd believed he might love enough to make a commitment—until he'd met Delsey. And because of him, Delsey could have died. He couldn't get his brain around it. He said slowly, the words painful, "Marsia and Veronica—you wanted to kill Delsey because you were afraid I'd fallen in love with her?"

Veronica looked at him, disdain clear on her face. "Can't you see Agent Savich is making this all up?"

Marsia said, her voice cool, unruffled, "Agent Savich—this new facial-recognition program you described, couldn't it be wrong? It wouldn't be accepted in court, would it?"

"Maybe not, but now that I'm sure who it was—and it was Veronica—we'll be able to prove it, you can count on that. We'll be able to prove you and Veronica hooked up well before you met Rob. Credit card receipts, cell phone records, emails, your neighbors at your studio—there's not going to be any hiding that, Marsia. I am wondering how long it took the two of you to plan all this."

Marsia waved it away. "There is no plan, there has never been. That's absurd. As for Veronica, yes, I know her. We met quite by accident at a coffee shop in Chevy Chase some time ago and discovered we liked each other. I found her stories about Mrs. Rasmussen interesting. She told me what it was like to work for her. She is, after all, a legend. And, in time, she told me about Rob." She smiled at Rob, reached out her hand and lightly laid it on his leg. "When I needed to have my kitchen remodeled, I checked around, heard

Rob could be trusted to do a good job. I recognized his name, of course, and thought, why not? And that's how Rob and I met. There are no deep, ugly secrets here, only two adults finding each other and getting together." She smiled up at him. "I have nothing to hide and neither does Veronica. I think your facial-recognition program is simply wrong, and you will have to deal with that."

Savich said, "And it's a coincidence you had breakfast with Veronica Wednesday morning at the *Flying Cow* in Foggy Bottom?"

"I don't know how you found out about that, but considering there are eyes everywhere in Washington nowadays, well, no matter. Yes, we do try to have breakfast on Wednesday mornings—nothing special in that. I did tell her about this girl Rob had just met, but I remember I laughed, said it was a passing thing, since he's a man after all, and that's the nature of the beast. Veronica laughed, too, said it sounded to her like Rob was a great deal like his father. We didn't speak of it further.

"It's Veronica's nature to protect people—Mrs. Rasmussen, and all her friends, me as well, I think. She's an honest person, believe me, she would never shove some girl in front of an oncoming car. Our conversation on Wednesday? Again, there was only the merest mention of this girl. Nothing more to it."

"There was a great deal more to it," Savich said. "Actually a lot more than anyone here might imagine."

60

Everyone burst out talking at once. It was Glynis's voice that won out over the others. "Dillon, you're saying Veronica Lake, Grandmother's Veronica for fifteen years, tried to kill this girl Rob met on Tuesday? That sounds farfetched to me. Hardly possible."

Savich smiled. "I agree with you. I would also say what she did was stupid. She panicked, and that rarely turns out well."

He raised his hand to quiet everyone.

Rob was staring fixedly at Savich, as if he couldn't bear to look at Marsia. "What do you mean, there's more than anyone can imagine?"

Savich could see dread in his eyes. Perhaps Rob had sensed that something was never quite right in his relationship with Marsia, and it was beginning to dawn on him that their entire relationship had been an illusion fostered by a very talented woman.

Savich said, "To begin with, Marsia and Veronica have been close since before you met her, Rob. Perhaps it started out as a joke when Veronica talked about you, the long-lost bad boy, the marriageable Rasmussen who could be worth untold millions if Venus were to take you back fully into the fold. I suspect it was more than a joke for Marsia. However it came about, between them, they arranged for Marsia to meet and seduce you, Rob, and to do anything she needed to marry you.

"The fly in the ointment was Venus Rasmussen. They had to be very careful in trying to maneuver her into welcoming you back, Rob, and giving you back your full share of the family's wealth."

There was stunned surprise, shocked voices. Savich raised his hand to shut them down again and continued. "Do you know, Veronica, Venus hardly even remembered it was you who started bringing Rob up in your conversations. You reminded her what a nice bright boy he'd been and that it was such a pity he'd had to leave. You wondered what he was like now, if he had changed. Because you knew Venus, you dropped it, gave her time to mull it over. You supported her when she wanted to reconnect with her grandson. She was eighty-six, after all, you told her, there was no reason to wait. And so emails were exchanged, and they met.

"Of course you encouraged Venus's relationship with Rob, Veronica, and you undermined Alexander as subtly as you could, poked gentle fun at Guthrie for his drinking and his womanizing, shook your head mournfully whenever you spoke of Hildi and Glynis, in short, you set the stage for the return of the prodigal son to the queen herself. You were pleased they quickly became close, though you had little to do with that. You watched and waited.

"And Marsia did her part. She attached herself to Rob, drew him in, encouraged him to rekindle his relationship with Venus." He turned to face Marsia. "Did you and Veronica wonder which of them would contact the other first? Your marrying Rob should have been enough for you, you might have succeeded at that, if not for Delsey.

"Rob no doubt told you Venus had given him back his full share of stock in Rasmussen Industries as Guthrie's son. I would bet it was you who hatched the idea of killing Venus. She was the only remaining obstacle to your big prize—incredible wealth—and you didn't want to wait for it. Given Venus's excellent health, it could be years. Rob Rasmussen and his new wife would inherit a fortune."

Alexander looked back and forth from Veronica to Marsia, clearly disbelieving. "Wait, are you really saying Veronica gave Grandmother the arsenic? *Veronica?*"

"Of course. Who else in the house could have done it? Other than you, of course, or Guthrie. The symptoms of arsenic poisoning aren't immediate. She and Marsia were counting on that fact. After a bit of research on metalwork, I discovered arsenic can be mixed in with copper, tin, and other metals to create varieties of bronze. It makes casting easier, gives a silvery sheen to the metal surface, much like some of the sculptures we saw in your studio, Marsia. It won't take long to find your supplier."

Alexander said, "You're saying Veronica put the arsenic in my bathroom?"

"Yes, but not at first. They hoped to kill Venus with the arsenic without anyone knowing, without anyone suspecting she'd been poisoned. Her natural death would not be unexpected, and they wouldn't do an autopsy that might detect arsenic. But Venus didn't cooperate. She stayed alive and grew suspicious, and that alarmed them. I think that's when Veronica and Marsia decided to implicate someone else, in case it was discovered Venus was being poisoned with arsenic, and who better than you, Alexander, since you were in line to inherit control of Rasmussen Industries, and sat squarely blocking their road to even more power?"

Alexander said, "But what about Vincent Willig? Why did he come out of nowhere and try to shoot Grandmother, here at our house?"

"They were afraid that simply planting the arsenic wouldn't be enough to allay suspicions, Alexander, and Venus was still alive. They needed to act quickly. Perhaps if she were shot and killed before an investigation got under way, they could still have their prize. They arranged for Willig to shoot Venus before she had a chance to call us at the FBI. Luckily she beat them to the punch, but just barely—no one expected us to be there. Putting Willig's number on your cell phone, Alexander, was an extra precaution, another nail in your coffin."

Hildi said, "But who was this man, this Willig? How did either of these women even know a criminal, an ex-convict?"

Savich smiled. "Do you know, when I set MAX my laptop to work to do a deep background on Marsia Gay, I found nothing at all questionable. But Willig had to fit somewhere, so I set MAX digging into genealogy records. I found a distant cousin of Marsia's mother, Eleanor Metzer. She divorced her husband, remarried and had a son—and suddenly all the pieces slotted neatly together. The son's name was Vincent Willig.

"He and Marsia grew up in the same town, must have known each other. I imagine Willig called her when he was let out of prison, and the timing was perfect. I wouldn't be surprised if she seduced him, to tie him to her, no reason to take any chances, and promised him the moon. Asking Willig to kill someone wasn't a problem because Willig was a psychopath, the perfect tool. The fact that he wasn't very bright was a plus because that meant he didn't think too deeply.

"Sherlock pointed out that in the end it wasn't Vincent's stupidity that brought him down, it was sheer bad luck. Sherlock and I didn't leave when Vincent thought we did. And that was why we got Willig. I've got to say, Marsia, you still kept your head, you didn't panic.

"Veronica saw him lying in that hospital bed, knowing he wouldn't be willing to go back to prison for life. You faced your biggest crisis. If he rolled on you, it was over. And he tried to, that afternoon when Venus offered him a hundred thousand dollars to give us the name of whoever had hired him—of course, no one believed him."

Veronica opened her mouth, but Savich held up his hand. "No, don't bother to deny it, Veronica. It couldn't have been anyone else but you who killed him. Were you smart enough not to drive your car with its GPS to the hospital? You worked as a nurse's aide for several years while you were finishing your psychology degree at Smith. More than enough time to learn how hospitals function, what the nurses' duties are, where the drug supplies are kept."

Marsia had sat in the beautiful antique wing chair, her legs crossed, her capable hands folded in her lap, no expression on her face. She hadn't moved. Veronica, on the other hand, was wringing her hands, her expression frantic, clearly not knowing what to do.

Time for the kill shot. Savich said to her, "When Marsia told you about Rob meeting Delsey, you saw your beautiful dream evaporating. You weren't about to let that happen. You didn't think through what you were doing, you acted. Luckily for Delsey, you failed.

"Do you know, it's very possible Delsey will never forgive Rob for keeping his relationship with Marsia from her, and that would mean you brought down your house of cards needlessly."

Veronica looked at Rob, dislike clear on her face. "If

he's anything like Alexander, like his father, he'd have talked her around. I only wanted—"

Marsia said, not raising her voice, "Shut up, Veronica, please shut up."

Savich continued to Veronica, "Venus told me you'd become her dearest friend. She didn't want to believe it when I told her what you'd done. She cared for you so very much. You broke her heart." He paused. "It turns out, your heart belongs to someone else—you're in love with Marsia."

61

Savich watched Rob finally turn to Marsia. He looked both stricken and confused. "You—you're gay, Marsia? You were faking everything?"

"Don't be absurd," Marsia said. "Really, Rob, we are very well suited, not only emotionally, but physically. You've never questioned that before. Why would you now?"

Glynis laughed. "Great nonanswer, Marsia. You're that good? Well, I suppose you'd have to be. Rob, don't be naive, she could have faked it without a problem. What a marvelous joke."

Marsia raised her chin, said pleasantly, "I am not gay. I find it distasteful."

Veronica gasped, her eyes laser sharp on Marsia's face, brimming with questions, with accusations. With hurt.

"Don't you see, Veronica?" Savich said. "Marsia set out from the beginning to use you, to seduce you, to manipulate you, just as she did Rob, and Willig. It was always you who were at risk. You were the one who gave Venus the arsenic, who took the risk of killing Willig, and who shoved Delsey in front of that limousine. Not Marsia, you. And you would have gained so much less than she, maybe nothing at all. Marsia never loved you. I doubt she's ever loved anyone."

Veronica's voice was a whisper. "Is he right, Marsia? That you never loved me?"

"For goodness sake, Veronica, don't be a fool. Just be quiet." She turned to Savich. "This is an amazing display of imagination, but I think it's time to bring this fabrication to a close. I want to speak to a lawyer, and if I were you, Veronica, I would do the same."

"I wouldn't listen to her, Veronica. She's protecting herself, not you. It's time for you to tell me why you've done this."

The room fell silent as slowly they turned to see Venus Rasmussen standing in the open doorway, dressed in an elegant Armani gray suit, perfectly presented, Sherlock beside her. He got a discreet whiff of Venus's signature Chanel perfume. Only he had realized Sherlock had slipped out.

Venus never looked away from Veronica, now pale as death, her pupils dilated and wild. "I really didn't want to believe Dillon when he told me you were the one who put the arsenic in my drink here at home. It made sense, of course, but I simply couldn't accept it, not after fifteen years of my affection and support. It was I who helped you set up your business, made certain you prospered. I couldn't understand how you could do something so—evil. That woman, Marsia, you fell in love with her, didn't you?"

Veronica took a step toward Venus, but Glynis grabbed her arm.

Veronica shook her off. "Does it really matter now, Venus? Listen, I didn't want to do any of it, it wasn't my idea. She told me she would tell you about me if I didn't do what she said."

"Veronica, I've known for a long time you're gay— the little things you'd say, how your face would light up sometimes when you were speaking to a woman on your cell phone. Of course I knew about your affairs over the years, discreet ones, but I knew. It was up to you to raise the issue with me if you wished. It made no difference to me. But it must have been lonely for you.

"And then you found Marsia, or she found you and she made all the loneliness fall away when she got her hooks into you." Venus turned to Marsia. "Such a pity for you that I didn't die, that I'm here facing you, the picture of eighty-six-year-old health. I heard Dillon say you were unlucky. Your bad luck was that he and Sherlock are dear friends of mine, and they walked through that door the very afternoon you had me scheduled for murder. Your relation Vincent Willig was indeed a psychopath. It obviously runs in the family."

Marsia looked Venus up and down. "You miserable old biddy. Why am I not surprised you made a grand entrance? It seemed too coincidental to me that you would be at death's door so conveniently when you'd hung on to life like a leech for eighty-six years." Marsia laughed. "I see, there isn't a new will. How rich. That ridiculous lawyer, he was in on it, obviously. Where is he, hiding in a closet?"

"No," Venus said. "Isabel took Mr. Sullivan down the back stairs. He's having cake and tea with Mr. Paul and Isabel in the kitchen." She smiled at each of her family. "I do apologize to all of you for upsetting you. Dillon thought a bit of playacting would help all of us get to the truth."

Savich said to Marsia, "We had to turn to you sooner or later once all that evidence against Alexander was handed to us, clumsily planted at best and far too obvious. We followed through with questioning Alexander as we were meant to. I'll bet that was Veronica's idea, wasn't it? You wouldn't have overplayed your hand in such a manner."

Marsia flicked a contemptuous look toward Alexander. "Oh, that ridiculous fool over there? Who's to say he wasn't stupid enough to leave the arsenic there? Perhaps both he and Veronica are behind all of this? I want a lawyer."

Savich said, "I have agents outside to escort you and Veronica to the Daly Center. You can call your lawyers from there." He punched his cell and called them in.

Venus waited until the two women were marched out, waited until she heard the front door close. She smiled at Savich and nodded, moved to stand behind a chair and faced her family. "Alexander, I never accepted that you were the one who was trying to kill me. Dillon didn't, either. I hope you now accept that I love you. I've always loved you. You will remain my right hand at Rasmussen. When I die, you will have controlling interest."

Venus turned to her youngest grandson. "And you, Rob, my dear boy, I am so happy you are back in my life. I have missed you, prayed for you, always wished you would return home. I am so pleased you have become a fine man, the man you were meant to be."

Rob roared to his feet. "You believe me a fine man? It was because of me you could have died! I believed I loved her, Grandmother, or loved the person I believed she was. And look at what I did—I brought her into your life."

Venus waved a weary hand. "Enough drama, Rob. Please, I am so tired of all the drama that's swirled around this house for the past week. You're back to stay, Rob. I will not let you out of my life again. If you wish to join Rasmussen Industries, you will be welcomed. If you prefer to continue on your own path, that is your choice as well. It's your life to live as you wish, with no meddling from me." She gave him a crooked smile. "Dillon speaks well of this Delsey Freestone girl. Would you like me to put in a good word for you with her?"

Rob gave her a huge smile. "I thought, Grandmother, you just promised me no meddling."

"All right, but if you need me—" She smiled at each of her family in turn. "All of you, I am so relieved and happy we're together again, with no more suspicions, with no more lingering doubts. The Rasmussens have won. I love you all. I hope at least some of you can stay for dinner."

Isabel lingered outside the doorway for a few moments and then hurried back to the kitchen, smiling hugely. "Mr. Paul, it's over. The family is safe, and together. This is your cue."

Mr. Paul rose from his chair and clapped his hands. "I do not think I will begin with my roast duck, but with espresso and my excellent éclairs. I think the family can use the sugar."

62

It was after nine o'clock when Cam, followed by Daniel, drove back toward Malibu to Missy's cottage. She was looking forward to finally getting some sleep. She turned her Toyota onto Colony Road and saw a shadow, looked hard, and realized it was Blinker. He saw her car coming and slipped behind some bushes four houses from Missy's cottage.

She was tired, she was frustrated, and the dam burst. She wanted to grab him, hold him upside down and shake him by his feet, do whatever it took to let him know he was messing with Missy for the very last time. She slammed to a stop, flew out of the car—with Daniel close behind her—and chased him down. She tackled him and flattened him facedown with all her weight, straddled his back, and slapped the back of his head.

"You moron! I can't believe you're back here again. I'm going to announce what you've been doing on *Good Morning America*, with your color photo. I'm going to tell your mother. Where does she live?"

"You think I'd tell you that?"

Cam smacked his head again.

Daniel came down on his haunches beside them. "Not a problem, Cam. I've got a file on him now. His mom is Carrie Bayley, and she owns a bakery in Cleveland. We can call her in the morning, tell her all about what her precious son has been doing. Maybe she'll haul you back home, Blinker. Hey, maybe better yet, we can save her the trouble. We can motor you a mile out in the ocean and toss your sorry self overboard." Daniel rose, lifted Cam off his back. She was red in the face, still breathing hard. He grabbed Blinker's arm and flipped him onto his back. He stood over him, arms crossed, staring down at him. "My boat's at my house up the road, not far at all."

"I hate boats, I get seasick! Listen, I'm more than one hundred yards from Missy's house! I'm not doing anything wrong, just out walking around, minding my own."

Daniel looked up the street, mentally calculated, and realized he was right. Barely. "Stop lying, you were planning on sneaking to Missy's house again, hoping Agent Wittier wasn't there to pound you. Again. What is it going to take to get you out of Missy's life once and for all?"

Blinker looked at Daniel's face in the dim moonlight, saw something that scared him. He licked his dry lips. "I couldn't sleep, no, really, I couldn't. I wasn't going to get any closer, I swear it. I just wanted to be near where she lives. Maybe see her if I was lucky, you know?"

Cam's rage evaporated. He was obsessed, fixated for some reason on Missy. He was only a sad little man, but still, an idiot. She said very clearly, "If I ever see you in Malibu again, Blinker, I will personally shoot you and bury your body in Topanga Canyon."

Blinker looked at her moon-pale face, at the fierce anger in her eyes, and whispered, "No, you won't. You'd go to jail if you killed me."

Cam said, "Nah, I'd haul your carcass to the canyon on a really dark night when no one's around. I'd bury you so deep no one would ever find you. And then Missy and I would drink a bottle of champagne to celebrate."

"I think it would be a beer for me," Daniel said.

Blinker looked seriously alarmed. He sat up, waved his hands at them. "Listen, you shouldn't treat me like I'm that guy killing all the actresses. I'm not into hurting anybody. I'm not even the only guy hanging around Missy. Look, Agent Wittier, I admire Missy, seeing her smile makes me happy. I'd never hurt her, well, or anybody."

Daniel's face was a study in frustration. He jerked Blinker to his feet, grabbed his shirt and shook him. "Let me put it this way, Blinker. Missy doesn't want to make you happy. She does not want to see you again, ever in this lifetime. You know why? Because she's dating me. I want you the hell out of our lives." He shook him again. "Do you understand me?"

"Missy is really dating you?"

"Yes." Another shake. "Answer me. Do you understand?"

"Well, yes, I suppose I have to."

Blinker looked like he'd burst into tears.

"Good." Daniel smoothed down Blinker's shirt, brushed him down. "Go back to Cleveland, bake cookies with your mom, sell her some bonds. Go, Blinker." They stood watching as Blinker, his head down, kicked pebbles out of his path on his way back to his car.

When they heard his car engine rev, Cam said, "Well, that perked me right up. Maybe he really will stay gone."

When Cam and Daniel pulled into the driveway of Missy's cottage, they saw Missy standing backlit in the doorway, wearing sleep boxers and a baggy shirt, her glorious hair tousled about her face. She looked relieved to see them.

Daniel started telling her about Blinker as Missy herded them into the kitchen. "Sit down, sit down. You both look wrung out. I'm going to make some tea. Too late for coffee. So tell me more about Blinker." They both sat down and Cam found herself looking at the bright red-and-white-checked tablecloth, thinking it would look good on her kitchen table back in Alexandria. She put that thought away and started doing a mental sort of the day, something she always did before bed at night. That's when it hit her square between the eyes. She jumped to her feet. "Daniel! What Blinker said—" She grabbed her cell out of her jacket pocket, dialed. Blinker picked up after three rings, wide-awake.

"Blinker, it's Agent Wittier. Are you home yet?"

"Yeah, like I'm Superman and can fly. I'm still driving. Look, Agent Wittier, when I get home I'll start packing, I swear. I'm calling my boss, taking a leave of absence. You good with that?"

"Yes. It's for the best, you'll see. Now, listen up, Blinker. You said you're not the only guy hanging around Missy. You saw someone else? Was he on her street? Another stalker?"

"He was a turkey, not discreet at all. I spotted him right away."

"Okay, I understand. When did you see him?"

"The first time I saw him around her house was a couple of weeks ago, then again the day before she took off for Las Vegas. I haven't seen him since she got back. Not to say he couldn't still be around because I spend my mornings working, usually."

"Describe him to me."

"Older, thirties for sure. He was tall, thin, and he always wore jeans and a hoodie with the top up to cover his head. I'm surprised Missy never noticed him, looking like he did."

"Blinker, Detective Montoya and I are coming to your place. I've got some photos to show you." She punched off, jumped to her feet. "Daniel, we have to go."

Missy grabbed her arm. "Let me throw on some clothes, I'll go with you."

"No, absolutely not," Daniel said. He gave her a long look, turned to Cam. "Let's go."

63

Blinker lived in an upscale apartment complex, complete with palm trees, bougainvillea, and manicured lawns. It was quiet and calm. As they climbed out of Daniel's Crown Vic, Cam said, "He's in 3C, there in the corner unit with all the windows. We've struck gold, Daniel, I know it."

Cam felt a moment of sheer envy when he showed them in. "Hey, nice digs, Blinker. How do you afford this?"

"He's a bond trader," Daniel said.

Blinker eyed them. "Well, you might as well come into the living room. So you come here late at night to show me some photos and the first thing you do is bust my chops some more? I wasn't lying, I'm leaving. You can look in my bedroom, suitcase open on the bed, my shorts already packed."

Cam said, "We're not here to pack for you, Blinker." She called up photos and handed her cell to Blinker. "Here, look at these photos. Have you seen this man?"

Blinker took her cell and put it under a living room reading lamp. When he shook his head, Cam swiped to another photo. Another head shake. When he looked at the third photo, he stared at it a moment, then nodded. "Yeah, I recognize him. But he looks different here, he looks dead. Is that a DMV photo? Like I told you, when I saw him, he was wearing a hoodie, both times. But that's him."

Daniel said, "This is important, Blinker. Are you completely certain this is the man you saw looking around Missy's cottage?"

Blinker nodded. "I almost told him to go away that first time, but there was something about him that was scary, and I chickened out. Then I was glad I didn't try to warn him off because I didn't see him again for a while. I thought he'd found someone else."

Daniel said, "How do you know he wasn't just out for a walk and happened to be going Missy's way? Did you actually see him following Missy home?"

"Yeah, that first time he did follow her home, sort of looked around before he left. The second time, Missy wasn't around and I saw him looking in the windows. I spotted him right away because he wasn't very polished about it, not like I am."

"Missy caught you and so did we, so you can't be all that polished, either," Cam said.

Blinker waved that away. "Bad luck, that's all it was. Who knew you'd be out so late tonight? And that first time, I didn't know Missy had an FBI agent sleeping in her second bedroom."

Daniel said, "You've already forgotten Missy chased you down in Las Vegas?"

Blinker puffed up like a proud papa. "Yes, she did. She's amazing. I let her catch me."

Cam said, "Let's focus. Tell us everything about this guy you can remember, Blinker, every detail."

"Okay, I remember I was getting a bag of Cheetos from that 24/7 market on PCH when I first saw him. Missy was in the store buying some stuff and I was hanging around, seeing what she'd do. When she left, I noticed him on the street. I saw he was looking at her. Even though he was keeping his distance, I knew he was following her, so, yeah, I tucked in behind him, watched him. He trailed her nearly all the way back to her cottage, then he waited a couple of minutes, you know, looking around, and left.

"I saw him again the evening before Missy left, not that I knew then she was leaving town. He was wearing the same hoodie, jeans, running shoes—that's how I recognized him. I waited to see what he was up to. As I said, he cased Missy's cottage, maybe trying to get a look at her. I left after he did, haven't seen him again.

"That's all I remember about him." Blinker stared at them. "Hey, do you think he's the sick dude who's killing off the young actresses?" Blinker looked about to faint. "Do you think he was planning on killing Missy?"

"It's very possible," Cam said.

Blinker weaved where he stood. Cam laid her hand on his arm to steady him. He whispered, "If Missy hadn't left for Las Vegas, he might have killed her, like all the others? Someone else was killed in Las Vegas when Missy was there, isn't that right? Maybe he couldn't get to Missy, so he killed someone else? That means I saved her, right?" He pulled away from Cam, stood straight, shoulders back. "Imagine that, me, John Bayley, mild-mannered bond trader. You won't forget I picked him out of your photo lineup, will you?"

"No, we won't forget," Daniel said. "You did good, Blinker."

Blinker sat down hard on his sofa. "This is scary, dude. You'll keep Missy safe, won't you? You'll get that guy? Will you tell Missy how helpful I was? Maybe she'll be grateful and—"

Daniel leaned down, gave his face a pat. "*Bon voyage*, Blinker. Have a nice life."

64

It took far too long to find the house Doc and Deborah had rented together because Cam and Daniel didn't have the address on file. They'd gone to Doc's old apartment, a half a block from the hospital, only to find it empty. It took fast-talking the hospital administrator to get them to the right address. Finally, Cam and Daniel pulled up a block from the new rental, Arturo right behind them. Their house one of many ranch-style homes built in the seventies, well maintained, its front yard lush with oaks and palm trees. Lights shined in many of the houses, and canned laughter sounded from a TV comedy through an open window. Doc's house was dark.

Arturo said, "With any luck, he's already in bed asleep."

Cam said, "I hope you're right, but there's a good chance he isn't here. He's not stupid, he had to know today didn't go well for him, that we were putting things together, Blinker aside. Maybe he figured he'd have to run someday, and he decided not to wait."

Daniel said, "No sign of Elman and his group. I say we go get him."

Arturo grabbed Cam's sleeve. "Look, in the side window—flames! Doc might be in there. Cam, call 911."

Arturo and Daniel ran to the front door, Cam on their heels, her cell phone to her ear. The door was locked. Daniel stepped back and kicked the door handle. The door shuddered, held. He kicked it again and the door flew open. Arturo called back as he ran into the house. "Stay here, I'll check the bedrooms!"

"No way," Daniel said. "Cam, we've got this. Keep a lookout for Doc." He took off after Arturo.

It seemed like forever but only a few moments passed. She wanted to go in after them but held herself back. What could she do to help them? The house was going up quickly, heat and smoke were pouring out at her. She heard sirens in the distance and prayed. She heard Arturo yell. She couldn't just stand there. She started into the house as Daniel came staggering out, carrying Arturo over his shoulder and dragging an unconscious man behind him. Arturo's jacket was on fire, flames leaping up from his back. Cam slapped at the flames as Daniel dropped the unconscious man and threw Arturo onto his back on the grass, smothering out the last of the flames. "He's inhaled a lot of smoke." He slapped Arturo's face. "Come on, you badass, breathe, no way do you want your ex-wife to get your pension. Arturo!"

Arturo heaved out a breath, choked, coughed as Daniel jerked him upright and pounded his back. Finally, through the coughing, he wheezed out, "What, Montoya, were you going to put your tongue down my throat?"

Daniel lightly tapped his face. "You wish, Loomis. Can you breathe okay?"

"Well, pretty good, but my back feels like it's on fire."

Cam pulled off his still-steaming jacket, ripped away his partly burned shirt and examined his back in the streetlight. It was bright red. She was afraid to touch him.

"Let's get them farther away from the flames first," Daniel said. "First Arturo. No, dude, don't you even think about trying to move." He and Cam pulled him beneath an acacia tree near the sidewalk. He let them, his head hanging forward, breathing fast.

"How bad is it?"

"Not bad, only a little red," Cam said. Arturo hoped she wasn't lying through her teeth, but it hurt so much he figured she probably was. He didn't move.

"I'm okay, see to that guy we pulled out. He's in worse shape than I am."

Daniel pulled the other man farther from the house and fell to his knees beside him. "He's alive, breathing. He's got some bad burns, and a head wound that's still bleeding." He grabbed Arturo's discarded shirt and pushed down on the gash, relieved to hear the wail of sirens.

Cam said, "The fire was just starting. Doc couldn't have left more than a few minutes before we got here. I've put a BOLO out for him already. The DMV has him driving a Volkswagen Beetle. The question is, where did he go?"

Daniel looked up at her. "And who is that guy who was in Doc's house?"

Before Cam could answer him, everything happened at once. Supervisor Elman, Corinne Hill, and Morley Jagger, their flashers flooding the neighborhood with red light, pulled up across the street as two fire trucks stopped in front, two ambulances screaming to a halt behind them. Neighbors poured out of their houses, everyone staring at the flames leaping out of the burning house, grabbing garden hoses to soak down their own houses. Elman set Hill and Jagger to keep them back.

Cam checked the man's pockets as the EMT quickly placed an oxygen mask over his face and examined his head wound. She found only some wadded-up Kleenex and a half packet of sugarless gum. "He has no ID on him," Cam said over her shoulder to Daniel.

Daniel squatted down beside her, looked at the EMT's nameplate. "Josh, will he make it?"

"Don't know," Josh said. "Pete, get a gurney over here, notify the ER at SMH that we're coming with a major head trauma, smoke inhalation, burns."

Another EMT was looking at Arturo's back. "The

detective's got second-degree burns, but he's not critical." She patted his arm. "You aren't going to have much fun for a while, Detective, but you'll be okay. You shouldn't need any grafting, good thing, that's a bitch." She jerked her head toward the unconscious man being lifted onto a gurney. "Were you the one who saved that guy's life?"

Elman walked over to them. "What in the name of heaven happened here, Arturo?"

Cam answered for him. "Arturo and Daniel went in there, pulled that man out. He's got no ID, and his head wound's bad enough to have knocked him out. He's about the same size and build as Mark Richards—Doc. My guess is Doc decided to run, but he didn't want us chasing him, so he found a man who was similar in build to him, knocked him out, and left him behind so he'd burn with the house. If not for a guy named Blinker we talked to tonight, we wouldn't have found out about Doc's house burning down at least until the morning, and we'd have assumed the burned corpse was Doc. It would have taken several days for the DNA to prove us wrong. By then Doc would have been long gone, probably on a beach in Mexico."

Daniel said, "I agree with Cam. After that lie detector test today, he knew it was only a matter of time before we got everything nailed down."

"I want to hear about this Blinker," Elman said.

"Actually, sir, you probably don't," Daniel said.

Elman stared back at the house, still spurting flames. It was going to burn to its foundation. He looked back at Daniel. "Hey, Montoya, your jacket's burned. Did it go through to your back?"

Daniel hadn't felt a thing, but now he did, and he didn't like it. "Yeah, I guess it did."

Elman called out, "Hey, over here. We've got some more burns."

Josh jogged over, stepped behind him. Daniel said, "Don't tell me what the jacket looks like, I don't want to know. Listen, I'm all right, you need to look at Cam's hands, she was beating out the flames on Arturo's jacket."

"No, I'm fine, a couple of blisters, not bad at all."

Josh helped Daniel out of his jacket, eased down his shirt. "I gotta say, Detective, it's a good thing you were wearing this jacket. It saved you a world of hurt. Still, you should come to the hospital, let the doctors have a look—"

"Thanks, Josh, maybe later."

Cam dusted off her jeans, clipped her Glock back onto her belt. She looked at Arturo, who was breathing hard, his eyes closed. She said a prayer, then turned to Elman and Daniel. "Doc isn't more than a half hour ahead of us, maybe less. He could be headed any-where—but probably the border."

"Unless he hasn't run yet," Daniel said. He straight-ened slowly, relieved he could. "I'm thinking he wasn't done here, that he went back to the person who put him in our sights."

"Where the end started for him," Cam said. "Agreed. I'll give Markham a call, warn him. You're sure you're good to go?" She didn't expect him to say no, and he didn't.

Arturo's eyes flew open and he coughed out a pitiful shout. "Wait! Where are you guys going?" The EMTs ignored him, lifted him into the ambulance, slammed the door.

"No answer. Let's go, Daniel, we've got to hurry."

Corinne jogged up. "Hey, wait, guys—is Doc the Serial?"

Daniel said, "I'll have to get back to you on that."

Elman said, "We should call for backup, Cam. No way are you and Montoya going after this guy by yourselves. Wait, where are you going?"

They were already running toward the Crown Vic, Daniel shrugging back into his jacket. Cam shouted over her shoulder, "Send units up the road to Theo Markham's house in Pacific Palisades. Tell them to come in silent. If they beat us there, tell them to wait for us."

65

After a nine-minute ride with his flashers on, Daniel pulled the Crown Vic to a stop on Minorca Drive a half block from the Markham house. They'd nearly gotten to the enclosed Markham estate when they saw a dark blue Volkswagen Beetle nearly hidden in bushes beside the road.

"Doc's car," Cam said, and checked it out. "He's still here, Daniel. We've got to hurry."

They saw the gate was locked, and climbed the six-foot wall. Before them was a sprawling two-story starkly modern glass and steel-beamed house, painted in a light stucco, a dozen skinny pillars lining the front. It was surrounded on three sides by thick oak trees, keeping it hidden from the neighbors. A huge swimming pool sprawled out beside the house. Incredible view, Cam saw, of both the famed golf course and the ocean.

"Some digs," Daniel said. "Your hands okay?"

She waved away his concern. "Your back?"

"Don't worry, I'll deal with it later."

Yeah, right, macho. "It's dark, Daniel. I'm afraid of what we're going to find inside."

"Doc standing over Markham's dead body?"

"And maybe his wife's as well," Cam said.

"He's already killed, and don't forget the man we found in his house, all he was to Doc was a means to an end. And now he's desperate."

"No backup here yet and we can't afford to wait. Let's go."

They ran bent over toward the garage, hidden in the shadows. One of the three bay doors was open. They stepped inside and saw a new Mercedes in one of the bays, a Beemer in another. The third bay was empty. The door to the house was locked. They went around to the front door, hugging the side of the house, barely visible in the faint moonlight reflecting off the swimming pool. A huge glass window stretched out beside the front door. They looked in, saw only darkness.

Daniel turned the lion's head knob on the front door. It was unlocked. "Not good," Cam whispered. "He left it open." She didn't want to think about what he'd left behind. They went in high-low, guns at the ready, but saw nothing at all. They paused at the foot of a grand staircase.

"Daniel, I heard something coming from upstairs."

They climbed the stairs as quietly as they could, straining to hear, and hugged the walls on opposite sides of the wide hallways at the top of the stairs.

They eased open doors as they walked, looked inside. Two of the empty bedrooms were probably for the two Markham sons off at UCLA, but all the detritus of teenage boys was gone, replaced by bedrooms so magazine-perfect, they looked dressed for Hollywood sets. At the end of the hall, Daniel opened the large double doors, listened, and heard a woman's groans.

When he turned on the light switch they saw a woman tied to a chair staring back at them, blood dripping down her face from a gash at her temple, her eyes frantic. A man's tie was stuffed in her mouth and pulled painfully tight around her head. Her hands and feet were bound to the chair with men's ties. She strained wildly, trying to speak through the gag.

Cam ran to the woman, went down on her knees to untie her hands and feet as Daniel undid the gag.

For a moment, she couldn't speak, trying to get saliva in her mouth. "You came," she whispered. "I thought he was going to kill both of us, but he didn't. He took Theo."

"How long ago?"

"Maybe fifteen minutes."

Daniel lifted her in his arms and set her down on an art deco chaise longue covered with lacy pillows. He crouched down on his knees beside her. "Mrs. Markham, you said he took Mr. Markham and that means we don't have much time. Did he hurt your husband? Was he still alive?"

"Yes, yes, I think so. But he hurt him, knocked Theo

unconscious, dragged him out. I don't know where he took him, I don't know."

Cam said, "We'll figure it out, Mrs. Markham. Tell us what happened."

They heard voices downstairs. "Our backup." Cam raced out of the huge bedroom and down the stairs, holding up her creds. Two young officers, their hands on their guns, stood spread-legged, staring up at her. "Cam Wittier, Federal Agent. We'll need an ambulance for an injured woman upstairs. And check the rooms downstairs and the grounds outside. Be on the lookout for a Caucasian man in his midthirties, tall and thin. Be careful, he's a murderer. He's holding Mr. Markham hostage."

As she stepped back into the bedroom, she heard Mrs. Markham's hoarse voice. "Neither of us was asleep. Theo's a night owl, he never goes to sleep until after midnight. He was still upset over Deborah Connelly's murder; it was bad, he was half out of his mind. I really tried to help him, not that he wanted much of anything from me, even comfort. He was still dressed, lying here beside me, not talking, staring up at the dark ceiling." Her breathing hitched. "The lights went on and I was blinded a moment, then I saw a man standing in the doorway, aiming a gun at us.

"I think I screamed, I'm not sure, but Theo, he leaped out of bed and started yelling. The man seemed crazy—he was yelling back at Theo, both of them cursing each other. I couldn't believe it—the man laughed and he told Theo to sit back down on the bed and be quiet or he'd shoot him right then and there.

"I've never seen Theo so angry, he was shaking with it, but he was scared, too. The man came up close and I saw him clearly. I didn't recognize him."

Cam quickly called up Doc's photo on her cell. "Was this the man?"

"Yes, yes, that's him. Who is he?"

"We'll get to that, Mrs. Markham. What happened after he approached you and Theo?"

"He told Theo to get some of his ties and tie me to the chair, and if he didn't tie me up tight, he'd shoot me." She was swallowing convulsively.

Daniel stroked her hands, trying to calm her, and kept his voice soothing. "That must have been terrible, Mrs. Markham. Then what happened?"

She closed her eyes a moment. "He didn't say anything while Theo was tying me to the chair. Then he told Theo to get on his knees.

"Theo was cursing him, but I could see how scared he was. I thought the man was going to murder him right in front of me. The man pointed the gun at his head, and then he said in a scary calm voice I'll never forget, 'Tell your wife about how you murdered Deborah Connelly.'

"I didn't understand, it was crazy. I mean, Theo had cast Deborah Connelly in a title role in his next movie. Why would he kill her? And then Theo yelled right back at him." 'I'm not the murderer, you are!'"

Tears streamed down her face, and she swallowed

yet again. "The man ran up to him and hit him in the head with his gun and Theo fell down, but the man kept hitting him, kicking him. Then he stood back over him and yelled, 'Tell your wife you killed Deborah Connelly and do it now or you'll kill her, too. Get up on your knees, face her!'

"Theo managed to pull himself to his knees, the man screaming at him over and over, 'Face her, you bastard, have the balls to face her!'

"Theo looked up at me and said straight out, 'I killed Deborah Connelly.' I made noises through the gag but he couldn't understand me. Then the man leaned down and hit Theo again, hard on his head this time, and he fell over and didn't get back up. I didn't know if he was dead or not. The man came up to me, bent down and put a knife to my throat. I knew I was going to die." Her voice clogged in her throat and she began shaking.

Daniel patted her arm. "I'm sorry, Mrs. Markham, but we have to hurry, and only you can help us. You have to tell us the rest."

Cam ran to the en suite marble bathroom and came back with a glass of water. "It's okay; you're okay. Drink this."

She slowly sipped the water, pulled herself together. "I'm sorry, I'm sorry, it was so horrible." She looked up at Cam. "That man didn't say anything else, only checked to see I was tied tightly. He grabbed my chin and held me still and I'll never forget what he said, never. 'I'll bet you were once as pretty as all the women your husband sleeps with. And now you know he's as much of a monster as you think I am. He admitted to you that he murdered the woman I loved and I'm going to see he pays for it.' Then he struck me on the head and I felt my skin split open." She touched her fingers to the wound. "I never passed out, though. I saw him look down at Theo and kick him again. He looked back at me and laughed. He sounded pleased, happy. 'You're far better off without this bastard. Consider it my present to you, that and your life.'

"He never said another word, dragged Theo to the door, and turned off the light. I heard him dragging Theo down the hall, heard him bumping down the stairs, the front door opened, then banged closed."

"Do you own a third car, besides a Mercedes and a BMW?"

"Wha-what? Yes, a Lexus SUV."

"Describe it, quickly, Mrs. Markham."

"It's white, last year's model, an LX 750."

Cam said, "Where can I find the license number?"

"It's my car and it's a vanity plate. HOLLY 7."

Cam called it in.

Daniel said, "Mrs. Markham, did the man say anything about where he was taking your husband?"

She started to shake her head. "Wait—after he hit me on the head I was really woozy, but I remember how he whispered something to Theo, even though I don't think he could hear him. He whispered something about how he was going to make him suffer where he'd suffered and then settling with him. Something like that." She closed her eyes tightly, as if it would blot out the words.

Cam heard ambulance sirens, not much time now. She hated to upset Mrs. Markham more, but she had to ask. "Did you know before he told you that your husband had been sleeping with young actresses?"

Mrs. Markham's shoulders straightened, her chin went up, and she looked Cam full in the face. "Of course I knew. How do you think I got him away from his first wife? I knew what he was, and I really didn't care, didn't worry about any of them, until this year, until Connie Morrissey."

"Why her?"

"Because I knew he put her in his house in the Colony, in Malibu. The way he sometimes said her name, I knew he loved her, because he'd loved me like that once. He changed after she was murdered, he was never himself again. He sold that house in the Colony he loved so much because he couldn't bear to keep the place where she'd died." She looked at them, and now tears spilled. "Did he really kill Deborah Connelly? Or did he just say it because he had to?"

"We'll find out, Mrs. Markham," Daniel said. "Do you think he took Theo back to Connie's house in the Colony?"

"No, I don't think so. Theo doesn't even have a key anymore. Why would that man take Theo there?"

Cam said slowly, "He wants to make him suffer

where he's suffered. Daniel, and that means he took him to where Deborah died."

Mrs. Markham ran her tongue over her lips. "Do you think Theo killed Deborah Connelly?"

Yes, of course he did. But to Mrs. Markham Daniel said, "We're going to find out."

66

Daniel passed everything ahead of them driving south on PCH back to Santa Monica, though there was little traffic this time of night. The ocean flew by on Cam's right as Daniel's Crown Vic shimmied at a hundred miles an hour past the last of the rugged cliff walls. It was warm, a perfect night, really, but Cam was too revved to pay much attention. She didn't tell Daniel to slow down. She knew she'd be driving just as fast.

She saw an SUV turning onto the highway from a driveway, managed to swallow a shout of warning as Daniel jerked the Crown Vic sharply right, spinning out onto the gravel and nearly sending them airborne, a dozen feet down to the beach below. He managed to ease the car to a stop and steer back onto the road, hugging the center stripe. Cam looked back to see the SUV stopped dead in the middle of PCH, probably too scared to move. "Well done, Mario."

He nodded, his hands white from gripping the

steering wheel. He sped up, not quite hitting a hundred miles per hour again, but he came close.

"Do you think Markham killed Deborah, Daniel?"

"I think he'd have confessed to murdering his own mother with Doc holding a gun to his head, but yes, it makes sense he murdered her. Do you have doubts?"

"No, not really," Cam said. "What really makes me mad is that Doc used us, pretended to help so he could find out what we knew, who we were looking at. We told him about Markham and his P.I. and he figured the rest out. Markham took Deborah's computer and cell phone—how would he know to do that? We never released that detail. Doc knew the killer had to be close to one of the victims, didn't take him long to realize Markham knew he'd killed Connie. So he figured it had to be Markham who killed Deborah. It's all about his revenge.

"The M.E. pointed out that Deborah's murder might have been a copycat. I didn't want to believe there were two killers, but Doc's going after Markham proves there were." Cam banged her fist on the dashboard. "I grieved for Doc, I felt sorry for him. Both of them were playing us."

Daniel shot her a look. "You were right about one thing, though. Doc didn't kill Deborah."

"Some consolation."

Daniel didn't say anything.

"What are you thinking?"

He smoothly executed a curve, then said, "I really

don't care if Doc kills Markham. They're both monsters." He drew a deep breath. "But it's Doc I want, Cam. I want to make him pay, for the rest of his miserable life."

Cam said slowly, "Because he was going to murder Missy."

"If Blinker hadn't been stalking her, freaked her out so much she wouldn't have pulled up stakes and gone to Las Vegas—"

"—She'd have been at home where Doc could easily get to her. In Las Vegas, he couldn't, not in a hotel with the twenty-four-hour casino traffic."

Daniel nodded. "So he killed Molly Harbinger instead. You know he drove there, Cam, and we'll prove it."

"If Missy and I hadn't met up in the grocery store, would he have tried for her again, rather than Gloria Swanson?"

"I know he would have. Hang on, we're nearly there." Daniel turned right, bulleted down a deserted block, swung a fast left, slowed to a crawl down the alley behind Deborah's house. Mrs. Markham's SUV, HOLLY 7, was parked in the alley close to the back stoop. It was quiet, after one o'clock in the morning.

The small house was as dark as its neighbors'. The crime scene tape was pulled from the back door. Cam touched Daniel's arm as he cut the car's lights and they slowed to a stop. "There, in Deborah's bedroom, I saw a light. Now it's gone."

Though she knew what he'd say, she whispered, "Backup?"

Daniel shook his head. "If he's got Markham, we can't wait. Whatever goes down, I want us to be the ones in control, not Elman, not anyone else. Just us, you and me."

He pulled a small flashlight out of the glove compartment. "Let's try the back door. I doubt Doc reset the alarm, if it was on in the first place."

They exited the car, taking care not to slam the doors, and crept along the walkway until they reached the kitchen door. Daniel tried the doorknob. It was locked.

Cam pulled out her lock pick set from her pocket, smaller than a change purse. A few seconds and the door lock sprung open. He shook his head at her, marveled. She turned the knob slowly and slipped in, Daniel behind her. They stood in the small night-shrouded kitchen, listened. They heard voices coming through the dining room.

Doc's voice was filled with rage. "Shut up, you murdering bastard, or I'll stuff the gag back in your mouth before I cut your throat."

Cam pulled out her cell, pressed record.

Markham's voice was low, pleading. "What can I say to make you believe me? I didn't kill Deborah. I honestly thought you killed her and that's why I hired the P.I. Don't you remember that party? You didn't want Deborah to have anything to do with us, you hated that she was an actress. I thought she finally threw you out and you killed her."

They heard a hand strike flesh, then Doc's hard voice. "You confessed!"

"I had to or you would have killed both me and my wife. But I didn't kill Deborah. She was starring in my movie. I had no reason to kill her."

"Did you really think I'd let you frame me for Deborah's murder after you killed her? Let you just walk away?"

"Didn't you hear me? You have no proof I killed her because there isn't any!"

Doc laughed. "It's enough that I know, Markham. You overplayed your hand, hiring that P.I., siccing the FBI on me whenever you had a chance. Oh yes, I know what you did, what you said, how you kept pushing me in their faces. I was in the inner circle, a victim. They felt sorry for me, all of them did, and they talked."

"You've got to stop this. I didn't kill Deborah. I didn't have a motive. Why won't you believe me?"

"Believe you? You're not even a good liar. I'm going to kill you, Markham, whatever you say. It's up to you if you want to go out a coward or die like a man, own up to what you did. You murdered the woman I loved." He was breathing hard, nearly beside himself.

Markham remained silent.

"Your wife won't grieve for you. She knows you cheated your way through eighteen years of marriage. Do you think she kept count of all the young actresses you stashed in your little house in the Colony? Deborah told me you charged Connie a bit of rent, to make it look good, and both of you denied you were sleeping together. What a joke. How many other actresses before Connie did you keep there? They slept with you, sold their bodies to you, so you'd get them roles? Your precious wife is still tied up. I could go back there, finish it for her. And I would. Up to you. I want the truth, now."

Theo Markham finally spoke, his voice low and flat. He sounded broken, in pain. How many times had Doc struck him, tortured him before they'd arrived? "I loved Connie more than anyone and you murdered her, sliced her throat. You're the monster here, not me. Connie had what it took to be a star, with or without me cheering her on. I loved her, do you hear me, you crazy bastard? And you killed her!"

Doc gave a small chuckle. "I really enjoyed killing her. Let me tell you about it. She was asleep, probably dreaming of some handsome young stud, not a middle-aged man she was having to suffer sleeping with to get her start in some idiot movie. You know what? There was a script open on the bed beside her. It was *The Crown Prince*, the role Deborah wanted and deserved. Her eyes popped open just as I sliced across her neck. She stared up at me with her big beautiful green eyes, and she never made a sound. I watched her die. Like you watched Deborah die, you bastard. There's one thing I want to know from you before I cut your throat and let you join your little slut in hell. How did you know it was me?"

"I saw you."

"No, that's not possible. I checked, you were at that splashy party at your house that night."

"I was only fifteen minutes away. I never drove into the Colony, I always parked outside, came in under the fence. I saw you leaving the house, and I went in and she was dead."

"How did you know who I was?" He slapped his hand to his forehead. "How could I forget that party at that degenerate's house six months ago? That producer's house, Willard Lambeth, that was his name. You telling me you actually remembered me, after six months?"

"Of course. The way you acted, your obvious disdain for all of us in the business, the way you treated Deborah."

"Then why didn't you tell the cops?"

Markham actually laughed. "You're so smart, who do you think they would have put at the top of their suspect list? Me, of course, they'd have painted me the jilted lover. I had no proof you were there, and I wouldn't have stood a chance. Even if they didn't convict me, I would have been ruined, my career, my marriage, over."

"You murdered Deborah for revenge, didn't you? You gave Deborah that part she wanted so badly in your damned movie, and you sent her out of the country. All that time you were planning how to set it up."

"You deserved to be destroyed, both of you. Like you destroyed Connie."

They heard a fist strike flesh, heard Markham moan in pain. Cam started forward, but Daniel grabbed her arm.

Markham was panting now, screaming back, "It doesn't matter. You're insane! You murdered all those helpless, innocent young women. I had to stop you. Even after all of it, you tried to kill Gloria Swanson. Because I was sleeping with her? Are you completely insane?"

There was silence and then Doc spoke, his voice dreamy. "Connie was my third, you know. She was the worst of them, really, taking up with you. You're responsible for her death, no one else. Do you know, each of them was better than the last? I fancied it was like a ballet, every move smooth and exact. They all died so beautifully, and I whispered to them to repent their sins but they couldn't, their throats were cut open."

There was the sound of a fist striking flesh again and another cry of pain.

Cam moved quickly along the narrow hallway, went down on her knees and looked into the second bedroom. Markham was duct-taped arms and legs to a chair. Deborah's desk chair, Cam recognized it. Everything else looked the same as Cam had seen it Wednesday morning. The chair sat in the middle of the room, Doc leaning over Markham, his knuckles bloody from the many blows. Markham's face was swollen and discolored, a deep cut over one of his eyes. A small maglite was propped up on a backpack, lighting Markham's bloody face.

Markham's words were liquid with blood. "There are hundreds, thousands of actresses. You said Connie was the worst because she slept with me. Everyone sleeps with someone. It's only sex. Why? Why my Connie? Why all of them?"

Doc raised the knife and both Cam and Daniel aimed their Glocks at him, center mass. Then he slowly lowered the knife and spoke, his voice emotionless, thin as parchment. "You want the truth? All right. Back at the beginning, before I understood how corrupt and venal this business is, I wanted Deborah to succeed. She wanted it more than anything, more than she wanted me, probably. Of course you know why Deborah didn't get any of those roles, you scum. It was because she was loyal to me, she didn't sleep with any of you lechers to get ahead. So I decided I would help her.

"You know what? I found I was quite good at it." His voice had dropped, became confiding. "It's not as well controlled as surgery, and I really am a superb surgeon. I didn't have to practice much to be a first-rate killer."

There was a long moment of silence. Cam thought if she could see his face there'd be a huge smile on it. He was revving himself up. They heard him announce, his voice excited now, "It's how I became famous, in the end. Time for me to go now, Markham, time for you to die. There are pretty young señoritas waiting for me."

Markham had gone beyond fear. His voice sounded

eerily calm. "They'll get you, you know they will, no matter where you go, they'll find you. They'll never stop."

"You think I don't know that? I know this part's over. There's always an end of the line. That's why I came for you, Markham. Did you think I'd leave you behind? They'll come for me tomorrow with more questions and their lie detector, and what they'll find is rubble and a burned body. They'll think my grief for Deborah drove me to kill myself. By the time they know better, I'll be gone, an obscure village doctor they'll never find."

Doc's voice suddenly caught, and he sobbed. "You know what, Markham, you evil bastard? If you hadn't killed Deborah, none of this would be happening."

Markham barked out a strangled half laugh. "Of course it would. You're a serial killer."

Doc's shadow lengthened and he raised his knife.

67

"Put the knife down, Doc. Now!" Cam jumped to her feet and raised her Glock.

Doc whirled around, shock clear on his face. He screamed, "No, it's impossible! You can't be here!" He shoved Markham's chair toward them and dove for the open window.

Daniel followed Doc through the window, rolled, and tackled him, landing with all his weight on his back. He grabbed his wrist, twisted it until Doc dropped the knife, and pulled his arms back to cuff them. Doc kicked himself up to his knees, twisted, and got an arm free. He held a small pistol in his hand.

"No!" Cam yelled. She and Doc fired at the same time. The bullet knocked Doc backward onto the ground. Daniel fell off him, onto his back.

She was at Daniel's side in a moment, saw blood spreading over his chest. She pressed down on the wound hard with both hands. He was struggling to breathe. She pulled her cell out of her pocket, dialed

911, forced herself to calm, and told the dispatcher to send an ambulance, officer down. She looked briefly over at Doc, lying still now, silent. She wondered if he was dead. She hoped so.

Harder, she had to press harder. "Stay with me or I'll make sure Missy makes your life miserable. Daniel, breathe!" She heard his breath bubbling, saw him spitting up as he tried to suck in air. He was bleeding into his lung.

His breathing eased. He whispered, "Where did he get a gun?"

"Not important. Be quiet and don't move an inch. Breathe, Daniel, help is coming."

"Cam, the gun—how . . ."

She leaned over him, whispered, "We'll have a talk about that later. We started this together, Daniel, and we'll finish it together." His eyes were vague, cloudy, and she leaned close. "Think about the dozen kids you and Missy are going to have. Daniel, focus!"

"Missy," he whispered, his voice liquid, and she'd have sworn his eyes brightened. She heard sirens. She kept pressure on his chest, the wet of his blood warm against the burns on her palms. "Hang on, Daniel, the cavalry's near." A moment later she heard the front door burst open as the EMTs came pounding through. His eyes were closed, his head to the side. She pressed her fingers against his neck. His pulse was thready, barely there. She kept pressing with the heels of her hands until the paramedics told her to move.

"He's got a bullet wound in his chest. I've been pressing down as hard as I could."

"That's good, now move." The paramedic quickly applied a pressure bandage. "On three," she said to the other paramedic behind her, and together they lifted him onto the gurney.

"Will he live?"

"He'd better," she called back before she closed the ambulance door. "I mean look at him. He's the whole package." Police were all around Cam now, more cop cars pouring in. Only then did she turn to look down at Doc. She'd thought he was dead, but there were paramedics surrounding him, busy trying to keep him alive.

She saw his eyelashes flicker. She knelt down beside him and leaned in close.

He opened his eyes, empty and vague as he stared up at her.

"Tell me one thing before you leave this earth. Where did you go when you left the hospital for those forty minutes the night Deborah was murdered?"

A ghost of a smile. "I went to visit Gloria Swanson. She wasn't home. I went back last night—didn't work out—but lots more nights—"

He died with a rictus of a smile on his mouth. She watched them start pumping on his chest and pushing air into his lungs. She watched as they put him on a gurney and moved him to an ambulance. She'd seen enough to know she'd heard his voice for the last time. She didn't move until she heard Markham yelling for her from the house, still bound tight to his chair with duct tape.

EPILOGUE

Missy and Cam stood by Daniel's bed in the step-down unit. They knew he was awake, saw his eyelashes flutter, but they didn't say anything, let him rest. They listened to the bubbling sound of the suction machine, a pleurovac, a nurse called it, connected to a tube in Daniel's chest.

"So many tubes and lines," Missy whispered. "I'm afraid to touch him." But she did, lightly stroking his forearm above an IV site at his wrist.

His eyelashes fluttered again. Missy leaned down, her breath warm on his face. "Daniel, open those beautiful eyes of yours and wink at me." He couldn't seem to make his eyes open, to reassure her. He felt like a boulder was sitting on his chest. It didn't hurt much now, but he knew it would if he tried to move.

He heard Missy say, "He's so pale, Cam. It's like he's hardly here." She sounded like she was going to cry and he hated that. He forced his eyes open but knew he looked vague, confused.

"Hello, Daniel," Cam said, leaning close. "Don't worry about a thing. You're going to be fine, your surgeon said you came through surgery like a champ. You only need time now, time to heal." She wasn't about to tell him about the hours they'd spent in the waiting room, afraid he would die.

Missy pressed the morphine pump into his hand. "If you have pain, you push the magic button."

Daniel tried to smile, to say something. He wanted to tell her she looked beautiful, but he felt strangely disconnected, no words in his brain. Cam was smiling down at him, so she was safe, and that was a relief. He whispered, "Doc?"

"He's dead," Cam said, nothing more.

"Markham?"

"He's in jail, but I doubt for long. His lawyers are proclaiming Markham is innocent, getting the word out everywhere in the press. They're using Mrs. Markham to make a hero out of him, how he saved her life by confessing with a gun to his head. For now, she's standing by him. We're going to need some physical evidence. We've served some warrants, started talking to those people at the party he slipped out of. But that's not for you to worry about. Your assignment is to heal yourself, all right?"

He felt the warmth of Missy's voice beside his left ear. "Cam told me she had you thinking about me, about us, to keep you going, back there. I had to tell her she was a bit premature, seeing as how we haven't even gone to the movies or out to my favorite Italian restaurant yet. You haven't even kissed me. Well, I can take care of half of that." Missy leaned down and lightly kissed him. "I'll give you a week to reciprocate." She smiled at him, but then her voice hitched. "Don't you ever let this happen again, Daniel Montoya. Do you hear me?"

He whispered, "I saw you dressed in your cutoff jeans and orange tank top, your hair all over your head. Snapped me right back."

Missy laughed, a small one, but it was a laugh. She said, "Look, Arturo's here. He's been bitching and moaning until they finally released him. He said he'd stop by, wanted to make sure you weren't going to fold up your tent and leave him to face Markham's lawyers alone."

He heard Arturo's deep voice. "Hey, dude, looks like I'm beating you out of this place. You've got to get well so we can rock 'n' roll with Markham. Your sheriff, Murray, agrees with me. You're needed."

Arturo's too-hearty voice faded. Daniel wanted to say something, but the pain spiked. He wanted to scream with it, but he didn't. The pain took over. Then he felt Missy's fingers lightly press his fingers on the morphine button. It was amazing how fast the pain began to recede. But as it backed off, it took his brain away with it. All he could manage was a vague smile in Arturo's direction.

Cam said, "My folks were here, Daniel. Mom left her famous chicken soup. The nurse said maybe tomorrow. Dad wanted you to know they'll be throwing a party for you when you get out."

The thought of chicken soup made him swallow bile. He heard a woman's voice, and somewhere in his brain he recognized she was the surgeon who'd taken the bullet out of his chest. He wanted to thank her, but the words floated away.

Dr. Soufret checked her patient's vitals, inspected the bandages over his chest, relieved there wasn't much fluid draining through the tube. She shoved her glasses back up her nose and looked at Arturo. "I hear both you and Detective Montoya were heroes. Congratulations. Now, all of you, let me reassure you that Detective Montoya will heal. I'll be taking the chest tube out soon, which won't be fun for him. Let's leave him alone, let him rest." She paused a moment, looked at Missy. "What's your name?"

"Missy Devereaux."

Dr. Soufret smiled at her. "He was mumbling your name over and over before he went under for surgery. All of you can come back later." She stopped in the doorway. "A warning. There's a swarm of reporters downstairs. Nurse Hopkins can show you the back stairs, if you wish."

Cam took a last look at Daniel. He would live. But five young women were gone, their lives ended by a madman. Six including Deborah, murdered by a man too much a coward to come forward, a man blinded by his hunger for revenge. It was almost too much to bear.

Arturo braved the reporters while Cam and Missy walked out of the rear entrance of the hospital into the bright warm California sunlight. Missy said, "I can't believe it's only been five days since I ran into you at the market. Look at what's happened."

Cam turned and hugged her. No way would she ever tell Missy she'd been in Doc's crosshairs. "You're going to be a star, Missy. It's your time."

EPILOGUE

Delsey punched Rob in the arm and gave Venus a fat smile. "Yes, I'm thinking of forgiving him, Mrs. Rasmussen, but I made him promise if he ever keeps anything from me again, he will bow his head and let me shave him bald."

Rob touched his fingers to his thick dark hair. "Delsey figures most guys would do about anything not to be bald."

Delsey laughed. "It started out as my mom's idea, to keep my dad on the straight and narrow." She ruffled his thick hair. "Since Rob's got such great hair, I think the threat might work on him, too."

Sherlock laughed. "Nice idea. Maybe we should try that, Dillon. Keep you on the straight and narrow."

He feathered his fingers through her beautiful hair. "As long as it works both ways."

Sherlock looked appalled. "Oh dear," she said.

"Would you shave my head, too?" Sean asked, looking back and forth between his parents.

"I'll see to it your hair is safe, Sean," Venus said, and handed him the cookie plate. She added to Delsey, "I rather hoped he would talk you around. He's got a lot of his grandfather in him."

"You must tell me about him," Delsey said. "After all, knowledge is power."

"Rob's grandfather was creative, as Rob is," Venus said. "But unlike Rob, he didn't build houses, he built a business, nurtured it, gave it every waking hour, made it into an international force. His business, our business, is thriving. It's your heritage, Rob, as much as it is Alexander's and your father's. It is my fondest hope you'll join us, give working at Rasmussen Industries a try." Her eyes twinkled. "Delsey, maybe you can help give him a little push. I think a good place to start would be on our development team here in Washington, in the home office. They design and build our new facilities, rehab our current ones. Your father enjoys working in that area, Rob, he could show you the ropes. He's started his AA meetings. It would help to have you near. And he could help you avoid flattening Alexander when he tries to throw his weight around. What do you think?"

"Yes," Rob said, "I'm willing to give it a try, Grandmother. What do you think, Savich?"

"Sounds like it might be perfect for you. Try it part-time for a year, Rob, then you'll know."

Rob arched a dark brow at his grandmother. "And what does Alexander have to say about it?"

"He rolled his eyes but didn't offer an opinion. I hope after all the drama of the past week he'll reevaluate what's important to him." She grinned. "If not, he'll learn."

Rob rose, sat down next to his grandmother and hugged her. "Thank you, Grandmother. You've got a deal."

"Excellent. By the way, Dillon, I took your advice and hired MacPherson back. He started today, drove Guthrie and me to church. I only wish he'd come to me when he learned how expensive his son's leukemia treatments would be. He said he didn't want to be a leech and he apologized for selling that story to the *National Enquirer*. His son's prognosis is excellent, so all's right in his world again."

That meant, Sherlock knew, that Venus would make certain MacPherson's son got the best of care. She looked automatically at Sean and closed her eyes a moment. Life was so uncertain at the best of times, and a child was so fragile. "Good," she said, "that's good of you."

Venus looked up. "Ah, Isabel, is our lunch ready? Mr. Paul has prepared the pulled pork sliders for our carnivore guests? And the spinach quiche for Dillon?"

"Mr. Paul wasn't certain if his quiche would be enough for Agent Savich and suggested he add his tofu dish, food for the gods, he called it."

No matter if the gods did eat tofu, Savich wasn't about to touch it. He smiled. "Quiche will do me fine, Isabel, thank you."

Venus added, "MacPherson loves Mr. Paul's pork sliders. I believe he'll be having some for his own lunch."

Alexander's smooth sarcasm floated into the room. "Well, the gang's all here, I see. I didn't realize Grandmother would feel compelled to feed you when a cup of coffee would have sufficed."

Savich looked up to see him standing lazily in the doorway, leaning against the frame, hands in his pockets.

Sherlock gave him her sunny smile. "It's kind of your grandmother to invite us for lunch, in the kitchen, of course."

Savich saw a flash of amusement in Alexander's eyes, he was sure of it.

Mr. Paul, resplendent in his white chef's hat a good foot high, sailed past Alexander and looked down at Sean. "This young gentleman admired my cookies, so I have decided to take him to Rockland Park after lunch and teach him some of the finer points of football— soccer, you Americans call it. He'll find it far superior to the barbaric game American football."

Sean beamed, but then he looked worried. "Mr. Paul, is it okay if I wear my Redskins sweatshirt?"

"You may. I will disregard my distress."

Sean turned to Savich and beamed. "Can I go with Mr. Paul, Papa? Learn the finer points?"

"Maybe we all can go, Sean. Mr. Paul, do you think it's too late for me and my wife to learn the finer points as well?"

Mr. Paul snapped his fingers. "Mrs. Rasmussen assures me you're a smart lad. I will try."

Sean turned to Alexander. "Will you come, too? Or do you still have a pain in the patoot?"

Alexander studied the little boy, the spitting image of his father. "So you've heard someone say I'm a pain in the patoot, Sean? It's true, I am. Ask anyone."

Sean nodded. "Okay, but what's a patoot?"

NOTE FROM THE AUTHOR

I hope you enjoyed *Insidious*. Please let me know at Readmoi@gmail.com or visit me at Facebook.com/catherinecoulterbooks.

Keep reading for an excerpt of

THE DEVIL'S TRIANGLE

the next installment in

Catherine Coulter and J.T. Ellison's

Brit in the FBI Series

Available Spring 2017 from Gallery Books

1

Kitsune stood on the Rialto Bridge and watched the sun flash against the waves of the lagoon. She enjoyed the early mornings in Venice, before the summer crowds flooded into the city. She watched pigeons peck the ground for yesterday's crumbs, watched a row of tethered gondolas bob in the heavy sea swell. There would be a storm soon—she tasted it in the air. She looked at her watch. It was time to go. Her client had instructed her to take a water taxi to the San Zaccaria dock, then walk to the house.

She should have been on her way before now, but she'd waited there on the bridge to see who was following her. Even though she hadn't seen anyone yet, she'd felt eyes on her, felt them since her plane had landed an hour earlier. At the airport's dock she'd caught a glimpse of one of them: a man—dark sunglasses, a slouchy work jacket. There were probably others, but where were they? She hated being in the open like this—a target—

and the large tube in her hand a target as well. She still didn't see anyone.

She bent down to adjust the strap of her sandal. From the corner of her eye she saw him. She was sure it was the same man she'd seen at the Marco Polo airport, still wearing sunglasses and a jacket. He wasn't very good at his job, since she'd spotted him, standing in the alley to the left of the Hotel Danieli, chewing on a toothpick like he didn't have a care in the world. But where were the others? She knew she hadn't been followed to Venice, she was sure of that, so why now? For some reason, her client didn't trust her. She felt a lick of anger. It was an insult to her reputation. Or perhaps someone knew what was inside the large tube and wanted it?

Ah, there he was, the second man, hovering near the dock, a cap pulled low on his head, wearing wrinkled jeans and scuffed boots. Both men were in their thirties, muscled, garbed in everyday working clothes. Thugs. One was tall, the other short. Mutt and Jeff. She saw no one else. Only two of them? Another insult. She took note of the small sign above Mr. Short's head—*Calle de la Rasse.*

Kitsune had learned the complicated layout of the Venetian streets, an integral part of her preparation, since she could run much faster than she could swim.

She checked the men out again. Both cocky, sure of themselves, but she could take them. Easily.

Not yet, though. The time wasn't right.

Their presence bothered her. Why the sudden distrust from her client? Her reputation was built on absolute discretion, always delivering what was commissioned and never asking questions. She had no false modesty. She could steal anything, anywhere—even the Koh-i-Noor diamond, that magnificent bloody stone that had nearly gotten her killed. A pity she'd had to give it up.

This client was paying her a small fortune, and half of it, five million euros, was already deposited in four different accounts in four different banks, as was her custom. She would receive the other five million upon delivery. All of it was straightforward, so why the two thugs following her?

Kitsune had been a thief for too long to ignore the prickle of unease that went down her neck. The tube was heavy, and she hugged it closer.

The breeze picked up between the Venetian buildings, blowing gently down the narrow canal. She continued forward, over the small bridge, up the walkway, past the arriving gondoliers, who watched her and wondered. Grant told her she moved differently, with singular grace and arrogance, and she looked like what she was—strong and dangerous—and then he'd held her close, stroked her long hair, and whispered against her temple that only the very stupid, or the very desperate, would mess with her. She felt a warm punch to her heart thinking of her husband of ten months, how the green of his eyes turned nearly black when he was kissing her. Soon, she would be with him again. She would give the prize to the client, and be gone.

She'd fulfilled the first part of the job three days earlier, when she'd pulled off one of the most fun heists of her career. She'd dyed her hair the deepest black, worn brown contacts, and used a semipermanent stain to make her skin appear two shades deeper, a process she didn't relish, but it helped her blend in beautifully with the population of Istanbul. With her forged credentials, which included a signature from Turkish military leader Hulusi Akar, the palace authorities had followed orders and assigned her to work security at the Topkapi Palace. It had taken her more than three months to work her way out of the harem complex and into special security in the Holy Relics exhibit, where Moses's staff was displayed.

Her arms had gotten tired carrying the H&K MP5 machine gun all day. Even with the strap around her neck and shoulder, the carbine got heavy, and being on alert for twelve hours at a time was exhausting. Despite the heat and grit and the hordes of tourists trooping in and out of the trea-sure-filled rooms in the palace, her assigned areas gave her a lovely view of the Bosphorus. The sun shined on the water, sprinkling diamonds, the sea breezes cooled her, and the tourists gathered nearby to take photos. She was careful, very care-ful, never to get in the shots. It wouldn't do to have someone post a photo of her on Facebook acciden-tally, have some government drone monitoring the Internet run the photos through facial recognition, and blow her cover.

She wondered again: did her unknown client really believe that what she carried in her hands was the very embodiment of power? That what she carried wasn't simply an ancient knob of wood but the actual staff of Moses? Or, as some called it, Aaron's rod? No matter what it was called, this staff was one of the most sought-after and priceless artifacts in the world, and she'd managed to break into the Holy Relics exhibit after hours and take the staff out of its lighted case after cutting the wires to the security alarm, and disappeared. And that brought a smile of satisfaction.

No more inky-black hair, no more dark brown eyes, the stain washed away. She was back to her blue eyes, her white skin, and her own dark hair.

Yes, it had been a clean, perfectly executed job.

One of her best, and she, the Fox, had a string of risky, daring jobs behind her.

The international news channels were still leading with the theft. No way was she going to take a chance of being caught in the crosshairs. She'd make the delivery, get her other five million, go home to Capri, and talk Grant into visiting Australia or America, anywhere away from Europe. He was due for a vacation, having spent the last three months in Afghanistan guarding a high-ranking British officer.

The house she was going to was only a drop site. She'd used this protocol many times—empty house, the owners probably on vacation. Clients rarely wanted the Fox to know where they lived. She wondered who would be there to receive the stolen staff.

A winding alleyway took her deeper into the neighborhoods, along the canals. And there it was, a simple, classic Venetian home—red brick, the second and third floors balconied, set between a narrow street and a small canal.

She went up the steps, knocked on the dark green door. Waited a moment before the thick, old wood swung open. An older man in a dark suit and silver tie told her to come in.

Inside, all was silent. She followed him through a small courtyard, a marble fountain at its center. He showed her into a parlor, to the right of the fountain. The door closed behind her.

The room was empty, the silence heavy. She heard voices, a man and a woman, somewhere nearby—above her, probably—speaking rapid Italian. The clients? Although she understood exactly what they were saying, it still made no sense to her.

The woman said clearly, excitement in her voice, "I wish I could see it, the Gobi sands—a tsunami sweeping over Beijing."

"We will see it on video," came a man's matter-of-fact voice. "All the sand, do you think? Could Grandfather be that good?"

"You know he is. And we will see the aftermath for ourselves. We will leave in three days, after things have calmed down."

The man said, marveling, "Can you imagine, we are the ones to drain the Gobi?"

Kitsune stood silently, listening. She shook her head. Drain the Gobi Desert dry? All that sand covering Beijing? By their grandfather? What she'd heard, it was nuts, made no sense. An image of Moses raising his staff, parting the Red Sea so the Israelites could escape the Egyptian army flashed through her mind. It was a famous image, given all the paintings and movies, and there were many who believed that was exactly what happened. But not her.

Kitsune held by her side a gnarly old piece of wood the Turks had stolen when they'd plundered Egypt in 1517, audacious enough or credulous enough to proclaim it to be Moses's staff. She didn't care if it was real or not, it didn't matter. Ten million euros would keep her in bikinis for a long time. She pictured Moses again, only this time she saw him waving his staff to send the sands flying out of the Gobi Desert. Such a strange image.

The voices faded away.

Moments later, the door to the parlor opened and a man came in. He was short, with dark hair and flat black eyes. This one, in spite of his well-cut dark suit, his perfectly polished boots, couldn't be the client. He looked coarse, crude, a lieutenant playing dress-up. Another thug, only this one with a bit of power, probably running the other who'd followed her. So the man and woman she'd heard talking wanted him to handle the transaction, then bring them the staff. Fine by her. All she wanted was her money.

He crossed the room to the small desk, picked up a silver lighter, and touched it to the end of a cigarette. He blew out a stream of gray smoke and said, in passable English, "I am Antonio Pazzi, and you are the Fox. You have the package?"

"Of course." Kitsune set the tube on the desk

and stepped back. Pazzi pulled a stiletto from his coat pocket, slit open the top of the cylinder, and upended it. The well-wrapped staff slid out into his waiting hand. He reverently laid it atop the desk and peeled off the packing. He looked at the staff, motionless, staring, but not touching it. Finally, he looked up at her, smiled widely, showing yellow tobacco-stained teeth. "I did not believe you would be able to steal this precious rod from the Topkapi. Your reputation is deserved. My masters will be pleased."

She saw him press a small button on the desk, and in the next instant she heard a door close, a boat's engine fire to life. So he'd signaled the client that she'd brought the staff? And they'd left. Pazzi handed her a long white envelope. "Five million euros. You will leave now."

As if she wanted to stay, maybe have a drink with this oily cretin with his yellow teeth. She wanted to open the envelope, but he kept smiling, herding her toward the door, and she felt that familiar shiver down her neck and went on red alert, her body flexed and ready to spring. Were the two men outside the door, waiting for her? Pazzi gave her a small salute, and at the last moment, he slipped past her and slammed the door behind him. She heard the key turn in the lock. In the next moment, another door opened, this time behind her. Mutt and Jeff stepped through, and both held guns in their hands.

"What a lovely surprise," she said in Italian, and, quick as a cobra, she dove at Mutt's feet. He had been expecting her to run, and he hesitated a moment. She rolled into him and knocked him backward, his arms flailing for purchase, and he fell against a chair. She popped back to her feet—Mutt on her left, struggling to get back up, and Jeff on her right, his Beretta aimed at her chest.

Kitsune fell to her knees, whipped out her two Walther PPKs cross-armed, and pulled the triggers almost before she'd squared the sights. Jeff fired at the same time. If she'd stayed standing, she'd be dead. Now he was the one who was dead, sprawled on his back on the floor, blood blooming from his chest. She'd missed Mutt, but his gun had clattered to the floor and slid under a red velvet sofa. He sprang to his feet and came at her, fast and hard, fists up and flying, trying to knock the gun away and kill her with his bare hands. He was fast, she'd give him that, but she was faster. A heartbeat later he was on the floor with a hole in his forehead.

Kitsune had never used guns, but in the past few months, Grant had trained her in them, and trained her well. And when he was satisfied, he'd given her the two Walthers. Almost as if Grant had known she would need them. She sent him a silent thank-you as she pointed the gun in her right hand over her shoulder, toward the locked door, just in case, and walked to the opposite side of the room. She listened but didn't hear anything. The house had gone silent. Too silent. As if someone was listening. She had to get out of there, now.

She heard voices shouting. She yanked open the door and ran down a long hallway ending in a staircase. The house itself was narrow and old, the walls cool gray stone. She had no choice but to run up the stairs.

She heard feet pounding after her, shouts growing closer. Kitsune burst through onto a rooftop terrace. Up this high, she saw that terraces littered the rooftops, and the Venetian houses were crammed cheek by jowl, separated by the small canals that crisscrossed Venice.

She didn't look down at the murky canal below, paid no attention to the shouts from the staircase, as men ran up to the terrace. She leaped across to the neighboring terrace. She felt a bullet whiz by her ear, and she dropped and rolled, was on her feet in a second, running to the next terrace. She heard the man leap after her, moving fast, gaining on her. She raced to the end of the rooftop and leaped again, barely missed a window box overflowing with pink and red geraniums, and skidded along the pebbled roof.

He followed her, shouting, shooting. People screamed through open windows, gondoliers looked at the sight and shouted, tourists stared up in awe as light-footed Kitsune soared over them like a bird in flight. Laundry lines tumbled into the water below. She was careful to avoid the electric lines; she'd be dead and gone before she hit the water if she grabbed one of those by accident.

She looked back, saw that it was Pazzi chasing her. She hadn't expected him to be so fast, but he was reaching his limits, and dropping back. With a yell of frustration, he took another shot. The bullet skimmed her arm, cutting the fabric of her shirt, stinging like mad. Blood began running down, turning her hand red. Not good.

She made a last desperate leap, grabbed a laundry line, swung down and smashed against the wall of a redbrick house, knocking the air out of her lungs, and dropped, hard, onto the deck of a water taxi.

The captain, gap-mouthed, stumbled back, and she pushed him overboard, roared the engine to life and took off. She heard shouts, curses behind her, but didn't look back. She pressed her right hand against the wound in her upper arm.

The boat shot out by the San Zaccaria vaporetto station. She was free now, in the lagoon, and she gunned it.

She was breathing hard, and bleeding, but for the moment, she was upright and safe, cool water splashing her, the wind tearing through her hair. She heard sirens. The police would be after her any minute now. She had to ditch the boat. It was a thirty-minute run to the airport, but that would be suicide; she could never fly out.

Think, Kitsune.

South, she'd go south, to Rimini, dock there, and start her way home.

She checked the gas, excellent, the tank was nearly full. She left the channel and headed into the open seas, leaving behind the wails of the sirens. She remembered she'd stuffed the white envelope Pazzi had given her inside her shirt. At least she'd been paid for the job. Or had she? She ripped the envelope open and inside she saw a folded sheet of paper. She opened it and saw a rough drawing of a dead fox. She felt the tearing pain in her arm as she wadded up the paper and tossed it overboard. Five million euros was that critical to them? But why had they wanted her dead? It didn't matter, she didn't care. There would be hell to pay.